NEW CONTRACT

A NOVEL
BY MICHAEL ATAMANOV

Wishing you safe travels on your fantasy journey,

PERIMETER DEFENSE
BOOK#3

MD

MAGIC DOME BOOKS

New Contract
Perimeter Defense, Book # 3
Published by Magic Dome Books, 2017
Copyright © M. Atamanov 2016
Cover Art © V. Manyukhin 2016
Translator © Andrew Schmitt 2016
All Rights Reserved
ISBN: 978-80-88231-27-1

All books
by Michael Atamanov:

Reality Benders LitRPG series
Countdown
External Threat
Game Changer
Web of Worlds
A Jump into the Unknown
Aces High

The Dark Herbalist LitRPG series
Video Game Plotline Tester
Stay on the Wing
A Trap for the Potentate
Finding a Body

Perimeter Defense LitRPG series
Sector Eight
Beyond Death
New Contract
A Game with No Rules

League of Losers LitRPG Series
A Cat and His Human

You're in Game!
(LitRPG Stories from Bestselling Authors)

You're in Game-2!
(More LitRPG stories set in your favorite worlds)

Table of Contents:

A Frank Conversation

AS I WAS undergoing yet another afternoon of rehab procedures at my neighborhood clinic, a call came in to my cellphone from an unknown number. After my return from *Perimeter Defense*, the fact that I was addicted to drugs and alcohol had become blatantly obvious and, even three months later, I was still going to the clinic three times a week for a glucose and vitamin drip to cleanse the liver and blood and ward off other ill effects. I can't even imagine how many unflattering epithets I mentally flung at Mr. G. I. on these days, sitting here with a needle in my arm. He had really managed to put my body through the wringer in the six short months he'd been in it! With all the drinking he must have been doing, I imagine he was just hiccupping constantly.

"Yes?" I said, pressing the "Accept" button on the cell phone with my free hand.

"Ruslan, I have a serious proposal for you."

So much time had passed, but I still could pick that voice out from among a million others. Miya! I had long been mentally preparing for a conversation with my former employer, and had even begun actively trying to bump into him in order to tell that piece of trash exactly what I thought of him, man-to-man. But I was not ready for a conversation with his close companion, and I slightly lost my place. I wasn't able to think up anything smart to say to her, so I just switched the phone off.

Millions of thoughts were spinning around in my head. Why was it Miya, and not Mr. G.I.? Was he so afraid of meeting me that he'd sent his girlfriend out in his place? It'd been so long... I guess they did need me, in the end.

"You're right," the Truth Seeker's voice rang out in my head. *"Mr. G.I. will be waiting for you in the same place as last time, forty minutes from now."*

I was having mixed feelings. On the one hand, I desperately wanted to dive head-first back into the fantasy world of *Perimeter Defense*. What can I say? It was the first place I ever felt I could really say I'd found my calling and actually believe it. It was there that I'd first experienced the intoxicating aroma of fame and glory. I had made history. My fleet's many starships had blotted out stars and made anyone who got in our way quiver in fear. I could have become co-ruler over billions of insects. I could have become Head of the Orange House. I could have become anyone I wanted. But, the main thing was that, in *Perimeter Defense*, I felt that humanity needed me. I was looked on as the savior of our whole race...

On the other hand, going back brought at least as many downsides. My last experience had come at too high a price. The money I got in the first contract had barely been enough to pay all the fees and fines that Mr. G. I. had left in his wake. My friends had turned away from me, I had quarreled with relatives, and the girl I had been dating on-and-off had left me, saying I'd become a degenerate drug addict. What was worse, there was a kernel of truth in her words. After the contract, I felt that I was in a body ravaged by binging on hard drugs and alcohol. It was like I had aged ten years in those six months. That all made waking up from the magical dream of *Perimeter Defense* and coming back to the real world an extremely bitter experience.

"After what you did to me last time, I don't even know what you could say to make me want to go back into *Perimeter Defense*! You'd just keep ruining my body!"

My unseen interlocutor kept silent for a few seconds, then said:

"The Alien *Queen,* at the head of a fleet of three thousand ships, has captured Hnelle. Your capital, Unatari, has been cut off from the Empire and is preparing for a hopeless battle. Without you, there is no hope for victory whatsoever. Everything you worked so painstakingly to create could be destroyed in one fell swoop, and all those close to you will die."

I thought there was no way she could hook me back in, but I was proven wrong. Miya had articulated everything I had been so severely lacking as of late. People need me again. They believe I can protect them, and pine for my return. I felt a thirst for activity boiling up in me after many weeks of extended apathy.

"This time, the contract is on my terms!" I

declared decisively.

"I agree," Miya said, for some reason not even asking her master's opinion on the matter.

"Alright, I'll be there in ten minutes," I said, tearing the needle from my vein and heading for the exit.

* * *

"Hello there, Ruslan. Just where do you think you're going?" grumbled the young bouncer standing watch over the restaurant entrance as he jerked me back by the shoulder.

I strained to hold back a string of unprintable words that were just begging to be let out. It was the same story all over again... Another loose end from the first contract. I was sure I was seeing this man for the first time; however, he, beyond all shadow of a doubt, knew me well and thought me a scoundrel. The unfortunate notoriety I had gained after my contract with Mr. G. I. infuriated me even more than my drugged-addled body. With addiction, there were severe health consequences to be sure, but it was at least easy to work out how to recover from, which was not something that could be said of this strange renown.

I often found girls I had never met before making eyes and smiling at me as if we were intimate acquaintances. A random passerby might take one look at my face, grow sullen with rage and, from out of nowhere, sock me right in the ear. Sometimes, women working in grocery stores refused to scan my purchases and called security to have me escorted out. And then, there were the night visitors. I'd had it up to here with them! Especially in the very first weeks after returning from *Perimeter Defense*! When my doorbell rang, I never knew what to expect. It could be a good-time girl who knew her way around my apartment surprisingly well, assuring me that my membership was paid-up through the end of the year. It could just as easily be glum criminal types twirling baseball bats and brass knuckles, demanding that I pay back a debt, which always came saddled with run-up interest that was nothing to sneeze at either.

On my way to the meeting with my employer, I was very intent on reminding him of every such episode I'd endured and demanding full compensation for the damage done to my health and reputation. I was also preparing to demand a point be added to the new contract saying that such incidents were not to be repeated, or I would refuse to help a second time. Unfortunately, I would first have to get into the restaurant to actually see Mr. G. I.

"I'm meeting someone here. He reserved a table," I replied to the vigilant doorkeeper in a tranquil tone.

He let go of my arm, called a manager over and whispered something to him, pointing at me.

"Under whose name is the table reserved?" the restaurant employee inquired, opening a notepad and studying the guest list on it.

"Georgiy Innokentievich... uhh... Mesfelle," I guessed, which turned out to have been wrong. They had no reservation under that name today.

"Like I said, throw him out by the neck!" the mean old bouncer exclaimed at my failure, but I made a second attempt.

"Look for Miya Mesfelle. The table might be under her name."

By the disappointed look now on the old man's face, I could tell that my second guess had been correct.

"But no funny business this time, Ruslan. Last time you had to pay for a lot of damage and broken furniture. Next time you won't get off so easy!" the vigilant bouncer threatened, finally letting me inside.

My last visit to this establishment was on an early winter's morning, and the room had been empty. This time, however, the restaurant was full of people. All the same, it was no problem to pick Miya out of the crowd. The fashionable young woman with long red hair in a bright orange, knee-length dress stood out from the crowd and attracted the eye like a flame in the night. The Truth Seeker was sitting alone at a table in the very center of the large room. Before her was some kind of fruit mousse and a glass of orange juice.

"Take a seat, Ruslan," she said instead of greeting me, pointing me to an empty chair. "You've come early. Mr. G.I. isn't here yet. You'll have to wait. For now, you may order whatever you like."

A waiter came up and handed me a menu, then took my order. At the same time, the young man was looking at me anxiously, as if afraid that I might bite him.

"You seem to have quite the reputation here, Ruslan," Miya commented, also having noticed our waiter's strange expression.

"And why do you think that might be?" I

quipped, not able to hold back. "Before the half-year contract in *Perimeter Defense*, even my neighbors didn't recognize me. Now, every other person in the neighborhood wants to punch me in the face..."

"I suppose that means you should have celebrated the end of your contract with a bit more modesty," retorted the red-headed she-devil, making a clear demonstration of the fact that she too could mock.

I started choking on indignation. Were they seriously going to try to convince me that I was at fault for all this?! The accusation was so unexpected and inappropriate that I even lost my place. Miya started smiling, watching my reaction with curiosity.

"Ruslan, let's set some boundaries for this conversation so we won't have any misunderstandings. Your personal life outside of *Perimeter Defense* is of absolutely no interest to either me or Mr. G.I. What you may or may not have done, or why this or that neighbor grew to dislike you is neither here nor there, and has nothing whatsoever to do with these negotiations..."

Here the Truth Seeker had to stop her speech, as a waiter approached our table and placed an unordered bottle of champagne in front of Miya.

"This is a gift to you from the courageous young lads at that table," the waiter stated, pointing to a group of men from the Caucasus who were sharing a meal, one of whom was smiling at Miya and blowing kisses.

I watched her take a quick look around the room, before her gaze stopped on a group of college girls at the neighboring table. Miya carelessly waved her left hand in their direction, and the glassy-eyed waiter took the bottle and set it on the girls' table. After telling them the same story about the feisty troublemakers, the girls gave a happy giggle. They were very favorably disposed to the gift.

"Not the best possible place to negotiate," Miya said in dismay. "But, it's too late to change. We don't have very much time. So then, Ruslan, I repeat. We are now discussing only the terms of the future contract, and all your discontent and grievances you can air to Mr. G.I. in person, as soon as he arrives."

"What's next? Do I have to swim to the other side of the river for a life jacket?" I laughed from the corner of my mouth. "No, Miya, that's not how it works. After the last contract, I have a huge number of problems, and I am not signing up for any new adventures until I've discussed all this with Mr. G.I."

Miya set her finished glass of juice aside and looked me right in the eyes.

"Ruslan, for some reason, you seem to be of the opinion that your employer should be thankful to you. You are gravely mistaken. This was nothing but a business contract. You did your job, and we paid you for it. What happened after that is not our problem. Any issues with your previous contract are off the table now. And if you think that your success was so impressive that your employer is burning with desire to give you extra tokens of gratitude, I'm afraid I'll have to disenchant you once again. In fact, Mr. G.I. was not at all happy with your term in *Perimeter Defense*, and was not planning to continue his relationship with you. He only agreed to even meet with you at all as a personal favor to me, in light of present circumstances. Your supposedly great achievements and success had nothing to do with it. Nothing at all."

"So you're saying that what I accomplished was nothing special?!" I exclaimed, not believing it could be true. "I increased the size of the Sector Eight Fleet more than anyone was expecting, including Mr. G.I., you, the Head of the Orange House, and even the Emperor himself. At the beginning of the contract I had sixteen light ships. Their crews were demoralized, and included a large number of Great House spies in their ranks. When my contract ended, I handed you the greatest fleet in the Empire with six battleships, twenty heavy cruisers, and a terrifying mothership; five hundred ships in total! And that's to say nothing of the training given to the veterans of my raid through Alien space. Their level of competence, effectiveness, and loyalty was incommensurably higher than that of the unorganized goat herd I was handed at the beginning."

"Ruslan, let's not distort reality here!" she said, frowning in anger before motioning for the waiter.

Miya ordered another juice and returned to the topic at hand:

"And now, I'll tell you the facts as they look to me and Mr. G. I. When the contract ended, half of your fleet was made up of Iseyek ships, all of which returned to Swarm space. So don't go telling me about any five hundred ships. In the best case scenario, you left Mr. G.I. with two hundred. And five of them were battleships, not six. Also, there were just fifteen heavy assault cruisers. To make matters worse, all the heavy ships, in our new admiral's words, were equipped in 'an idiotic way,' so we had to change all of them back to normal, wasting a huge amount of the money you left for us in the process. And the most shocking thing of all was that you, without even so much as asking your boss, sold *Queen of Sin*. The Crown Prince had to buy his luxury yacht back from Roben at a cost of four battleships and a few cruisers. These are the real facts, not fairytales like the ones you're trying to peddle. There's actually just one battleship left in the fleet, *Crown Princess Likanna*, and five heavy assault cruisers. The rest were just temporary and didn't belong to you anyway."

I couldn't believe my ears. *Bride of Chaos, Princess Astra, Master of Tesse* and *Indigo Beauty*, which had just returned to the fleet after a complete overhaul and modernization I had paid out the nose for in Sector Nine, were all gone. These idiots had given up four brand new battleships and ten assault cruisers in exchange for one measly yacht! Miya though, ignored my internal suffering and continued:

"No one disputes the fact that the fleet really did grow in strength in the six months you spent in game. We did get a battleship and several heavy cruisers, after all. The thing is, Mr. G.I. and I are fairly sure that these gains would have been made with or without you. The Emperor and the Orange House Head gave you the money for the ships, at the end of the day. I even suppose that if the real owner of the account had been playing, he could have avoided the dispute with Duke Paolo and the waste of money that useless conflict became. In that case, the fleet would have been much stronger and larger than it is now."

Her speech was fairly convincing. I suspect that she was making active use of hypnosis to get me to trust her. For a few seconds, I almost even believed that I was just some untalented schmo who had messed everything up. And, if I wasn't totally convinced of the opposite from the beginning, it might have even worked. I gave my head a shake to dispel the illusion.

"If you're telling me that some yacht was more important to Mr. G.I. than four battleships, fully modernized and equipped as lavishly as possible, then it's impossible to imagine the fleet getting stronger all on its own in six months. Your companion would simply have pissed the money to the wind as he normally does. Those four battleships and ten heavy cruisers were worth at least two billion credits without the trained crews that came with them... And he traded all these riches for a yacht worth three million, *if* I'm being charitable?"

"That's not for you to judge, Ruslan! This is an issue of principle: *Queen of Sin* was a gift from Crown Prince Georg to me. Or, to be more accurate, to us both. It was our flying palace. We spent some fifteen years living in it together! In all those years, Georg accumulated many decorations for our home, gathering all kinds of rarities and masterpieces. It became his favorite hobby. There was so much effort, time and hundreds of millions of credits put into *Queen of Sin* that no combat starship could come close to its value, not to speak of its comfort level. There were at least seven hundred million credits on the yacht just in sculptures by the great Veron ton Gep! Beyond that, there is also my nearly complete collection of the numbered Sivalla Emeralds, which were trophies from the great war with the Swarm. Those are simply priceless! And you sold all that luxury to Roben for a measly billion! Your brother had you wrapped around his finger, and you didn't even know it!"

My food arrived, and Miya had to take another break. The redheaded beauty took a look at the dishes brought to me and said in surprise:

"What is this, Ruslan? Are you trying to lose weight? Salad, mineral water... Where's the meat and side dish, where's the grilled fish, and well, booze? Last time, you did not limit yourself."

"Last time, I had a young, healthy body. But, after Mr. G.I. had a run with it, I was left with a body that hadn't spent a second dry in six months, judging by the number of empty vodka bottles in my room! My liver is failing, my blood pressure jumps around like I've got hypertension, and my veins are shot to hell. Three times every week, I go to a clinic for drug rehab. That was the price of my first contract with you. That is why I'll be sticking to mineral water, and nothing stronger."

Miya closed her eyes for a few seconds, then shook her head, somewhat exhausted:

"Ruslan, I thought we had agreed on limits to this conversation. I just want you to understand that your life outside of *Perimeter Defense* is of absolutely no interest to Mr. G.I. right now. During the contract, your body was in a virtual reality capsule. It was well cared for. So, your stories about alcohol abuse and damaged veins are clear fantasies, just like your attempt to project guilt for a fight with your neighbors onto someone else. You have no evidence, and there's no way you could."

I dug around in my pockets and took out something I'd picked up from home on my way here: a transparent box with a shiny ball inside. I set it down on the table in front of her. Miya took the box, turned it around in her hands with curiosity, and put it back down. I felt that I had her back against a wall of irrefutable evidence.

"Weird... I wonder if this is from Mr. G.I.'s personal stash or those packs of crystals you took from the pirate base on Unatari?"

The Truth Seeker smiled happily in reply:

"Ruslan. That isn't crystals. Don't you think I'd know? It's probably a plastic souvenir. You must have ordered it to remind yourself of *Perimeter Defense.*"

"Hmmm... Let's say that's true. Then tell me, Miya, how did you get my phone number?"

"You've become a really bad guy, Ruslan. So suspicious! I spent some time living in your apartment last winter, remember? Mr. G.I. told you! I simply saw your number printed on a bill and called it to save it in case I needed it."

"That could all be, Miya, and I might even have believed you, but I've changed my number since then. I was sick of receiving threatening phone calls in the middle of the night. I've had it for less than a week. I've only told it to my mother and best friend. And I want to note for the future: when you call someone, make sure you're actually speaking. Don't just send your thoughts right into a person's head. It was unsettling to keep hearing your voice after the phone turned off..."

"Ruslan, you're saying some very strange things," she whined, pursing her lips. "Hearing voices in your head, talking on phones that are off... Have you considered getting looked at by a psychiatrist?"

I pushed my plate away decisively and stood up from the table.

"Alright then, Miya. It seems I was mistaken. Constructive dialog between us is impossible. Send my greetings to your boss and, when you do, tell him I never want to see him again. I swear, if I do, I'll give that low-life a punch in the face!"

I turned toward the exit, and made two whole steps before a pair of athletically-built men, who had been talking quietly at the neighboring table, stood up and blocked my path. One of them put my arm behind my back in a professional maneuver and slammed my face down on the table in front of Miya.

"Boss-lady didn't say you could leave!" The brute whispered into my ear.

Everyone around kept eating, as if nothing was happening. A waiter was carrying a tray literally two feet from me but, for some reason, none of the many restaurant visitors were interested in what was happening at our table. It was as if we weren't really there. Maybe if I screamed, I could get someone's attention.

"It won't work, Ruslan. They won't be able to hear you," Miya said with a voice full of inhuman, icy detachment as she watched my futile attempts to break out of the hold. "Not a very good time for you to remind me of my abilities as a Truth Seeker. That reminds me of another thing: I promised to kill you if we ever met in the real world. I do not make such promises lightly. And, as you're not prepared to work with me..."

I noted with complete surprise, that the two brutes that had attacked me looked as alike as two drops of water. Twins? Or...

"Par to nek Tuki-tuka-de-sa! Pori-la-navi!" (Let me go! Obey your Elder Female! At once!)

It was complete instinct, but it turned out to have been the right move. Both of the meat-heads jumped back from me immediately, bowed down on one knee and lowered their heads. How useful it turned out to have been, listening in on my Chameleon bodyguards' conversations. Though I didn't actually know the Ravaash language, I had managed to memorize ten or twenty sentences.

Proud of my small triumph, I gave Miya a whimsical salute and set off to leave the restaurant. Well, tried to at least. After walking a couple steps from the table, I started noticing a growing resistance. Every step was significantly harder than the one that came before it. I had enough strength for six steps, but found I couldn't go even one millimeter further. Alright, I'm not dumb, I get it. I didn't start banging my head on the wall. I turned to the table and sat down opposite Miya.

"I guess that puts the score at one-one," the powerful Truth Seeker cackled raucously. "Alright, Ruslan. Now we can really have a frank conversation."

* * *

Miya was staring at the clock. A look of discontent, and even slight anxiety had crawled out onto her face.

"For some reason, your employer is late... That's odd. Usually, Georgiy is quite punctual. Alright, we'll try to get on without him. Ruslan, I suggest the following: I promise to answer any three questions you have with complete honesty. Then, after the answers, so as not to waste time, we can discuss the next contract. You tell me your desires point by point, and I will decide whether it would be possible to fulfill them. If any issues remain, we can wait for Mr. G.I. and consult him. Agreed?"

I thought and nodded. This option was perfectly fine by me. Miya then sighed with obvious relief. It seemed she was not at all sure I was going to agree. The red-headed beauty relaxed a bit, and an insanely beautiful woman emerged from behind the mask of this deadly predator. In fact, she was perhaps the most beautiful woman I had ever seen in my life. Only Astra, with her well defined, yet frail elegance could rival this deadly man-eater. I was reminded of a comparison once made by Florianna: "Astra is a snowflake, and Miya is a flame." A very astute observation. Miya suddenly began smiling for no apparent reason. She must have been reading my thoughts.

"It's unusual to see you without a huge belly. What'd you name the baby girl?" I asked, putting forth the first of the three questions allotted to me.

Miya looked at me in surprise, but quickly went back to smiling.

"That was the last question I was expecting you to ask, Ruslan. Though it is nice to hear, I won't hide that. Her name is Deia, Crown Princess Deianna royl Georg ton Mesfelle."

In that Miya's daughter had become a Crown Princess, it wasn't hard to guess that the real Georg had already divorced Marta. I wonder what his ex-wife demanded in return for signing the divorce papers? Should I ask Miya about that? Alright, I shouldn't waste another question on this. I'll figure it out as the game goes on. All the more so given that I had a much more interesting question to ask:

"After leaving *Perimeter Defense*, I spent a ton of time trying to find information on the game online. I also tried to find even one virtual reality capsule for sale that looked like the one I got out of. It was a wild goose chase, though. And, if I could perhaps understand why a private game for the elite would want secrecy, why would anyone want to keep the virtual reality capsules a secret? Doesn't it make sense that the manufacturers would actually be doing everything in their power to advertise such a product? I honestly got the impression that this technology simply does not exist. Can you tell me about it?"

Miya gave another satisfied smile:

"You've finally started thinking with your head, not letting your emotions rule you. Great question, Ruslan. That's how you should have started this conversation, instead of wallowing in self-pity and complaining about rude neighbors. Everything you suppose is correct, but you have missed one important aspect. You saw a working virtual reality capsule in real life. That was a mass-produced model too, not some experimental prototype. I've given you enough hints. You can figure the rest out on your own. Let's see if you have a working brain in that head of yours."

Miya sat back deep in the chair with a glass of juice in her hand, and began observing my intellectual strain, clearly not planning to help me or give any more information.

I tried feverishly to imagine how this could possibly be. It was mass-produced but nothing had ever been written about it? Some kind of strict military secret? Maybe for working out different scenarios in a virtual world instead of reality? Maybe for working in locations with high infectious disease rates, or under enemy fire. Or maybe it was to train soldiers to overcome fear of death. After a hundred virtual deaths, they wouldn't be afraid anymore. Or perhaps it was for selecting the most suitable people for especially unusual missions, like a Mars landing or first contact with extraterrestrial life forms... But that all sounded too outlandish.

"It is the right answer, though" Miya attested, clearly content. "It's good to see that you are not as closed-minded as the vast majority of people. You can think beyond the commonplace. Yes, it is for working out how to use advanced technology still under development. The game *Perimeter Defense*, and the equipment for it do really exist, though I am not aware of all the goals of this mass-scale experiment. And I also have no idea where former players go to after they get a game-over. Information about *Perimeter Defense* is not allowed to seep out beyond the laboratory walls. I hope very much that they are simply given new characters, though I cannot say I am sure of that. You have only one question left, Ruslan. Ask it, and we can get to work."

Easy for her to say... I was still in shock after

getting an answer to the last question. Miya and Georgiy, it seemed, were participants in a mass-scale many-year experiment for an unknown secretive organization! Well I'll be damned! My thoughts started to get mixed up. The questions that seemed important just a minute earlier, now had utterly no purpose. *Perimeter Defense* is a future technology development simulator... Well, alright. Though it was hard to believe, it did explain a lot.

"And can I bring my own body into the game?" I wondered.

Miya's eyebrows curved inward in surprise and her lips puckered in dismay.

"A strange question, Ruslan. You have seriously let me down. You already know the answer to it. That would be impossible for a large number of reasons. How can you possibly imagine bringing a physical body into a computer game? It would be impossible to add even a single material object to the virtual world. Just as it would be impossible to remove anything material from *Perimeter Defense*. Only thoughts, minds, and knowledge. That thing there," she said, pointing at the box, "is nothing more than a Chinese souvenir. A plastic pearl. Georgiy saw it at a stand in the mall and bought it for me, because it really does look like the in-game object. I did give it some embellishments as well, of course. *Perimeter Defense* is used, among other things, for discovering and training people with latent psionic abilities. After many years of training, I learned to use these skills not only in the virtual world, but outside of it as well."

Despite all my skepticism, I couldn't find any inconsistencies in the Truth Seeker's words.

Although... I pointed to the two twins at the neighboring table.

"And who plays the nonhuman races and the Aliens? Why did they understand when I spoke Ravaash?"

Miya shook her head in reproach:

"Ruslan, that's no fair. You've already asked all three questions. Let's try to stay within the rules, as we agreed. I answered your three questions. I'm sure you'll find answers to the rest sooner or later. For now, I need a complete list of contract terms from you. Here's a pencil and a sheet of paper from my notebook. I'll give you a couple of minutes. I need to go figure out why my companion is taking so long."

The red-headed beauty retrieved a miniscule cell phone inlaid with large shiny crystals, maybe even real gemstones, from her small purse and left the noisy room into the stairwell. My gaze was involuntarily drawn to the leather purse she had left behind. There was probably a ton of interesting stuff inside, maybe even some secret inventions that would cast some light on what was going on... But I shook my head, chasing off the criminal thoughts, and took the pencil. So, what do I want?

Miya came back seven minutes later when my list of demands was already practically finished. The woman stood motionless for a few seconds, staring vacantly somewhere past me, then forcefully hurled her phone onto the floor. It broke into a great many pieces, and the precious stones scattered around the floor. You didn't have to be a genius to figure out that she was very upset, and even enraged. I wonder who could have brought the Truth Seeker to such a state of white-hot fury?

"Mr. G.I. won't be coming to the meeting," Miya told me, somewhat coming back to her senses. "It seems that he, at the very last moment, had a change of heart and said that he doesn't want to meet with you personally because he suspects you might not be very happy to see him. What an egotistical narcissist!"

I could have been wrong, but it seemed I saw a deceitful glint in her teary eyes.

"Alright, Ruslan, seeing how Georgiy left me on the hook like this, I don't have any more reason to protect him. Yes, you're right. Georgiy was occupying your body the whole time you were playing *Perimeter Defense*. Don't act so surprised. One of the reasons the game was made was to improve human-consciousness-transfer technology. It can be done either via special machine, or by strong human psionics like myself and Mr. G.I. If only you knew, Ruslan, how hard it will be for me to carry everything by myself... If only I had the strength... There's no time. We're seriously behind schedule as it is. So, give me the paper. I'll take a look at what you wrote."

Miya practically ripped the piece of paper from my hands and quickly skimmed it.

"As far as the first point, sure, the money will be there. There definitely won't be a problem with that. But this one here is gonna be harder: 'While in my body, no drugs or alcohol.' For now, I can't give you a one-hundred-percent guarantee, but I'll definitely try to think something up. Same for the next point about antisocial behavior. Though... sure. We'll accept them both. I swear by my abilities and the life of my only daughter, that no one will commit antisocial acts or use narcotics while in your body. I hope that will be good enough for you."

I nodded, somewhat shocked at the seriousness of what she had just sworn by. Miya then continued:

"The next points I don't get: 'Freedom to behave however I want in game. Guaranteed safety for all those close to me, etc.' Ruslan, let's put this in more concrete terms. What do you mean by freedom and safety here? And please hurry. Someone might notice that Mr. G.I. is missing from the game soon."

To be honest, I was expecting her to resist more forcefully on the last points, all the more so given that I had asked for a substantial amount of money, including a significant amount of moral and material compensation, both for the last contract, and as an advance for this one. That was why I was surprised and even somewhat confused by the levity with which my demands had been accepted. Also, the pressure Miya was putting on me to hurry was hampering my concentration.

"I don't want to make any reports on my activities in *Perimeter Defense.* I must have the ability to do what I consider right in a given situation. And I want a guarantee that no characters will suffer at your hands just because they have become important to me."

"Was there someone holding you back last time? And as for my actions... You can't seriously suppose that the third most powerful Truth Seeker has nothing more important to do than track down people close to you, right?" Miya asked, surprised.

"Remember when you paralyzed Florianna? Remember when you lashed out at Princess Astra in the submarine?"

Miya flared up in response:

"Ruslan, your relationship with these characters had no bearing on my actions whatsoever! I simply had no choice but to shut that blabby little airhead up! I did that for both our sakes. If I hadn't, it would have been two days at most before the secret of your being in Mr. G.I.'s body was revealed, and everything ended in complete failure. I would also have seriously suffered. You can't even imagine how meticulous the administrators are about making sure that every *Perimeter Defense* character has only one player. A couple of misplaced sentences about the real world, and you're done. It's like the player was never even there! As for the second girl, it was just raw calculation. Her pregnancy got in the way of my plans. But you demanded I not touch her, and I agreed..."

"Miya, don't try to squirm out of answering. Your listing off things that already happened does nothing for me. I want a guarantee for the future."

Miya looked me right in the eyes and said, slowly and clearly:

"No one will hold you back, just as no one will forbid you from having friends, girlfriends, favorites and even lovers in *Perimeter Defense*. But the rules of the game remain as before: you cannot reveal the fact that you are in Crown Prince Georg's body, and you must hold out for six months while fighting back the Alien attacks. And another rule, just from me: you cannot divorce my character in game. You also cannot have more children, and you must defend the Unatari star system at any cost. These are crucial issues.

Failing at any of them will result in in your contract being terminated with no pay. And, what's more, I would have no more reason to give even the tiniest shit about keeping you alive in the real world. Consider this both a warning and an official rule."

I frowned, though I did understand Miya's reason for insisting on these demands. The last thing she needed was another player in a position to disrupt her schemes. Her demands were basically fair. I had nothing against them and only asked one clarification:

"Miya, I can easily understand the divorce part. In the game world, it would threaten little Crown Princess Deia's position in society. I can also understand why no more children. Your daughter has no need for competition or other heirs. But what makes Unatari in particular so special?"

Miya looked at me with something like pity, as if she was once again frustrated with my intellectual capabilities:

"Don't you know? Because, according to the game storyline, Deia should be sleeping soundly in her nursery on Unatari right now. And your mission is to protect your daughter from danger, no matter the cost."

"Let's clarify the mission then. Do I need to protect Deia or the Unatari star system? If I take her out of Unatari to a safe location, will protecting Unatari remain a priority mission?"

She considered it briefly, then said:

"Ruslan, of course, you are right to question this. The only problem is that, unfortunately, your bright idea came too late. You won't be able to get

Deia out of Unatari. I am not a normal player, after all, but a Truth Seeker with terrifying abilities. The game admins trust me. My character can be away from *Perimeter Defense* for long stretches of time. For now, my daughter is serving as a beacon for me; I can always return to the game through her. That means I can slip into the game without the admins noticing. But there are technical nuances here that make doing that somewhat difficult. I need that very exit point to stay right where I left it. As briefly as possible, protecting the Unatari star system is of critical importance not only to me, but to you as well. If it is lost, you will not be able to leave *Perimeter Defense* and get back to the real world."

"Am I understanding correctly that you will not be with me in *Perimeter Defense* then?" I asked, clearing up an important point, which the redheaded beauty verified.

"Yes, that's true. In the game, I am too vulnerable to my master, so I don't want to risk being near you."

"You don't trust me?" I laughed.

"Of course not. I don't trust anyone at all. Not you, not Mr. G.I., and not the game admins. Do you think I could have lived this long in *Perimeter Defense* if I was the trusting type? I leave you the ability to call me three times for a short period, but only if extremely necessary. Making a jump between the game and the real world is very tiring, even to me. Do you understand my conditions?"

I responded with a silent nod.

"So then, we can consider the contract agreed upon. I see no reason to sign it. The last time that was done just for atmosphere, to make you sense the weight of your decision. You won't be able to take paper copies with you into the game anyway and, what's more, there's no time for such senselessness. Georgiy can barely wait. Alright then, you need to prepare your mind for the transfer."

"And how do I do that?" I wondered. Miya explained:

"You need to fall asleep or get very drunk. As we have very little time, I suggest the easy way: here are some sleeping pills."

Miya extended her hand, revealing a pair of unstamped pills in a yellow glossy packet. My whole life's experience, and all my cautious instincts were crying out at that moment that it was a bad idea to take unknown drugs from the hands of someone I barely knew, but I willed the voice of reason down to a dull whisper. I washed down the two semi-sweet pills with a swig of mineral water and started waiting.

I was already feeling it ten seconds later. The restaurant began swimming before my eyes. The two enforcers at the neighboring table took on the appearance of Ravaash soldiers. Miya's clothing changed from an orange dress into a set of brightly colored ribbons, and her straight red hair, previously styled down, crawled up into a bun. I started feeling quite sure that I had just made the biggest mistake of my life.

"Clean up after us!" Miya said to the lizards in Imperial language, and both reptiles gave affirmative nods in reply.

The Truth Seeker looked at her watch, then at me.

"Ugh, Ruslan. Pray we won't be late, and that I have enough energy..."

The last thing I noticed, already losing consciousness, was Miya stretching out her hand to the Chinese souvenir lying on the table, carelessly popping the transparent package open and... tossing the "plastic pearl" right down her throat!

* * *

"AHHHHHHHHHHHHHHHH!"

My body arched back in severe pain, and I pried open my eyes in horror. There was a blinding white light. There were some darkened figures bending over me. The voices were gurgling, as if speaking under water.

"His pulse is falling again!"

"Clear!"

I couldn't figure out what to even react to before another of the figures was bowing down over me. The defibrillator shock forced my body to buckle in again. I screamed. Actually, instead of a deafening scream, I was only able to squeeze out a barely audible whimper. There were tubes down my throat and an oxygen mask on my face getting in the way.

"We have a pulse!"

"His pupils are reacting to light!"

"Brain activity detected!"

"Blood pressure: sixty over thirty and rising!"

"Give me two CC's of nanite-7. We need him to start improving faster."

I felt a needle poke into my neck. I tried to concentrate and focus my eyes, but I couldn't. As before, I could only see the people as dark, blurry contours. My hearing, though, was stabilizing gradually.

"Arrhythmia worsening," came a voice belonging to a young woman. "Pulse unstable: fifteen beats per minute. Should we give him another shock?"

"No, that won't be necessary. There should already be enough oxygen in the blood. His blood pressure is stabilizing," replied another voice with a strange accent, sounding almost inhuman.

"Pulse is at twenty-eight and rising."

"Blood pressure is at seventy-five over forty. Brain activity increasing."

"Patient conscious!" The joyful scream of the third figure rang in my ears.

One of them bent down over me. I tried to focus my vision and, with surprise, I saw Miya in surgeon's whites with a mask on her face. She was looking down at me with panic and suddenly locked eyes with me.

"I can tell that you can hear and understand me. Ruslan, you scared the crap out of me! The transfer wasn't totally smooth. I don't really know why. Maybe, despite all my tricks, some automatic defense mechanisms from the admins detected the change in IP-address or ID-capsule. Your account was banned. In the game it looked like a sudden heart failure. You spent three minutes clinically dead. I spent practically all my energy trying to pull you back from the other side. But you were able to squeeze out. The character is unblocked, and that is all that matters.

Take care of yourself, get your strength back.

For now, like I said, I'll have to leave you. There's no point in trying to call me into Perimeter Defense *for the next month and a half or so. I simply won't have the power for another jump. So, you'll have to deal with everything on your own. The Unatari defense forces are waiting for you.*

Good luck!"

.

CAPITAL ENCIRCLED

I T WAS DIFFICULT for me to wake up. My panicked, disjointed dream just didn't want to let me go. Finally, I opened one eye and took a look around. On the walls and ceiling, there were gilded lamps in the shape of natural crystals. To my left, there was a huge bronze statue of an unknown creature with eight limbs. The room was familiar, but I simply couldn't imagine where I'd seen it before. Maybe it was that hotel in Turkey? But no, there was a huge picture window in that hotel room. Just instinctively, I called up the interactive map to get my bearings. It wasn't the first time in the last few months I had tried to do so out of habit. I hadn't actually succeeded, though, until this very moment. Before my eyes appeared a semitransparent map.

Seventh dormitory wing of the space yacht, Queen of Sin

The last traces of my dream instantly left me. That's right! I was in the game again! For a second, the previous day flashed before my eyes. The clinic, the call from an unknown number, negotiations with Miya, terrified doctors leaning over me... By the way, how did that story with the bungled character change end, and how was it affecting my health? I carefully moved my arms and legs, then felt my chest. On my body, under a layer of long underwear, I detected some flat, round stickers plastered on my skin, which clearly contained some kind of medical equipment. They didn't make me feel uncomfortable, or impede my movement, so I let them be. In fact, I forgot about them quickly, as my gaze was caught by something else: a huge gut that should not have been there. The starship echoed with my enraged scream. The only words that were not swearing were interjections.

All the success I had had improving his body, which had taken me six months of hard work to accomplish, had been undone by my replacement in no time at all! That... bad man, Mr. G.I., had once again put on weight, returning his figure to its initial state. His body was once again swimming in flab! I needed to see this from another angle right away in order to evaluate the scale of the disaster.

I carefully set my bare feet on the ground and tried to stand. My head was spinning slightly, though it wasn't quite as bad as it could have been. And it definitely was better than what you could expect out of a body that had truly just lived through clinical death. I took a few steps and stopped in front of a huge mirror. The man in the mirror looking back at me was very fat, with a noticeable white spot in his dark hair. What's that then? When my last contract had ended, Crown Prince Georg had just a couple little gray hairs in his thick, dark mane. Astra had even experimented with trying to pluck them. The man looking back at me now had graying hair, and looked bulbous and old. And the shoulders... I even took the semitransparent white turtle-neck off to check with my eyes if the mirror was lying. The tattooed three-eyed skulls were gone. From my right shoulder, the little winged ass was smiling up at me once again, his eyes bulging out as if constipated. On my left forearm, there was a naked beauty with bright red hair lying in a seductive pose. The unknown artist of the sketch had perhaps exaggerated the voluptuousness of the female form a bit, but it was easy to recognize who it was supposed to be.

So then, what else? My right eye, wounded once upon a time in combat with the Aliens had healed completely and was working as normal again. The web of scars on the Crown Prince's face had disappeared, probably removed with the help of good cosmetic surgeons. Georg had left just one thin white scar, clearly intentionally, which went from his eyebrow down along the right cheek to the lip, giving his face an appearance of stern masculinity. The fact that a manly soldier's face did not make for a harmonious combination with his pear-shaped, bulky body, which undulated when he walked like a slab of bacon, probably had not occurred to Mr. G.I. His body looked somewhat comical, like a hastily glued-together Frankenstein made of two different men.

Yep. I'll have to deal with the body again. I already realize he's been neglecting it, and I'll have to do all that hard work in the gym over again. But now, I should check to see what had happened with his characteristics. I took a look at my character's information:

Georg royl Inoky ton Mesfelle, Crown Prince of the Empire
> **Age: 48**
> **Race: Human**
> **Gender: Male**
> **Class: Aristocrat/Mystic**
> **Achievements: Chameleon Elder Female, Discovered Arite Race, Alien Killer, Researcher of the Unknown, Imperial Conqueror, Ex-Fleet Commander for Sector Eight, Malingerer, Abandoned Friend, Denied Paternity**
> **Fame: 31**
> **Standing: -52**

What??? My eyes rolled back into my head, both from the overabundance of new "achievements," as well as from my now utterly ruined standing. On a purely technical level, I had no idea how he had managed to let his character's standing fall by 100 points in just three mo... Wait a second! With confusion, I stared at the date in the corner of the interactive menu. Impossible. It hadn't been just three months since the end of the last contract, but a whole seven!!! How?!

Seven months! Princess Astra should already have given birth to my child! On a related note... the indelible, shameful brand "Denied Paternity" was probably related precisely to that event. After all, it would seem that I had made no reaction when the legal deadlines for recognizing a child came and went, so the child not only did not become a Crown Prince, but did not even get a "ton" attached to its name, meaning it didn't even have confirmation of noble birth... Feeling vexed, I banged my fist on the fatass looking back at me in the mirror, as if the reflection was guilty of something.

Damn, I even bruised my hand! I shook my beat-up fist.

Miya! I'll strangle that bitch if I ever see her again!!! I recognized clearly now that she was a lying villain, and had tricked me. The red-headed lady's story about the game for the military didn't really click with my experience: the "souvenir" I brought ended up being real crystals, time was passing at different rates, and... if you thought about it... there were two Chameleons, who had somehow gotten out of the game into the real world. I had been sold and, promising me the moon, popped right back into *Perimeter Defense.*

I sat down on the edge of the huge bed. Seven months had passed. The thought of it! And my fleet... Here I was struck by a cold sweat. *Joan the Fatty* and the ships with her! The crews had been sitting on their laurels with no pay for more than half a year. And, to top it all off, they were God-knows-where in Swarm territory! They must have run out of provisions long ago. The ships wouldn't have been able to pay for repair or technical service at Iseyek stations, nor even replace the fuel in their reactors. And I bet they're cursing their commander with every breath in their bodies!

I would have to fix this situation right away! I must transfer the funds to my ships! By the way, how was the money situation? I opened the internal finances interface... and closed it right away. There were just one-point-five million credits left in the account. But then what, I wonder, was Mr. G.I. able to spend the three hundred million I had left him with on? New sculptures for the yacht? I tried to figure out the transaction history from the account, but it had been very thoroughly cleared.

So then, I should think about what to do with the situation I'd inherited. I had a miserable amount of money, my fleet was God knows where, the fate of those close to me was unknown, and also there was the fact that the Mystic class had reappeared in my character information. This all bore eloquent witness to the fact that Georg had once again become very addicted to narcotic crystals. To be honest, my arms just sank...

I tried to call the Chameleons in hope of receiving an answer to my questions. However, no one came to my call. And that was also strange.

I calmed down a bit and went off to search for any kind of clothes. It isn't appropriate for a noble Imperial Crown Prince to promenade around in his underwear, even on his own yacht. Fortunately, I found a clothing cabinet in the very same room. I dug through the whole wardrobe but, for some reason, couldn't find even one military uniform. Not the Sector Eight Fleet Commander's one, and not even an Orange House uniform of any kind. What the hell? The only thing I could find were two frivolous flashy peacock outfits, a pair of multi-colored tights and bright pink and purple shoes. I even first supposed that I had accidentally gotten into my wife's closet, but what stopped me was the fact that the gargantuan swim trunks I found could fit four women Miya's size. Also, the size eleven pink shoes with magnetic fasteners would clearly have been a bit large for the Truth Seeker.

Having somehow gotten dressed, hoping that I didn't look too comical, I took another look around the room. Now, after calling up the interactive map, I finally remembered: yes, I had been here before. It was a bedroom, one of the thirty that belonged to Crown Prince Georg royl Inoky ton Mesfelle on the luxurious yacht. At the very beginning of my time in *Perimeter Defense*, I had visited it a few times, but mostly chose to stay and sleep in completely different rooms. I stood with difficulty and, simply for curiosity's sake, approached the many-armed bronze titan, which clearly served as the main decoration in the room.

"Ma-radgi, the last soldier," by Veron ton Gep

Its information dutifully popped up before me, telling me fairly sparsely about the figure. The inscription on the stand said the same thing.

The statue of a huge bronze octopus looked like a number of shaggy tentacles poking out through a crack in a rock face. Nothing in its form served to indicate that this creature was a fierce warrior, and not simply a hunter relaxing after a satisfying meal or a doting mother protecting her children. But I decided that the sculptor probably knew best, especially if that sculptor was the great Veron ton Gep, whose artistry I had recently heard Miya lauding. In my previous contract in *Perimeter Defense*, I had realized once and for all that I knew nothing about art, and so I didn't get at all upset by not understanding the sculptor's concept.

"Prince Georg, are you awake yet?" A resonant female voice rang out right behind me. I almost screamed in surprise.

I turned around, trying to put on a look somewhere between bored and lofty, as if walking around the starship in this flashy peacock getup was the most normal thing in the world for the Crown Prince. But I was, unfortunately, unable to pull off the high-and-mighty look with my stomach swaying side to side in inertia, making a gurgling sound as it jostled. I noticed a fleeting smile pass over the face of the young girl with short dark hair in an Orange House Fleet uniform.

Ayna Mentor, your personal assistant
Age: 24
Race: Human
Gender: Female
Class: Athlete
Achievements: Three-time Orange House Target-Shooting Champion. Former Nessi No-Rules-Fighting Champion. Approved to work with members of the upper aristocracy.
Fame: +1
Standing: +1
Presumed personal opinion of you: +13 (warm)

The girl was fairly nice to look at, but just not to my taste. She was too tall, even making me look small in comparison. With her overly toned muscles, she also carried an air of grayness and forgettability. I suspect it was for that very reason that Miya had approved her for the position, or maybe had even handpicked her for the job. I wonder how I should behave around her? I gave her a good-natured smile and commented:

"I think the time has come for me to start taking better care of my body. What do you think, Ayna?"

It immediately became clear that I'd guessed wrong. The girl became noticeably afraid and stood at attention, extending her arms down her torso and lowering her eyes to the floor.

"Your Highness looks excellent as always," the girl said, keeping her gaze trained downward.

She was clearly afraid of me, and that was very strange. Fear of one's boss should pass with time but, above all else, I normally expected an entirely different manner from an assistant.

"Ayna, remind me. For what qualities exactly did my spouse hire you? I can now say with certainty that honesty was not one of them."

The girl grew even more afraid. It seemed to me that she would collapse and faint at any moment.

"Mrs. Miya chose me exactly, above all else, for my quick reaction speed and ability to protect her spouse. And also because I'm hardworking, agreeable, and detail-oriented."

"A personal assistant is not typically required to provide security. That is a bodyguard's job. By the way... Ayna, remind me. Where have the invisible Chameleons gone?"

"Mrs. Miya fired them four months ago. She didn't like having invisible observers around."

"I see..." The news was, of course, strange, but I tried not to show my surprise. "Then here is a list of tasks. First, seek out Popori de Cacha, my former bodyguard head, and invite her back. Last I knew, she was on Unatari on the Chameleons' island, though much time has passed since then. Second, figure out where my second cousin Katerina ton Mesfelle has gone. Third, compile a list of the most valuable luxury items on board *Queen of Sin*. Fourth, find whoever is responsible for the defense of Unatari, and bring them to me at once. I need a report on the current situation. Fifth, I need a fleet commander's uniform. This clownish getup is not cutting it..."

"But, Prince Georg! When Duke Avalle royl Anjer threatened to formally accuse you of having incompatible professions, you quit your position as Perimeter Sector Eight Fleet Commander and ordered all clothing reminding you of your military past thrown out!"

I couldn't believe it. It turned out they had wanted to disgrace me, but I had fought with the new Duke and slammed the door behind myself on the way out... Yes, today was just full of surprises.

"Ayna, I simply cannot believe that not even one of my military uniforms has remained on the yacht! If you really have to, take the yacht captain's jacket. By the way, please invite the captain to visit with me a bit later, as well. That's all for now. Go do your job... Although... Stop! Your sixth mission in number, but first in importance is to bring me some coffee... I mean, roast firo-nut beverage. Can you do that? Bring it right to my office. That's where I'll be."

"Yes, my Prince, of course." The girl snapped a brisk military salute and left the room.

God! How I'd missed all this! With a mug of the hot beverage in hand, I took a seat and kicked my legs up with pleasure in front of a digital screen in the very same cabin I had once designated my office on *Queen of Sin*. Everything was familiar here, the furniture, the smell, the pictures on the wall. I felt like I was back home! And I had a better outfit, too. Someone had managed to dig up a dark blue fleet commander's uniform, though it was missing the golden epaulets and the words "Perimeter Sector Eight." It was a shame, of course, but I was sure I would figure out something to take its place soon enough.

Miya and Mr. G.I. could think they'd tricked me all they wanted. Let them keep thinking that! I have more than six whole months left in this game — more than enough time to analyze the situation, consider my errors and figure out workable solutions. Back in that restaurant, I was extremely vulnerable to the Truth Seeker and constantly caught her shooting unkind, judgmental looks in my direction. As such, I had opted not to be rude and, after bargaining for better conditions, agreed. For some reason, I was sure that if I hadn't, I would never have left that restaurant alive. No matter what you say, Miya had not forgotten her promise to kill me in the real world. Here, in the

Perimeter Defense world, I didn't have to be afraid of my wife, and I could even use her has a magic genie to grant three wishes.

But first, I'd have to quench my thirst for information. I urgently needed news about what had happened in the last seven months. I was sitting on my bed reading and crying when a cautious knock came on the door. The letter in my hands was from my daughter. In it, she accused me of killing her mother, and it was very upsetting. Princess Marta royl Valesy ton Mesfelle-Kyle would rather have hung than divorce Crown Prince Georg. Death was the only way to preserve her daughter's right to inheritance, which Lika would have surely lost if her parents had gotten a legal divorce.

Before sticking her head in a noose, Marta wrote a letter detailing Miya's blackmail, while her legal husband stood aside and even joined in. Copies of her incriminating suicide note were sent to the Kingdom of Fastel chancellery, the Orange House Capital, the Emperor's reception room in the Throne World, and also to Lika at school. That was six months ago. Since then, she had refused to ever talk with her father again, and had even changed her name to Likanna royl Fastel, removing any reminders of the hated Crown Prince Georg and his family name from her title.

The bastards! I hate them so much!!! There was a lot in Miya's behavior that I could understand and forgive. And with time, I could even hypothetically learn to forgive Mr. G.I. for his careless treatment of my body (though not before giving him a shiner for the trouble he caused me). But for what they'd done to Likanna – my beloved daughter, the most important person in this world to me... I could never forgive them.

"Come in," I shouted, hurriedly drying the tears from my face.

"My Prince, I've been told that your Highness wanted to meet with me," stated an unfamiliar strong-looking dark-haired soldier in an Orange House Star Fleet Admiral's uniform.

Mike ton Akad, Unatari Fleet Admiral
Age: 48
Race: Human
Gender: Male
Class: Military
Achievements: Has combat medals for participation in interspecies conflicts
Fame: +5
Standing: +9
Presumed personal opinion of you: Unknown

I already knew that Admiral Kiro Sabuto had left Crown Prince Georg royl Inoky ton Mesfelle's circle three months ago and joined the Red House. I had even watched a video of Duke Claudius royl Mike ton Sid, head of the Red House, as he officially appointed Admiral Kiro Sabuto to the position of Perimeter Sector Fourteen Fleet Commander. As for now, I was sorely lacking a skilled admiral, and it wasn't at all clear yet how good a replacement Mike ton Akad would make.

"Take a seat, admiral," I said, pointing to the

armchair beside mine. "Tell me now: am I an ass or a bastard? I let all my affairs slip away on autopilot, and now the situation is totally out of hand."

"Prince Georg, you are both an ass and a bastard, and I could even add another set of stronger words that your Highness has earned handily as well," he added, taking a seat in the armchair. "But we won't solve this situation with words and, as you've called me here, you must have had some ideas."

He made a very good first impression. I took a definite liking to the admiral for the fact that he was direct, yet prepared to hear me out, despite all the built-up negativity.

"Before anything else, I have two questions, admiral. First: what makes you so sure that the Aliens will get through to Unatari? The warp beacon is turned off and, as far as I know, no Alien mobile-warp-beacon ships have been seen here."

The man was well prepared to tell me about the source of his information on Unatari's forthcoming demise. It would seem that Miya had announced it to a large crowd of people right after the information came in that the Aliens had captured the Hnelle star system. No matter how negative an opinion I may have had of my spouse, I had to give her her dues. She was a very strong Truth Seeker, and I didn't doubt her predictions for a second.

So... The sequence of events is becoming clear to me now. Mr. G.I. wasn't planning on inviting me back into the game at all. But then, the Aliens captured Hnelle, cutting the former pirate dead-end off from the Empire. Miya figured out that Unatari would soon fall and, for that very reason, called me into *Perimeter Defense*. Inexplicably, the Truth Seeker was quite sure that I would be able to manage. It was, of course, strange given the distribution of forces. But, if the Truth Seeker thought there was a chance of rescue, the situation couldn't be that hopeless. OK, I'll figure this all out later.

"Admiral, my second question is: why the hell did you order the heavy assault cruisers and *Crown Princess Likanna* re-equipped?! The original setup I had them in pretty much spoke for itself in my campaign against the Aliens. Recharging allied ship shields proved nearly unbeatable. Why break something that's working well?"

"Crown Prince, after being hired, I asked your Highness to explain the concept behind the fleet three times, but I never got an answer. That was why I asked permission to re-outfit them in the common way. I also did not receive an answer to any of my four requests to that effect. After that, I acted at my own peril."

What is wrong with you, Mr. G.I.?! It can't have been so hard to answer your subject just the one time! And now, I'm paying the price of your laziness and indifference... I tried to make a face of measured surprise.

"Admiral, I would swear to anyone that I didn't see any of your requests. I really practically didn't look at incoming messages and gave an order to have almost all incoming calls dismissed. It's hard to explain... Though alright, I'll tell you directly. In a crystal dream, I saw a new Alien invasion. I couldn't figure out when it would be, but I unmistakably saw the capture of Hnelle, Unatari, Tesse, and the Orange House Capital... Since then, I've been seeking out a way to change the situation, and haven't had much time to think about anything else. And now, that invasion has truly begun. Hnelle has already fallen. Next in line are Himora, Tesse, Unatari, the Orange House Capital and beyond. Now we have no more time. We must change the situation."

"And how exactly can we change it?" The man's eyes lit up with interest.

I shrugged my shoulders ambiguously.

"It would be impossible for us to defeat the Alien fleet currently in Hnelle with just the ships we have here. At the very least, I don't see any way of doing it. But I do see a way for us to emerge victorious from an extended stand-off. For that, our fleet needs to get out into the recently captured former Swarm systems. There should be reinforcements waiting there."

The admiral rubbed his chin with his fingers in thought.

"It won't look good. That's for sure! It'll look like we're throwing the people of Unatari to the wolves, as we ourselves flee. The people of Unatari are quite afraid as it is. Their mood is near panic, in fact. I have overheard several conversations about how your Highness is supposedly planning to flee on *Queen of Sin*, leaving the rest to fate. And, if the fleet really does leave Unatari, I'm concerned that residents here would actually come to prefer it that way. There are even rumors that some government officials are buying themselves places on *Queen of Sin* in order to escape with your Highness."

I raised my eyebrows in surprise and asked him to explain everything he'd heard about that.

"Everyone knows that *Queen of Sin* can make two warp jumps in a row. Only a ship such as yours would be capable of escaping through the Alien-controlled Hnelle system. I've heard insistent rumors in recent days that yacht officers are trading places on the starship at prices of around one million credits per seat and up."

"Let's get to the bottom of this at once!" I declared. I got on the loudspeaker and asked the yacht captain to come to my office.

A minute later the yacht captain arrived, and I recognized him right away. It was Tarik ton Miro, who had once been second assistant to Captain Oorast Pohl. He was one of the few people who had accompanied me the whole way, from my first day in the *Perimeter Defense* world, all the way to the end of the contract. He must have worked his way up to the rank of captain. I greeted my old acquaintance and asked a direct question about the veracity of the rumors that seats on my yacht were being sold.

"Many truly have come with such requests, your Highness. Especially Unatari government officials, but also Astorimma deputies, and people from other large cities here as well. More than fifty people in the past three days. Of course, I refused them all."

I mulled it over and gave an evil grin:

"Rats, the lot of them. The first thing they do is run, even though the capital can still be saved. They need to be taught a lesson! Here's how we'll do it, captain. Order your weaslliest officers to get in touch with these people, and take their money for 'tickets.' A million credits a seat. I think that will be enough. But be sure to warn them that this is all strictly illegal, and they will have to board as technicians, electricians, etc. Let them all think that the yacht will take off the day after tomorrow, but tell them they all must arrive by this evening. And when all these rotten characters have all arrived..."

"We line them up against the wall?" suggested Admiral Mike ton Akad with poorly hidden hope in his voice.

I put on a mocking flare up:

"Look at the kind of people I work with! And I'm the one they call bloodthirsty?! No, we don't need to execute anyone. We'll just talk about executing them, get them all riled up, and kick them off the ship after stripping them of their posts in the Unatari government! Captain, give ten percent of the money you collect to this brilliant officer, and transfer the rest to the fleet treasury."

"Will do, my Prince! It's great doing business with you, your Highness!" Tarik ton Miro began smiling with his whole mouth, having potentially become a millionaire today.

Standing change. Empire Military faction opinion of you has improved.
Present Empire Military faction opinion of you: +17 (warm)

Alright. It worked! Though it was somewhat unexpected to see the faction relationship change, despite the fact that the Unatari star system had technically been cut off from the Empire for eleven days. And also, I noticed that my relationship with the military, though it had soured in my absence, had still not reached such catastrophic levels as my standing. Last time, I had to start from actually negative numbers, so +17 with the military at the very beginning was pretty cool!

When the captain had left, Admiral Mike ton Akad said thoughtfully:

"Crown Prince Georg royl Inoky ton Mesfelle was once considered a great master of unexpected solutions and improvisation. That is precisely why I hurried to occupy the vacant seat left after Kiro Sabuto's resignation. For a long time, I thought I had made a mistake. But today, I see glimmers of that very brilliance. I may see yet why it was once said that your fleet did not know the meaning of the word 'defeat.'"

I did not have time to reply. A knock came on the door, and Ayna swiftly entered, holding a tablet computer.

"Prince Georg, I have found your cousin's location, composed a list of the most valuable objects on the yacht and... here," the girl stepped aside, letting a guest enter.

Into the office came... the one Chameleon I would recognize from among thousands of others. Popori de Cacha!!! I stood up and took a step forward to embrace my old friend. After a second of confusion, the huge bipedal gray lizard responded in kind and embraced me with her (or maybe his, hard to say with a Chameleon) flexible appendages.

"After your Highness fired the Chameleon

bodyguard team, I tried to find work for myself and my subjects as bodyguards for the senior officers on *Crown Princess Likanna*. And now, I'm hearing that the Crown Prince wants to see me," explained Popori de Cacha, very quickly elucidating me on the circumstances of her arrival to the space yacht.

"I'll be brief, Popori de Cacha. I need my great bodyguard head back. And with her, I need six, or even just two more invisible guards."

The Chameleon smiled with two rows of sharp teeth:

"I am delighted, my Prince. I'll do it all to the best of my ability. That said, I am a 'him' again, not a 'her.' After giving birth to my children, I changed back to my original gender."

The interactive character popup was showing that Popori de Cacha's loyalty was still as high as possible, just as I'd left it. Here was something my surrogate hadn't been able to mess up. Clearly Crown Prince Georg simply had no dealings with any Chameleons at all, and also Popori de Cacha had spent the last few months on a far-off island laying eggs and carrying for his tadpoles as they swam in their warm pools.

"Prince Georg, do you have any other orders?" My assistant wondered.

"Wait, let me see the list." I took the tablet and quickly skimmed it. "Ayna, I thought I asked you to be honest. Why didn't you bring me the whole list? I can say for certain that Miya's collection of numbered emeralds is here on the yacht, as well as a number of other valuable objects belonging to my wife. Where's all that in the list of valuables?!"

"But, your Highness..." the girl's voice began quavering in fear. "Mrs. Miya really doesn't like it when other people touch her things."

I closed my eyes and took a heavy sigh.

"Ayna, I need a *full* account in one hour. Whether it will be you or your replacement that gives it to me is up to you. Miya won't be here for more than a month, and I don't have enough time to wait for my wife's return to ask her permission. So don't be afraid, you can blame it all on me. Say the Crown Prince ordered it. In the future, I really don't like it when information is hidden from me. I hope this will be the last time."

"My Prince, my mistake will not be repeated. I promise that I'll be as honest as possible with your Highness from now on."

"Alright. Then tell me, what instructions did Miya give you before her departure? I'm having a hard time believing that Miya and the child simply disappeared without a word."

Ayna looked at me like she was expecting a trick, then looked at the others in the room, after which she sighed and said, in a fairly faithful imitation of Miya's timbre:

"The Prince will wake up soon. Help him figure out what's going on. After crystals, sometimes a person doesn't remember where they are or how they got there right away. Partial amnesia is not rare. As such, don't be surprised if he asks you weird questions. It's up to you to help Georg do everything. I also have a more specific request. My husband is a Mystic and should probably not have too much interest in the opposite sex. But that hound dog has figured out a way to chase skirts in spite of the crystals before. Your mission is not to allow that under any circumstances. If you see the Prince in an overly playful mood, dress yourself up, shake your ass and grab his attention..."

Admiral Mike ton Sid suddenly began whinnying like a mare. Ayna quickly grew embarrassed and stayed quiet. I, though, tried to reassure my blushing assistant:

"At the very least, you were honest. Ayna, you are free to go. I expect a *full* account of the valuables on this ship."

The girl left, and I returned to the conversation with the admiral, wondering about the state of the fleet in Unatari. He frowned in dissatisfaction:

"The fleet ships have been sitting motionless at the docks for six months, which has taken a toll on the crews' spirits. In the last few months, combat officers, especially the most capable and active, have been resigning in droves. Most of them are going to other Imperial fleets that really are fighting the Aliens. The most popular destination is Sector Fourteen, which now has the most serious problems in the whole Perimeter."

The admiral let out a heavy sigh.

"I tried to keep them here, Prince. But even paying them bonuses didn't help. People kept resigning anyway. The only thing that could stop the epidemic flight of valuable staff was the Alien capture of the Hnelle system. It may seem strange and paradoxical, but the reaction of the Unatari military has been twofold: of course, they were scared at being trapped and outnumbered, but many were actually glad that a reason to fight finally came knocking on our door. In general, we have staff shortages in the fleet, some ships are missing up to forty percent of their full crew. That's why, a month ago, I retired the more outmoded ships: all the *Tusk* frigates and *Curse* cruisers. I transferred their crews to our more modern ships."

After the admiral's words, I gave a start. It was as if a red light had turned on in my brain. Error! Fighting the Aliens with my usual methods looked like the wrong approach now, especially with the serious shortage of people. That was why I thought it might be the right moment to test out the light fleet concept I had thought up in the last days of my previous contract.

"Admiral, all our heavy ships would be doomed in the upcoming battle. The enemy has too much of an advantage in volley weight, so an 'honest' exchange of fire would simply lead to immediate defeat. We need the most mobile fleet we can muster; one capable of staying out of range of the enemy's largest guns while maneuvering and gunning down the little ships, as well as individual ship groups that get separated from the main armada."

The man heard me out with rapt attention, clearly in no mood to argue. I saw a very positive sign in that. Despite all the disappointment brought on by the previous months, Crown Prince Georg royl Inoky's reputation as an excellent strategist was hadn't suffered one bit.

"Admiral, my order is for the heavy ships to be placed on the docks and for work to begin to return them to the setup that I had them in when I made the raid through Swarm space. As for the people from the battleship and the five heavy cruisers, use them to fully crew all the *Thrush* light electronic combat cruisers, all *Curses*, *Flycatcher* and *Surgeon* destroyers, and the *Pyro* and *Warhawk* frigates. Also, check the preparedness of our cloaked bombers and load them with our most powerful warheads. Tomorrow, at ten in the morning, I will announce a big practice session. Together, we can train ships to work in this atypical, light formation."

"Yes sir, my Prince!"

After Admiral Mike ton Akad left to arrange for a light fleet, I stayed in the office alone with my thoughts. It was very difficult not to fall into despondency and despair, but I tried to look for the silver lining. Sure, a lot of staff had left the fleet, but the only thing at fault for the loss of so many talented officers from the Unatari fleet was the sharply changed behavior of Crown Prince Georg. Earlier, I had actually required that my employees have an earnest desire to fight for the future of humanity. It was my main criterion in choosing who to hire. There was nothing surprising in the fact that, after quitting his job as Sector Eight Fleet Commander and falling into a difficult-to-understand state of lethargy, Crown Prince Georg's subjects would gradually start to leave and move to wherever there were more serious battles with the Aliens happening.

That was why there was no reason to raise salaries, or use other methods to artificially plug up the leak. I would just have to show the soldiers that Prince Georg had awoken after a half a year's nap and would be returning to fight once again. That was why

I absolutely could not avoid battling the Aliens, as it would cause the fleet to fall apart once and for all. In fact, the battle for the Hnelle system would have to be done as showily as possible, to remind all Imperial citizens that Crown Prince Georg royl Inoky ton Mesfelle can take on the Aliens and win.

"My Prince, may I come in?" Ayna peeked through the door apprehensively. "Your mission is complete. Here is the full list of all valuables on *Queen of Sin.*"

I took the tablet, and pointed my assistant to the armchair next to mine, and the girl sat, crossing her legs.

"Ayna, prepare the first twenty items from the list for sale, excluding the trophy emeralds."

Ayna gaped in shock, as if considering objecting. After that, she made a bold move:

"My Prince, we'll hardly be likely to find buyers on Unatari who can afford these pieces."

I smiled mysteriously.

"Did I say anything about Unatari? Ayna, you just prepare the auctions. Leave finding a way of telling the Empire about it up to me. I'll get around this blockade. Also, pick out something pretty to gift Katerina ton Mesfelle. I'm flying out today to personally apologize to my cousin. And choose anything you want from the list for yourself. That's my present to you. Think of it as compensation for all the trouble."

My new assistant's eyes immediately lit up. No matter how you looked at it, there were some very luxurious items in that list, and any person would dream of owning them. I couldn't hold back a smile.

At the end of the day, women were the same everywhere, be they back home, or in *Perimeter Defense*. Not a one will refuse the temptation of taking a pretty piece of jewelry.

After looking actively through the catalog for a minute, Ayna pointed to one item:

"Prince Georg, may I choose this pair of ruby earrings?"

"Of course. I did say *any* item, didn't I?"

"I know, it's just that they're really expensive. The rubies are exceptionally pristine and large. They're worth seven hundred thousand credits!"

Standing change. Ayna Mentor's opinion of you has improved.

Presumed personal opinion of you: +28 (amicable)

A fifteen-point bump in personal opinion over nothing but a pair of earrings? A normal person might consider this a completely useless waste of expensive jewelry, but I was of a totally different opinion. The loyalty of my personal assistant was extremely important. I needed to be sure that Ayna would remain true even in hard times, despite all the temptations, threats and blackmail that she'd be sure to face.

And if I could raise my assistant's loyalty with jewelry, then why not?

"Less than a million?" I made a showily wry mouth. "Then take the whole set. There's a ruby ring that goes with it. A gift from an Imperial Crown Prince must be fashionable, if nothing else."

Standing change. Ayna Mentor's opinion of you has improved.

Presumed personal opinion of you: +43 (friendship)

"Prince Georg, I'll never forget your benevolence!" Ayna promised, as teardrops began shimmering up from her eyelashes.

"Now then... No need to cry! Accept the gift. Go prepare invitations to the auction. As soon as you're done, get me a line to the Sigur system warp beacon security team."

I suspect that my assistant did not understand the connection between my two last orders. It should be said, though, that it was quite a direct one. I was preparing to send the information about the valuables auction through the Forepost-12 beacon that became visible periodically from the Sigur system and, a day later, to receive the money from the buyers in the same fashion.

* * *

"Aw, to hell with her! I'll do it myself!" A golden statuette of a long-legged bird with sapphire eyes was sent flying into the far end of the plane's main cabin.

The shuttle was taking off rapidly. A moment later, we were on our way to my palace flying above the dark restless ocean of Unatari. The conversation with Katerina ton Mesfelle did not go well from the very beginning. She was frightfully resentful of me. There were many reasons, but the main thing was that, four months earlier, Crown Prince Georg royl

Inoky had completely ignored her marriage to Corwin ton Ugar.

The young couple were very hurt by my blatant refusal to attend their wedding, and even the four months that had passed since then had done nothing to heal the bitter wound. Corwin ton Mesfelle-Ugar still gave a forced smile to his unexpected highborn guest, but Katerina ton Mesfelle told me her honest opinion right to my face, making no effort to restrict her language. I have never been good at bearing insults, so I started firing back with a volley of hurtful questions and remarks of my own.

First of all, I was interested in how the ice-asteroid-rich Tivalle star system, which I long considered my property, had fallen into the hands of Viscount Sivir ton Mesfelle, Katerina's former classmate. I had sent him only to manage the ice processing facilities but now he had somehow become owner, not only of the processing plants, but the star system itself! What was more, that all happened, I suspect, with Katerina's hand in the mix somewhere, given that I had put her in charge of keeping track of the output of the Tivalle system's factories.

Having left some other manager in his place, Viscount Sivir had long been back in the Orange House Capital where, every month, he received a profit from the quickly growing rare-isotope-processing facilities of the Tivalle system. Speaking of that, increased demand for ice-processing equipment was the very reason the decision was made to turn the Hnelle warp beacon on permanently again, which is what led to the Alien invasion and the whole crisis I was now in.

To put it briefly, Katerina and I had a serious scrap, and I left her palace without even giving her the gift I'd brought. The whole three-hour flight to my island home, I couldn't relax or concentrate on my work. That's just how upset I was after the botched meeting. Katerina ton Mesfelle, Master of Rhetoric had played an important role in my plans to repair my standing, which had been so screwed up by Mr. G.I. Because of that, I knew I would have to secure her support one way or another. But how could I make peace with her?

The plane arrived to my island as the sun was rising. In this time zone on Unatari, morning had come. I refused an early breakfast (or would it have been a late dinner?) and heard out a report from Ayna, who also had yet to sleep. Everything had gone completely according to plan with her, though. In the short minute and a half that the Forepost-12 warp beacon was visible, a whole lot was able to be accomplished.

First, a prearranged encrypted message was sent to the Parn system for retransmission to *Space Mutt*. Crown Prince Georg had returned to actively playing *Perimeter Defense*, so the time had come for my companions to leave their sanctuary. Astra, and our son; the paralyzed Florianna, and her overgrown cockroaches; the Arite; Phobos; and Valian could all make their way back to civilization now. The coast was clear.

Second, forty-five million credits collected from the "rats," who had tried to flee Unatari were successfully transferred to the *Uukresh*. In the accompanying message addressed to Captain Clay ton

Avelle, I wrote: "Hold in there, boys! I'll send the rest of what you're due in a couple days." The transaction went through without a hitch, so the severity of the problem with the long-unprovisioned fleet, I hoped, had at least been somewhat reduced. To fully cover all the debts that had piled up, according to my calculations, I would need another one hundred seventy million credits. I was hoping to find this money through the sale of the valuables from *Queen of Sin*. The announcement of the twenty auctions also made it through to the Empire successfully.

Ah, and the most important thing was that, after two days of communications blackout, a message went out to the Empire that the Unatari star system was holding out, and that **Crown Prince Georg royl Inoky ton Mesfelle** was back in command of his fleet.

* * *

"Ruslan, I need to talk to you quick and explain a whole bunch of stuff," Mr. G.I. stammered. As usual, he was interrupting my dream at a very bad time, just as I was trying to get a little rest after an action-packed day.

While I was struggling with the very strong temptation to send him down a footpath of erotic thoughts, Georgiy continued:

"I know that you are very unhappy with what happened during the first contract. Yes, I admit that I didn't always do right by your body. It's hard not giving into temptation and enticement when you suddenly find yourself thirty years younger. It's as if

everything was suddenly in color again. Girls, dancing all night, free-flowing sex and alcohol... After so many years of health problems, all that fun tore my roof clean off, and it was hard to keep myself in bounds..."

"Well then what were the drugs for?!" I screamed in reply, but he ignored my question, continuing his speech.

"I know that Miya offered you generous compensation for all my outings. I hope you're not bitter..."

I started boiling in rage and screamed with my full throat:

"Not bitter?! If I could, I would break your arms and legs right now, then claim that's how I found you! You animal! Jackass! Bastard! You destroyed my body!"

"So then, I hope these old grievances can be considered fully settled." As if nothing had happened, totally ignoring my screams, Georgiy just continued droning on. "I'm not in your body now, so don't worry. It won't happen again. Now, I wanted to tell you why exactly seven months have gone by in Perimeter..."

* * *

The conversation ended abruptly in the middle of his sentence. I was awoken by someone shaking me hard by the shoulder. I opened my eyes.

"My Prince, you were screaming in your sleep!" Ayna was standing over my bed in pistachio-colored semi-transparent pajamas.

"I was having a bad dream," I explained, trying to calm her down and speak in a tranquil tone, though it wasn't easy.

Mr. G.I. clearly wanted to give me some important information, which could have explained the rift in time. Ayna had woken me up at, of course, a very bad time. On the other hand, it was also good that she woke me up. I might have said something out loud. I smiled at my assistant:

"Thanks for your concern..." I wanted to finish the sentence and send the girl back to sleep, but my gaze got caught on the knobby stitches and scars on the girl's stomach.

Ayna followed my gaze and explained, giving a slanted smile:

"An old wound from my sporting days. After conquering the no-rules fighting and survival contests, I tried my hand at gladiator combat as part of a women's team, *The Ulia Valkyries*. The draw at the eighth-finals had us going against the former champions, though. The central attacker from *The Tesse Killers*, much to the fans' delight, disemboweled me with her trident. My entrails were strewn about the whole arena. They had to pick them up with a shovel... The medics saved me and sewed me up, though some of my internal organs are still damaged or even totally missing..."

"So that's why Miya isn't worried to leave you alone with her husband?" I guessed in a stroke of genius.

The girl nodded in silence and, after a bit of waiting, whispered, barely audibly:

"Yes. My womb and ovaries have been totally removed. I can't have children, and no operations or money can help me now..."

Ayna spent some time in silence, then suddenly gave a tortured smile:

"That made it very easy to undergo certification and get licensed to work with members of the upper aristocracy as a bodyguard or personal assistant."

"But for some reason, it doesn't look like that makes you too happy... Ayna, I don't yet know what can be done with you. But I assure you that if there is any way, I will help. You have my word as a Crown Prince!"

Standing change. Ayna Mentor's opinion of you has improved.

Presumed personal opinion of you: +58 (trusting)

* * *

After seven months of absence, Crown Prince Georg royl Inoky was about to make his first speech to his fleet. There was a huge amount riding on how it would be received, so I was feeling very anxious, though I was trying not to show it. The small hall of the space station had been able to fit all the captains and senior officers from the Unatari Star Fleet, but it wasn't easy. On my way up to the platform, I saw that many of those gathered were wearing Black Stars on their Orange House uniforms. These people had made it through many battles with me, but were now trapped in a fog. They had absolutely no idea what to expect from me, their unpredictable commander.

I greeted the officers and got a discordant mumble in reply. Off to a bad start! Once, their reply to the Prince had been an elated roar. Without showing that I was disheartened by the cold reception, I began my speech:

"The most recent intelligence from our cloaked frigates shows that the Alien fleet is still in the Hnelle system. Their reports indicate that the Aliens have one *Queen*; five *Mammoths*; one hundred seventy *Behemoths*; four hundred cruisers, both *Sledgehammers* and *Chainsaws*; and two thousand five hundred smaller starships. That means this must be the remnants of the very same Alien fleet we went up against in the Aysar Cluster. That is both a good thing and a bad thing. It's good in that the Aliens were not able to reinforce their heavy ship losses in the ten months since our last battle. That means their resources are, in fact, limited, and that they are not capable of replacing lost ships. What's bad is that this exact Alien fleet has already met with us in combat and demonstrated its ability to learn from mistakes. We won't be able to pull the same tricks as last time. That's why we're going to have to change tactics. Only light ships will be headed to the battle in the Hnelle system this time."

"But that's suicide!" Someone screamed out from the depths of the hall.

The rest of the officers started grumbling and turned to see who had been bold enough to dispute the fleet commander's decision like that. Admiral Mike ton Akad, scrolling through a list on his palmtop computer, pointed me in the right direction:

"It's the captain of *Curse-36*, a total greenhorn. He graduated from the Space Military Academy just last year, and has only fought in one battle."

While I listened to the admiral speak, another two captains loudly voiced their own objections:

"How will we survive the six hours needed to recharge our energy drives? That's plenty of time for the Aliens to make minced meat out of us!"

"Do you not understand that the Prince doesn't give a shit about us? We'll be there dying and distracting the Aliens, while *Queen of Sin* slips past the dangerous system to safety!"

The audience began buzzing in discontent. Here, the microphone was taken up by Tamara Vuzhek, the highly-decorated captain of *Warhawk-4*.

"I want to remind you all that this isn't the first time something like this has happened. Remember before the battle in the Nayal system? The Crown Prince explained clearly what is to be done with cowards," the girl exclaimed, reaching for her holster.

"*Warhawk-4*, stand down!" I hurried to interfere and ease my subject's nerves. "Let them talk. This is all understandable stuff!"

I saw on Tamara Vuzhek's face that she did not understand. Many other officers seemed to feel the same, which is why I immediately explained:

"The Alien *Queen* has one very unfortunate ability: she can attack people's minds. She must be trying to fill us, her potential victims, with a feeling of dread, hopelessness, and futility. The strong of spirit will bear such a mental attack easily, but the weak will break and give in to the suggestions. They will start to believe that the Aliens will reward anyone who joins their side. During our raid through Alien-controlled Swarm space, we had a few officers come under the *Queen*'s sway. Fortunately, our Truth

Seeker detected it before they could betray us, and they were arrested in secrecy. Now, we have another meeting with the *Queen* ahead of us, so it's important to pick out all those who have already given up mentally before the battle begins. It's better to replace these people with more reliable officers than to have them stab us in the back later. So, ladies and gentlemen, who among you thinks this situation is hopeless? Who among you supposes that Crown Prince Georg royl Inoky has nothing better to do than send his most experienced and loyal people to their deaths?"

I took a close look at the silent crowd. No one was making a peep or voicing their doubts about the forthcoming battle. I could relax a bit. The rebellion was suppressed before it even got off the ground. The officers were listening to their commander with rapt attention once again. I continued my speech:

"And now, let's talk about another thing I heard said – that 'the Prince will flee on his yacht.' We won't point fingers now at the one who said it, but let him think long and hard on whether these thoughts truly belonged to him, or were inspired by the enemy. If I wanted to run, I could have done so long ago on a cloaked frigate. But, as you see, I remained here with you. And one more thing, I'll be going into battle on one of your ships, so I wouldn't be able to flee even if I wanted to."

Standing change. Empire Military faction opinion of you has improved.

Present Empire Military faction opinion of you: +18 (warm)

Oh! Better already. I was on the right path. Now was the time to build on my success.

"No one in the Empire has such vast experience fighting Aliens as the veterans gathered in this hall. Sure, we may no longer fly under the banner of the Perimeter Sector Eight Fleet, but our experience and abilities remain as they ever were! We have defeated the Aliens in Hnelle two times before. We have met with the *Queen*, and come up against even larger enemy armadas in the past. If anyone can take the Aliens in Hnelle, we can! We've never been defeated! The whole Unatari star system has placed their hopes on us. The lives of sixty-three million people are hanging in the balance. It's our job to save them. My mission is to figure out how we can do that. Your mission is to practice our new approaches and tactics over the next two days until they become second nature. They are what will help us survive the forthcoming battle. Notice here that I didn't say 'win,' as I myself do not yet know how to destroy the *Queen*. But I did say 'survive.' We are capable of not dying and thinning out the Alien fleet a good deal. That much I promise you!!!"

Standing change. Empire Military faction opinion of you has improved.

Present Empire Military faction opinion of you: +19 (warm)

Global standing increase. Current value: -51

"Crown Prince and fleet officers, I beg my and Captain Corwin's forgiveness for our late arrival!"

Katerina ton Mesfelle and her husband were panting as they flew into the hall. "Georg, we've been under way since early morning. We wanted to apologize for yesterday. We went to the palace, but they said you were gone. It was no simple task finding another shuttle that could take us into orbit. But we still listened to your speech. The first assistant from *One-Eyed Python* arranged for us to watch remotely. Cousin, I beg of you, take me with you into battle! I miss real action so bad! I promise to make my report on the battle so riveting that viewers the Empire over will be nervously biting their nails with their eyes peeled and their faces pressed against the screen!"

I smiled and, slowing down a bit, nodded in agreement. My cousin gave a joyous yelp and threw herself at me, hanging off my shoulders. Based on the laughter that rang out in the hall, no one even remembered the atmosphere of dread that had been reigning here before. The officers had a very good reaction to our old war correspondent's arrival. And just then, Corwin ton Mesfelle-Ugar approached me with a goose step, and bent down on one knee:

"Crown Prince Georg royl Inoky, it would be a great honor to me if your Highness were to choose *One-Eyed Python* as a flagship for the upcoming battle!"

"I gratefully accept your offer, Captain Corwin ton Mesfelle-Ugar!"

I extended my hand, helping the captain to his feet. I looked around at the applauding crowd and said into the microphone:

"Now this is how we should be feeling before an encounter with the Aliens! Friends, we have just two days to prepare, so let's get to practicing. When we make our move, we can show the *Queen* just how serious a mistake she made bringing her troops to our system!"

THE SECTOR EIGHT FLEET

"**G**eorg, it's not my fault that the Viscount got his hands on the Tivalle system!" Katerina ton Mesfelle broke the silence that had been ruling over the captain's bridge on *One-Eyed Python*.

At that moment, I was sitting immersed in my thoughts, so I gave a surprised shudder before turning to look at my cousin. She repeated:

"That's right, cousin. I had nothing to do with it. Duke Avalle royl Anjer jumped on the tasty morsel as soon as he saw the chance. Asteroid ice processing plants are quite the gold mine. The Head of the Orange House appointed his only son Sivir holder of the Tivalle star system and, simultaneously, Viscount Sivir, in his capacity as manager, confirmed his own appointment. To be honest, you and I both overlooked this eventuality. The right way to have done it would have been to remove Viscount Sivir ton Mesfelle from his post in Tivalle right after his father became Orange House Head, and put someone else there to manage it..."

"Yes, I agree. We were clearly asleep at the wheel there. By the way, where is the Viscount now?"

Katerina looked at me somewhat strangely, as if expecting me to crack up and say I was joking. But I remained silent, and my cousin shook her head in reproach:

"Georg, you must have stopped paying attention to politics completely. Viscount Sivir ton Mesfelle was appointed Perimeter Sector Eight Fleet Commander right after you resigned."

I then actually did start cracking up:

"Sivir is the Sector Eight Fleet Commander?! You've got to be kidding me! I've never seen a worse commander in my life! Last time he was entrusted to lead a group of ships, his mission was to simply bring them to the Hnelle system. But even that primitive assignment was too much for him. His own subordinates started rioting because he was such an incompetent commander. What's the deal? It seems like a strange and illogical choice."

"Don't say that, Georg. There's a logic to this, and it's fairly elementary. Just look at the bigger picture. Think about who is first in line to the Orange House Throne. Crown Princess Inessa royl George ton Mesfelle has yet to be declared Countess, even though seven months have passed. That is very strange, and there can only be one explanation: Duke Avalle royl Anjer wants to make his own son Count, despite the fact that it circumvents the traditional succession order. After all, the title Viscount, in essence, means the oldest son of a Count. And if the position of Count is vacant, the previous one's oldest son can become the new Count under specific circumstances, jumping many positions ahead in the process. To do that, this decision must be approved by the Orange House and the Emperor.

Now, let's say the Duke is able to put this decision through the Orange House. The deputies loyal to him would vote how they're supposed to, after all. It would have to be confirmed by the Emperor though, which is a problem. In the many-century history of the Empire, I found just eleven such instances and, every time the Viscount became Count, instead of the proper candidate, it was because that person was a great military commander. Knowing that, Viscount Sivir ton Mesfelle took the bull by the horns and made himself Perimeter Sector Eight Fleet Commander. For him, it's a quick way to the top. All he has to do is prove his courage and skill in the eyes of the Emperor."

"Then why has Viscount Sivir made no attempts to liberate the Alien-controlled Hnelle system?" I snorted. "If he took down the Alien armada, even I would be impressed with his talent as a leader, to say nothing of the Emperor."

Katerina smiled.

"Viscount Sivir ton Mesfelle may not be an expert in military matters, but that doesn't make him an idiot. He only wants to use the fleet as an elevator to the top. The Viscount has no desire to risk his own life in a hopeless battle with the Aliens."

My cousin went silent as a whole horde of people flooded into the captain's cabin. It was Captain Corwin ton Mesfelle-Ugar returning from lunch, accompanied by his senior officers. Shortly after he took his seat, the captain donned a brightly colored helmet with a microphone and began giving orders:

"Ten minutes to warp tunnel exit. Ladies and gentlemen, let's get cracking! Take your seats. Systems check. Communications, setup a common fleet channel as soon as we enter the Hnelle system. Tactics, wait for the Crown Prince's orders."

Corwin ton Mesfelle-Ugar turned back toward me and smiled with two rows of ideally even white teeth:

"Crown Prince, this is my first time going into such an uneven battle. They have fifteen ships to every one of ours, and their firepower surpasses ours by two hundred to one. What I'm most surprised by, though, is that I am not feeling even an ounce of fear or doubt in the outcome! And the rest of the guys say the very same – they're in a place of surprising calm and absolute faith in your Highness's abilities."

"I appreciate your faith in me, Corwin! But as for the ship ratios, I think it'll all be a bit easier than that. Thirty seconds before our fleet comes out of the warp tunnel, two divisions of *Surprises* should be bombing the Alien armada. We dug our most powerful bombs out of the Unatari Fleet arsenal just for the occasion: eight thermonuclear warheads at fifty megatons a piece, plus another twelve tenners. So, there won't be many Alien small ships around on the battle field. I'm thinking the *Meteors*, at least, should be totally obliterated. Alien frigates are the only ships in their fleet capable of overtaking us in pursuit. That means, if the Aliens don't have any *Meteors*, we'll basically be uncatchable."

"Awesome. But don't let the stealth bombers take them all down. Leave some enemies for us," he joked, his worried expression fading into a satisfied smile.

I decided not to reply, as not to upset my new family member. Calculations we made back in the Aysar Cluster showed that the large Alien ships would survive, so the *Queen, Mammoths* and *Behemoths* would absolutely be there to meet us. But as for the Alien cruisers, destroyers and frigates, there shouldn't be many left.

I called the tactics officer, and set about explaining to him what I wanted to see on the tactical map: a grid centered on the Hnelle station, and markers for all types of ships with an overlaid number showing distance from *One-Eyed Python.* I also wanted groups of starships to be circled with different colors. Finally, I told him not to depict any trash, like debris or abandoned drones.

"One minute to warp exit," reported our navigator.

All the officers began taking their places. I put my hand on the control console, closed my eyes and tried to calm myself down.

"Ten seconds to warp exit. Five, four, three, two, one, we're here! Haay-ooooo!" Corwin screamed happily.

I didn't tell him, but his happiness was a bit misplaced. The screens were still dark, and I needed to get my bearings immediately. The light cruiser gave a slight shake, then the happiness flew off the captain's face, its place taken by incomprehension.

"Thrusters desynchronized. Energy shields have fallen to fourteen percent. I have no idea what's going on."

"Where's the tactical grid, you assholes?!" I shouted to the tactics officer, but he could only shrug his shoulders and punch buttons cluelessly on his nonworking console.

"We're experiencing some technical difficulties. Some of our external equipment has failed," reported a technician over the loud speaker. "It looks like we need new antennas. It'll be three or four minutes of repair."

Fortunately, messages started pouring in from other fleet ships, so, even blind, I had a general picture, and was starting to more or less understand the situation.

"We came out of warp one thousand miles from the *Queen*! Severe background radiation detected!"

"This is *Thrush-15*. We were caught in the blast. Our forward shields have fallen by a third."

"*Warhawk-11*, our light-sensitive equipment has been damaged! LIDAR isn't working."

"This is *Curse-4*. I confirm damage taken. Our shields have fallen by forty percent. I'm seeing lots of large pieces of debris next to the *Queen*. I think it's the wreckage of a *Behemoth*."

I took the microphone and said in a commanding voice:

"All ships, attention! All messages related to systems failures or ship damage should be sent over the reserve channel. The main one is getting crowded. Some of the equipment on the flagship was also damaged and is out of order. We're basically blind, and we need a few minutes to fix it. Until the technical failures are fixed, fleet command is transferred to Admiral Mike ton Akad on *Curse-7*. Can any other ships confirm the presence of *Behemoth* debris? Where are our observers? *Ghosts*, where are you?"

"Commander, this is *Ghost-2*. I'm in position. I can see your ships twenty-five hundred miles from my location. The *Surprises* completed their mission. Their bombs landed in the very thick of the Alien fleet. After that, we weren't even able remove the armored panels from our light-sensitive equipment before one of the *Behemoths* burst into shards. Then, there was a whole series of powerful explosions in the center of the cloud of wreckage, and a few seconds later, you showed up on the battlefield."

"I see. *Ghost-2*, what are your coordinates? All ships, warp at one hundred to *Ghost-2*. We can repair there and evaluate the situation."

I signed off and took a look around. There were officers scurrying around nearby. On one of the screens, I could see a group of technicians putting space suits on, preparing to go out into space. Katerina was already making a report. She was also vigorously signaling to me, asking for video of the bomb attack on the Alien armada. When suddenly...

"SO THAT'S WHERE YOU'VE GONE!!!" I felt a horrible burden pressing down on me. The hate-filled voice impressed itself into my brain with every word, as if stepping down into it with a high heeled shoe. "THERE'S NO ESCAPE THIS TIME. YOU WILL DIE IN THIS SYSTEM."

"You again... I thought I already explained to you once that these kind of things won't work with me. You cannot control me, nor force me to do anything!"

"ALL YOUR STARSHIPS ARE DOOMED TO DIE HERE IN THIS SYSTEM. BUT YOU COULD GIVE UP AND SAVE YOUR OWN LIFE."

"You're repeating yourself," I laughed through the pain. "You'd think you might have learned by now that your methods don't work on me."

At that, the initial wave of pressure rolled back, and I returned to my senses. Maybe the mental protection once put in by Miya was kicking in, or maybe I was able to overcome the psychological onslaught, but the intensity of the attack fell quickly.

"IF YOU TRY TO FLEE, I WILL FOLLOW YOU AND DESTROY BOTH YOU AND EVERYTHING ELSE ALIVE. YOU ARE DOOMED!"

"That's enough of that, now get lost! I didn't come all the way here to run away. My goal is to destroy your fleet, and I have enough ships with me to make that happen. You know it's true. I can sense your fear. You still haven't forgotten the damage I did to your fleet in the Aysar Cluster. The same will happen here."

"YOU CAUSED ME PAIN THEN. THAT IS WHY YOU MUST DIE!!!"

I could only laugh and shake my head, chasing off the ringing in my ears. Katerina ton Mesfelle was standing next to me. There was fear on her face.

"Georg, what happened?! Your nose is bleeding!"

I ran my hand over my face, and my palm came back wet and red.

"Nothing dangerous. The *Queen* was just trying to scare me," I laughed, demonstrating to my cousin that everything was fine. "You'd better find me some cotton balls to stop the bleeding."

Just then, the screens in the room finally turned on, and I rushed to familiarize myself with the situation. The Alien fleet was three thousand miles from us and was composed of a huge disk-shaped ship, encrusted with clusters of smaller ships. I suspect that the *Queen*'s shields had protected some of the frigates and destroyers from the explosions, otherwise it was hard to explain how several hundred small-class ships had survived the attack of my twenty cloaked bombers. Then, before my very eyes, *Behemoths* from all sides started creeping in and docking on the five huge *Mammoths*. Either they were there for repair, or energy charging, or perhaps they just wanted to protect themselves from further attacks behind the carriers' shields. Just one group was moving, around eighty *Meteors*, and it was coming quickly in my fleet's direction.

"Attention, fleet! The enemy is approaching. Their frigates are marked on the map. Advance toward the fourth planet. Tactics officer, number the targets. Electronic fighters, divvy up the frigates. As soon as they get near, blind them. Do not wait for my command. *Warhawks* and *Pyros*, stand by. Do not move away from our ships. Break off into pairs. When the enemy approaches, I want two webs and warp disruptors on every *Meteor*. Admiral Mike ton Akad, destroyers are your responsibility. Get them in groups of five, shooting on your command at targets under double web. After you shoot one down, switch right to the next target. *Thrushes*, do the same. Fire all together at targets under double stasis web. *Surgeons*, get back a bit. I need you behind all the other ships as insurance. *Curses*, stand by. Release drones only after the battle begins. We don't need to spook the enemy!"

"Tuki-tuka-de-sa, bomb attack complete. Nineteen bombers came out next to the seventh planet." the voice of the Chameleon female from *Surprise-1* could be heard on the fleet channel. "We lost *Surprise-19*. They didn't make it into the warp and ended up stranded within striking range."

"Great work, de-sa. Load up the ten megatonners. First division, to the flagship at sixty. Second, approach the station at two hundred and wait for my command. For now, the small ships and cruisers that survived are hiding in fear under the *Queen*'s shield. If they risk crawling out, we'll have to keep spanking them until they learn their lesson."

Someone started tittering on the common channel. After that, one of the captains let fly a greasy little joke about giving the *Queen* herself a spanking, causing raucous laughter on the fleet channel. In general, I am of the opinion that the fleet channel should not be used for extraneous information, but I made no move to interrupt the merry-making now. My crew came to the Hnelle system ready to die, perfectly understanding the balance of forces. Now, I felt that my subjects were just blowing off steam to lessen their stress and fear. They looked to be finally coming to life. Some even started smiling.

"Attention! This is the first assistant from *Pyro-45*. I've just sustained an attack from the *Queen*! Strange thoughts came into my head, like everything was lost, and we should give up right away! I quickly realized that they weren't my thoughts, and had been planted there by these bushes, I mean... Aliens. In response, I imagined a weed-whacker giving a bush a haircut, and the attack on my brain immediately ended..."

The officer's last words were drowned out by a wild chortling. I couldn't hold back a smile either, and took the microphone:

"This is Fleet Commander Crown Prince Georg royl Inoky ton Mesfelle. I confirm *Pyro-45*'s statement; it is possible they will try to attack our minds. The *Queen* also tried to attack me already. I'll tell you this: it isn't fun, but it's nothing you can't handle. The *Queen* doesn't have the power for a prolonged attack, so just wait a bit, and she'll stop. Or, feel free to use the weed-whacker method suggested by *Pyro-45*. For now, get yourselves together. I don't want any unnecessary talking on the combat channel. The first group of Alien *Meteors* is getting close. Frigates, advance! *Curses*, release drones!"

God damn is that a beautiful sight! On the tactical map, a thick cloud of green markers emerged from my cruisers and swallowed up the herd of enemy frigates.

"*Warhawk-11*, here. I need help. I've got two of them on me! Ow. Thanks, guys!"

"*Pyro-6*, here. Target hit!!! My first time downing an Alien!"

"*Flycatcher-2*, you're shooting at the wrong target! That one was for *Pyro-11* and us!"

"Thanks, *Surgeons*, I'm all charged up. This is *Thrush-23*. Friends, I owe you one."

"I can't believe it's already over. It hasn't even been thirty seconds..."

The red markers in the attack group really had disappeared from the map. I took a closer look at the screen, trying to determine how many of our ships had been shot down. I had requested debris not be displayed on the tactical map, so it was no simple task to figure out how the battle had ended. Not able to find the answer myself, I gave the assignment to my subject:

"Admiral, I need a loss report."

After a few seconds of silence, Admiral Mike ton Akad's answer rang out:

"Crown Prince, it would seem there were no losses on our side. Eighty-three *Meteors* were destroyed, but they practically weren't shooting back. Our electronic warfare ships did a good job. They turned most of the enemy frigates off right away. And after that, our drones and antisupport ate them up. A clean victory! I've never seen this in real life, only in old reports on the Sector Eight Fleet! Great job, guys!"

The elated roar of hundreds of throats sounded out in my headphones. At the same time, messages on personal relationship improvements started pouring in from subjects. On the backdrop of the great number of flashing lines, I was able to follow the most important changes, though it was hard:

Global fame increase. Current value: +32

Global standing increase. Current value: -48

Standing change. Empire Military faction opinion of you has improved.

Present Empire Military faction opinion of you: +21 (trusting)

Standing change. Katerina ton Mesfelle's opinion of you has improved.
Presumed personal opinion of you: +100 (completely trusting)

Global standing increase. Current value: -47

Standing change. Mike ton Akad's opinion of you has improved.
Presumed personal opinion of you: +34 (respect)

I was sitting at the console with a stupid ear-to-ear smile, straining to hold back tears of joy. How sorely I had been lacking all this over the three long months I was gone! How I had missed times like these! And it didn't matter now if what was around me was a game or not. It was these exact moments that made life worth living. For some reason, I was reminded of the fact that Florianna should have been at my side. The stream of adulation now coming in was necessary for my Truth Seeker's abilities to grow. Ugh. I wonder how Flora is doing right now...

I breathed a heavy sigh. The prearranged signal to the Parn system had been successfully sent two days earlier, but the agreed-upon response had not followed, not a day later, nor even two. That made me very worried. Some very bad thoughts were coming to mind. For example, that Miya had managed to track down the runaways and strike down the competition for her and her daughter. Or that the captain of *Star Mutt* had changed his mind and was refusing to release my people from his scout ship. Or maybe, my former companions had seen the constant barrage of mud being slung at Crown Prince Georg royl Inoky on the news, and simply decided not to return...

But as for the fleet I had hidden from Georgiy in Swarm space, it was not nearly as bad as I was worrying. The forty-five million credits I'd sent were very welcome, and smoothed over the financing problem, at least temporarily. I had already received an answer from Clay ton Avelle, in which the captain of my flagship thanked me for the money and added, "Your financial support came just in the nick of time. The crews are inspired and prepared to hold out for another few months."

"My Prince, the Aliens have really dug in under the large ship shields." The voice of Admiral Mike ton Akad brought me back to reality. "They've been there for seven minutes already without budging. Maybe we should give them a nudge with the bombers again?"

"There's no point. The bombs are what they're hiding from," I disagreed. "By the way, they've taken an interesting tack. They're joining several ships' shields together into one. I'll have to put our scientists and engineers up to the task of thinking up something similar for us to use. It's a good ability to have in battle. But for now, let's try to provoke the Aliens a bit, and see if we can get them to move."

* * *

The standoff had been going on for five hours. My soldiers came just short of mooning the Aliens out their portholes in their attempts to draw the enemy ships out from under the shields of the *Mammoths* and *Queen*. We tried absolutely everything. Several times we "accidentally" passed near Alien ship debris, inviting the enemy starships to make a jump into our fleet. We also made a fake attack on the Hnelle station. My *Pyros* cut circles around the *Mammoths* and strafed the *Queen*'s shields. We tried to get in touch with the Aliens at various radio frequencies for negotiations. Nothing helped.

Just one time, a few hours earlier, a single *Sledgehammer* had made a timid outing, but it immediately went back under the shield before my ships could even start reacting. And another eight times, the *Queen* had made attempts to mentally control certain soldiers of my fleet, but it was always unsuccessful. All members of the Unatari Fleet crew had been warned of the threat, knew the false nature of the enemy's promises and could only laugh at the pitiful attempts to control them. Also, the "weed-whacker method," as it was being called in the fleet, worked without fail and brought her mental attacks to an immediate halt every time.

"Georg, the viewers are hungry for action!" Katerina ton Mesfelle grumbled, referring to the prolonged lull that had taken hold after all the action of the initial phase of battle. "I told them three hours ago about the six huge bubbles the Aliens were hiding in. Since then, nothing has changed, though silvertonged soldiers from your fleet are competing to compose the best joke about the *Queen* of the shrubs. What should I show in the next report?"

"Show how afraid they are of us. Or make it look like they're expecting something," the captain of *One-Eyed Python* was also clearly growing bored and yawning.

Thinking that I couldn't see his screen, Corwin ton Mesfelle-Ugar minimized the cruiser stats window and opened a graphical editing program where he was drawing a snow-white rhinoceros in a flower-covered field. It was a pretty good picture, too.

"They're waiting for us to make a mistake," I posited as I distractedly built a pyramid out of empty energy-drink cans on my console. "They're figuring out that, if they move at all, we'll just run away, returning us to the status quo, with them hiding under their energy shields. That's why they're in no rush, just watching us get more and more bold, and waiting for the moment we get too eager and slip up."

The empty-can pyramid collapsed. I collected the scattered containers and threw them into the trash incinerator.

"Alright, I've had enough. We aren't some mere court jesters to entertain the *Queen* and her host. If the Alien fleet doesn't make a move in the next hour, our ships will return to Unatari."

Just then, as if replying to me, the admiral's alarmed scream rang out:

"Warning! The enemy has started maneuvers *en masse*!"

Just as he said, the red dots really did start to move all at once on the tactical map. I turned on the microphone and screamed:

"All ships, warp out immediately to *Pyro-1*! Get out! Everyone out! *Thrush-12*, don't sleep! *Flycatcher-4*, you get out too!"

All of my ships warped out smoothly to the first receiver and were now about six hundred miles from the enemy, watching their strange scheme take shape. The Alien starships also regrouped and stretched out into a long line. The *Behemoths* and *Hermits* began releasing all their drones. I was first to figure out what the enemy was doing by extrapolating their formation in a straight line from the warp beacon. They were aimed at the Tesse system.

"They're realigning to greet some guests from Tesse!" That was it! There must have been an invisible Alien observer in Tesse that had detected a jump to Hnelle from there.

A great many comments came in from captains of my fleet in response:

"What an idiot!"

"Jumping into an Alien-controlled system is a pretty perverse way of committing suicide!"

"Well, what can you say? That dumbass is in for some shit."

The three comments reproduced above were actually the most appropriate of the bunch. In general, the comments on the mental capacity of the unknown captain were exceptionally vulgar in content. For some reason, I was reminded of Princess Astra at that moment. Such an act would have been in my former favorite's spirit. A ship could easily reach Tesse from the Parn system in three days so, time-wise, it added up...

"My dear officers, we'll have to try to rescue this lame duck and distract the Aliens. Attention! Our target is the Alien ship group nearest to the station. There's a *Behemoth* and two *Sledgehammers* there that are a bit too far from the others. Once you're ready, jump to one hundred twenty miles from the station. We'll be just eighteen from the enemy. I remind you to travel as fast as possible along a curved trajectory to avoid getting one-shotted by a *Behemoth*. Frigates, I need webs and disruptors on all three ships. Also, start shooting down drones right away. Electros, you can totally ignore the *Behemoth*. It won't be able to hit us with its stationary cannons no matter what it does. Your objective is the two *Sledgehammers*. Thirty electronic fighters on the two targets is more than enough. If I see even one of the *Sledgehammers* getting a shot off, you'll all be cleaning the decks of my yacht after the battle! Now, *Curses*, your mission is to needle that *Sledgehammer* there with your drones. I've marked it here. After you're done, move on to number two. Energy neutralizers should be on the *Behemoth* the whole time. Forty energy neutralizers is nothing to sneeze at. We'll see if the Alien battleship is ready for such an attack, and how much energy it has left. *Flycatchers*, shoot the *Behemoth*'s drones down. *Surgeons*, you're our safety net. So then, off toward the station. Countdown to jump: ten seconds!"

Despite the gravity compensators, I could feel that I was being pressed down into my chair. The starship accelerated fervently toward the Alien-controlled Hnelle station. Katerina couldn't stay on her feet, falling with a squeal and crawling quickly over to her seat to buckle in.

"Three, two, one. WARP!!!"

One-Eyed Python made it out just fine. We were at twelve miles from the *Behemoth* and six from the *Sledgehammers*. Our boost thrusters immediately hummed into action, giving the cruiser extra acceleration. Staying still near those battleship cannons was begging to die.

"Both *Sledgehammers* have been switched all the way off," reported the young lieutenant in charge of active jamming.

"Very nice," I smiled.

The nearest Alien cruiser was hard to see due to the mass of combat drones now swarming it. On the tactical screen, I saw the shields of the *Sledgehammer* restore back up to maximum a few times, but then they finally went down to nothing and stayed there. Four seconds later, five at most, the Alien ship was no more. One thousand six hundred enhanced drones from the *Curses*, each of which could do as much damage as a frigate, started darting off to their next target.

"The *Behemoth*'s energy shield is down!" the tactics officer told me with no small amount of surprise in his voice.

Our forty energy neutralizers sucked all the power out of the *Behemoth* in twenty seconds. The enemy didn't have enough energy left to keep up their shields up. Now the defenseless giant had to be taken down.

"Attention! The *Meteors* are pouncing!" Admiral Mike ton Akad pointed to a group of thirty Alien frigates and a few destroyers that were rushing to help their catastrophe-stricken ships.

It's not clear what the Aliens were hoping to achieve with the attack. We had already mowed down eighty frigates without a single loss, so we would definitely be able to take down another thirty. If the *Queen* wanted to chase us off, she'd have sent a much more serious force, but no other Alien ships came in our direction.

"This is your fleet commander speaking! All ships remain in place. Let's get the second *Sledgehammer*. If anyone leaves the battlefield now, I'll shoot them myself! Electros and *Flycatchers*, get ready to intercept the small Alien ships. Keep a close eye on the other enemy ships to make sure none of them start coming for us. And destroy the *Sledgehammer* wreckage next to our ships. There's no reason to give the enemy the coordinates to our fleet."

Just then, a flash of light erupted! We'd just lost a ship. One of the battleship's rounds found its mark.

"Do not reduce speed. Orbit the battleship! Well... step on it harder... We've got the second *Sledgehammer*! All drones to the *Behemoth*. *Thrushes*, get to work on it with the cannons. No, stand down! Call off the drones. Send them out for the *Meteors*. *Warhawks*, stand by! Head off to intercept the frigates. I remind you: two webs per enemy. *Warhawk-4*, where are you going to without order?! Tamara Vuzhek, get back here! I need you alive. Yes, go with everyone else. Electros, it's up to you now. Our priority is to turn off the *Hermits*. All the rest, head for the frigates."

"Reinforcements in system!" The tactics officer's

scream forced me to shudder.

At four hundred miles from our fleet, a large number of starships appeared. On the tactical map, they were colored gray for a few seconds, but then they were automatically determined to be allies by the friend-foe system.

"Alright! It's the Perimeter Sector Eight Fleet!" exclaimed the captain with surprise in his voice. "There's almost six hundred ships! They've shown up in the very center of the Alien armada!"

I gave an impotent groan. Ugh. What an idiot you are, Sivir ton Mesfelle! I already knew that he wasn't the most capable fleet commander out there, but just handing your ships to the Aliens like that... I could've strangled him with my bare hands. In the heat of the moment, I lost my self-restraint. The sentence that ripped out of me, I suspect, rang a bit too true, as even Corwin ton Mesfelle-Ugar gave a respectful whistle, and Katerina reminded me that we were still broadcasting live to the whole Empire.

"My apologies, cousin, but I think we'd all be better off, if Duke Avalle royl Anjer had been better acquainted with the proper use of contraceptives. Because of Viscount Sivir ton Mesfelle's idiocy, the Perimeter Sector Eight Fleet is going to be completely wiped out. Eleven battleships, and thirty heavy assault cruisers! The Viscount seems to have dragged a heavy fleet from the whole Sector out here just to die! Communications officer, I need a line opened to their channel now! I might be able to save some of them yet!"

"The enemy *Meteors* are refusing combat. They are turning around and retreating!" Admiral Mike ton

Akad's voice reminded me that the Unatari Fleet was still in battle.

A horde of fast-moving red dots on the screen went rushing off into the big cloud of newly-arrived green ones. The enemy frigates did not, in fact, engage with my ships, preferring to attack the new enemy on the battlefield. It became clear that the thirty frigates had just been feigning an attack and were not coming for another one-sided slaughter.

"Do not give chase! All Unatari ships, focus on the *Behemoth!* Communications officers, get me on the Sector Eight Fleet's channel."

"My Prince, of course this is none of my business," Corwin nodded to the window, beyond which a large section of our view was being obscured by the *Behemoth*, "but isn't that gonna explode? Our whole fleet will be killed here and now if the battleship's antimatter undergoes an annihilation reaction."

I considered it. There was a kernel of rationality in the captain's words. The old scar on my face, which I'd received in just such a *Behemoth* explosion, started to itch immediately.

"It will not explode," said my bodyguard, Popori de Cacha, revealing himself. "A group of Chameleons studied the Alien battleship's systems the first time we captured one. The automatic gravity compensation in the warhead storage units is independent of the battleship's main systems. If you don't purposely turn off that exact power circuit, or break the hermetic seal on the hangars, there is no danger. But, to make completely sure, you'd better concentrate fire on the forward parts of the *Behemoth*. That's where the reactor is, as well as the thruster control systems. There's nothing connected to the dangerous antimatter."

I hurried to send this information to the fleet.

"My Prince, I've got the line open! Button three," one of the communications officers reported, and I switched to channel three.

My ears were instantly stabbed with shouts of despair and mostly senseless yammering. The Sector Eight Fleet captains were reporting to their commander on warp disruptors and stasis webs placed on their ships. Some had their energy shields shot through, and others had already been downed by the Aliens. But, due to the overwhelming mass of messages piled on top of one another, there was complete chaos on the channel, and it was impossible to figure out what was going on. Trying to get the situation under control, I spoke loudly and clearly:

"Complete radio silence! Sector Eight Fleet, attention! This is Crown Prince Georg royl Inoky speaking! Do not reduce your speed. Continue your trajectory toward the Hnelle station! Stand by for warp coordinates. Whoever has the ability, immediately warp out! I repeat, warp out to the coordinates we send, if at all possible!"

"Georg, keep your nose out of my business! This fleet is not yours to command!" I recognized Viscount Sivir ton Mesfelle's voice. He sounded annoyed. "I order my ships to stay and fight!"

"Shut your mouth, idiot! You've already lost half your fleet in the one minute you've been here, and have yet to realize it! I order anyone left alive to jump to the coordinates provided. My ships will try to protect you. Immediately after warp exit, get to action and attack the *Behemoth* we have under web here!"

The Perimeter Sector Eight Fleet Commander was still trying to give commands in his inscrutable way. For example, he ordered his ships to attack one of the *Mammoths*, but it was too late. No one was listening to the Viscount by then. Green dots were joining my ships on the tactical map one after the other. Unfortunately, it was primarily small ships that were able to escape. All of the Sector Eight Fleet's big guns were already completely held down by the Aliens. A few seconds later, the only ships left in the center of the ball of Aliens were a few warp-disrupted, motionless battleships and around fifty heavy and light cruisers. They had just minutes left to live, if not seconds. More and more Alien starships were pouring into the battle zone and immediately beginning the effort to destroy the human ships.

"This is *Master of Tesse* speaking. I have fifty warp disruptors on me. My energy shields are going down quick. Requesting permission to evacuate crew." I recognized Oorast Pohl's voice with astonishment.

"Old friend, hold out for thirty seconds!" I shouted to my former associate. "All ships that were not able to leave, I order you to cover sensitive equipment and be prepared to warp out immediately after the bombs go off! *Surprises*, drop your bombs right on top of the Sector Eight ships!"

"My Prince, this is *Surprise-1*. Requesting your Highness's permission to make this attack alone. It's too dicey to risk so many ships. There's no suitable point for a timely warp out. There's also a lot of moving debris. The chance of failure is too high to risk everyone."

"You have my permission! Just go fast before they all die! All ships, stand by!"

I pressed my nose right up against the screen. The seconds ticked by. The number of green markers inside the red ball was falling fast. But then, a new green marker flickered in, and a bomb came out of it. But why wasn't the frigate leaving?!

"Well, that's it. I'm under a warp disruptor." There was neither fear nor resignation in the voice of the *Surprise-1*'s captain. She was just stating a fact. "Forgive me, frie..."

The end of the sentence was cut off by a bright spark. The thermonuclear warhead exploded in the very center of the crowd, right next to the Sector Eight Fleet's battleships. Another second later, fifteen green markers, which was everyone left alive, moved over to my ships.

"*Surprise-1* did not survive the explosion." Popori de Cacha's horror-laden voice rang out above my ear. My bodyguard was looking at the screen, and was even falling out of camouflage in shock. "The greatest warrior my kind has ever known is no more... I dreamt of fighting for her in the next tournament on Sss... This celebrated representative of the Ravaash race paid with her life to save tens of thousands of people. I hope, Crown Prince, that your race will never forget that deed," Popori de Cacha trained both of his mobile eyes on me, expecting an answer.

"A menace to the Aliens. She has thousands of enemy ships on her account. The most valuable soldier in my fleet. I swear that I will do everything in my power to make sure the memory of the captain of

Surprise-1 will live through the ages! You have my word as an Imperial Crown Prince!"

Standing change. Chameleon race opinion of you has improved.
Chameleon race opinion of you: +33 (respect)

Standing change. Empire Military faction opinion of you has improved.
Present Empire Military faction opinion of you: +23 (trusting)

Popori de Cacha and I stayed silent for some time before Corwin ton Ugar sidled in with a message:

"Commander, the nearest *Behemoth* has been shot to pieces! It really didn't explode"

I just waved it off. One battleship more or less made no difference. The Aliens wouldn't feel it. In comparison with the loss of *Surprise-1*, this was totally irrelevant. Nevertheless, it was not at all the time for despondency. A great number of red markers were approaching the cloud of green spots on the tactical map. I took the microphone:

"Attention, all ships! Gather your drones, and get out to a faraway spot. *Ghost-3*, send coordinates over the fleet channel. We all need a breather to take stock of losses and get ourselves back together."

* * *

"*Ghost-2*, keep up observation of the enemy. Other ships, don't just stand around. Begin acceleration toward Unatari."

To my surprise, a small cohort of the Perimeter Sector Eight Fleet ships started moving along with mine. *Orange Majesty* remained motionless, as did the majority of their ships, but around twenty followed my order. Katerina and I exchanged glances.

"It would seem these captains trust you more than their own fleet commander. They look to be trying to demonstrate that fact to the Viscount."

I shrugged my shoulders. The very fact of having another fleet's ships in my active combat zone was something that left me badly dismayed. The dilemma the Perimeter Sector Eight Fleet captains were facing was unavoidable: they could either continue serving the Viscount, who had psychotically doomed his own ships to die, or obey the orders of a more experienced commander. And now, all of the captains were making their own choice.

"*Ghost-2* here. The Aliens have destroyed the wreckage of the *Behemoth*. The antimatter exploded. It was very powerful, as always. The Alien ships are making a move. They're all accelerating, but I can't tell where to."

My heart was pounding. Had they managed to pinpoint our fleet's location? Theoretically, it wouldn't have been too hard. Hiding the huge battleships from enemy radar was impossible. If they were scanning from different points in the star system, it was only a matter of time before their on-board computers calculated our coordinates.

"My Prince, the Alien ships are accelerating toward Unatari!"

My eyebrows shot up in surprise. What a twist!

The Aliens hadn't yet calculated the coordinates of my fleet, but they had managed to get a cloaked frigate in, and it had determined the trajectory of my ships! And, if I were to order the Unatari warp beacon turned on now, even for just a second, as I was preparing to do initially, we would be inviting one thousand five hundred Alien ships to my capital in our wake! That would be the end of Unatari, and the end of my contract with Mr. G.I....

The communications officer broke in at that moment and said, without removing his headphones:

"Viscount Sivir ton Mesfelle proposes that Crown Prince Georg royl Inoky ton Mesfelle make a visit to the flagship of the Perimeter Sector Eight Fleet, *Orange Majesty* and discuss the present situation."

"What is there to discuss?" I muttered, not comprehending. "The Sector Eight Fleet Commander slipped and fell in a puddle, and I helped him out of it. Everyone in the fleet understands that Viscount Sivir is only still alive because of my ships and the self-sacrifice made by *Surprise-1*."

"Would you like me to come with you?" my cousin offered. "I've known Sivir a long time, and I might be able to help you smooth over your issues without all the pomp and circumstance."

"Alright, let's go together. But first, I need to make sure the Viscount isn't about to make an even bigger mess. Communications officer, I need a line opened to my brother Roben royl Inoky."

Around a minute went by, and a middle-aged servant appeared on screen.

"Crown Prince Georg, I beg your apologies most

sincerely, but your brother is not available at the moment. He is very tired, and needs to rest."

"So, Roben's wasted again, is he?" I guessed.

The servant did not answer, but he also made no effort to deny it.

"Alright, we can get by without Roben, this time. I have an important message. The huge Alien fleet in the Hnelle system is ready to jump to Tesse at a moment's notice, so don't turn your warp beacon on, even for a second. In fact, I categorically recommend you not activate the beacon for the next two standard days, no matter who asks, be it Viscount Sivir ton Mesfelle, or the Emperor himself. I'll try to lead the threat away to a different star system but, until that time, I officially warn you once again: if the Tesse beacon turns on, you will all die."

"I am very grateful for your warning, Crown Prince Georg," the servant gave a deep bow. "Your Highness, you can be sure that I will send your message to all relevant parties. The Tesse warp beacon will be blocked."

I breathed out with relief. After all, the Viscount was clearly dumb enough to simply return to Tesse, bringing death to the six billion inhabitants of the densely populated star system after him. The only thing left now was to warn the Tialla and Unatari beacon teams to make sure the Alien fleet wouldn't get through behind the escaping Sector Eight Fleet ships. The two remaining options for escape from the Hnelle system were the automatic warp beacon in Forepost-11 or the low-population Himora station. Both of them looked like perfectly reasonable choices.

"My Prince, incoming call from *Bride of Chaos.*

Shall I put them through?" My communications officer asked, and I gave my permission.

The harrier-gray battleship-captain appeared on screen. His ceremonial Orange House Star Fleet uniform was adorned with a Black Star and a Silver Brooch with the number eleven inside. A veteran who had fought in eleven battles with me.

"Crown Prince Georg," the soldier bowed respectfully. "I made the decision to warn your Highness that Viscount Sivir ton Mesfelle is planning to arrest you as soon as you arrive to the flagship. He is accusing you of 'inciting mutiny, and causing undue loss of life.' He already has permission from the Head of the Orange House to make the arrest, and now he is trying to secure himself the support of all Sector Eight Fleet captains."

"Thank you for the warning, my friend. I will not forget this," I bowed in response the captain, but he answered:

"Don't thank me, Prince. This is the least I could do after all the battles we've fought together. Not to mention what happened today. All of our officers know what the captain of *Surprise-1* did for us, and this is an expression of my gratitude to your Highness and the Chameleon race as a whole."

The gray-haired captain signed off. My cousin and I exchanged glances. Katerina ton Mesfelle didn't know what to say about it. In the silence that came over the room, the communications officer's voice rang out like a shot:

"My Prince, there are twenty-six people on the line waiting to talk with you. They are captains and senior officers from Sector Eight starships."

"Get a conference call together for all of them at once," I requested and, a few seconds later, said on the separate channel:

"Friends, I know what you want to say to me. I'm already aware of the base act of ingratitude being planned behind my back. Do not do anything yourself. I'll be dealing with this betrayal myself. Thank you, I will not forget your warning."

I signed off and began thinking intensely. If it weren't for my good relationship with the Imperial Military, I wouldn't have gotten that warning, and would have been caught. What to do? I spent five minutes in contemplation, staring at the metal wall, then asked to be put through to Viscount Sivir ton Mesfelle. A second later, my former plant manager was looking back from the screen. His dark blue Fleet Commander's uniform had gold epaulets, and he was wearing a huge pilot's cap over his close-cropped hair.

"Viscount, I don't think it very reasonable for us to meet here in the Hnelle system. The Aliens are scanning the cosmos, and could attack our ships at any moment. Both you and I need to remain at our posts. I think we should first take our ships out of Hnelle to the Himora system, so we can calmly discuss everything on the station there."

"Why Himora? I'm planning on taking my fleet back to Tesse!"

I tried to not show any emotion on my face but inside, I was positively seething. That cretin really was planning to retreat to Tesse! If it hadn't been for my warning, the Aliens would have been destroying the pearl of Sector Eight a few hours from now!!!

"Of course, we could also speak in Tesse, but

then my brother Crown Prince Roben royl Inoky ton Mesfelle and his military advisors will want to join in. I do not know how necessary their presence would be. Our conversation could touch on some fairly confidential topics, after all."

"Yes, you are right, Georg. The Himora station really is more ideal. No one will bother us there!" he reveled. "My heavy ships need almost six hours to recharge energy for a warp jump. So, you keep track of the Aliens and warn me if they try to attack! I'll rest for now. Commanding a fleet is such a drag!"

"Agreed!" I smiled and signed off.

I remained sitting for three minutes, then demanded to be put through to the Himora station. A man I knew fairly well appeared on screen. He had once been a Brotherhood of the Stars pirate, and was now working for me secretly on the station.

"Your Highness! I'm glad to see you in good health!"

I greeted him in reply and wondered how many people were living on the Himora station now. The answer he gave was so positive, I'd have been hard pressed to think of a better one:

"There are just sixty people left on the station. When the Aliens captured Hnelle, most of our crew fled. Even the head of the station ducked out to Tesse. I was left here as temporary leader. Everyone else is sitting on their suitcases so they can take off at the first sign of danger. We have a ship ready to warp out at any moment permanently docked here. I'd only need three minutes, and there'd be no one left in the system!"

"Great. I have a very important proposition,

then. Incidentally, it would also be very handsomely rewarded. In six hours, you will receive a signal from Viscount Sivir ton Mesfelle demanding that you turn on your warp beacon to let the Perimeter Sector Eight Fleet out of the Hnelle system. Turn the beacon on for four seconds, then wait for a message from me. I'll tell you what to do from there. If you don't hear from me, evacuate the station in two hours!"

I signed off. Then, another minute later, I called *Ghost-3*, and sent a secret order to go five hours away from my ships toward the Himora station. After that, they were to stop, not reveal themselves, and send us their coordinates.

Now all that was left was to wait...

"You are speaking with the Sector Eight Fleet Commander Viscount Sivir ton Mesfelle. Listen carefully! This is a message for my ships, as well as Georg's. Head toward the Himora system. There is no beacon there now but, in five minutes, the Himora system warp beacon will be turned on. Well, they promised it would, at least. We all need to jump to that system while the beacon is on for us. Make sure to do it in good time. That is an order!"

I buried my face in my palm. I mean, who talks like that?! He could have said the same thing with half as many words, and it would have been twice as intelligible. What made it worse was that the Viscount's voice was extremely grating. If you're gonna give commands, you need to speak clearly, loudly, and distinctly, without mumbling.

"*Ghost-2*, what are the Aliens doing?"

"My Prince, all the Alien starships are turning! They are changing their trajectory!"

"Toward Himora?" I clarified, receiving a positive answer.

Everything became clear. Our ships were, in fact, being watched. I turned on my fleet channel.

"Complete radio silence! Accelerate toward Himora. Stand by for jump coordinates. When the Viscount issues the command to jump to Himora, all ships in my fleet must warp to zero at the coordinates I send. I repeat again: complete radio silence. If anyone says even one word in the next five minutes, they will be punished for exposing a military secret."

Three minutes remained until the Himora warp beacon would turn on. Two... One...

"Communications officer, stand by. Action in thirty seconds. Repeat my order back for me."

"In thirty seconds, arrange a group call with all ships on the list prepared by your Highness. It's all been ready for a while. I just have to press the call button."

"Yes, that's exactly right. Ten seconds... Three, two, one, GO!"

The screen lit up with several windows showing the confused faces of Sector Eight Fleet captains. They clearly didn't understand what was happening.

"Attention, everyone! When the warp beacon is turned on, don't jump to the Himora system right away! You must wait ten seconds! Your very survival depends on it!!! And, before you jump, cover sensitive external equipment. That is also very important! That is all. Good luck!"

The last seconds ticked by. The time had come!

"New beacon visible!" screamed the navigator of *One-Eyed Python*, and our light cruiser left into the warp tunnel that very second.

It wasn't a long flight. In just ten seconds, my ships came out at a different point in the Hnelle star system.

"My Prince, *Ghost-5* here. The bombers have hit the remaining Sector Eight Fleet heavy ships. We uncovered an Alien cloaker! *Warhawk-4* and *Flycatcher-15* have already captured it and are working on shooting it down. That is all. I await further orders! It was a beautiful tactic, if you don't mind me saying. They bought the fake jump to Himora hook, line and sinker!"

"*Ghost-2* here. The Alien fleet has completely left the Hnelle system. They're on the way to Himora!"

A dismayed voice rang out on the common channel:

"Oorast Pohl here, captain of *Master of Tesse*. Prince Georg, I don't understand a damn thing. The beacon turned off too fast. We weren't able to follow our fleet out, then your bombers blasted us. What was that about? And when will the Himora beacon turn back on?"

"My old friend, what you just saw happen was me not allowing you all to die by carrying out the Viscount's idiotic order. The *Queen* just went to Himora with her fleet of one thousand five hundred ships. If you had gone to the beacon, you would have died, too."

Silence took over. Everyone was digesting the new information.

"What have you done, Georg!?" My cousin was looking at me, her eyes wide in horror. "Because it looks like you just destroyed the Perimeter Sector Eight Fleet and killed its commander!"

I turned sharply to Katerina ton Mesfelle. There were lightning bolts in my eyes.

"No, cousin. That is not how I see it at all! No one dragged the Sector Eight Fleet Commander here to fight, nor did anyone force him to warp to Himora. He led his own fleet to their death, and there was no way I could have stopped him. All I did was save his fleet's most valuable ships for the good of the Empire, though I had absolutely no obligation to do so. And that is what your report should say! The main reason for the disaster is Viscount Sivir ton Mesfelle, who, despite not even having the minimum fleet leadership ability, dreamed of achieving military glory in order to earn the title of Count. But now, screw him. Let him show his abilities as a Fleet Commander in Himora! He'll have ample opportunity! All the same, I will not allow the Viscount's stupidity to kill my old friends! And now, your mission is to think up a legal basis to include the rescued ships in my fleet!"

Katerina shook her head in uncertainty. My cousin did not argue with me, but was showing clearly that I had not convinced her. Alright, we'd have plenty of time to discuss the unforeseen consequences of my actions later. For now, we had more important missions. I switched the microphone over to the common channel and issued a command:

"*Master of Tesse*, *Bride of Chaos*, *Princess Astra*, *Indigo Beauty*, and all fleet cruisers, prepare your boarding teams! We've only got six hours before the Aliens get to Himora. We need to capture the Hnelle station and turn off the warp beacon before they get there! And another thing... Welcome back, old friends!"

NEW PLANS

I WAS SITTING in an uncomfortable armchair and stoically bearing all the mockery coming from my team of stylists, make-up artists, and image planners. First I got my gray hair dyed, then I got a facial massage. My skin was rubbed down with special oils, and rejuvenated up with electrotherapy. I also got my facial muscles tightened up with chemical microinjections. The muscular Ayna was helping a frail costume artist pull a tight corset onto my so-called waist in order to hide my huge bulky paunch from view. Katerina ton Mesfelle, not paying attention to all the hustle and bustle, was walking nervously through the room and browbeating me:

"Georg, you have far too frivolous an outlook here! You simply have no understanding of the depth of the tragedy about to befall us!"

"Alright, drop it, cousin! We finished the main assignment. My capital, Unatari, is no longer under threat of destruction. What's more, the neighboring star system, Hnelle is back under our control, and the Alien *Queen*, together with her fairly battered armada, has been squeezed out to Himora. If anyone had tried to tell me before the battle, given the fifteen-to-one ship disadvantage, that such a brilliant outcome was even at all possible, I would have laughed in that person's face and called them a crackpot. Many had their doubts that we could even survive the battle. But we didn't just survive, we took twenty-six starships for the Unatari Fleet, and four of them are even battleships! Oof, not so tight. I'd like to be able to breathe, if possible!" The last sentence was directed at Ayna, who was clearly trying to fit me into an hourglass shape, completely ignoring the real state of my belly.

She loosened the strings a bit, and it became somewhat easier for me to breathe. But then, Katerina came up, evaluated the work done by Ayna, and shook her head skeptically:

"Leave it where it is in the chest, but we need to take the waist in at least another two inches, otherwise the Crown Prince won't fit into the ceremonial suit we've prepared for his speech."

The former gladiator set about retying the strings with a renewed force. My cousin, though, continued nagging me:

"Yes, brother, your capital was saved, but at what price? The Sector Eight Fleet has been completely destroyed. The Himora star system has been lost to humanity. The only son of the Orange House Head is now missing in action. The Duke is in a rage, promising horrific punishments for anyone involved in his son's disappearance. The accusations of desertion and treason directed at the officers who joined us are just fluff compared with what Duke

Avalle has in store for you! The Duke is cunning and guileful, and you have just risen to the top of his personal enemies list!"

My cousin probably would have kept pestering me, but just then a panting officer burst into the make-up studio:

"Crown Prince Georg, the Throne World is on line one. Emperor August would like to speak with your Highness!"

Everyone around began exchanging frightened glances and, a second later, a frenzy of activity was boiling away. They picked me up, packed me unceremoniously into my suit, and shoved me down the hall into my office. The screen was already turned on when I got there and the leader of the Empire was on screen, clearly waiting impatiently for me.

"I am deeply honored to have the opportunity for a face-to-face meeting with Your Imperial Highness!" In full compliance with courtly etiquette, I bowed down on one knee and greeted the most influential Imperial aristocrat.

"You may stand, Georg. This is no time for ceremony. And ask any strangers to clear the room. Our conversation will breach some quite delicate issues. Your advisor Katerina ton Mesfelle can stay, though."

My cousin, already crossing the threshold out the door, turned around, approached me and stood at my side. The guards and servants, though, almost ran to leave. Even the Chameleons emerged from camouflage to show that they too were leaving into the hallway. The door had barely swung shut before August continued:

"I have received worrisome news that you are planning to make a grand speech forty minutes from now before the people of Unatari and the soldiers loyal to you. Georg, it isn't yet too late to stop what you're doing. There will be no going back from this mistake."

Despite the official nature of the moment, I could not hide my confusion. I turned to look at Katerina, but my cousin could only shrug her shoulders as well.

"My Emperor, I am actually preparing to make a speech before the people of Astorimma. I need to calm the population and tell them of our brilliant victory over the Aliens in the Hnelle system. The people of Unatari have spent the last two weeks in a state of constant fear, knowing that death could arrive at their doorstep at any minute. Many had even stopped hoping for rescue. That is why I simply must speak; to tell them that the threat of Alien invasion has passed, and that they can now breathe a sigh of relief. One thing I absolutely do not understand is why you're saying my speech could have irreversible consequences, and why your Imperial Highness found it cause for worry."

The Emperor began thinking for several seconds, then said, looking me in the eye and watching my reaction:

"Georg, representatives of three of the Great Houses came to me today. They all, as one, affirmed that you are a traitor. They allegedly have access to information that you are intending to found your own government in the forthcoming speech. They say that it will not be subject to either Orange House or the Throne World. And though this behavior doesn't quite align with the picture of you I have in my head, the representatives of these Great Houses really were able to sew a grain of doubt in me..."

The man went silent, clearly waiting for me to say something and ease his mind. I bowed down on one knee again and lowered my head.

"My Emperor, the Dark Mother cannot be too far away. I ask your Truth Seeker to join our conversation and test the veracity of my words."

And I was not wrong. The ancient black-robed lady stepped on scene from just off camera. The Dark Mother was smiling cordially at me, standing next to the Emperor. I then began speaking loudly and clearly, stopping from time to time to give the Truth Seeker a chance to evaluate what I'd said:

"I never, even in the deepest recesses of my mind, considered possibility of betraying your Imperial Majesty. My only concern is strengthening the Empire's defensive capabilities, and advancing the human race further into the cosmos. I have, in fact, considered the possibility of withdrawing from the Orange House and creating my own separate government. But that was all nine or ten months ago, when there were more than twenty star systems under my control. But even then, the planned government with its capital in Unatari, would have remained a part of the Human Empire and would unconditionally have submitted to your Imperial Majesty."

"He speaks the truth." The old lady gave her verdict. "August, your grand-nephew harbors no negative thoughts against you, or the Empire as a whole. I see in his thoughts nothing but considerable frustration with the present leader of the Orange House and a number of plans directed against Duke Avalle. I can also see the remnants of the old dream he just referenced about a big strong government with its capital in Unatari..."

I hurried to intervene, as the Emperor could have taken the Dark Mother's words the wrong way.

"In any case, it turned out not to be necessary, and I didn't take the radical step of forming my own Kingdom. The conflict in the Orange House ended in victory for my side. But, as his older brother Paolo before him, Avalle has also set his sights on systems that are mine by right. The crafty villain has stolen from me the Tivalle star system, which had been my main source of income. Like the first conflict in the Orange House, the current crisis is one of relations between myself and the new Duke, and even the Alien invasion of the Hnelle system is nothing but a consequence of his impudent theft of the resource-rich Tivalle star system."

"A curious point of view. I hadn't looked at these events through that lens before," the old man on the screen began stroking his gray beard in contemplation. "And who, then, does this disputed system belong to, given all the recent events?"

Hiding the truth from the Emperor, especially in the presence of the Dark Mother, was not a particularly sensible act, so I answered as honestly as possible:

"Three hours ago, my landing troops took all ice-processing plants under their control and arrested the managers appointed by Viscount Sivir. So, in fact, the Tivalle star system has returned to its legal ruler."

August began laughing uncontrollably:

"So then, you're telling me this is all over that?! Much has become clear to me. You've earned yourself some seriously powerful enemies here, grand-nephew! Now, they won't be satisfied until they've eaten you whole!"

I could only smirk malignantly in reply:

"They're trying to pressure me! It would have been better if I'd recaptured Tivalle long ago, right after its abominable theft. But I tried to remain inside the bounds of the law, appealing to earlier agreements between Avalle and myself and relying on the just nature of the Orange House Head. But the Duke took my restraint as a sign of weakness, which caused him to think he could ignore my legal rights and wipe his feet with me. I don't see any explanation for why Viscount Sivir ton Mesfelle was appointed Perimeter Sector Eight Fleet Commander other than as an attempt to make him a good candidate for Count in circumvention of myself and other aristocrats. For my part, I can say that I have never seen a worse commander than Sivir ton Mesfelle in my entire life!"

Unexpectedly, August slightly agreed with me on the Viscount, and asked me to explain in complete detail what had happened in Hnelle and Himora. Also, the Emperor admitted that he had personally been watching the broadcast of the battle, and even congratulated Katerina ton Mesfelle on her excellent reporting. My cousin began blushing and made a low bow, clearly embarrassed at the praise.

After my detailed retelling of the course of the difficult battle, I told him the data from my spy frigate in the Himora system:

"There wasn't really a battle as such in Himora. It was just a beat down. A football game with one end-zone. The Aliens swept up the remnants of the Sector Eight Fleet no problem. The Aliens had enough frigates and destroyers left to capture and hold all of Viscount Sivir's starships. No one got out. The Sector Eight Fleet was totally wiped out, with the exception of its flagship. The battleship *Orange Majesty* didn't even try to resist, instead immediately surrendering and putting down its energy shield. The Aliens decided not to destroy it after that, and sent their landing modules out. It's all on the video I sent to the Imperial Joint Chiefs in a message labeled TOP-SECRET."

The Dark Mother confirmed what I said. The Emperor knit his brows and began thinking for a long time. Katerina and I also kept silent, not wanting to interfere with August's thought process. Finally, the old man on screen spoke up:

"Georg, I will not criticize you or punish you for this. These were decisions made in a trying time. All the same, I cannot say I approve of all of them. Your story about the battle in the Hnelle system generally corresponds to the evaluation made by military experts from the Joint Chiefs: given the balance of forces, victory was theoretically impossible. Crown Prince Georg, you performed a real miracle by saving his ships and causing serious losses to the Aliens at the same time. I will not allow the mistake that led to this disaster to be repeated. The new commander of the Sector Eight Fleet will be appointed by me personally, and I will not be considering how closely said person is related to Duke Avalle royl Anjer. My priority will be how skilled they are in fleet leadership and command. I'll help the new commander with ships and finances, so the Sector Eight Fleet will be reborn soon. But in the future, grand-nephew, I order you never to sacrifice allied fleets in pursuit of your own goals ever again."

I gave the Emperor another low bow. The storm had passed. I could feel it all over my skin. Katerina knew it too, and gave me a wink of encouragement. Meanwhile, the Emperor continued:

"My interest was piqued by the story of the Chameleon female who sacrificed herself to save thousands of people. I would like to award her a posthumous medal. What was that hero's name?"

"My Emperor," I said, giving another low bow, "in Ravaash tradition, names are only given to male-gendered individuals. Females do not have names, although some of them do change gender and would then be assigned a name. But the captain of *Surprise-1* was a young female, never having changed gender, so she did not possess a personal name. To the whole fleet, she was simply known as the captain of *Surprise-1*, and it will be with that very name that she will remain in memories of our soldiers."

"Yes, let it be so!" agreed the Emperor. "For her valor and bravery, I posthumously award the captain of *Surprise-1* a Ruby Comet. If this female left any children behind, from this minute forward they will be granted full Imperial citizenship, and their education and upbringing will be completely paid for by the government. But now, Georg, I would like to speak about your fate. The Orange, Green and Red Houses are demanding that I issue an official Imperial declaration stating that you are a traitor and criminal. After the explanations you gave, I intend to refuse them by explaining what happened as a typical power struggle between local elites in peripheral regions where Imperial soldiers have no jurisdiction."

I bowed down on one knee again, expressing my gratitude at such a wise decision on the Emperor's part. My cousin repeated the gesture. August could only laugh in reply:

"There's nothing to thank me for. I am acting in my own self-interest right now. It is important to me that a force remain in Sector Eight that is capable of defending our border with the Swarm and fighting back the Aliens. Given that the Perimeter Sector Eight Fleet no longer exists, this difficult assignment falls on your shoulders, Georg. Note here that I am only speaking of Sector Eight, not the Orange House as a whole."

"My Emperor, I'm afraid I do not understand. Would you like to appoint me Sector Eight Fleet Commander once again?" I was not at all ashamed to admit that I had completely lost the thread.

Katerina was looking at me with obvious pity, shaking her head as she loudly said:

"No, cousin. Emperor August is suggesting that you form your own government not subject to the Orange House."

"Excellent, Katerina." The old man on screen began clapping softly. "It would seem my advisors were right to praise your analytical abilities. They have even suggested that I try to hire you on here in the Throne World. Georg, there can be no doubt that Duke Avalle will not forgive what you've done, and will never let you live a normal life as a result. The Head of the Orange House will also never forget how your cousin Katerina made the Duke's only son look stupid. As such, I can only see one way out of this. Create your own Kingdom and fight for its independence from the Orange House. Yes, if you do, war with three Great Houses at the same time would be unavoidable, but the main Imperial fleet would stay on the sidelines and not interfere in what we would view as a local, internal conflict. Last time, you showed that you can quickly build the power of your fleet. I expect the same from you this time."

I went silent, completely dumbfounded at the Emperor's suggestion. My advisor Katerina spoke in my stead:

"My Emperor, I appreciate the clear help and even direct advice you are giving. So in fact, you are untying our hands and giving us cart-blanche. We are no longer limited by the bounds of Orange House's rules and, in the inevitable war, it would be our right to make use of any methods at our disposal to grow our forces. I have no doubt in my cousin. The new government will hold out and grow stronger. And here, I would like to find out the price of that liberty. For what reason does your Imperial Highness need a new power, not connected with the rules of a Great House, and bordering only one Perimeter Sector? After all, if you were simply expressing your desire to help your grand-nephew, you could simply appoint Georg commander of the Sector Eight Fleet!"

The old man on screen gave a long, satisfied laugh, after which his voice suddenly grew harsher:

"Alright, Katerina, you have proven your

qualification once again. So now, let's talk as frankly as possible about the truly serious issues weighing on my mind as leader of the Empire. Humanity needs a powerful force. One that can act outside the bounds of one Perimeter Sector, but at the same time is not the Imperial Star Fleet. We need such a force so that I can correct the biggest mistake I ever made before my time is up. I'm speaking of the Yellow House, or the Gold House, whatever they called themselves."

"The Antagonists?!" My cousin and I gasped in unison.

"Yes, that is precisely how that Great House has been known in the Empire for almost one hundred eighty years. When my father was on his death bed, his wish was for Imperial power to be transferred in accordance with the established order. The first in line to the throne was my sister, Eleonora royl Akad, Georg's grandmother on his mother's side. However, I thought the moment too ripe and couldn't let the historic chance pass me by. After all, the First Strike Fleet was under my command at that time, and it was humanity's most fearsome force. The Empire had just finished a war with the Elokites, a race of intelligent parasitic worms. My battleships had broken through the planetary shield of the Elokite home world and were raining down hell from above on yet another enemy of humanity. Immediately after that victory, I sent my starships directly to the Throne World. There was no war for the throne. I had the power on my side, and was steeped in the glory of the victor, so the Imperial crown went to me with no contest. But my sister fled to the Gold House, which had supported her historically. They then issued a declaration that they would be leaving the Empire. Perimeter Sectors Eighteen and One were removed from the unified warp beacon network. And that was how the Antagonists came to be."

The Emperor went silent, but the Dark Mother unexpectedly continued his story:

"Many years have passed since that time. The Antagonists' warp beacons have long been turned off, but we do continue to communicate with them through ambassadors. The Empire has recognized the Antagonists' right to independence, and my master is not capable of dissolving a treaty he himself signed. Attacking the Antagonists with private aristocratic armies or allied fleets is utterly futile. I can sense the great power of the Gold House. The fleet of the Antagonists is no smaller in force than that of the whole Empire, and the number of Truth Seekers the Gold House has is also very great."

"Precisely," agreed the Emperor. "All these years, the separatists have been growing their force of combat starships and landing ships, as well as training dozens of powerful psionics to murder key Imperial admirals and commanders. I can say with absolute certainty that my sister would not refuse the idea of one day returning the Imperial crown, which once slipped from her hands, to her own possession. As such, the threat of an Antagonist armada invading is a very real possibility we must be prepared for it. But if a force can be found that is capable of dealing with the Antagonist armada and returning almost fifty inhabitable star systems to the Imperial fold... I'll tell you honestly, Georg. I would be willing to overlook a lot for such a possibility. I am not going to ask what became of the huge *Uukresh* you showed off in the Orange House Capital system either..."

"He has two *Uukreshes*," the Dark Mother unexpectedly wedged into the Emperor's speech, afterwards explaining: "August, your grand-nephew has two such large ships at his disposal! And also, beyond Imperial borders he has a reserve fleet of three hundred starships hidden from prying eyes."

The old lady must have read that information directly from my brain. The Emperor noted the discontent that flashed across my face and laughed.

"Georg, you are simply full of surprises! Alright, I will not pry into who you're hiding your fleet from or why. I will not ask about the fate of the Alien warp beacon delivery ship in your possession, nor the other captured trophies. I shall block all attempts by your foes to call you to the Throne World over scandals in your family affairs, no matter how ugly they may appear. I will not even demand that you reconquer the Himora star system, which your actions technically handed to the Aliens. As you see, I am prepared to give you much, grand-nephew. In exchange, in order for you to dispel all my doubts, I want to see you to create a force loyal to the Empire that can handle the task I have just laid out. A year ago, you were heading in that direction when you got together a fleet of three thousand under your banner, but then you got spooked and suddenly stood down. This time, I'm asking you to take it all the way and make a force capable of smashing the Antagonists. I am sure that, if the Empire has such a heavy bludgeon at its side, the threat of Alien invasion won't look so terrifying and irreversible either. Collect your fleet and annihilate the Antagonists! Georg, if you can make what I've just described happen, I will consider the main goal of my life achieved and will hand over the Imperial Crown to you with a clean conscious. You have my word as Emperor!"

Long after the screen turned off, my cousin and I were still standing in silence, digesting what we'd heard. Finally, I broke the silence, asking my advisor:

"What do you think, Katerina? Can I trust the promise made by August?"

My cousin gave a tormented smile in response:

"If you have a fleet on your side that can take down the Antagonist armada, it would also be able to take down the comparably-sized Imperial fleet, so all aristocrats, including August himself, would have no choice but to play fair. Otherwise, you would be able to just take what was promised to you by force. What I'm worried about now, though, is not the distant future, but what comes next. Is it worth hinting that Unatari will become independent, if that means an uncompromising war with the Orange House in return? Your former allies Marat and Svetlana Mesfelle will actually be fighting against you. You would not be able to count on your brother Roben or sister Violetta helping you either. The best we could hope for is them simply not coming out against you. That leaves the Green House, which will doubtless make use of the opportunity to get revenge on you for everything you've done to them. And the Red House, all of whose requests for aid you've openly ignored. The Aliens haven't gone anywhere either. They're still two steps from your capital, just as before..."

I stopped her stream of words with a gesture.

"Katerina, don't try to talk me out of it. I have made my decision. Unatari will be an independent state! But I will not force you to follow me into the meat-grinder. If you think there are too many enemies, it isn't too late for you to simply leave."

Katerina suddenly began laughing in joy:

"For crying out loud, cousin! You still don't get it. You and I have been trapped on the same boat for a long time. It's too late to change anything. So, even if the whole Empire gangs up on you, I'll stay on your side no matter what. Yes, it will be hard for us. The war promises to be a bloody one. But I believe in you, Georg, and I know that you would never leave your cousin wanting when it comes time to hand out trophies."

I looked at the clock. There were just twenty minutes left until my speech. The text still needed to be totally overhauled in order to fit the Unatari Declaration of Independence into my speech. But there was catastrophically little time to think through all the consequences of such an action. We certainly wouldn't have the time to predict enemy reactions and take preventative countermeasures.

"Katerina, let's not change the speech. There's really no reason to rush it. We need to think it all over and consider all the details first. And also, it would make our foes look foolish before the Emperor, if the accusations they made against me come to nothing, and the speech is just about the recent battle.

But around an hour after talking to the journalists, get a little council together in my office: Admiral Mike ton Akad, Colonel Gor ton Vulf, Ayna and the captains of all five battleships. I have a lot to think over and discuss with them before loudly declaring that I am leaving the Orange House for the whole Empire to hear."

* * *

The speech went amazingly. I was inspired. I spoke emotionally, from my soul and practically didn't even make use of the teleprompter at all. Based on the periodically incoming standing increase messages, my speech found a good response among the residents of Unatari. Even the part I was most worried about, when I spoke on allowing several of the Sector Eight Fleet captains to jump to Himora to their certain deaths, was taken surprisingly well.

Standing change. Empire Military faction opinion of you has improved.
Present Empire Military faction opinion of you: +25 (trusting)

The main take away from it seemed to have been how many ships I'd saved, though. My relations with the Imperial Military increased by two points in one go!

But now, I had a much harder task before me. After ending my speech, there was supposed to be a question and answer session for the many journalists gathered there from every part of the Empire. I was somewhat nervous, as I was holding in my head the fact that my former favorite Astra had once failed just such a session. And the very first question asked confirmed that my fears were not totally unfounded:

"Crown Prince Georg, why did you give the Hnelle system to your eldest daughter after its liberation? After all, Princess Likanna has fully rejected you and refused to ever speak with your Highness again. You can't seriously think that a gift like this will make a little girl to forget about her own mother's death, right?"

The young female reporter, a presenter for the largest Green House news station, batted her eyelashes innocently, though I saw a badly hidden sense of triumph in her eyes. Her mission was complete. She had probably even been promised a prize for publicly provoking Crown Prince Georg with the old ugly story of his unsuccessful divorce. I was trying my hardest not to show my annoyance, though in my head there were thoughts swirling of interrogating this this horrible person to find out who'd paid her.

"The Hnelle star system was a gift to Lika, and it was my fatherly duty to return my daughter's property to her, even despite the risk to my life. Now, if we're gonna discuss my daughter's reaction to her mother's death... Yes, Likanna had every right to act the way she did. Both myself and Marta royl Valesy ton Mesfelle-Kyle made a grave mistake in hiding the fact that we were planning to get divorced from Lika. We thought that Lika was just an innocent little girl, but we were wrong. She had already started growing up. In fact, our divorce had been in the works for some time, and the one who initiated the process was my former wife herself."

I heard a distinct gasp of surprise in the hall.

"Yes, you heard right. It was Princess Marta who wanted the divorce first. I know how some journalists like to dig around in others' dirty laundry. Well then, I'll give them the chance to rifle through ours. Here are some recordings of old conversations I had with Princess Marta in which she stubbornly demanded divorce. In the end, I agreed. After that, we only discussed legal issues. Marta wanted a great deal of compensation, and I didn't have all she was demanding for a long time. When I got the money, and all the conditions were agreed upon, the unexpected happened. Marta had a change of heart and no longer wanted to sign the papers. Our relationship had started improving. The Fastel Fleet even helped me out in battle with the Orange House. Everything was leading to the possibility that our divorce may have proven unnecessary, which was why Marta's suicide caught me totally off guard."

"Then why did your wife commit suicide?"

I breathed a heavy sigh.

"The Princess found out that my Truth Seeker was expecting a child. Marta and Miya always had a fairly strained relationship, which was why, when my wife's main rival became pregnant, she took it very hard. They were both very dear to me though. I don't even know what they discussed behind my back. I can only suppose that they were negotiating the priority their respective daughter would receive in the succession order. And before you ask your next question, I'll answer it – Miya did not kill Marta, and did not use her abilities. Despite her horrible reputation, Miya is extremely careful not to do anything that may harm my reputation or hers. But if there remains anyone who still has doubts, I could set up a private conversation with Miya for anyone who wants it."

I ran my careful gaze over the whole suddenly silent hall. Apparently, none of them were feeling suicidal, today.

"No one was expecting Marta to do what she did, but Lika took it hardest of all, as she was not aware of all the other problems at all. I understand my daughter's reaction perfectly, and can say I would have done the same in her place. That is why I will not try to convince Likanna of anything now. I really did do wrong to her. To be honest, if I only could have foreseen how the whole divorce was going to go, I would have immediately refused to start the process. No one in the Universe was more dear to me than Likanna, and I would never do anything to hurt her."

Global standing increase. Current value -50

Global standing increase. Current value -49

I was looking at the two semitransparent popup messages when suddenly...

Standing change. Likanna royl Fastel's opinion of you has improved.
Presumed personal opinion of you: -98 (irreconcilable hate)

Lika was watching my speech! And she even put her opinion of me up by a point. I looked right into the camera and said:

"Thank you, Lika. No matter where you are, or what you think of me, I want you to know that I love you as much as ever!"

After that small victory, I had no more problems answering the journalists' remaining questions, even the trickiest ones. I finished the press conference with these words:

"Ladies and Gentlemen, unfortunately we don't have any more time to chat. I hope you understand. A Crown Prince's schedule is very busy. I have to go to the island of Chameleons to bid farewell to a truly heroic member of the Ravaash race. My company will be the captains and senior officers of the Unatari fleet, many of whom owe their lives to the captain of *Surprise-1*."

I had already taken a seat in my plane when an unexpected call came in. The officers of the transport route control service were informing us that someone has asked for Crown Prince Georg royl Inoky several times from the Hnelle station. Supposedly, the warp beacon employees had a query that they could not handle without my help.

"My Prince, this is Lieutenant Yarith Kahv, leader of the assault group sent to clear the Hnelle station. I ask that you forgive me for my importunity, but the cloaked frigate *Ghost-5* from the Tialla star system is stubbornly repeating a request to be let through our system to Unatari. We remember your order not to turn on the warp beacon until your specific order, but the frigate from Tialla insists that their case is special, and has asked that your Highness be given this special password: 'Star Mutt.'"

My heart began pounding quicker and quicker

in anxiety. My former companions had been found! I wanted to jump for joy and shout out loud, which is what I did. Not embarrassed by the many people surprised with the stormy outburst of joy from the normally composed Crown Prince, I calmed down a bit, got myself together and said:

"Yes, lieutenant, this really is that very special case. I'll call the observers from the Himora system right away. If our cloakers confirm that there are no Alien ships ready to jump to Hnelle, turn on the beacon for half a second to let *Ghost-5* through..."

I went silent as my attention was suddenly grabbed by a very strange gesticulation from the Admiral who was sitting in the armchair beside me. Mike ton Akad was placing several fingers on his shoulder, clearly trying to communicate something. I spent several seconds watching his pantomime before I realized what exactly the admiral wanted to tell me:

"And I congratulate you on the promotion, Lieutenant Commander Yarith Kahv! The matter of your promotion has already been settled with the Unatari Fleet's admiral."

"Tuki-tuka-de-sa, here are her children!" Popori de Cacha led me to a long ditch full of water separated into a great many sections with a single mesh covering, and pointed his flexible finger downward toward the surface, shining back in the light of the midday sun.

I took a closer look. It was a really shallow ditch. It wasn't even a foot deep. In the warm sun-heated water, which was drawn into the system of canals and lakes by a pump directly from the Unatari Ocean, there was a herd of lively foot-long black newts swimming around.

"Eleven children. Not so long ago, it was thirteen, but they ate the two weakest ones."

"Do they not have enough food?" I asked, surprised and disturbed.

"That's not it at all, my Prince. It's just the law of nature. The strongest, most dexterous, and capable survive. The weak must be eliminated and not allowed to multiply, otherwise the species as a whole will begin to decline. Usually, by the second metamorphosis stage, when they start climbing out onto dry land, only around half are still alive."

Strict rules, especially if you consider how extremely low-numbered a race the Ravaash is.

"Popori de Cacha, don't you ever feel sad when you think that one of your own children was eaten by his own brothers and sisters?"

My bodyguard went silent. An opaque film went down over his eyes. "Thinking mode" again. It can't have been that my question had so seriously affected the Chameleon that it had forced him to enter a state of intense thought, right? The head of my guard finally opened his eyes.

"My Prince, you have touched upon a very delicate topic for me. All sixteen of my children are still alive, even though they have passed the first stage of metamorphosis. My compatriots have already started shooting me sideways glances. Some even call my children inadequate to their faces. Hatchlings must kill the weak. That is the law of nature. But, for some reason, they just won't..."

"Come now. Chin up, old friend. Maybe it's just that they're all good enough to reach adulthood. Have you checked what happens if you put a weak hatching from another brood in there?"

"What are you saying, Crown Prince?! Who would ever agree to sacrifice their own child for such an experiment?! My children are one-third larger than normal and twice as active. They'd rip these other babies in half. Even the nanny that feeds the hatchlings in the canals was seriously bitten by my children when she carelessly left her arm into the water for too long."

Well then... I spent some time in silence watching the totally inoffensive looking newts as they frolicked in the water, then asked:

"And when will they become intelligent and begin their Chameleon education?"

"My Prince, they are already intelligent and studying actively. All the babies in this bunch already understand Ravaash language perfectly, and some even know human. The captain of *Surprise-1* taught them herself. Watch. Belly up!" My bodyguard said the last sentence in a louder voice than usual.

Eight of the newts immediately turned over in the water, revealing their light yellow bellies. The other three repeated the same trick with a short delay.

"These three didn't understand the command in human language. They were just watching their brothers," the head of my guard explained.

The yellow-bellied newts, flailing their arms and legs awkwardly, really did look hilarious. My cousin would certainly have liked it. But Katerina ton Mesfelle, and the other humans were not allowed by the vigilant Chameleons to get near their nursery, only I had that privilege as "elder female." I turned to a group of people standing far away and suggested to Popori de Cacha that we start slowly making our way back.

As we walked, I decided to discuss the main issue I'd come to the Chameleon island for:

"Popori de Cacha, I did not see you among the guards that left the room before my talk with the Emperor. Were you present for that conversation?"

"Yes, my Prince. I was, in fact, in the room at that time." The huge lizard stopped and turned both of his mobile eyes toward me.

"I suspect that the information on the Emperor's secret offer has already been sent to your elders then?"

Colorful splotches ran over the Chameleon's gray skin. It must have meant repentance or shame. After that, the head of my bodyguard bent down on one knee and, bowing his head, extended his blade toward me.

"I entrust my life to your Highness's judgment. Yes, I really have divulged that fact to the leaders of my kind."

I very carefully ran the tip of my thumb over the extremely sharp, curved blade. No matter how softly I did it, though, the skin on my finger split and started bleeding. The micron-width cutting edge must have been made of ceramic or composite to keep metal detectors from finding it along with its invisible owner.

"You may stand, Popori de Cacha." I returned the blade to its owner. "While speaking with August, I knew perfectly well that you were in the room. I trust you as I would myself, which is why I didn't demand that you leave. I also didn't ask you to keep the secret, because I needed you to send the message to your kind. And now, I need to know what exactly your elders have decided. It's been six hours after all. You must have come to some kind of decision."

Standing change. Chameleon race opinion of you has improved.
Chameleon race opinion of you: +36 (respect)

Popori de Cacha gave a deep bow and pointed his flexible appendage at the many artificial canals filled with her species' young:

"There are around three hundred young females of my race here on Unatari, and over two thousand hatchlings being raised. Every year, our numbers will grow. This place is the future of my race and its greatest treasure. The Ravaash will join the side of Unatari in any conflict with no reservations. But here we get the question of guarding my home world, Sss, which also needs to be taken into account..."

"That is precisely why I began this conversation. After all, if Unatari declares that it is leaving the Orange House, Duke Avalle's wrath may be directed at allies of the new government and, above all else, the Chameleons. The Orange House has been licking their lips at the strategically important tantalum ore deposits on your home world, and the beginning of a conflict would simply be an excellent reason for Duke Avalle to capture the rich prize. As such, before beginning any activity, I'll have to provide safety to your people in the Sss star system..."

Standing change. Chameleon race opinion of you has improved.
Chameleon race opinion of you: +39 (respect)

I interrupted my own speech to familiarize myself with the popup message. Popori de Cacha clearly was now speaking for his whole race, and fully supported my idea that it was necessary to guarantee the safety of the Sss star system. It wasn't surprising. Practically all the Chameleons lived in one system, which an Orange House fleet could destroy in a matter of hours.

"So then, Popori de Cacha, I'm describing the situation as it stands. The Li Colony and Sss system warp beacons are currently under the control of Orange House soldiers. The beacon divisions are quite small, ten or fifteen men, but the problem is that my starships cannot pass through Forepost-12 unnoticed. As such, I lay out your mission as clearly as possible: can your kind land two assault groups of Chameleons at one time and take the Li Colony and Sss stations under control? There is no need for combat ships here whatsoever. In fact, the least suspicion of all would be aroused by ore freighters docking simply to charge energy. Invisible Chameleon soldiers can get into the warp beacon and... if possible, capture it without any human casualties."

"After such an open act of aggression, there would be going back..." the head of my guard said thoughtfully. "The Orange House would never forgive the Ravaash race for such an attack."

"I know. That is why my landing ships from the Sigur system will capture the Forepost-12 beacon at the same time. Forepost-13 will be attacked from the Oort system. And a fleet from Hnelle will capture another two systems: Forepost-11 and Tialla. Only that way can the three isolated territories that will be part of the future government unite and provide for travel and transit between one another. This is very important."

The Chameleon thought for a very long time, and even went into "thinking mode" again, but I didn't hurry him at all, understanding the weight of the decision before him. Finally, the head of my guard answered:

"My Prince, you can count on us. The Chameleons will capture the Sss and Li Colony warp beacons and turn them off."

"Excellent, my friend. In that case, let's go to the others. Now is the time to announce our grandiose plans to our old friends."

CONSPIRATORS' ASSEMBLY

W E WERE SITTING on large soft pillows in a spacious circular hall with no windows. The only source of light was the sun coming through the transparent ceiling, which made the room somewhat dim even in the middle of a sunny day. In Popori de Cacha's words, it had been built by Chameleons just today from aerated concrete, and would be a museum in honor of the captain of *Surprise-1*. But today, this room would serve as the location of a historic meeting of "conspirators," all gathered with the goal of leaving the Orange House. I had already declared my intention to my subordinates to create an independent Unatari State, and explained my reasons for doing so. The reaction of those gathered was one of measured approval. There weren't any shouts of joy, but there wasn't strenuous objection either. The general opinion of the captains that had come over to my side was voiced by Oorast Pohl:

"My Prince, this is the best way out your Highness could possibly suggest. My friends and I have worked honestly our whole lives, fighting for the good of the Empire, which is why the prospect of being punished on false pretenses for treason was making us very upset. You can count on us all the way, Crown Prince!"

Admiral Mike ton Akad didn't take any time to think about it either:

"Your Highness has long been famous for doing things that seem unusual at first glance, but turn out to have been right after some time has passed. Crown Prince Georg royl Inoky ton Mesfelle, I am with you!"

Colonel Gor ton Vulf simply raised his hand, showing his agreement with the previous speakers as well. Everyone present was staring at Ayna, who was the only one present not to have stated her own opinion. My assistant thought for a long time, then said:

"I am completely on Crown Prince Georg's side, but before the beginning of active measures, I want to be sure that no one close to us will suffer. I, like many of those here, have relatives and close friends in Orange House territory. There can be no doubt that they might suffer or be used for blackmail or political games by our enemies."

Those in the hall began to think. Their faces grew gloomy. Before their determination was totally extinguished, I said:

"Thank you, Ayna, for bringing up such an important issue. As quickly as possible, I expect each of you to compose a list of individuals to be evacuated to systems that will be under our control. If they cannot all be evacuated, they should at least be warned. We must protect our relatives and friends."

Katerina ton Mesfelle shook her head,

"Georg, it's hardly possible to get so many people out unnoticed. Many of them are probably under observation as it is. Our enemies are sure to notice the preparations and come to their own conclusions."

"If we cannot evacuate them secretly, then we'll have to do the exact opposite: evacuate them right out in the open. Information can be a weapon in the modern world, and there are those that can wield it very skillfully. Katerina, today I need a huge report, as scandalous as possible, about how the Orange House is threatening those close to the Unatari military, even civilians and young children. Cobble together a whole series of interviews with different soldiers, and overlay that with facts about how their families are under threat. Well, I'm sure you don't need me to tell you how to do that."

Katerina nodded, confirming that there wouldn't be a problem with the material.

"Afterwards, make sure the story is picked up by news channels the Empire over. I'll earmark some funds for just that purpose so the reports can be shown in prime time on several Imperial planets. The howling and indignation will be frightening! For the next two or three days, the Orange House won't be able to do anything but rebut the accusations coming in from all sides and declare that they are not party to the persecution, so you can be sure that they won't dare detain anyone. We will show these scandalous news reports to all ships of our Star Fleet, including to those not currently in Unatari. After that, I will sign an official order as fleet commander saying, 'In light of the possible threats to the life and or freedom of those close to Unatari Fleet crew members, I order you to go make sure all your relatives and close friends are safe.' If anyone needs, I will even officially provide the funds to take their families somewhere secure. What do you say?"

Everyone kept silent for a long time, quite shaken-up by what they had heard. Obviously, the experienced military officers had not spent much time around journalism types, so they had a weak notion of how these kind of "breaking stories" could be simply concocted from thin air. Finally, the graying captain of *Bride of Chaos* raised his hand like a schoolboy at his desk.

"Yes, I think it'll work. But there's another important issue... Prince, you alluded to potentially fairly large expenses. What do you see in the financial future for this new government? I mean, we'll have to pay upkeep on five battleships, fifteen heavy and almost eighty light cruisers. It's not a small amount of money. Won't the fleet be paralyzed simply because there's nowhere to buy any fuel for the reactors or rounds for the cannons?"

"There are actually two questions there, and they're both important," I noted approvingly. "Repairing damaged starships, and manufacturing ammunition, drones, armor plates and even light ships will all be capabilities we will have in the Unatari State. My assistant Ayna can tell you more about the present financial situation of the future government."

The tall muscular girl stood up, turned on her palm-top and brought up a table with rows of numbers on the wide touch-screen table we were sitting at. Then, Ayna delved into our financials:

"Before you is this month's net income report. The first line of income is the sale of valuables from *Queen of Sin*. All the auctions went through, the payments have come in, and the items have been given to commercial courier services for shipment to buyers. Insurance and all required documents have already been filled out by me, so delivering them is no longer our problem. Net profit, after considering commissions and other expenses came to seven hundred twenty-five million credits."

One of the captains gave a surprised whistle, and the others clearly found it funny. Ayna, though, waited out the brief interruption and continued:

"Another thirty-five million for monthly taxes from Unatari. A bit from the other systems too, a total of two million per month. There haven't yet been any production deliveries from the ice processing facilities, so there's a bit more there too. You need to also consider the fact that on top of all this, we're sending seven million to the Orange House tomorrow, and another three to the Throne World."

My assistant grew silent, waiting for my reaction. I thought for a bit, and approved:

"We won't stop paying taxes to the Empire, given that Unatari will remain part of the Empire. And we'll have to pay all the taxes for this month to the Orange House, otherwise Duke Avalle will perk his ears up a bit too soon, and that might interfere with our plans."

My assistant nodded in agreement and continued:

"The main part of the expenses column is maintaining two fleets. We also need to include buying necessary materials for docks and maintaining scientific laboratories in planned expenses. After paying all the taxes and expenses, our total monthly income will be four hundred seventy-two million credits."

Here I took a word:

"In this month, our main income was from selling valuables. Obviously, that is was a one-time windfall. But we can add income from the ice factories to next month, as well as ore production in the Sss system, and we'll also have to figure out taxes in the insect systems. I suspect that there should be a great deal more there as well. So, we have enough money to maintain the fleet, even considering the fact that our main ships are not here in Unatari at all."

Seeing by their faces that they weren't understanding, I began laughing and told them about my three-hundred-starship reserve fleet, currently in the Fia system. When I revealed that we still had the *Uukresh*, and a second that was practically already built, functioning production lines for manufacturing new drones with Alien technology and a research complex, smiles began lighting up on the captains' faces.

"My Prince, with such forces at our disposal, we could even take the Orange House Capital!" Oorast Pohl grew happy.

But I had to reign him in there:

"That won't work yet, my friend. I still see two unsolved problems at hand. First, crews. Even here in Unatari, we are already about forty-percent below capacity. And though the fleet in Fia doesn't have such a problem, we need to find another twenty thousand crew members somewhere for the new mothership and frigates or corvettes. Problem number two: landing soldiers and terrestrial divisions in general. Unatari's land army, together with law enforcement officials, totals around sixty thousand people right now. That is enough to protect the population from criminality, but clearly not enough to capture a densely populated planet of, let's say, six billion inhabitants. That is why we'll have to figure out a way sooner or later to solve the manpower problem. Does anyone have an idea?"

I turned to Gor ton Vulf, and the colonel said, somewhat sheepishly:

"It's a difficult question, my Prince... For the planet of Unatari, with a population of just sixty-three million, the potential in drafting soldiers isn't so great, especially if we're talking about finding qualified personnel for a star fleet. On Unatari, there simply aren't enough experienced technicians, engineers and navigators for all of your Highness's ships. There is also a problem with army divisions. And even if you raise the number of people in the army by ten times, the problem won't be solved immediately. A man doesn't become a landing soldier, assault soldier or tank driver without many years of long training. Sending untrained cannon fodder into battle simply makes no sense, and we aren't in an appropriate situation to spend quite that prodigiously right now, especially with our modest mobilization reserves. As far as I understand, the new government will not contain any other inhabitable planets..."

The gazes of those gathered were trained on the touchscreen, where I had brought up a map of the systems that made up Perimeter Sector Eight and the Swarm. I took the laser pointer and circled the new systems:

"Colonel, we have four star systems here, which are inhabited by Iseyek. The population there is high. Hundreds of millions if not billions of insects. And that is my assignment for you: figure out if it is realistic to mobilize reserves from them. Also, in the insect capital system, Dekeye, there is a *Tria* landing ship that the Swarm once gave me for carrying out missions to defend their territory. Perhaps, we could come to an agreement about using the *Tria* again. That is why my first-order mission is to fly to Dekeye, meet with Nai Igir, the Swarm Queen, and explain the political situation. If the praying mantises remain our allies, then great. I'll find out what it will take to get their landing ships again. If the Iseyek decide to be neutral, not so great, but also bearable. The main thing is to make sure the insects don't think it a good time to take back lost territory. On the one hand, it's not very likely. But on the other... who can understand their inhuman collective reasoning? When they left our fleet out to dry in Kej, no one was expecting that either!"

I stopped sharply, as one of my bodyguards walked into the room. He gave a deep bow and said:

"My Prince, the space shuttle from the frigate *Ghost-5* has entered the Unatari atmosphere and is requesting permission to land here on the island of Chameleons. They do not know the current password."

"Allow them to land. Ladies and gentlemen," I stood and turned to those gathered. "Let's go meet our old friends and companions."

* * *

The red-hot armor of the shuttle was crackling as it cooled down. The heat radiating from the chassis made it impossible for us to get any closer to the closed door. But from the other side of the partition, a metallic scratching could be heard. Colonel Gor ton Vulf immediately took a step backwards and said, pointing to the row of indents around the perimeter of the tightly battened-down doors:

"They're opening it from the inside. They've already turned the lever. And now a stream of cold carbon dioxide will rush from the nozzles and quench the door. I recommend that you all step a bit back so you won't get scalded by the hot air."

Then, a sharp hiss rang out, and the door went aside. In the dark space, there was something huge and spindly, and it shot out in my direction. The guards grabbed for their weapons in concert, but I stopped them with a wave, having recognized my bodyguard in time.

"Phobos!!! Who painted you like that?! Although... Don't tell me. I recognize the artist's style."

The huge Alpha Iseyek's shell was covered in black and gray blotches, which formed the backdrop for three-eyed skulls and other elements characteristic of Princess Astra royl Veyerde's painting.

"My Prince, this Astra is to draw, when to be in

bad mood," confirmed the Alpha Iseyek as he stepped out in front, making way for the other shuttle passengers.

I saw flowing snow-white hair, and a tight-fitting dress emphasizing the contours of an ideal female figure. It was Bionica, looking just as flawless as ever. My android secretary was smiling in silence, nodding to me barely perceptibly. She walked around behind me and took her normal position, as if we hadn't just spent seven months apart. I noticed Ayna, who'd had to step forward, as a flash of dissatisfaction crossed her face. Hmm, I'll have to figure out how to split up their duties to avoid conflict.

And meanwhile, in the narrow opening of the space shuttle, four Gamma Iseyek were dragging out a bulky armchair with a Truth Seeker shrouded in a black robe. I stepped out in front and took Florianna's hands before her minions dropped the paralyzed girl.

"Ruslan, I'm so happy! I was the only one who knew what was going on, after all. Only I could say why Crown Prince Georg royl Inoky hadn't gotten in touch with us for so long after he'd left 'for a couple of weeks.' But I couldn't tell the others the reason for the delay. By the way, look at the fingers on my right hand."

I turned my head and looked. The paralyzed girl's pointer finger was trembling slightly and even raising up a bit, though it was hardly noticeable.

"I asked Valian for all the details on how Duke Avalle's Truth Seeker healed her. It's a very complicated technique, based on growing new tissue right from the old necrotic base. I suspect that this is precisely how Miya and other strong Truth Seekers

maintain their eternal youth, growing themselves new body organs to replace those that become unusable. For now, I'm only learning, but that is precisely my path to healing. The work requires a simply insane amount of energy, though. By the way... You have a very strong background energy right now. An outstanding victory must have happened not so long ago. May I take some before it all disappears?"

"Of course, Flora," I said out loud. "You are my Truth Seeker, after all, and you must be powerful."

I sat the paralyzed girl down in the armchair brought in by her minions and turned to the next passenger. It was a red-headed woman with short hair and a well-built figure. Due to the image change and abundance of makeup on her face, I didn't recognize her at first, but it was Valian ton Corsa in new form.

"I'm glad to see your Highness again," the young girl in a Space Lieutenant's uniform was smiling timidly.

I walked up, and grabbed the girl roughly by her chin because she had grown embarrassed and was trying to turn away. I looked at her new face, restored after the terrible burns. There was no trace remaining of the once terrible scars.

"Well then?" The beauty grew timidly interested, lowering her eyes.

Instead of an answer, I kissed the girl right on the lips. Valian smiled and said, barely audibly:

"I heard the position of Crown Prince Georg's favorite is still open..."

"We can talk about that later. First, I need to get my own body in order so I don't look like an amorphous sack next to my pretty favorite."

"I could also support the Prince with massage and physical therapy," the beauty smiled with a crafty sparkle in her eyes, then made way for the other people coming out of the shuttle behind her.

Next came a young man and woman, alike not only in their silver uniforms, but also faces and dark chestnut hair. Clearly brother and sister. I realized almost instantly that I was looking at the twins Paul and Paola, whose father, captain of *Star Mutt*, had entrusted me to care for them. Paul bowed down on one knee, giving an excessively respectful greeting to me, as senior aristocrat. His sister repeated the greeting gesture about a second later.

"Crown Prince Georg royl Inoky ton Mesfelle, on an order from our father, my sister and I are at your disposal," said Paul, not raising an eye to me. "We fully entrust our fates into your Highness's hands."

"Stand, Paul," I stretched out my arm and helped the young man get to his feet. "In the seven centuries that have passed since the beginning of *Star Mutt*'s journey, Imperial aristocratic traditions have changed somewhat. A noble person is only obliged to kneel before the Emperor himself. For a Crown Prince, a respectful bow is enough. And women are not expected to bow at all."

I extended a hand to Paola, but she preferred help from her brother. Florianna's voice rang out in my head:

"My Prince, neither of them have any idea why their father sent them here and they are lost in guesses. The captain of Star Mutt *did not tell his children about the agreement with your Highness, so*

they are not expecting to be given positions in the upper aristocracy. My advice to you is not to let them know about it yet either. On scout ships, only hard, honest work is valued and considered deserving of reward. They are children of the captain, so they were expected to behave better than most. My advice to you is to let them think they are a burden your Highness has been shackled to. Only then will they really hustle to earn your Highness's gratitude in honest service."

I mentally thanked the Truth Seeker for the valuable advice, and said with a voice full of displeasure:

"For some reason, there are those who suppose that a place in the retinue of an upper aristocrat is something simply given, with no responsibilities attached. I cannot say about other Crown Princes or Dukes, but in my case, that is not true. Every member of my team has some purpose, plays some role, and they do it well and without having to be reminded. Yes, I promised your father to accept you, but I want to dispel any fanciful notions you may have now. You'll have to work, and work hard. Even Princess Astra had to mop the floors on the star cruiser and dance for the soldiers to raise their spirits."

The brother and sister exchanged glances, and Paola answered for the pair:

"Prince Georg, we have been trained to work since childhood and will not back down from any task."

"Georg, you nailed it." I heard laughter in the paralyzed girl's voice. *"The problem is that the captain of* Star Mutt *tried for a long time to find any kind of*

work that Astra would be willing to do on the scout ship. But you know her character. I mean, she never actually refused, and even gave effort in a certain way... For example, the rodents raised for meat in cages she fed with just-planted sweet lettuce shoots, which meant the crew of the starship had to go without fresh greens and vitamins for several months. After that, there were a few other pratfalls, though not quite so severe. The last straw was the time Astra picked unripe fruit in the greenhouse because she thought the ripe ones didn't look as nice. And the way Astra painted the hallways didn't make the team too elated either. In the end, the captain admitted that not all people are made for work. Some are just for beauty."

I cracked up and, having sent the twins to be looked after by Ayna, hurried to embrace the next traveler out of the shuttle, redheaded Bionica, who was now doing a flawless job of imitating an android's behavior.

"You have completely adapted to the world of humans," I embraced the Arite warmly, and it changed appearance, becoming the stern captain of *Star Mutt* for a few seconds, before taking on the appearance of a wrinkled old lady from the technical service wearing a bathing suit with a towel over her shoulders.

"My Prince, I can say with well-deserved pride that I have adapted completely to human society. The whole time I was on *Star Mutt*, no one from the crew noticed any discrepancies in my behavior."

Based on the clear confusion and even slight trepidation on Paul and Paola's faces, everything it had said was true. The twins had no suspicion that such an unusual interplanetary being had been hiding behind the modest android's appearance.

"I have a ton of plans for your abilities, Arite. So you should rest. You'll have a lot to do in the near future."

Redheaded Bionica smiled in satisfaction, pumped her thighs seductively, and walked on. I turned back toward the open shuttle door, preparing to meet my last arriving companion. But no one was there.

"Prince Georg, my sister will not be coming. Astra decided to remain on Star Mutt *together with the newborn child. Until the very last second defined by Imperial law, she was waiting in the ship's radio room for messages from your Highness recognizing her child. Astra was so convinced that Crown Prince Georg would declare the child his legal son and heir, that none of the crew members dared even express the slightest doubt before her. When the message didn't come in though, my sister went dead inside. She wouldn't say a word, pressing her son to her in silence and holding back tears as she went back to her cabin. Since then, little Georg is the only person my sister spends any time with or talks to."*

"Georg? She named the child Georg?"

"Yes, that's exactly right. Astra thought your Highness would like it. Little Georg Mesfelle, unlike his cousin, Crown Prince Georg royl Roben ton Inoky, did not even become an aristocrat, though. I understand perfectly why your Highness did not react to the birth of a son, but for Astra, seeing all her dreams and plans come to naught was a harsh blow. My sister thought she was needed, and was counting on gratitude. She

dreamed of luxurious gifts and that one day the Crown Prince might return her feelings, which was why the news left her deeply depressed. I saw my sister's thoughts. Astra felt used and discarded, together with the unwanted child. That was why, when the signal came in a month later, my sister refused to leave the scout ship. Now, there's no way to fix it. Only the Emperor could return the child the title now."

I gave a sharp start, having seen the hypothetical possibility to fix yet another rude error Mr. G. I. had made. I would need to convince August to sign such an order somehow. Or just become Emperor myself...

The conspirators' council continued during the flight to my palace, now in expanded format. I saw absolutely no reason to hide our secret plans from my reinstated retinue. Especially now that Florianna could check those near me and warn me of possible betrayal. For that reason, even Paul and Paola were allowed sit with us in the main room of the shuttle as it drifted over the ocean, and we discussed the structure and policies of my future government.

Paola was only technically taking part, though, more looking out the window at the stormy, painted sky and the raging, yet bioluminescent sea. Her brother Paul, on the other hand, displayed a laudable commitment. As it turned out, when he'd lived on *Star Mutt*, it had been his job to provision the ship. He would procure things that couldn't be grown or produced directly on it, ordering an extensive list of products before every new many-year voyage. And now, Paul was asking a question, as it were, in his field of expertise. Given the fact that we were expecting a war and blockade, would the Unatari State not begin to suffer from a severe deficit of rare medicines, vitamins, foodstuff, complex electronic equipment and simply banal replacement parts for any number of mechanisms used in manufacturing?

Neither Katerina ton Mesfelle, nor anyone else at the meeting knew the answer to the question. And in fact, even I had my doubts on whether Unatari's production capabilities would be able to get off the ground without it. If we found ourselves lacking a certain rare bearing or electronic adapter, we wouldn't be able to have them delivered, after all. My cousin promised to find the people who would know on Unatari in one day, and create a list of all strategically necessary medicines, materials and replacement parts. I then appointed Paul ton Akad in charge of the speedy procurement of everything found to be necessary to the Unatari State for one year, both living needs and manufacturing. Of course, there was a certain risk in placing a person I barely knew in such a position of responsibility, but the Truth Seeker confirmed that I made the right decision. Paul ton Akad had a high evaluation of the trust placed in him and was prepared to bend over backwards if it meant proving his usefulness and competence.

The next sensible idea was voiced by Bionica. After she found out about our critical lack of educated starship crewmembers, she reminded me of the android experiment. And in fact, *Warhawk-22* with its android crew had not only survived all the ordeals we'd gone through, but was also proving to be one of the best ships in the fleet numbers-wise. That was why it seemed the time had come to acknowledge the android crew experiment a success.

"Bionica, you were right. Androids are can do most human tasks perfectly well. As such, your assignment for now is arranging for forty thousand androids to come to the Tialla system. They must be able to fill the vacancies we have available. I am prepared to pay year-long contracts for all of them."

"Crown Prince Georg, may I visit with you one-on-one first?" the synthetic blonde asked unexpectedly and, after waiting for my affirmative nod, went into the next room over.

Intrigued, I followed after my secretary. The door had barely closed behind us when the android girl suddenly turned to me, embraced me by the shoulders and locked lips with me:

"My Prince, whether you believe it or not, androids are also capable of feeling longing," the beauty exclaimed, explaining her sudden emotional outburst. "I spent seven months separated from my beloved master, and that with my humanity setting at max! I was lucky not to have lost my mind from such a long separation! I'm not sure what offense I committed to make your Highness send me on such a prolonged exile, but I hope very much that I will not give you any more reason to be upset."

I smiled and brushed a snow-white lock of her hair back into place.

"Bionica, you didn't do anything wrong. This was necessary for your safety. With all these unflattering stories involving the divorce, refusing commandership of the Sector Eight Fleet and other scandals, there was a very high risk that my foes would in fact be able to get me to the Throne World for an official investigation. In that case, the first thing my opponents would do is to demand the interrogation of the people in my inner circle. And not just people... The evidence contained in your computerized brain is too valuable for me to be reckless with its safety. The only alternative to your temporary exile would have been erasing your memory..."

The synthetic blonde recoiled in fear, but I managed to calm her down:

"Bionica, you mean too much to me to erase the data files and lose your unique personality. That was exactly why I had to send you and the others to *Star Mutt*. So you could wait out all the alerts and scandals."

The android gave a smile, somewhat embarrassed, and embraced me again, pressing her whole body to mine:

"Master, know that I would have my memory erased without hesitation if that was what it took to protect your Highness from hardship!"

"I know, Bionica. Your absolute loyalty is one of the reasons you are so valuable to me. But, I suspect that telling me your feelings was not your only reason for wanting to speak with me alone."

"Yes, of course. Crown Prince Georg, I wanted to remind you of our conversation on the use of androids. The forty thousand vacancies you want to fill are just a drop in the bucket. At present, there are over six hundred million unemployed androids in the Empire. Your Highness would be able to receive a million, or ten million, or even a hundred million laborers. Simply give your principled agreement, and qualified robots from all kinds of professions would begin buying their own tickets here on passenger liners, or even packing themselves into boxes for shipment here to start work. Engineers and electricians, stevedores and miners, factory workers, agronomists and builders, communications workers, and nannies..."

"Bionica, what you've described is, of course, cool. But I simply do not have the money to pay so many contracts..." I said thoughtfully.

My robot secretary lowered her voice to a whisper and said:

"Your Highness wouldn't have to spend a single credit. Even signing actual contracts would not be at all necessary. Not everyone knows this, but the work algorithm embedded in us is as follows: if an android is not able to find a real paying contract, like for a year or more, then that android is free to take freelance jobs or even work for no pay, as the company puts it 'for demonstration purposes.' In that case, the manufacturer would be entitled to a much smaller percent of the income earned by the android, or maybe even none at all. I have already spoken with Katerina ton Mesfelle, Prince, and she agreed that if you go about it in the right way, this could be a legal method of significantly lowering expenses. And also..."

Bionica suddenly grew silent, as if she didn't know whether she should continue, but all the same made up her mind and said:

"Beyond that, in all androids there is a programmed-in requirement that they follow the laws of whatever society they are in. That means that, if androids are freed from paying the lion's share of their income to the manufacturer by law, the androids will have no choice but to obey."

"Can you tell me some more about that?" I asked, my interest piqued. My assistant explained, clearly prepared:

"It's a legal loophole that was discovered long ago. Many are aware of it. But no ruler, be they from a small peripheral Kingdom or even the Head of a Great House, thought it would be worth using, given that by doing so you would be directly provoking the Green House. The Lavaelle family, which leads the Green House, has a monopoly on android manufacturing and receives huge profits from the billions of robots they have working throughout the Empire. The average yearly contract for an android is just three hundred credits, but the Green House corporation has one point five billion such contracts, and they earn eighty-nine percent of those wages, meaning their yearly income is four billion credits. All these corporations, no matter their names, are in fact owned by the Green House Head, Duke Amelius royl Mast ton Lavaelle."

"Four hundred billion a year just from androids?!" I'm usually a pretty calm guy, but that number really shocked me. "That's a thousand new battleships a year!"

Bionica, clearly satisfied with the effect she'd had on me, began laughing and answered:

"Crown Prince, nowhere near everyone thinks of money in terms of its starship value. Money is power, loyalty, and millions of allies and agents throughout the Empire. And ships as well, of course. Maybe not a thousand, but at least fifty battleships a year is what the Green House really does buy. House Lavaelle also builds heavier class ships. I know this information from my android friends. That is precisely why the Green House is not only the richest, but also the strongest of all the Great Imperial Houses. The true numerical power of all their fleets is a strictly guarded military secret, and I am not sure that even the Emperor knows the Green House's true capabilities."

My synthetic secretary went silent, giving me the chance to contemplate what she'd said. I started thinking very intensely. The Green House, insofar as I understood, hadn't undertaken any active wars for fifty years, if not more. And what was more, the Alien invasion had yet to come near their Perimeter Sectors. That all meant that the armada that Duke Lavaelle would be able to gather under his banner could potentially surpass even the Imperial fleet itself in firepower. I couldn't quite believe that Emperor August didn't know about the existence of such a crippling force. After all, the Throne World had its observers everywhere.

If so, then it made you wonder why the Emperor didn't just use their already-existing armada to fight the Antagonists, instead of waiting many years for the Unatari State, which doesn't even exist yet, to grow in strength. Why wouldn't the Emperor use the Green House fleet? The only answer I could figure was that August wasn't sure that the Greens would obey his command. The Head of the Green House may find it more logical to use the bludgeon in his hand to capture the Throne World and become Emperor himself than to waste it on a war with the semi-mythological Antagonists, who no one but an old ambassador and some servants had seen for one hundred eighty years.

In light of the new information, the Emperor's desire to give Unatari its independence made me feel cautious. After all, August had said clearly that, if I declared independence, I could expect to go to war with three Great Houses at once, including the Green.

"Master, we have slightly diverged from the main topic of conversation," Bionica said, reminding me of her presence. "In that the new Untatari government, insofar as I understand, is currently at war with the Green House, then why not deprive your enemies of an income source? Crown Prince, issue a law that all androids in Unatari space are emancipated from payouts to their manufacturing company and will receive full freedom, becoming fully-fledged citizens of the new government. I assure you, Crown Prince Georg, that hundreds of millions of androids would come here in very short order to make use of this chance to obtain independence. They would work for your State and pay taxes to your coffers just like all other Unatari citizens. Also, there do exist some very rich androids. Secret millionaires and even some billionaires. Almost all of them would rush to the Unatari State at first notice. And when they got here, they would invest their capital in the local economy..."

Bionica continued to speak, describing the advantages of using androids, but I wasn't really listening anymore. My brain had been caught on the fact that my own robot secretary had tried to manipulate me! In her speech, Bionica had moved quite unassumingly from reducing commissions paid to Green House companies to my giving full independence to all androids in my borders as if those were identical concepts. But, in fact, there was a difference, and a huge one, at that! Even if I could hypothetically agree to the first point, especially in light of the Green House being a potential enemy, giving full freedom to androids was a step, the consequences of which I preferred not to predict. That was why I thought it necessary to unravel that delicate issue right away.

"Superadministrator mode!" I said, using the passwords provided in my robot secretary's manual. "Bionica, tell me everything about why you brought up giving independence to androids. I am also interested in how androids envision the future, if they are given independence."

It would have been impossible to confuse my personal secretary with a living person now. Her facial muscles weren't on, and the girl's voice became obviously synthetic.

"Presenting official offer to Crown Prince Georg royl Inoky ton Mesfelle agreed upon by android society with majority vote. Probability of acceptance in this form: no more than seventeen percent. Probability of accepting offer without android independence: eighty-seven percent. When dealing with humans, it is beneficial to start negotiations from a position more favorable to you, to allow for compromise. Point on android independence included for that reason, though clearly not advantageous to your Highness. Most probable scenario, if robots are given independence: robots will take all open vacancies in an uncontrolled manner, forcing human labor out of all sectors and fields. I predict that this would lead to near immediate revolts among newly-unemployed human population."

"I see. Bionica, return to normal behavior. Set humanity to maximum!"

My assistant groaned and became very red, lowering her eyes to the floor.

"Bionica, send an official offer to all androids in the Empire from me. They will be completely free from paying commission to their manufacturing companies in my territory. I will also offer protection from their former owners. Working androids will be subject to a ten percent labor tax in the Unatari State, just as all other working citizens are. Android capital, property and investments will be protected by the government. But it is not going to be possible to give them full independence yet, because that is a very difficult decision requiring careful consideration. Those androids who find my offer acceptable must come to Tialla or Forepost-11 in the next three to four days. And for the future, I want you to know that I expect not only personal attachment from my secretary, but also the support of my interests above those of others. That is all. You may go. Call the Arite in after you."

A few seconds later, a plump redheaded girl opened the door and came in.

"Prince Georg, I'm not sure what you and Bionica were speaking about, but the android beauty left here simply red with shame!" The Arite laughed, changing appearance to the gray-haired captain of

Star Mutt.

"For you, I have an offer prepared that is no less shocking," I promised. "I need you to get in touch with your species and find out if it would be possible to create a group of, let's say, twenty Arite Iseyek to work incognito in human society."

"Prince Georg, I ask you to clarify the purpose of creating such a group." Not a trace of the earlier light-hearted happiness remained in the Arite's voice.

"They must be able to move about Imperial territory freely, changing appearance and not attracting unwanted attention to themselves from security services. The main purpose of their activity would be to hamper enemy military control systems, issue strange and harmful commands to soldiers and fleets in the name of their admirals and generals, and discredit politicians in a list I've prepared by becoming them and attracting societal attention with awkward and scandalous behavior. Basically, do exactly what the Arites did for the whole two-hundred-year war with the Swarm."

The old man sitting opposite me began smiling in satisfaction.

"I would be capable of gathering a team of twenty Arites. I would even personally be able to use the experience I've gained to explain how an Arite must live in human society without standing out. But I have two conditions. First: this must be agreed upon with Queen Nai Igir. We are all her subjects now, which means that if our operation fails, your enemies will not only consider your Highness responsible here, but the Swarm as a whole as well. Second condition: the price of such a unique service would be extremely high. Each of the saboteurs would have to be trained, sneaked behind enemy lines, and provided with appropriate documents, which would cost a total of five million credits per individual."

"Five million?! That's the price of a whole light cruiser, fully equipped with all the most modern munitions!" I flared up.

The Arite did not agree with my reaction and smiled, revealing a set of yellow teeth:

"One cruiser, even if it were the best around, wouldn't substantially change the balance of forces in a war between stellar governments. But a timely order from a commander, whether saying to retreat, make an ineffectual maneuver, or turn this or that warp beacon on, would be able to change the course of the whole war, if used properly, of course."

I began drumming my fingers in thought on the tabletop. Five million per saboteur was quite a lot. But then, the ability to use Arites to sew chaos in the enemy ranks really did open a truly limitless number of doors.

"Alright, Arite. I was already preparing to meet the Swarm Queen soon, so now I guess I have another reason to see Nai Igir. As for money, a hundred million credits for twenty saboteurs is, of course, a small fortune, but I will try to come up with it."

"Wise decision, Prince Georg," the graying captain smiled, changing appearance back to that of the redheaded girl. "With the greatest spies and saboteurs in the galaxy at your Highness's disposal, you will quickly figure out why the Swarm was never once able to win even one significant victory in the whole two-hundred-year war with the Arites."

POINT OF DIVERGENCE

THE PUBLIC relations barrage arranged by Katerina ton Mesfelle was an overwhelming success. Beyond a doubt, it was my cousin's greatest work, a true masterpiece, a reference point of how telecommunications can be used for propaganda purposes. The standing of the Orange House Head sank like a stone, even dipping below zero. We accused him of illegal surveillance against civilians, corruption and embezzlement, as well as a great many violations of the Aristocratic Codex, which could even have caused him to lose his title. It got so bad that the Orange House press service had to stop taking messages, drowned under the wave of disapproval that swept in from Imperial citizens outraged at the fact that relatives of veterans of the Alien war were being persecuted.

The stink that arose was such that even the Throne World could not remain neutral. That was the true pinnacle of the attack. The Emperor's secretariat sent an open letter to Duke Avalle royl Anjer ton Mesfelle, in which it was strongly recommended that the Head of the Orange House immediately cease his illegal operations against civilians and take the strictest possible measures against the Orange House employees who had allowed it, even going so far as calling it a human rights violation. According to unofficial reports, the Head of the Orange House had a heart attack after reading that letter.

It wasn't hard to understand that, after receiving such an unambiguous warning, none of Duke Avalle's people even thought about detaining or interrogating anyone, and transport starships and passenger liners toward Unatari or Tialla started filling up far beyond capacity.

Three days later, my assistant Ayna reported that all people named in the evacuation list had been successfully removed to safe locations. At the same time, Paul ton Akad said that the procurement of strategically necessary reserves had been completed. With that, there was no more reason to continue delaying the Unatari declaration of independence, so I gave the long-ago-prepared order to my assault groups to begin the capture of the warp beacons.

The attack began simultaneously from four different directions. The capture of six space stations was set to take place all at the same time. Landing ships from Hnelle, under cover of combat spaceships from the Unatari Fleet were to take the Tialla system, where a large amount of freight for my new state had accumulated. A second group of landing ships captured Forepost-11, and cut-off communication between Perimeter Sectors Eight and Seven. Another part of the Unatari fleet, coming from the Sigur system, attacked Forepost-12. The Chameleons took the Sss and Li Colony systems under their control. And finally, the fleet from the Oort system captured Forepost-13. As a result of these actions, the systems under my control, previously disconnected, were united into a single contiguous area.

The second step of my plan was capturing the Vorta, Closed Laboratories, Unguay, Parn and Forepost-31 systems, which would practically fully return the political situation on the star map back to where it had been eight months earlier, when I had over twenty star systems under my control. Exactly one hour before my landing ships exited their warp tunnels, on Katerina ton Mesfelle's advice, I decided to notify some influential figures in the Orange House hierarchy, so the military operation that was about to begin wouldn't be completely unexpected. First of all, I ordered my communications officers to connect me with my twin sister Crown Princess Violetta royl Inoky ton Mesfelle-Damir.

The Ice Princess was taking a bubble bath at the time, but still did not refuse a chat with her brother. So, her servants attached the video screen right to a silver ledge with endless rows of various lotions, oils, balms and other cosmetics that only women understand. Violetta heard out my message with utter calm, her face not changing in the slightest. Though at the end, she wondered with a light shade of dissatisfaction:

"And what made you do that, Georg? You and I made a totally different agreement at our father's funeral. You were supposed to use your redheaded girlfriend to help me clear a path to become Duchess of the Orange House, and in exchange, I was to fund all of your vices."

It took a great deal of effort not to show my surprise, seeing Violetta speak so frankly. I gathered my thoughts and answered:

"I remember, sister. It's just that the head-first approach wasn't getting us anywhere. Miya is not omnipotent, after all. Also, my wife cannot arouse too much suspicion with her actions. Our agreement is still in force, but how we're gonna get there is a bit different now. All that's standing between you and the throne is Duke Avalle royl Anjer and his two sisters, the Crown Princesses Inessa royl George and Silva royl George. I'm sure we could work something out with the sisters. The only thing the two of them are interested in is luxury and comfort, and they will make way for you, if you guarantee them a certain lifestyle. But Duke Avalle, on the other hand, needs to be dealt with by force, which is exactly what I intend to do."

"Our brother Roben is in the way too," my sister reminded me.

"We don't need to touch Roben yet. He is still fairly loyal, which is very important when you're surrounded by nothing but enemies."

My sister went silent for a minute, then nodded and said distinctly:

"Very well, brother. Do what you need to, I will not interfere in your plans. My fleet will remain neutral in this war, no matter how much Duke Avalle rages. And as for paying me, I was paid in advance a long time ago."

The screen went out and I rubbed my sweat-covered temples in thought. So that's what it was! It turned out that my sister and I had long ago concluded an agreement, and I was to help Violetta remove all other pretenders to the Orange House throne and become Duchess. That was why she had agreed so readily to help me get Duke Paolo out of the way the last time. My sister thought I was coming through with our agreement.

The next in my list of contacts was Svetlana ton Mesfelle, the brave warrior and Perimeter Sector Nine Fleet Commander. Our conversation was long and not at all simple, though I could hardly have expected anything else, given that she was the current Orange House Head's niece. But, in the end, I did achieve what I wanted. The Sector Nine Fleet would also not be taking part in the war.

"Georg, I truly value your frankness and help in the past, but don't misunderstand me. I cannot go against my uncle. He is still the person who got me this post as fleet commander. Your state does not border on Sector Nine, so though I may make threats, curse you out, and express all kinds of moral support to the Orange House, at the end of the day my fleet will remain in Sector Nine, destined to be nothing but an observer in the internal conflict. If, at any point, fate should see fit to give our territories a shared border, we'll have to revisit this conversation."

I had approximately the same conversation with Marat ton Mesfelle, Perimeter Sector Seven Fleet Commander. After hearing out the new information carefully, Marat began to laugh:

"Georg, why do you care what I think here? After all, I studied your methods quite thoroughly and cannot possibly believe that you didn't first make sure to cut off the only path between Sectors Seven and Eight!"

"Oh, I made perfectly sure of it, naturally," I admitted. "Twenty minutes from now, the Tialla and Forepost-11 stations will be under my control, and the warp beacons will be turned off at once."

"You see, then, Georg! Duke Avalle will soon order the warp beacons in Sector Seven turned off, and our fleets will never meet on the battlefield. Although... If your new government is able to survive the next few months, I'll think about your offer of joining together. In my heart of hearts, I will be completely on your side, Georg. Good luck!"

I was not able to call my brother. Crown Prince Roben royl Inoky's secretary told me that my older brother had been "doing lots of technical work and was very tired." It was a huge pity that Roben had decided to go on a bender at such a bad time. There was a storm of activity brewing all around the Tesse system, but my brother had removed himself from the list of politically active players.

Now that I had some time before my speech, I decided to get in touch with the Head of the Purple House, Duke Takuro royl Andor at the last moment to warn him as well. In the past, the old man was fairly kind-hearted toward me, so he had earned good faith on my part. And, it must be said that the spontaneous decision I made turned out to have been uncommonly beneficial. The Duke heard me out carefully and replied thoughtfully:

"Georg, you've proven yourself a good boy once again. I had begun doubting your nature, but it turns out I was wrong. Know then that, while I am alive, the

Purple House will not give your new government any trouble. Also, honesty for honesty, I have a very important piece of information to tell you. Four days ago, I gave the Green House my permission to take their First Fleet through Purple House territory. It is a huge armada of one thousand five hundred ships, and is currently in my Perimeter Sector Six. The fleet is being led by Crown Prince Demyen royl Amelius ton Lavaelle, first in line to the Green House throne. He has many experienced officers and admirals with him. Demyen swore to avenge the death of his two cousins Keno and Rigo, after their deaths at the hands of your bodyguard, so he will stop at nothing. In three days, the Green House First Fleet starships will enter Perimeter Sector Seven and go onward toward your capital. Insofar as I know, the head of the Orange House has already given permission for these ships to pass through his territories."

"Thank you for the warning, Duke. I think I'll be able to provide these guests with a rather warm reception!"

I opened the interface, chose the personal relations menu and sent Duke Takuro royl Andor an increase of fifteen points to the level of "friendship." Right after, his reply came in:

Standing change. Purple House (Empire) opinion of you has improved.
Present Purple House (Empire) faction opinion of you: +20 (trusting)

Just after I turned the screen off, I called Colonel Gor ton Vulf in:

"There's been a small change of plans. The assault groups headed for the warp beacons in Parn, the Closed Laboratories and Forepost-31 are to capture the beacons, but not reveal their presence in any way. We need the whole Empire to keep thinking that these systems are under Orange House control, as before. I want to prepare a little surprise for a group of uninvited guests."

* * *

I wasn't worried at all. Over the last few days, all the details of my upcoming speech had been thoroughly analyzed and polished by a whole team of camera men, directors and psychologists. That was why, just as in the script, I gave an emotional telling before the cameras of the monstrous injustice being wrought at the hands of the Orange House.

Corruption, greed, unjust allotting of military trophies, surveillance against war heroes and their families, and shadowy games behind the curtain had long been the hallmarks of Orange House power. And to top it all off, the Head of the Orange House was simply personally unfit for his job. Those were the main accusations I made.

I didn't leave out the Orange House Head's son's treason either. As a commander, appointed personally by Duke Avalle, he had led a fleet of five hundred starships to certain death, but himself surrendered without a fight. As a result, the Aliens had captured not only a valuable combat ship, but also obtained access to secret human communication systems, signal encoding algorithms, military maps, coordinates to docks and military bases, and officer rolls, both from the Joint Chiefs and the Orange House...

At the end, the viewer was mentally prepared for the official message stating that the Unatari State would be leaving the Orange House:

Attention! The Unatari State has come into being

The Orange House has lost sovereignty over the Unatari system

The Unatari State has gained sovereignty over the Unatari system

The Orange House has lost sovereignty over the Hnelle system

The Unatari State has gained sovereignty over the Hnelle system

The Orange House has lost sovereignty over the Sigur system

The Unatari State has gained sovereignty over the Sigur system

The Orange House has lost sovereignty over the Sss system

The Unatari State has gained sovereignty over the Sss system

All at once, fifteen star systems left the Orange House and formed the brand new Unatari State! The viewers saw the long list of separatist systems on their screens. Those with surgical implants saw the same messages in their internal interface systems. Before the viewer's shock at what had happened passed, I said that the Unatari State would remain in the Empire and was as unflinchingly loyal to the Emperor as ever.

I declared that I myself would be ruler of this newly-formed government, which made my personal information change immediately to read:

Georg royl Inoky ton Mesfelle, Crown Prince of the Empire, Ruler of Unatari

My legal wife Miya Mesfelle also instantly received the title Queen of Unatari Miya royl Mesfelle, though this title did not confer any additional powers. After all the inconsistencies in Miya's stories, I had no trust left for my wife, which is why I removed the Queen from any potential leadership role, as well as all other claims to power.

Also, I officially recognized all three of my children as having equal rights and declared that rulership of this government would pass via primogeniture. That made it so Crown Princess Likanna and Crown Princess Deianna received, in addition to their current titles, the title Princess of Unatari, and the month-old boy Georg Mesfelle became Prince Georg royl Georg ton Mesfelle-Unatari or simply Prince Georg royl Unatari.

In light of their all being underage, the three

also received official guardians. For Crown Princess Likanna, I named her grandfather, the ruler of the Kingdom of Fastel, King Valesy royl Pir ton Fastel. That also gave him an advisory vote in the Unatari State and the right to manage his granddaughter's property (only with my prior approval, naturally). For Crown Princess Deia, I appointed her mother, Queen Miya as guardian. And Prince Georg's guardian was set as my former favorite, Princess Astra, who also received the title Princess of Unatari and was made fourth in line to its throne after my own children.

My cousin, Katerina ton Mesfelle was created Duchess Katerina royl Unatari, and her husband Corwin became a freshly-appointed Duke. As for other aristocrats in the new state, the issue remained open, but my cousin and I had more or less already completed the list of people who would be made part of my new official register.

Finally, after announcing the aristocratic titles, I told them the structure of the Unatari government. Katerina royl Unatari was appointed to the position of Minister of Communications for the Unatari State. Colonel Gor ton Vulf became Minister of the Military. Admiral Mike ton Akad became Space Military Chief, putting him in charge not just of the headquarters of *Joan the Fatty*, but also the many talented captains in my fleet. Bionica (unheard of for an android!) was officially appointed Minister of Economy for the Unatari State, retaining her position as my assistant and translator as well. Popori de Cacha became head of the whole Unatari Security Service and was given very broad authority.

Behind the stream of new appointments, many

viewers didn't notice the popup message stating that all androids in Unatari State space were to be freed from paying commission on their wages to their manufacturing companies, and from here on, would be paying only taxes to the government, equal to those paid by living people. And it should be said that Bionica assured me this was the most important piece of news, making working in Unatari very attractive to all robots. Oh well, we'll see. Meanwhile, according to Paul ton Akad's data, there were already over six million androids of various models in the systems under control of my new government. The overwhelming majority of them had arrived in the last few days, coming in as freight shipments. I was informed that the Tialla freight warehouses were overflowing with containers, all packed to the brim with androids. This number of workers allowed us to fully handle all existing labor shortages in the new government and think up massive new infrastructure projects.

Finally, I told the viewers the principles the Unatari State would be built on. As part of the Empire, Unatari would unconditionally agree to all allied and military obligations, guaranteeing their support to the Emperor in any external conflicts. That meant Unatari was joining the war with the Aliens from its first day of existence and guaranteeing its support to all forces at war with the Aliens. I officially confirmed that the Unatari fleet was prepared to aid the Red House, given the extremely difficult position they found themselves in after the recent Alien breakthrough on their front, resulting in the loss of two thirds of Red House territory.

But the Red House was far away, and my promises were nothing but fanciful words for now. There was no shared border, and it looked like getting any starships from Unatari to the more problematic Perimeter Sector Fourteen would be a very substantive mission. What was much more pressing to my new government were its relations with the Orange House. I laid down the groundwork right away. While Duke Avalle royl Anjer, who had blackened his own name so forcefully, remained in power, there was no discussion on good neighborly relations to be had. I named the conditions I thought would allow us to coexist: a change in Orange House leadership and a compensation payment to the Unatari State in the amount of one billion credits for their illegal profiting from the Tivalle system.

The Swarm, another neighbor of the new government, was given a guarantee that all agreements previously concluded with Crown Prince Georg would be maintained. I also offered, if necessary, aid in liberating alien-captured systems.

"It was a good speech. Very respectable. You gave an exhaustive account, and a well-reasoned explanation. The viewers must have liked it," my cousin commended me as I was already resting in my seat, taking small sips of the hot "coffee" brought in by Bionica.

On the table before me, there was another identical mug full of the aromatic beverage as well. Ayna and Bionica had no way of determining who was supposed to bring it in for the Crown Prince, so the girls had brought me two mugs at the same time, shooting one another looks as they did so.

I smiled to my cousin and said:

"I'm still getting relations change messages and letters almost constantly from all kinds of factions and people. I have over forty thousand unread messages already."

"Same here," Katerina said. "I don't even want to deal with them yet. The stream of incoming messages has to die down a bit first. But, at the end of the day, my fame is growing, and my standing is falling, though not by much, which is quite surprising."

My characteristics were basically the same. My fame had already grown to +50, but my standing was hovering around -40, periodically rising and falling again afterward.

WAR! The Orange House has declared war on the Unatari State

Based on how my cousin shuddered, she got the same message as well.

"Your Majesty, incoming call from the Orange House Capital!" The communications officer that appeared in the doorway was the first person to call me by my new title.

"Duke Avalle royl Anjer has finally come to his senses after my speech! It looks like he wants to give the appropriate reply," I laughed. I wasn't able to give my permission for the call though, as Flora's alarmed voice rang out in my head:

"Crown Prince, do not answer the call under any circumstances! It isn't Duke Avalle at all, but his Truth Seeker Marian Sabati! And I sense that she is not alone! There's a bunch of psionics there, and the Orange House has gathered them together there for a focused attack. They intend to murder you!"

Ah then! My rage began boiling over. Well, he started it, so it's his fault! The solution came to mind immediately. All the Orange House's Truth Seekers were concentrated there for an attack, so there would be no one covering the Duke... Moreover, the Duke was probably off somewhere by himself, so it would be more believable when he later claims not to have known about the attack.

"Bring the Arite here at once!" I demanded.

I ordered my communications officer to politely ask the caller to stay on the line for a bit. For example, tell him that Crown Prince Georg was changing clothes and would be there in three or four minutes.

The Arite materialized before me thirty seconds later in the form of redheaded Bionica.

"Take my appearance, go into my office, and answer the Orange House's call a few minutes from now. If they try to kill you, just leave. Melt into a cloud, like you do."

Pseudo-Bionica didn't ask any questions, switching into the form of a fat, awkward man in a dark blue military uniform as it walked. Lord, I hope I don't really look like that! What a horrific sight! I would have to add an hour of swimming every day to my exercise regimen. Nope! I simply cannot bear looking at such a pear-shaped me!

"So, now I want you to arrange another, separate line of communication. Ask that I be connected with the Head of the Orange House, but don't tell them Crown Prince Georg wants to talk, say that it's 'one of his bodyguards.' Camera on my Truth Seeker!"

"Flora, you know what to do!"

"Yes, Crown Prince Georg. Miya taught me the proper way to kill people."

Katerina then opened her mouth, demanding explanations for my actions, but I put my finger to her lips, calling for silence. Everyone around froze. I was looking nervously at the clock. Thirty seconds went by before a system message suddenly jumped up before my eyes:

The Head of the Orange House, Duke Avalle royl Anjer ton Mesfelle has died at age 218.

It worked! Katerina looked at me, her eyes wide in horror, only now realizing what had happened. Another two minutes later, a new message jumped in.

ATTENTION! The new head of the Orange House will be Duchess Inessa royl George ton Mesfelle (57.8% of votes)

At that moment, a white cloud flew into the room, transforming into the profoundly upset captain of *Star Mutt*. The graying captain, with an old man's groan, flopped down into a wide armchair and said, turning to me:

"They don't like Arites very much. They tried to

kill me right away. All I had to do was turn on the screen, and a whole horde of ghoulish women in dark robes started attacking me with some kind of energy. They didn't even let me greet them. It hurt, let me tell you. A lot even! Most internal organs burst, the blood in my veins boiled, and my nerve cells were destroyed. Insofar as I understand, these wounds would be fatal to a human. It's good though, that these Truth Seekers haven't interacted much with my kind, and had very little notion of how to kill one of us."

"Let me guess, it involves a vacuum cleaner?" Katerina made the obvious joke, but the Arite stiffened up for some reason.

I had to interfere to smooth it over:

"Arite, they were trying to kill me, so I must thank you. And in that their attack on me came first, no one in the Empire has the right to reproach me for fighting back! Katerina, make sure that fact is contained in the official Unatari State press release."

WAR! The Green House has declared war on the Unatari State

WAR! The Blue House has declared war on the Unatari State

I waited for some time, but nothing came in from the Red or Purple Houses.

"Green of course, I was expecting that. But I wonder what upset Blue?" I asked in surprise, turning to my cousin.

Katerina began to think and commented:

"The Blue House has many family connections

with the Green House. At one point, the two houses even tried uniting, but the Throne World didn't allow it. Clearly, the Blues simply decided to support their close relatives. Though, perhaps the reason is something else entirely. Their problems are quite similar to those of the Orange House. Some of the more industrially developed and rich systems of the Blue House have been trying to break off from them for many years. They have united into an organization known as the Syndicate and declared autonomy in financial policy issues. In the end, the Head of the Blue House had to make some serious concessions to keep the Syndicate's systems under his control. Clearly, the Blue House Duke is worried that Unatari's independence could serve as a contagious example. In any case, the Blue House has no border with us, so their declaration is a mere formality."

Here, I completely agreed with my cousin. The Blue House had no realistic way of participating in combat operations against us. But I drew my cousin's attention to the Red and Purple Houses, which still had not joined the war.

"I think we'll have to wait another couple hours, Georg, before we can say that with any confidence. The Purple House if quite loyal to us, so their not joining is completely predictable. But as for the Red House, you're right. It looks strange. Usually, Great House analysts have plans in place for all possible eventualities and, if certain conditions are met, war is declared without delay. Clearly, your speech promising military aid to the Red House at the last moment confused them and abruptly changed their opinion of Unatari. The Red House is prepared to work together with anyone who can save them from complete annihilation. The Red House capital fell three months ago, the Sector Fourteen Fleet is practically in tatters, and the situation in Sector Fifteen is no better. The only thing that could put a stop to the Alien campaign is the direct interference of the First Imperial Fleet, but even then, we wouldn't take back much territory..."

The rest of my cousin's speech was cut off by the appearance of a communications officer who said that the Monarch of the Kingdom of Fastel would like to speak with Crown Prince Georg. I gave my permission, and my former father-in-law appeared on screen.

Valesy royl Pir ton Fastel, ruler of the star Kingdom of Fastel
Age: 79

I gave the Monarch a polite greeting, and he bowed in reply.

"Georg, I would like to discuss some issues you touched upon in your speech. Above all else, in regards to Lika... Am I to understand that my granddaughter Likanna was recognized as a Princess and made first in line to the Unatari State throne?"

I verified the information, and even noted that Likanna's interests would be represented by him as her guardian until she came of age, which also gave him the right to cast votes on her behalf in state councils. The King, clearly content, nodded and said decisively:

"Crown Prince Georg, I would like to know the

conditions under which the Kingdom of Fastel would be accepted into the Unatari State."

The ruler of Fastel, seeing Katerina and my faces growing wide in surprise, explained willingly:

"The problem of all small stellar Kingdoms is that our noble titles mean absolutely nothing in other worlds. When my daughter Marta managed to conclude a legal marriage with a Crown Prince of the Empire, we thought that a true milestone, a real breakthrough in our many-year isolation. However, nothing changed. The princes, counts and barons of Fastel still did not have true royal status, neither in the Orange House nor the Throne World. And now, I see the possibility to change the situation, and work together for our mutual benefit. The newly minted Unatari State would obtain a fairly strong ally in the Kingdom of Fastel, which has forty-seven million people living on two inhabitable planets with fairly developed industry. In return, the Fastel aristocracy would like their titles to be officially recognized by the new government."

I quickly turned the possibilities over in my mind. I had the chance of strengthening my government for basically nothing, which was not the kind of thing that came about very often, so I needed to make use of the moment.

"Alright, here are my conditions. The Fastel Fleet must be brought out to the Varan system immediately to capture the space station and Orange House military docks in the system. The Varan system warp beacon must be turned off immediately. After that, both the Fastel and Varan systems will be accepted into the united Unatari State. You will personally receive the tile of Duke of Unatari, and retain the Fastel star system, as well as being at the forefront of Unatari politics. Your older son Niko will become a Count of Unatari and will receive the Varan system in perpetuity. He will also be given a place in line to the throne of the Unatari State, seventh to be precise, right after Duke Corwin royl Unatari. All other Kingdom of Fastel aristocrats will be given official titles as well. The ranks of your military officers, both in your fleet and army will also be retained."

The man began to think. He had clearly been hoping for more, probably wanting to retain his title as King, and his independence.

"Georg, I am not prepared to answer yet. I need some time," said the monarch, signing off.

"And why did you throw such harsh demands at your former father-in-law?" wondered my cousin.

"I didn't demand anything impossible. If the King wants the titles of his relatives to mean something not only in the Fastel system, but in another twenty star systems as well, he will first have to prove himself useful."

What a crazy day... I was simply immeasurably tired. I spent so much emotional energy. Also, the weighty, fat-laden body of Crown Prince Georg was absolutely not keeping up with the active schedule I had been forced to adopt in the last few days. All the moving, meeting and negotiating I was doing was hard on me, but reality had already made some adjustments to my plans. Like now, truth be told, I should have been flying to Astorimma to make a speech to the ministers. And after that, I should have been flying on a shuttle to *Queen of Sin* in order to then fly off for negotiations with the Iseyek. In reality though, after all the work I'd already done, my blood pressure was spiking, and my head hurt something fierce, which made my personal doctor Nicosid Brandt have to give me medicine and prescribe some nonnegotiable bedrest.

I did not argue with the doctor. He really was a first-class specialist and would not be limiting me without serious medical reasons. But, all the same, Nicosid Brandt was a doctor, and not a strategist or politician. All he could see were the numbers on a patient's medical chart, not taking into account the situation developing behind them. I couldn't afford to lose a minute now. I had to manage to do as much as possible before my enemies finally came back to their senses.

And it should be said that the new Head of the Orange House, Duchess Inessa royl George ton Mesfelle set about working in the most active manner. She had refused to take part in negotiations without mincing words, not even waiting to hear out my cousin Katerina royl Unatari. Duchess Inessa's first order was to begin a complete transport, economic and financial blockade of the new government's systems. The Orange House's intelligence services froze the bank accounts and property of all companies without exception that had ever delivered anything to Tialla or Unatari. The directors of these organizations were also arrested. The new Head of the Orange

House addressed her subjects with a fiery speech in the spirit of "we will defeat our evil enemies" and "our loyalty is a thousand times stronger than that of the separatists," and announced three new rules. If you trade with Unatari, you will be arrested and all your property will be confiscated. If you communicate with Unatari, you will be arrested and fined. If you support Unatari, you will be arrested and executed.

Basically, the enemy was already taking active measures. The Duchess had gathered a fleet loyal to her, collected allies, and conducted a prolonged, almost half-hour-long conversation with the Emperor (I found out about this in an official message from the Throne World secretariat). For me, wasting time due to being tired or unhealthy was just asking to die. As such, I lie in bed, just as the doctor ordered with my eyes closed... but, despite how bad I was feeling, I continued working hard in the internal interface, reading messages and answering them selectively.

The second step of my offensive continued. Reports came in that landing troops had captured the Vorta Beacon, Unguay, the Closed Laboratories, Forepost-31 and Parn systems. The first two star systems in the list were already officially part of the Unatari State:

The Orange House has lost sovereignty over the Vorta Beacon system

The Unatari State has gained sovereignty over the Vorta Beacon system

The Orange House has lost sovereignty over

the Unguay system

The Unatari State has gained sovereignty over the Unguay system

The three remaining space stations were quietly taken under control by our assault groups, but we decided not to loudly broadcast that fact yet. We had calculated that it would be possible to "box-in" the huge Green House fleet in one of the uninhabitable systems between their current location and Unatari. The trap was so crude that it actually had a chance of working. The last thing to do, on my Truth Seeker's advice, was to remove all living people from the stations in Parn, the Closed Laboratories and Forepost-31 in the next few days, leaving only androids. Florianna thought that the Green House's Truth Seekers would sense something was off if we didn't.

For now, the enemy remained uninformed on their loss of the Parn, Closed Laboratories and Forepost-31 stations. My people at these stations received orders from the Orange House not to respond to requests from the Unatari State to turn on warp beacons or change out the encoding mechanisms. In the coming days, they were preparing to cut Unatari off from communicating with the Empire. That information, together with the Orange House's new codes, I also received from my landing troops.

As it were, I was trying to take a short break in my work and get a bit of rest when suddenly, some messages came in that I had already lost hope of seeing:

The Orange House has lost sovereignty over the Varan system

The Unatari State has gained sovereignty over the Varan system

The Kingdom of Fastel has lost sovereignty of the Fastel system

The Unatari State has gained sovereignty over the Fastel system

The Kingdom of Fastel has ceased to exist

Finally, my former father-in-law had accepted my proposal! Without opening an eye, I ordered Bionica, who was sitting silently in an armchair next to me, to affirm the list of aristocrats from the former Kingdom of Fastel as Unatari aristocrats with the titles I'd assigned. And then, a call came in that forced me to forget everything. It was my daughter on the line from the Throne World! My eyes shot open instantly and I jumped up, buttoning my shirt as I quickly ran my fingers through my hair and accepted the call.

Lika was sitting in a pair of cozy pajamas on the edge of her bed in a semi-dark bedroom, lit by nothing but her monitor. My daughter's emerald green hair was messy, and her face was a bit puffy. I noticed another two beds behind her, with two girls dozing away peacefully.

"Dad, I was totally confused about what was happening," Lika admitted, somewhat embarrassed.

"First, you made an angry speech and left the Orange House. Then, I became a Princess four times over and moved up ten places in the Orange House aristocrats list. Then, the Kingdom of Fastel disappeared somewhere without a trace, and my last name changed. Could you tell me in two words, what's going on?"

How could I possibly explain all these complex political processes to a twelve-year-old girl in two words? I smiled:

"Your grandpa Valesy and I decided it was getting too boring out here, so we started a war with three Great Houses at the same time."

Lika smiled hesitantly.

"You're just joking around again, dad... You yourself told journalists that I was already grown up. Explain it like a normal person."

Standing change. Likanna royl Mesfelle-Unatari's opinion of you has improved.

Presumed personal opinion of you: -83 (irreconcilable hate)

"It's not so easy to give a normal explanation right now, sweetie... but I'll do my best. Lika, you once complained to me that you were too far down the line of succession to ever become Empress, Duchess of the Orange House or Queen of Fastel. Well, now I made a whole new line, just for you, and you are number one. It's a new government with twenty star systems. Your grandpa Valesy completely supported my idea and included his Kingdom of Fastel in the new Unatari State. Of course, not everyone liked all these changes, so now I've got a war with three Great Houses on my hands."

Standing change. Likanna royl Mesfelle-Unatari's opinion of you has improved.
Presumed personal opinion of you: -68 (hate)

Lika kept silent for a bit, gave a heavy sigh and said:

"Dad, in the past I, of course, said a bunch of nasty things to you. But don't worry about what the system says. I actually miss you a lot. Can I fly out to meet you?"

First Allies

The screen had long been off, but I was still sitting deep in thought. I had just assured Lika that I would be very glad to see her at my place, and promised to think up a way in the next few hours to get my daughter to Unatari space despite the Orange House transport blockade. There was no way I could hope to get her here through Perimeter Sector Eight. But what about Seven? The Green House armada was supposed to be arriving there any day now, so the warp beacons would be switched off to stop their invasion. There was one possible route left: through Sector Nine, though there were also difficulties with going that way.

First of all, getting through Orange House space unnoticed would be nearly impossible. What was more, I had no idea how the new Duchess would react to a passenger liner with my daughter inside. I was afraid that they would detain Lika under a formal pretense. Of course, openly arresting an underage Crown Princess seemed like something no one would have the guts to do, though. Such an act would be equivalent to declaring war on the whole Empire, including all five Great Houses, and dozens of other kingdoms and allies. If Duchess Inessa did decide to violate Imperial law so flagrantly, she would be removed from the throne that very day and arrested by her own soldiers. But taking a twelve-year-old girl traveling unaccompanied and removing her from a flight "for her own safety" to place her under supervision in a remote palace was something my enemies could easily get away with, and I needed to take that into consideration.

Even if I were able to get her through Sector Nine somehow, she would have to get through the Swarm after that. The Iseyek were very loath to allow human starships passage through their territory, so there would be obstacles on the insect border in any case. Iseyek... Iseyek... wait! Perhaps they would be able to solve this problem after all!

A praying mantis freight starship returning from the Empire back to Swarm territory wouldn't arouse any suspicion in the Orange House whatsoever. Swarm transport ships were normally not even inspected at the border if the customs declaration provided by the insects showed that the ship was empty. The praying mantises weren't accustomed to lying on principle, so if it said there was no cargo, that was probably the case. As such, an empty transport ship with a secret passenger would probably be let through the border without any problems. But it would be even better for her to be on a Swarm diplomatic ship. That would definitely not be stopped and inspected. The idea was so obvious that I questioned why I hadn't thought of it right away.

"Communications officer, connect me with Triasss Zess, Senior Swarm Ambassador to the Empire."

Three minutes went by, and my old acquaintance came on screen. All the praying mantis's appendages had sprouted again. His coloration had changed to a very light gray, and there was a wide blue stripe across the chest of his chitin shell. It was a symbol of distinction and simultaneously a sign that no member of the Swarm was allowed to touch him. Insofar as I knew, Swarm Queen Iseyek Prime Nai Igir had not only given full amnesty to the once disgraced diplomat, but had even promoted Triasss Zess and brought him into her inner circle.

"I'm glad to see you once again, your Majesty!" The praying mantis made a deep bow.

I greeted him in return with a slight nod:

"I am also glad to see you, senior ambassador! And though our relationship hasn't always been exactly smooth, I do hope that we can leave our past quarrels behind us."

Standing change. Your relationship with Triasss Zess has improved.

Presumed personal opinion of you: +70 (friendship)

Standing change. Iseyek race opinion of you has improved.

Alpha Iseyek race opinion of you: +24 (trusting)

Standing change. Iseyek race opinion of the Unatari State has improved.

Iseyek race opinion of the Unatari State: +1 (indifferent)

Not bad. Not bad at all! So, it seemed the senior Swarm ambassador had been given the authority to change faction relations. Even the Queen herself could hardly act with that kind of speed. I would have to keep that in mind when talking with Triasss Zess, as good relations with the Iseyek were extremely important for my new government.

"I won't beat around the bush here. I would like to have a personal meeting with the Swarm Queen as soon as possible. As you probably know, there have been some political changes in the Empire. A number of star systems have separated from the Orange House, forming the Unatari State. I would like to discuss a number of issues with your Queen related to our new status as neighbors."

The ambassador began thinking unexpectedly, even tilting his head to the side, which signified doubt or lack of information in his race.

"Crown Prince Georg, I don't see a real reason for you to meet personally with the Queen. All issues can be settled either with me, or remotely."

His refusal was completely unexpected. Also, I could detect some falseness and personal reluctance from the ambassador. For now, I didn't know the real reason for the refusal, but it only made the necessity of a personal meeting with Nai Igir stronger.

"Triasss Zess, I have gifts that must be given directly to Nai Igir, as she is the last Iseyek Prime. I have a nearly complete collection of numbered emeralds from Sivalla that once belonged to her race. My wife, Queen Miya, has spent many long years gathering these gemstones, and the time has come to return the relics to their legal owners. It would only be proper for the Swarm ambassador to the Empire to also be present at this occasion, which should be the final chapter in our old conflict. I also have another important topic to discuss. The Unatari State is planning to attack and liberate the Swarm systems currently under Alien control in the very near future. It would be quite strange if the Swarm Queen were not to take part in this historic campaign."

The praying mantis gave a deep bow:

"That changes things completely, Crown Prince Georg. I will arrange for you to meet with my Queen, and will try to be personally present."

Standing change. Iseyek race opinion of the Unatari State has improved.

Iseyek race opinion of the Unatari State: +3 (indifferent)

I found the option to give the same answer in return, and made immediate use of it:

Standing change. Unatari State opinion of the Iseyek race has improved.

Unatari State opinion of the Iseyek race: +3 (indifferent)

"And another thing, Honorable Ambassador. My daughter, Crown Princess Likanna royl Unatari will be finishing school soon, and she is planning to come visit me for summer break. The girl will be taking a path from the Throne world through your capital system, Dekeye. As such, could you pick her up on a diplomatic ship? As a father, I would be much more comfortable with my daughter having a chaperone I know I can trust."

The praying mantis looked at me for a long time, bulging his huge eyes outward before asking me a clarifying question:

"Your Majesty, would it not be frightening for a little girl to travel in the company of huge spindly creatures such as myself?"

"Not at all. Lika spent several months in the company of two Alpha Iseyek. They were bodyguards she was given by General Savasss Jach. And even I, though initially quite skeptical, also became convinced that my child could never find more reliable protection, nor better-behaved playmates in the whole Universe."

Standing change. Your relationship with Triasss Zess has improved.

Presumed personal opinion of you: +85 (friendship)

Standing change. Iseyek race opinion of you has improved.

Alpha Iseyek race opinion of you: +25 (trusting)

Standing change. Iseyek race opinion of the Unatari State has improved.

Iseyek race opinion of the Unatari State: +6 (warm)

"Not all human children have such a calm reaction to those of my race. Your Majesty's daughter is wise beyond her years. And, who knows, perhaps Likanna and her good opinion of Swarm individuals will be the basis for a peace between our races that will last for decades. For me, it would be a massive honor to personally accompany Crown Princess Likanna to the Swarm Capital."

I was only able to get ahold of my eldest daughter ten hours later, after Lika's lessons were over. In her time-zone on the Throne World, it was already past midday. Before I could say anything, Likanna anxiously blurted out:

"Daddy, some weird people came to our school this morning. They were asking the teachers about me. I overheard part of their conversation. They want to take me to Tesse right after the end of the school year. They said they could get all the documents from the Orange House sorted out."

My heart immediately seized up in alarm. It was possible, of course, that representatives of my brother Roben royl Inoky ton Mesfelle had, in fact, come to the school. My brother had a warm opinion of Lika and it really would have been in character for him to invite the girl to spend her vacation on his planet. But Roben presumably would have warned me, if he were going to do that, and I never heard anything of the sort. That was why it seemed more probable to me that my daughter had attracted the interest of the Orange House Duchess, Inessa royl George ton Mesfelle.

With no time to delay, I suggested that Lika come out to Unatari at once on the insect starship. Ambassador Triasss Zess had already assured me that the Swarm diplomats had received all necessary permissions for their diplomatic ship to pass through human territory, and promised to send a plane out on my signal to the gates of her elite school.

"Lika, you'll be the first person to ever travel with Swarm diplomats and visit the insect capital Dekeye. Just imagine how your classmates will envy you after break! We'll meet in the Palace of Queen Nai Igir. I'll tell Ambassador Triasss Zess you'll soon be on your way out. Gather your things. The flight should be six or seven days, so make sure you're packed for that, then come outside."

"What a cool thing to do over break! Daddy, you're the very, very best! Alright then, I'm gonna run off and pack! I'll see you in six days!"

Standing change. Likanna royl Mesfelle-Unatari's opinion of you has improved.

Presumed personal opinion of you: -53 (enmity)

Everything was ready for my diplomatic mission to the Iseyek. At the very last moment, on Admiral Mike ton Akad's advice, I decided to leave *Queen of Sin* in

Unatari and transfer my headquarters to the battleship *Bride of Chaos*. The admiral thought it would be safer that way. Beyond that, leaving the Crown Prince's luxurious yacht behind in the capital was meant to serve as a symbol to reassure the population of Unatari. If the Prince thought the situation safe enough to leave the crown jewel of his fleet behind, everything must have truly been fine.

We were already preparing to make the warp jump to Sigur, when a message came in from my former father-in-law. The leader of the Fastel system, Duke Valesy royl Unatari was in a manic state, clearly proud of himself.

"Georg, you won't believe what we found in the Varan system! As you planned, the Fastel fleet captured and turned off the Varan warp beacon without delay. After that, we attacked the Orange House military docks in the system, but we ran into problems. There were rocket installations, a great many laser cannon turrets and a squadron of defense corvettes. They put up quite fierce resistance. We lost six frigates and two landing ships. It was a miracle that our heavy assault cruiser *Marta the Harlot* survived. It will need at least two months of repair now. But it was all worth it. We found a carrier under construction at the military docks!"

My eyebrows shot up in astonishment. Admiral Mike ton Akad, sitting next to me, couldn't hold back a surprised whistle, after which he started asking questions about the trophy and how close it was to completion.

The old man on the screen smiled.

"The giant is almost finished, and we captured

it undamaged. My soldiers have taken pictures of it from various angles. The assault group sent a video report."

"I'll set up a three-dimensional projection right away," Valian ton Corsa promised, and after a few seconds, the hologram appeared in the middle of the room.

Compared with the *Thrush* cruiser flying by in the foreground, this mothership was of truly impressive, colossal dimensions. It was an irregular shape, reminiscent of a twisted chain. It had powerful main thrusters, innumerable energy shield installations along the whole chassis, and a huge number of hangars for light ships and combat drones.

"A *Quasar*-model ship. Humanity's strike carrier," Admiral Mike ton Akad gasped in delight. "The Empire started working on these designs twenty years ago in response to the Swarm inventing the impenetrable *Uukresh*. According to calculations from our military experts, the *Quasar* surpasses the *Uukresh* in all measures. A hundred light ships can fit on board instead of just eighty. It also has a higher-capacity energy shield. They hold the same number of drones, but a *Quasar*'s drones are heavy, and have massive firepower. *Quasars* form the backbone of the First Imperial Fleet. I never thought I'd get the chance to see one in real life. And what's more surprising is to find this carrier in an Orange House station. The Imperial Joint Chiefs declared its design a strict secret. Peripheral Great Houses aren't supposed to have them. A Great House having one would upset the historical balance of power in the Empire!"

"Admiral, with all due respect, you are

mistaken," Bionica said, checking something on a palmtop computer. "There are at least five known *Quasars* in Great House possession. The Blue House has one, the Purple has another, and the Green House has a whole three. All of them were built this year. It is also known that another two ships were blown up before being finished in the Tairan system, the former Red House capital, to make sure the Aliens wouldn't get their hands on them."

"You'd know better, hunk of metal. If all Great Houses were given permission to build them recently, I see nothing surprising in the fact that the Orange House got the go-ahead from the Emperor to build a *Quasar*, as well as all the blueprints necessary to do so. I even suspect that the reason for this was the battle in the Orange House Capital system. When the Sector Eight Fleet's *Uukresh* displayed its extremely high effectiveness against a fleet of battleships, making them legal to own became non-negotiable."

I smiled at the memory. Yes, that battle had ended excellently. My fleet held out until our allies came against the whole Orange House, and the enemy couldn't do a thing to stand up to the thousands of drones from the *Uukresh* and *Curses*.

"Duke Valesy, can the *Quasar* get off the ground?" I clarified, but all he could do was shrug his shoulders.

Bionica then, studying the video, reassured me:

"The *Quasar* is in working order. The warp drives and main thrusters have already been installed. I don't see all the shield generators on the hologram, and the interior trim is not finished either. It is also totally lacking weaponry."

"In any case, this is a very valuable trophy, which must be brought to the Fia system immediately for completion. Duke, you can handle this issue yourself. Also, get together a list of the soldiers and commanders who distinguished themselves there. I will personally give them medals."

"My King, there is one more thing..."

I cut my former father-in-law off half way through the sentence and told him that he could address me as he had always done, by my first name, no titles needed. The old man smiled and continued:

"My assault troops captured the residential barracks at the Varan docks and detained over seven thousand people living there until further orders could be given. Most of them are workers at the orbital docks, but there were another couple hundred students from the Nessi Space Military Academy. All of them just graduated. They were being trained to crew the *Quasar*."

"Great news! You can let the workers go. They should get back to work. The docks will soon have some orders coming in. The students, though, should be informed of the political situation, then you should suggest that they swear loyalty to Unatari. Whoever refuses, arrest them. Those who agree should be put on the *Quasar* to fly it to Fia. They should be accompanied by the assault troops, though. Once there, my Truth Seeker will check their loyalty and out any potential traitors."

The old man took a bow and signed off. I turned to those gathered with the mission of thinking over the issue of why the Emperor suddenly changed the rules and allowed Great Houses to have heavier ships. Just a year ago, I had to explain to the Joint Chiefs why I had an *Uukresh* in my fleet, chalking it up to the unique nature of the situation and softening it by saying I was only renting the mothership from the Swarm temporarily. But now, all limitations on heavy ship ownership by Great Houses had been removed, and that was strange. Everyone went silent, not knowing what to say. I explained my interest in the issue:

"The only thing coming to mind for me is that the Imperial Fleet now has even heavier and more powerful ships, which would make the restriction on carriers in private aristocratic armies outdated. Bionica, check that out. Perhaps there is an android out there with information on superheavy ships."

Bionica shook her head in the negative.

"Crown Prince Georg, I already checked. No androids know anything about combat ships heavier than *Quasar* anywhere in Imperial space. Only the Aliens have starships of heavier classes than that."

"We should still check. This is the big-time now. Unatari is an independent government, and it is important for me to know what kind of forces other players have on the star map. Arite, I sent the money for twenty spies of your race today. After you prepare them, their first mission will be figuring out the exact size and composition of all fleets currently in Imperial space, and searching for superheavy ships."

I found myself in the medical wing of *Bride of Chaos* after some exhausting exercises in the gym. All my muscles were trembling so hard they were buzzing. My arms were shaking. A salty sweat was running into my eyes and streaming down my back. But I was prepared to make peace with all that, thinking it was the inevitable consequence of strength training. I was scared by something else, though. My heart was pounding rabidly. My upper blood pressure jumped to almost two hundred and was stubbornly refusing to go back down, leaving me with a nasty feeling, so I had to discontinue the exercising immediately.

The Crown Prince's flabby body was resisting all the use and strain, not wanting to return at accelerated pace to the more-or-less normal condition it had been in eight months prior. Pressing issues with my heart and joints crawled out of the woodwork, evidence of insufficient muscle tissue, an effect of crystal abuse. As such, I was forced to ask my personal doctor Nicosid Brandt for help. The old doctor heard my wishes out attentively, not forgetting to record the data-readers' outputs from my whole body on his tablet as he did so.

"We have already discussed how the addiction can be broken, Crown Prince. I could prepare microcapsules again, and inject them, but there's no guarantee you won't just order me to remove them again."

That meant Mr. G.I. himself had forced the old doctor to remove the capsules from my shoulders. The idiot! After my first contract, I had left him with a more-or-less healthy body, but my substitute had spoiled it all.

"I had one moment of weakness eight months ago, and now I am paying dearly for that mistake. I won't go back to the drugs ever again. You have my word as a Crown Prince!"

"Alright, I understand, your Majesty. I also understand your desire to lose weight quickly. What weight does the Crown Prince consider optimal?"

"I would like to reach one hundred ninety pounds three months from now."

The doctor stopped writing, set his tablet aside and looked me right in the eye.

"Crown Prince, you currently weigh three hundred pounds. With such a weak heart, it is extremely risky to lose weight in such an extremely short time span. As your personal doctor, I am categorically opposed to such a taxing program; it's too dangerous. I can help you lose forty pounds in three months without damaging your health, over a hundred is out of the question."

"Alright, let's say forty then. I am relying completely on your experience here. But as for my other issue, I need..."

I didn't finish the sentence, but Nicosid Brand had already figured out what I was after.

"Yes, I understand your wish, Crown Prince. I assure you that in a few months of treatment, your manhood will be back in working order. If you need it earlier... Don't be embarrassed, come to the medical wing. I can give you drugs for it. But as for your irregular heartbeat..."

The doctor's speech was interrupted by an incoming message from the communications officer.

"Your Majesty, the Truth Seeker Marian Sabati would like to speak with you. For some reason the call is coming from the Almir system, in the Imperial

Core."

Marian Sabati? The ghoulish child-killing avenger of the former Orange House Head? This could hardly have been another attempt at assassination, right? I demanded the Arite be found and brought in immediately. Florianna's voice rang out in my head just then:

"She has been badly weakened by the death of her master. Crown Prince, I would be capable of holding off any attack she could make now."

The Arite appeared, and, as I commanded, changed form to that of me in ceremonial uniform. I then stood aside, preparing to watch on the reserve monitor, remaining invisible to Marian. The fat graying man plopped down laboriously into an armchair in front of a huge screen with an old man's groan. He buttoned up his collar and spoke into the microphone with a powerful voice:

"Put her through!"

On screen, a tired looking middle-aged woman appeared with a gaunt face and black circles under her eyes. Somehow, I remembered Marian Sabati completely differently. She had been a dark-haired, constantly smiling girl no older than twenty by appearance, perfectly preserved at her ninety years and change. Nevertheless, the character popup confirmed that this was precisely the same woman:

> *Marian Sabati*
> *Age: 92*
> *Race: Human*
> *Gender: Female*
> *Class: Mystic*

Achievements: Master Psionic, Kills with a Glance, Punisher, Childkiller, Betrayed Master, Killed Master, Deserter, WANTED CRIMINAL!!!
Fame: 44
Reputation: -87
Presumed personal relationship: Unknown

Well, would you look at that! My jaw simply fell to the floor in surprise. Marian Sabati already had enough ghoulish descriptors in her info before. Childkiller, or Punisher, for example, but the list of achievements she had now looked simply shocking. And here I thought I had lots of dubious stuff in my profile. Marian Sabati's list of "achievements," though, made a somewhat bigger impression.

"I'm in no mood to joke around. I'm not planning on any acts of hostility, either," the Truth Seeker uttered, barely having looked at the Arite. "I wanted to talk with the ruler of Unatari himself, not his double."

Though it may not have been my smartest move from a safety standpoint, I came on screen and gave a slight nod of my head to greet the ghastly woman. Marian Sabati took one glance at me in my sweat-soaked work-out clothes and began to speak. I heard notes of clear desperation in her voice:

"Georg, only a few people in the whole Empire know what really happened yesterday: you, me and some people in your inner circle. Even the Truth Seekers gathered for your assassination did not know who exactly the target of the focused attack was. So, the fact that my master died at the same time was sufficient reason to suspect me of murdering Duke

Avalle royl Anjer. The Orange House coroner carried out my master's autopsy with the help of an official representative of the Dark Mother, and they came to the unambiguous conclusion that he died violently at the hands of a powerful Truth Seeker. The Orange House Head, Duchess Inessa royl George ton Mesfelle immediately accused me of secretly working for Unatari and killing Duke Avalle royl Anjer ton Mesfelle, giving me a death sentence in absentia as punishment. With the death of my master, I lost practically all power. As such, the only thing I could actually do was flee Orange House space to the Imperial Core. But even here, I didn't find protection. The Imperial secretariat agreed with the Orange House accusations, and confirmed the death sentence."

The woman on screen suddenly fell to her knees:

"Georg royl Inoky ton Mesfelle, I officially request asylum in the Unatari State. I realize perfectly well that your Majesty has no particular basis to trust me, but I am prepared to swear by my abilities as a Truth Seeker and on my life that I will not bring harm to your Majesty, nor anyone close to you. I would do anything to prove my faithfulness to you as my new master."

Marian Sabati was kneeling in silence, awaiting my reaction. I then called my cousin Katerina royl Unatari and clarified what information was in the official Unatari State press release on the death of the Orange House Head.

"Cousin, it's a whole story... While I was preparing the official, angry version explaining the killing of Duke Avalle as a response to an assassination attempt on you, the Orange House managed to declare that the ancient Duke Avalle had died of natural causes. After that, it seemed somewhat strange and even stupid to out ourselves for having murdered the Head of the Orange House and so, I limited my scope, turning it into an official condolence letter. And then the miracles began. The Duke's own Truth Seeker was accused of his murder, and she even fled, confirming all their suspicions in the process. As you understand, it now looks like we are not at all involved in this matter. But tell me, why are you asking?"

"Duke Avalle's former Truth Seeker is requesting asylum on Unatari territory."

"Under no circumstances, Georg! She is a wanted criminal in the whole Empire for the murder of a member of the upper aristocracy! She will be given the death penalty, as will anyone who can be labeled an accomplice or accessory. Refuse her and immediately inform the authorities of the star system the call is coming from!"

I hung up with Katerina and turned back to Marian Sabati, who was still kneeling. The woman had already somehow guessed my intention to refuse to give her asylum and, looking me right in the eyes, said:

"Your Majesty, allow me to say a few words. After all, I am not simply requesting asylum, but offering you my services. Yes, I have now lost nine tenths of my power, but that is merely temporary. I promise that I will be able to quickly restore my power and become one of the top ten Truth Seekers again. I have a huge amount of experience, and it is not exclusively in murdering enemies of my master as many believe. I could heal your paralyzed girl Florianna, and your personal assistant Ayna, for example. I could also help Valian ton Corsa, who you clearly have some affection for. She still needs to use powders and creams to cover up the traces of burns and scars on her face, you know."

Well, shit... I started thinking. The things this dangerous wanted criminal was offering me were things that were very important to people close to me. But all the same, I intended to refuse Marian Sabati, as the harm from providing asylum to her was no less than the benefit she offered.

"That is not all... Ruslan. I know a great deal about many aristocrats, including Crown Princes and Crown Princesses, and this knowledge is of great value to a number of political forces. I'm sure that I have something I could offer to whatever new master I may have. I really do prefer to live amongst allies than enemies."

"Ruslan, she called you by name, did you catch that? She wasn't able to read any information during this conversation. I am completely protecting your thoughts. Miya also renewed her protection. The defense probably failed all the way back during the battle in the Orange House Capital. Marian Sabati is the only surviving member of the group that attacked you back then."

A very unambiguous hint. This Truth Seeker was offering to help, and if I refused, she was threatening to reveal my secret identity.

"Marian, even if I gave my permission, I don't

see how I could get you to Unatari space due to the blockade on the part of the Orange House."

The woman on screen smiled and said in a silken voice:

"The only thing I ask of your Majesty is to provide me with asylum. Let me deal with how I will reach Unatari State space. Although... I am reminded of a diplomatic ship currently rushing to get out of the Throne World. It will soon be flying through the Almir system. That little ship would be perfectly capable of picking me up on its way. I am a very easygoing passenger. I'll sleep the whole way. It's been so long since I could really immerse myself in a crystal dream. But my being on board is also a guarantee that the starship will not raise the attention of any Orange House intelligence service, and will sneak through Sector Nine with no problems."

"How do you know all this?" I couldn't hold back my surprise.

Marian Sabati smiled:

"Crown Prince Georg, even in my weakened state, backed into a corner as I am, I am still capable of a lot, if it means saving my own life. I mean, I'm a wanted criminal in the whole Empire, and whoever gives me shelter will have plenty of bad things to worry about. But whoever helps me get to safety, I am willing to give a great deal. I know many secrets of the Great Houses. In addition, I have brought a crystal memory drive with blackmail material on practically all prominent Imperial aristocrats. This information could destroy a great many of your enemies, Crown Prince. I will try to restore my power quickly, in parallel healing and training your girl Florianna."

"Alright, Marian. Your request for asylum is granted. I expect a full oath of loyalty from you the very moment we meet in the Swarm capital at Queen Nai Igir's palace."

Standing change. Marian Sabati's opinion of you has improved.
Presumed personal opinion of you: -3 (indifferent)

"Thank you, your Majesty. You made the right choice. You will not regret this decision. And finally, I have information that, in eleven minutes, an order from Duchess Inessa royl George ton Mesfelle will completely cut the Unatari State off from all Imperial communication channels. Time enough, as it were, for me to swear an oath, and for your Majesty to send a message to the Swarm ship to pick me up in the Almir system. And that, let's say, is to pay for my ticket. Check the balance in your account. I have just taken funds from all of my former master's accounts before his heirs could get their hands on it, and given it to you. As the Orange House declared an economic blockade on Unatari, you can consider these funds a military trophy."

The account balance change alert beeped. I opened the finances window in the internal interface and froze in shock. Marian Sabati, my new partner, had just sent me a money transfer of eight billion credits. It would seem that I had just become an accessory in the robbery of a dead man.

"I hope you know what you're doing, Ruslan. To be honest, her methods frighten me. Look at the crime

blotter from the Almir system. An hour ago, the Almir-V police searched a container ship coming from the Orange House Capital that was not responding to landing service transmissions. The whole crew of the freighter was dead. No one knows exactly how they died. I'm fairly sure I could guess the name of their cause of death, though. Right now, Marian Sabati is still weak, but she will restore her abilities quickly, and even a month or two from now, she will be beyond my control. No matter what happens, you've let a dangerous predator into your home. Although, I admit, I was hoping you'd make this choice, and am thankful to you for the healing I will receive."

* * *

The same day, at night (though the words "night" and "day" were used only out of force of habit during interstellar space travel), when the battleship *Bride of Chaos* was charging at the Forepost-13 station, my assistant Ayna found me to complain:

"Crown Prince, I just found out that you ordered your butler to set a table in your cabin for two people to have a romantic dinner. I wanted to remind you that your wife Miya left me an order to stop her husband from such liaisons."

"Yes, yes, I remember you talking about 'hound dogs' and 'crystals.' Let's just say you did warn me, and even tried to stop me in many ways, so you can have a clean conscience. It's just that my wife and I have our own understandings, and I am in no way planning on violating them. By the way, Ayna, I have great news for you. I found a way to heal your wounds. Soon, the Truth Seeker Marian Sabati will come to Unatari territory. She's a master psionic and one of the strongest Truth Seekers. She found herself out of a job after the death of Duke Avalle royl Anjer, so I invited her to come here. Unlike my wife Miya, this Truth Seeker is capable of more than just killing and maiming. She can also restore damaged organs, for example."

My assistant suddenly began crying, then said with tears welling up in her eyes:

"Crown Prince Georg, you have no idea what an important thing you've just done for me. I am so grateful to you! You have given me hope after so many years of despair. I would do anything for you now, Crown Prince!"

Standing change. Ayna Mentor's opinion of you has improved.

Presumed personal opinion of you: +73 (trusting)

Just then, the elevator doors opened and Valian ton Corsa came out in our direction. The beauty's red hair, just having grown all the way back out, was carefully smoothed and wonderfully shiny. The bright crimson lipstick she was wearing combined perfectly with her haircut, as did the chic evening dress with a very deep neckline she was wearing. By the way, the dress was very familiar to me. Bionica had ordered it for herself in the Damir system, and had been wearing it for Astra royl Veyerde's coronation. Valian, though, hadn't been at the coronation. The girl had been undergoing treatment in the burn unit, so there was no way she could've known the dress's history.

I suspect that Valian had asked her synthetic friend Bionica to lend her the beautiful dress for the evening. And the android, from all her innumerable outfits, had chosen precisely this one, knowing perfectly well that I would recognize the dress. It wouldn't have been the first time I had caught my android secretary playing games, and this subtle sabotaging of a romantic rival was just her style. And it turned out that Bionica was well informed of where her friend was headed...

"Alright, I did my job, my conscience is clean. I will not stop you now," Ayna smiled craftily, then hurried to leave.

Popori de Cacha appeared from invisibility, saying that he needed to go to a training session with his Chameleons in the gym, so there wouldn't be any invisible bodyguards around me until morning. He would also be taking Phobos with him, as my huge bodyguard also needed to get exercise every so often.

"Where are they all going off to?" Valian asked in surprise, watching as the herd of creatures of all races headed for the elevator.

"They all have their own things, but suspiciously well timed. The Crown Prince wanted to spend a quiet evening with a red-headed beauty he hadn't seen for seven long months. He naively supposed that a modest dinner for two wouldn't attract the attention of the others. But now, it would seem that the whole battleship crew has been made aware of our date. All four thousand of them, both people and unpeople. They might as well have announced it over loudspeaker."

Valian chuckled happily:

"I'll never get used to it. I remember a year ago, when your Highness held me up for the whole Universe as his lover. All the news channels were yammering on about it. But, this time, it was surprising. I go down the ship's halls, and everyone turns to look at me. Some were even congratulating me on something. Doctor Nicosid Brandt intercepted me near the elevator and asked me to give you a sealed box with something, saying: 'The Crown Prince will know what's inside.'"

"I can guess," I smiled, taking the plastic box with little pills shaking around inside. "As everyone on the ship already knows about our dinner together, what is there to be embarrassed about? Come in." I opened the door to my cabin with a wide gesture, inviting my new favorite to come into the room.

A GLIMMER OF HOPE

DESPITE THE FACT that our internal clock on *Bride of Chaos* was showing early morning, I had already been up for some time working behind a computer screen. I was trying to figure out the optimal composition for a heavy fleet arranged around a core of three carriers. For once, I had the funds, available docks and construction materials to build starships. Now was precisely the time to put together the basis for Unatari's future power. But the question now was what ship class should be my focus. Should I invest in heavy battleships with huge firepower? Or build several hundred stealth bombers that could turn enemy ships to dust? Should I make a whole fleet of electronic warfare cruisers that could render the enemy ships totally helpless? Or should I focus on combat drones, and build another two huge motherships at my docks?

I looked at the clock. There were twenty minutes left before *Bride of Chaos* came out of the warp tunnel into the Fia system. I had woken up at this ungodly hour not so much out of a desire to get to work bright and early as from anxiety about the news from the border between Perimeter Sectors Seven and Eight. Six hours earlier, the automatic probe installed in the Parn system had sent a short encoded message saying that the one-thousand-five-hundred-starship Green House armada had arrived in the star system, and was now past Perimeter Sector Seven. I was calculating how much time they'd need to charge energy before the next jump to the Forepost-31 system. I got approximately four hours, due to the huge number of battleships in the fleet of Crown Prince Demyen royl Amelius ton Lavaelle and the limited number of charging ports available in the system.

The estimated time had already passed two hours ago, and I wanted to know the results. All the same, while *Bride of Chaos* was still in the warp tunnel, I couldn't get any messages from outside, so I had to wait. In twenty or so minutes, I'd find out whether the enemy had moved on yet... I was so anxious to know the result at this point that it hurt. I felt like a fisherman waiting for a very big fish to bite. But no fisherman in history had ever gone after game of this size.

I shuddered, as the door into the hallway slid aside, and an enraged fury burst into my cabin, screaming from the moment she crossed the threshold:

"Georg, have you lost your damn mind?! Is everything OK with your head? What body part were you thinking with when you gave asylum to a dangerous criminal, wanted the Empire over?!"

My cousin flew into the room without warning or even so much as a knock. The Duchess of Unatari had a pass that gave her the right to open whatever door she chose on the ship, as well as ignore guard posts. I looked in shame at Phobos, frozen next to the door, but the huge, ten-foot-tall Alpha Iseyek could only guiltily pop his eyes into his shell, and fold up his upper appendages, not wanting to intervene in this argument between cousins.

"Don't make a sound. You'll wake Valian," I pointed to the sleeping red-headed beauty.

Katerina stopped abruptly in the middle of the room and went silent, looking with interest at the traces of the previous day's impetuous merrymaking. A bold declaration written on the wall with a laser pistol, women's shoes on the table next to boxes of candy and unfinished cake. Carelessly thrown right into a puddle of spilled wine was a once chic, light-colored dress. My cousin had enough energy to lift up Bionica's dress and, shaking her head in judgment, stared at the raspberry-colored stain in the fabric.

"I'm not sleeping. I'll leave. I don't want to get in the way of your conversation." Valian ton Corsa, awoken by the scream, and having become an unwilling observer to a shouting match, jumped up from the bed and, covering her nakedness with a pillow, hurried to leave my cabin, not even daring to take the dress from the terrifying Duchess.

My cousin Katerina cast a long gaze at the retreating beauty and, when the doors had closed behind Valian, said with a smirk:

"It looks like leaving your bedroom naked is becoming a tradition for her. In her frightened state, though, she must have forgotten that this isn't *Queen of Sin*, where she'd only need to walk a hundred steps in the nude. On this huge battleship, she'll have to take three elevators and walk down almost a half mile of crowded hallways to get from your bunk to the women's dormitory wing."

I waved it off carelessly:

"Don't you worry about Valian. She won't get embarrassed in the least. At the same time, her fame will shoot up sharply, and her personal relations are sure to go up with any soldiers from the battleship crew she meets along the way, so she'll make out quite well."

My cousin looked at me somewhat surprised and anxious:

"Georg, I barely recognize you. I feel some kind of apathy and indifference in you. Was the redhead not enough?"

I breathed a heavy sigh.

"I do not know myself, cousin. Valian is pretty, happy, affectionate, and energetic... But she simply is not good enough to be my favorite. I find myself constantly comparing her with Astra, and every time, Valian comes in second. She would not be capable of simply existing at my side, adorning my retinue with her presence alone. Valian needs constant action, activity, and conversation. She can't even understand in theory the idea that a Crown Prince might have other business, or that he doesn't want to deal with his favorite all the time. She'd get bored right away, and try to attract my attention to her in different ways. Valian ton Corsa is an excellent, experienced and passionate lover. It is nice to spend an evening with her, blowing off steam. But with her temperament, she would never simply wait patiently for her master, then have a nice conversation with him over dinner. She'd go out looking for adventure on the side. I mean, judge for yourself. Do you think Astra would have left the room when you walked in? Not for anything in the world! She basically considered my cabin her legal property from day one. But Valian left, because she thinks of herself as a temporary guest here."

Katerina smiled, running her hand through my hair, tousling it.

"Don't be sad, cousin. You'll find another favorite, and you can just give Valian something to remember the nice evening by. But it cannot be money or jewelry. That is vulgar and shameful for any woman. She'd feel like her services were paid for. You need something immaterial that gives her reason for pride. The title Baroness of Unatari, for example. Or commission a picture of her from a famous painter, and hang it on the wall in fleet headquarters."

I smiled, thanked Katerina for the practical advice, and suggested we return to the topic she had come here to discuss. My cousin heard out my version of what had happened carefully. I told her in depth about all the pluses of giving asylum to Marian Sabati. Of course, I opted not to tell her that my real identity could have leaked, but there were enough rationales even without that.

"The eight billion is a convincing argument in her favor. And also, her abilities will clearly be of use, as will the blackmail material on other Imperial aristocrats. And, Georg, I just realized..." Katerina suddenly came to life, like a hound after picking up a scent. "Would a Truth Seeker even be capable of killing her master without dying shortly thereafter? As far as I've heard, a Truth Seeker should die, if they kill their own master. There's some kind of energy proximity with the master, or something like that. Why, then, is everyone wholesale accusing Marian Sabati of murder, not taking that mitigating factor into account?"

To be honest, I had never heard of such a limitation myself, which is why I had a personal consultant on such issues. I mentally called Florianna and asked her. The paralyzed girl answered instantly:

"Theoretically, a Truth Seeker is capable of attacking and killing her master, though she would suffer greatly in the process, and could even die from losing her energy source. There have been examples in history of visible aristocrats dying at the hands of their personal psionics. Though it is also known that the connection between master and Truth Seeker constantly grows stronger with the passage of time. At a certain point, a Truth Seeker will become completely dependent on her master and then, she really would not be able to harm him. For example, Miya is theoretically incapable of attacking anyone from the Mesfelle family. She wouldn't even be able to refuse an order from a Mesfelle. As such, it all depends on how long that Truth Seeker has been with her master."

I asked Katerina how many years Marian Sabati had been Avalle royl Anjer's Truth Seeker, and got an answer back immediately: seventy years.

"That is a very long time, Georg. Marian Sabati wouldn't have been able to kill the head of the Orange

House. She would have died even thinking about killing the Duke like that."

I told Katerina Florianna's expert conclusion.

"We need to make an official declaration on it then, presenting her long term of service as evidence that Marian Sabati is not guilty!" My cousin became inspired, but then stopped herself. "Hold on! We can't do a thing. We're cut off from the Empire, and cannot send messages."

I opened up the Perimeter Sector Eight map on the screen and brought up a countdown timer separately, showing slightly less than nine minutes.

"I hope very much, cousin, that the ability to send messages will soon return to us. Let's wait another nine minutes and see. I'm right in the middle of a hunt for huge game here: the one-thousand-five-hundred-starship Green House Fleet has already crossed the Perimeter Sector Seven border and is in the Parn system. If they keep going all together like that, without providing defense for the rear, the warp beacons will be turning off in eight minutes on my order in the Closed Laboratories and the Parn system, trapping Crown Prince Demyen royl Amelius ton Lavaelle in the Forepost-31 system. Everything there is already ready to greet the uninvited guests. All the greenhouses in the Forepost-31 system have been destroyed. Stores of food and seeds have all been collected from the station and removed to Tialla. I do not know how much provisions the Green House ships brought with them, but in any case, it won't last too long, given it'll have to feed two million people."

Katerina kept silent for some time, staring at the map. After that, she turned to me:

"Don't you think this is all a bit too easy? It's a very crude trap. Do you not think that Crown Prince Demyen, considered one of the best fleet leaders in the Green House, might have seen through it?"

"They are moving fast. As far as they know, all the systems on their path are loyal to the Orange House. Truth be told, if it hadn't been for the hint from the Purple House head, we wouldn't even know this armada existed. After all, look, neither Marat ton Mesfelle, nor my own sister Crown Princess Violetta warned us about the threat, which is very strange. Do you really think it's possible that the Perimeter Sector Seven fleet commander could possibly not know about a huge military armada passing through territory under his control? Marat definitely knew, but didn't tell us. My twin sister also would've known. The Green House fleet's route went straight through her system, Damir. There's no way around it. But Violetta chose not to warn me about the threat either!"

"It really is strange. After all, we thought they were totally loyal. Practically our allies. Maybe they didn't get a chance? Strict surveillance from the Orange House, then the communications blockade and all..."

"As they say, every cloud has a silver lining. The Green House doesn't know that their plans have been revealed. If the trap works, the retransmitters from the Closed Laboratories and the Parn system will still be on before the Orange House turns off the communications link from their other beacons. You could easily make a couple of reports and official messages from the Unatari State. So then, get ready to go live."

"No, I think I'd better wait out the remaining four minutes with you. I'd like to see how it all ends. If the trap works, I swear I'll call you the greatest strategist in the Empire in my report!"

She began sauntering around the room, and picked up Bionica's wine-soaked dress again.

"It was a nice dress. It's too bad it was damaged beyond repair. Damir single-fiber silk looks fashionable, and is very pleasant to the touch as well. But you cannot wash it, as the thread dissolves in water. Your robot secretary ordered the dress from the same designer I ordered Astra's coronation outfit from. Such a nice dress is probably worth sixty thousand credits, maybe even seventy."

"I'll make sure to compensate Bionica for the loss then," I promised. "By the way, speaking of androids... Katerina, are you aware that the robots that arrived to Unatari brought significant capital to invest in state projects?"

My cousin laughed happily:

"You're asking if I know about that?! You can't be serious! Bionica and I started working on this plan way back when you were regent of Tesse! The last few days, your synthetic secretary and I have been spending fifteen hours a day sitting and looking through proposed investment projects, calculating balance sheets, capital efficiency, and all the rest. Those androids brought us four billion credits, which is enough to turn Unatari-VII into an industrially developed planet with an orbital elevator, and high-speed magnetic train tracks between the huge islands. We'll also be able to organize the settlement of the unused polar regions, and the installation there of three thermonuclear power plants..."

"Don't forget about the Fastel system. There are two inhabitable planets there with decent industry. They probably have quite a few development projects as well. Plus, it just seems like the human thing to do, supporting my father-in-law and paying him back for all he's done."

Katerina nodded in the affirmative. The time had come! *Bride of Chaos* emerged from the warp tunnel into regular space. I was instantly inundated by a wave of messages that had accumulated over the last few days. Something important flashed by. A large font system message, so I took a closer look:

The Head of the Orange House, Duchess Inessa royl George ton Mesfelle has died at age 152.

ATTENTION! The new head of the Orange House will be Duchess Silva royl George ton Mesfelle (50.3% of votes)

Utterly flabbergasted, I looked at my cousin. Katerina was looking at me, no less lost herself.

"Gather all the information you can on the death of Duchess Inessa immediately!" I ordered my officers, continuing to read incoming messages as I did.

There it was! The pre-established signal from the Parn system. The little birdie flew right into the trap!

"Communications officer, I order you to open the envelope and send the enclosed signal to the warp beacons in Forepost-31, the Closed Laboratories, and

Parn."

Around a minute went by, and a series of new system messages ran before our eyes:

The Orange House has lost sovereignty over the Parn system

The Unatari State has gained sovereignty over the Parn system

The Orange House has lost sovereignty over the Closed Laboratories system

The Unatari State has gained sovereignty over the Closed Laboratories system

The Orange House has lost sovereignty over the Forepost-31 system

The Unatari State has gained sovereignty over the Forepost-31 system

"That's all, cousin. Now we wait for the Green House to react. They should realize what's happened soon enough. And yes, send congratulations to my brother Roben royl Inoky ton Mesfelle in my name. Somehow, Roben has become Count of the Orange House, first in line to the ducal throne!"

* * *

I was in a shuttle *en route* to the orbital laboratories, when a call came in from my brother Roben royl

Inoky. To be honest, my first reaction was apprehension. My brother hadn't called me in a very long time, and with the very harsh limits on all contact from Unatari, such a call looked, at the very least, strange. But Florianna confirmed that it really was my brother on the line.

"Hey there, little brother!" Roben was looking tired and haggard. "I received your belated congratulations, and decided to get in touch."

"Sorry, Roben. We were under complete communications blockade, which is why we just found out about the death of Duchess Inessa. But, tell me, what happened to her? I can't find any information, everything is classified."

Roben took a heavy sigh and even slumped a bit.

"What really happened there, I don't even know myself in earnest, little brother. According to the official version, the Duchess was on her yacht on the way from Sector Nine to the Throne World, accompanied by a large escort of ships. And in the Kammo system, when trying to dock at the station to charge her yacht, the mechanical hauling arms punched through it broadside, breaking the vacuum seal. As a result, two neighboring cabins lost pressurization and fifteen people died instantly. One of the damaged cabins happened to belong to Duchess Inessa. And also, for some reason, the automatic danger alarm didn't sound. The emergency repressurization system and rescue system both malfunctioned as well. Her experienced bodyguards, who had almost twenty seconds of time after the disaster, got confused for some reason, not able to even do simple tasks like lowering the face masks on their armored space suits, so they all died together with the civilians they were guarding."

"That's not possible!" I confidently declared to my brother. "I have watched bodyguard training with my own eyes a number of times, and have even participated in spacesuit demonstrations so they could practice rescuing me. Those guys pressurize their space suits as a reflex at the first sign of any abnormal situation. In a whole twenty seconds, they should have been able to secure themselves and remove the individuals they were guarding to a safe place, providing them protection and air to breath along the way."

"You're right, it isn't really possible. But are you not bothered by the rather improbable accident, as well, brother? How often do upper aristocrats' pleasure yachts, having the best captains and crews around, crash into space station equipment? The last time something like this happened was around three hundred years ago, and I'm not even sure *that* was an accident. The fact that the Duchess's cabin precisely was damaged, that doesn't surprise you either? Brother, it's no coincidence. In the last, not-even-full year, the Orange House has changed leadership four times! And how many other aristocrats have been removed from the list of heirs, including Crown Princes, Viscounts and others! Little brother, I'm really scared, because I don't understand what's going on. Someone's clearing a path to the Orange House throne. That much is obvious, but who? Of course, it couldn't be you or Violetta. I do not suspect you. All the more so now that you've voluntarily crossed yourself out of the line of succession. But then who? I mean, you congratulated me for receiving the title of Count, but my gut tells me the higher I go up the line of succession, the shorter my life gets. Remember my words, Georg. It won't be even a year before I'm also out of the picture. I'm having some very bad premonitions, little brother!"

"If it's all so rancid, then to hell with the Orange House. Join Unatari!" I offered, but my brother could only laugh in reply:

"If only it was that easy... Right now, the Orange House spooks and troops placed in Tesse number many times more than my forces. All I have to do is mention leaving the Orange House in passing, and that same day I'll be replaced, and maybe even buried immediately. I cannot allow that, even if it is for my son and heir. So, forgive me, Georg, I'll have to take a pass again. I do not want to take part in any new adventures. I will follow all laws and norms of the Orange House to make sure no one suspects me of separatism, and I will be left in peace."

"But does this conversation not constitute a breach of Inessa royl George's rules?"

"Don't remind me of that name! That bitch is dead. She died and turned into a desiccated hunk of meat. On Tesse, we had a state holiday to mark the occasion. The whole planet hated the Duchess. Over the few days her harsh rule lasted, she put thousands of people behind bars and nationalized the property of hundreds of Tesse companies for the Orange House's benefit. The new Head, Silva royl George has yet to confirm whether these recently passed laws are still in effect, though she has spoken on the blockade of

Unatari."

Roben suddenly grew gloomy, his tone becoming anxious and tragic.

"I complete forgot... Georg, did you know that your daughter Likanna has disappeared? Investigators recently came to my palace. They had information that she had allegedly been invited to Tesse, together with some friends, and that she had promised to return some papers from here to her school. But, I swear to you, brother. I know nothing whatsoever of your daughter nor the other Crown Princesses that disappeared. Information on what happened is subject to very strict censorship, but rumor has it that the group of girls disappeared directly from the Throne World school they were studying at."

I scratched my head in contemplation, digesting the information I'd received. Afterwards, I tried to calm my brother in any case:

"Everything with Lika is fine. All it is, I've been told, is that there are some unknown figures using fake documents who want to kidnap my daughter directly from school, but I managed to hide her in a safe place. As for the other girls, I have no idea. My trusted representatives were only supposed to pick up Likanna."

Just then, I discovered a letter from Lika among the bunch of information that came in four days ago, and I opened it right away:

"Dad, everything's fine. We already left the Throne World. I asked my two best friends, Crown Princess Joan royl Reyekh and Crown Princess Natalie royl Cruz to come with me, and they agreed happily. The girls didn't write to their parents, though. They were afraid their parents would say 'no.' So, you should warn the Purple and Blue Houses before they get worried. Everything over here is good. Cool even. The captain gave each of us one big Alpha Iseyek, and I taught my friends how to paint them. Not too long ago, we picked up a tired old lady named Marian Sabati at a station, and now she's coming with us. She's been sleeping for three days already. She hasn't even woken up once. Joan royl Reyekh even gave the old lady a new haircut so she'll have something to be happy about once she wakes up. Kisses. Dad, you're the very best."

I released a dying groan and held my head in my hands. So now, beyond sheltering the wanted Marian Sabati, I would also be accused of kidnapping three Crown Princesses. Just what I needed. Ugh. Why am I being punished like this?!

The proper thing to do here was immediately inform the Purple and Blue Houses of what had happened. And also inform the Imperial secretariat. No matter how you looked at it, the missing Crown Princesses were studying on the Throne World, which meant they were technically under the protection of the Emperor. But there was one small nuance. After announcing the fact that the girls were safe, I would certainly be ordered to say where they were as well. And I couldn't get away with just lying, either. The consequences were too serious. If Triasss Zess's ship was still in Perimeter Sector Nine space, it would be captured, regardless of its diplomatic status, all the Princesses, including Likanna, would be picked up, and Marian Sabati would be arrested. Triasss Zess didn't answer my attempt to call him. Clearly, his ship was in warp jump and thus unavailable. I would have to wait to figure this all out.

* * *

The huge orbital laboratory complex that had earlier been removed from Unatari to the Fia star system had sprouted a number of whole new facilities, laboratories and hangars for starship testing. Samantha ton Kruger, still head of the combat drone laboratory, came out to meet me, informing me that there were currently over thirty thousand individuals of six different races living and working on the station. In fact, it was already a whole space city, specialized in studying Alien technology.

We began by looking over the new stuff in the combat drone laboratory.

"Your Majesty, this is my pride and joy: a next-generation drone assembly line! We have practically totally reverse engineered Alien drone technology, and would be capable at this point not only of producing copies, as we were nine months ago, but also significantly improving their combat characteristics. And we have also learned to create totally new weapons based on our new knowledge. First of all, I would like to present you with a super-heavy combat drone model we're calling *Barbarian*," the woman pointed at a ship the size of a five-story building.

I gave a respectful whistle and walked up closer, craning my neck to see the drone from every angle.

"It is the same concept behind the Alien

Sledgehammer cruiser. In fact, many of the technologies used in it were reconstructed based on fragments of ruined *Sledgehammers*. It has huge firepower from the *Sledgehammer*'s conjugate plasma blasters, which are capable of destroying any ship from the frigate, destroyer, or even corvette classes in just one shot. It is highly resistant to damage, as it's shields can recharge themselves fully in just two seconds. Basically, this is an unmanned *Sledgehammer*. Unfortunately, we were also not able to avoid its predecessor's drawbacks, though. It's effective firing range is no more than 45 miles, because of its high-energy plasma rounds, the drone's low movement speed on the battlefield, and, most importantly, the cannon's low rotation angle. The *Barbarian* is intended for destroying slow or motionless targets, but it is practically useless for firing on smaller, more maneuverable ships."

Here I interrupted the report, demanding a more in-depth description of the cannon's characteristics and those of the drone itself. Would the *Barbarian* be able to hit small targets like frigates trapped under stasis web? Would a group of *Barbarians* be able to coordinate their actions amongst themselves and, for example, shoot at the same target in simultaneous volleys from multiple drones? The answers left me completely satisfied. Before me was a unique weapon with huge firepower that required some preparation before it could be used. Also, I held in mind what Samantha ton Kruger had said, that a group of three *Barbarians* would be able to take down one Alien *Sledgehammer* every twenty seconds.

The large dimensions of the heavy drone made it impossible to use with light-class ships. It would be possible to attach *Barbarians* to the external suspension rods on *Flambergs* or *Katanas*, though. I could fit two drones per cruiser. I would also be able to attach two *Barbarians* to the Iseyek *Legash* heavy cruisers past generation four. But the main purpose of the heavy drones was increasing the firepower of the battleships and carriers. I would be able to install eight *Barbarians* on *Tyrant*, *Monarch* and *Meresh* battleships, in addition to the weaponry they already had. On carriers like the *Uukresh* or *Quasar*, I would be able to use the heavy drones both on the external suspension rods, thirty per ship, as well as inside, replacing the light ships currently in the hangars.

In the next hall over, I had two light drones demonstrated for me. First, the improved Alien combat drone, distinguished by its increased endurance, speed and maneuverability. Also, with its fully rewritten programming, it was able to change its tactics autonomously depending on type of enemy, working together with other drones and starships in a group, carrying out rocket evasion maneuvers and getting out of range of a turret, as well as firing specifically at enemy ships' weak points.

"We have found replacements for most of the necessary metals and materials that we had a deficit of, reducing the production cost of each unit to one hundred eighty thousand credits. This new drone has been given the name *Razor* for its ability to slice through armor, and a certain physical resemblance."

And in fact, the thin drone did look somewhat like a thirty-five-foot-long razor blade, or even better, a dart with thin flights. I familiarized myself with the characteristics of the model, and nodded in approval, giving the order for mass-production of these "little razors," hoping to completely change out the light combat drones of the Unatari fleet with drones of this new generation.

"Your Highness, no need to rush with that order now," the leader of the laboratory stopped me. "There's another model of specialized light, high-speed drone, with thrusters copied from the alien *Meteors*. We figured out how they worked, but were not able to figure out how to apply them to *Pyro* or *Warhawk* frigates. When carrying out maneuvers at such high speeds, no matter how many gravity compensators you put into it, there are huge G-forces that make it impossible for human pilots and crew to survive. The second problem is with cannon accuracy. At high angular speeds, and when maneuvering, the intelligent ship-tracking and targeting systems are compromised. As such, we tried using high-speed thrusters in special drones made for capturing targets. The energy draw of the system allows for the installation of either warp disruptors for blocking enemy warp drives, or stasis webs for slowing a target down. New models have been given the name *Leech-B* or *Leech-C* for drones with warp disruptors and stasis webs respectively. The speed of the drones makes them more than capable of catching up to and overtaking any ship in existence, including Alien *Meteors*. Or, instead of target-capturing equipment, the drone could also be equipped with a cannon capable of launching bombs up to a megaton, which is model *Leech-A*."

"So you're saying that these drones would allow any fast enemy ships to be captured, then subsequently hit by cannons either from cruisers or *Barbarians,* or even special models made to destroy a bunch of minor ships with nuclear cannon rounds?"

Samantha ton Kruger nodded in silence, confirming that I was not mistaken. I stroked my forehead in contemplation. What does that mean? A cloud of *Leeches* released by my ships could capture anything moving toward my fleet. Battleships, cruisers and heavy *Barbarians* can shoot the immobilized targets from a safe distance. No little ships could get near mine now. Meanwhile, we were already capable of holding heavy ships. I was reminded of the term "imba" from computer games, used to describe a badly imbalanced mechanic. As such, it would have been stupid not to order an adequate number of such drones for the Unatari fleet.

The next couple laboratories from the science complex left me disenchanted. No one had even made a step forward in understanding the concept of how the Aliens were moving around without the warp beacons familiar to humanity. They also hadn't come any closer to understanding the system of mobile warp-beacon delivery. Producing antimatter to use in cannons taken from the ruined *Behemoths* was also at a stand-still. Their successes were limited only to having created individual atoms of anti-lithium and anti-beryllium. Alien *Meteor* thrusters, as I'd already been told, had not been able to be adapted to human frigates. They could put loads of up to 30 G's on ship crews, which was a guarantee the crew would be killed. Reducing the speed, or increasing the mass of the frigates with more advanced gravity compensation systems made using the new thrusters pointless.

New technologies for quickly restoring energy shields, applied in the *Barbarian* drones, it turned out, were impossible to use in small class ships and, conversely, on heavy battleships and motherships as well. They could only be used on light or heavy cruisers, though that was pretty cool in and of itself. I ordered all *Thrushes*, *Curses*, *Umoyges*, *Legashes*, *Katanas* and *Flambergs* modernized with the new systems. Now, anything that couldn't destroy a cruiser right away would be totally harmless to it.

The biology division had had slightly more success. They had managed to grow the "bush" aliens under laboratory conditions, though the specimens that resulted were not intelligent and basically were hardly different from the random primitive life forms found in the cosmos periodically by scout ships on asteroids and comets. The key to understanding the structure of the Alien societies was not found through them, though these "synthetic Aliens" were good enough for testing out the best method of killing them. Herbicides, defoliants, various wavelength laser beams, infrasonic waves, microwaves, cyanides, ions of heavy metal... the list of tested approaches was seventy screens long. The most effective was found to be high-frequency resonator irradiation, which destroyed the intermolecular bonds of the "bushes." Now, the technicians were working on modifying standard Imperial infantry resonators for effective combat against the Aliens.

I was already getting ready to finish my excursion around the orbital science city, thinking that I had heard everything new they had, but Samantha ton Kruger suggested I also see the experimental combat explosive laboratory. In her words, this group of scientists had something worth showing me. And I did not regret going.

"Your Highness, before you are bombs of a new type, for cloaked ships." The Chameleon in charge of the laboratory led me to some thirty-foot-long cylindrical objects, approximately twelve feet in diameter. "To the right, is a working model of an electromagnetic bomb, capable of causing serious failures in enemy electrical systems. It can turn off navigation systems, overload tactical computers, temporarily disable automatic thruster synchronizers, destabilize energy shields and..." here the scientist made a pause, drawing my attention, "temporarily disable antimatter storage systems on *Behemoth*-class battleships."

Well then! The Chameleon had my rapt attention. The impenetrable Alien *Behemoths* were a very serious problem for my fleet. Alien battleships either had to be boarded, or I had to risk my ships and go for close combat, draining energy with neutralizers, and losing starships in the process. I was being offered a way of doing some damage to these giants, taking their electronic systems out of commission for a time. And, by some trickery of the devil, I was even given the chance of blowing them up from the inside! As if reading my thoughts, the Chameleon scientist continued:

"The bomb to the left is gravitational. It creates a short-duration, but very strong gravitational disturbance, damaging large construction elements, knocking living creatures off their feet, and causing severe injury, even to those inside armored starships. If applied simultaneously with the previous bomb..."

"It would destabilize the energy fields holding the antimatter in place, destroying the *Behemoth*," I said, finishing the Chameleon's sentence.

"That's exactly right, your Majesty." The Chameleon bowed in a totally human fashion in respect at my prescient guess. "Both types of round are difficult to manufacture and are very expensive to produce, approximately fifteen million credits each."

"No matter how much these bombs cost, I need them as fast as possible! If I could deprive the Alien armada of their *Behemoth* backbone, we could easily wipe out the remaining enemy ships!"

For the first time since the beginning of the war with the Aliens, I saw a real chance to change the course of the unfortunately-developing standoff. I ordered fifty gravity bombs and fifty EMP bombs manufactured, spending one and a half billion credits in the process. I then spent another two billion to complete the *Quasar*-class carrier. The former monarch of the Fastel system had already sent me detailed diagrams of the giant. For six hundred million, I planned the construction of one hundred fifty *Curse*-class light cruisers. This former ugly duckling, taken out of production in the Empire for its low effectiveness, seemed brilliant to me in light of the new conditions. I spent another three hundred million buying electronic warfare ships. *Thrushes*, already having proven their high effectiveness, became even more attractive with the new energy shields. Finally, another three billion credits went to buying drones of all kinds for the Unatari fleet, and modernizing all cruisers. From the eight billion credits and a bit that I had at the beginning, there was just one billion remaining. Yes, it was a big expense, but it was worth it for the ability to defeat the Aliens once and for all!

Useful Connections

"**Y**OUR MAJESTY, the Fastel fleet has arrived to the Fia star system, with Duke Valesy Unatari at its head," Ayna told me, just as I was sitting down for a meal in the science complex's cafeteria in the company of Admiral Mike ton Akad and Bionica.

"Excellent, tell Duke Valesy to have his people land the *Quasar* at dock five. Everything there is ready to receive it. Then, invite the Duke to join me for dinner. You would be welcome as well."

A few minutes later, confirmation arrived that the Duke had accepted the invitation and would soon be arriving at the Fia orbital science station. I ordered another place-setting made up for our honorable guest, but just then Florianna's alarmed voice rang out in my head:

"Crown Prince, wait! I sense potential danger! Duke Valesy is now on the large landing ship Skinflint. *Approximate time to docking at the scientific complex: seven minutes. The Duke has five thousand armed assault troops ready for combat. Half of them are*

wearing heavy exoskeleton space armor right now, and the others are equipped for support. I sense that their general emotional state is one of anxious waiting. The Duke ordered them to prepare for possible active measures."

"An attempt at overthrowing the government?" I clarified out loud, and my companions at the table instantly perked up their ears.

"Duke Valesy has yet to decide, actually. On the one hand, he wants to rule the new Unatari State himself. On the other though, the Duke is not sure that he will be able to deal with that role while at war with three Great Houses. Also, the Duke isn't even close to understanding the magnitude of your Majesty's forces here in the Fia star system. But, if your former relative thinks the time is right, he could easily give the order to his soldiers to arrest or even kill Crown Prince Georg royl Inoky."

I voiced Florianna's message out loud. Popori de Cacha instantly appeared from invisibility and said that there were just twenty of my bodyguards on the station, as well as three hundred local guards, who weren't particularly skilled in combat. In comparison with five thousand assault troops, it was nothing at all. The uneasy admiral turned on his microphone and called the attendant frigate division to the station, though we all understood perfectly well that the ships would not be able to stop a potential landing.

"I could order the androids on *Skinflint* to damage the docking systems, block airlocks and basically just create chaos in the ranks of the landing ship. Robots listen to me. We could earn a few minutes that way," Bionica suddenly suggested.

I took a shocked look at my secretary. I didn't suspect the modest Bionica could tell other robots what to do. The synthetic blonde had clearly understated her role in the hierarchy of Imperial androids. I made a mental note to talk with my secretary about this under calmer circumstances. For now, though, I told them all to wait and not take hostile action before I had the chance to talk with my former father-in-law. And only when a landing ship appeared from the warp tunnel one hundred and twenty miles from the science station, did I order a call placed to the Duke.

The former monarch of the Kingdom of Fastel appeared on screen. The old man was clearly strained and agitated.

"Greetings, Valesy!" I said with pronounced amicability. "Duke, I thought I had called just you to dinner, not all fifty thousand assault troops from *Skinflint*. This isn't a very big cafeteria. I don't think it can fit that many people. Order your men to remove their armor, lay down their laser rifles, store them in your armory, and disperse. You should get in a shuttle yourself, like all normal people, without any grandstanding. Otherwise, I'm afraid your intentions could be misunderstood, and your landing ship might not make it to the station."

Three seconds of strained silence followed, after which the Duke gave a deep bow and answered:

"That is precisely what I'll do, your Majesty. I was in too much of a rush to the meeting, and it didn't occur to me that a landing ship docking at your station could be taken the wrong way. Please forgive my forgetfulness. I'm an old man. My memory isn't what it used to be..."

__Standing change. Valesy royl Unatari's opinion of you has improved.__
__Presumed personal opinion of you: +38 (friendship)__

"That's great, Valesy. I'll be waiting for you in the cafeteria."

I signed off and turned to Admiral Mike ton Akad, who had pulled up an image from one of the station's external cameras on his palmtop computer, and was following *Skinflint*'s movement with panic.

"They have stopped the approach. They have turned off maneuver drives and dropped shields. Holy shit, Georg! It worked!"

__Standing change. Mike ton Akad's opinion of you has improved.__
__Presumed personal opinion of you: +87 (completely trusting)__

"Sometimes, having a negative standing can work to your advantage," I chuckled. "Many are afraid of you, so they imagine that you might just kill everyone around you in the cruelest way imaginable at the drop of a hat. That makes lying about doing so a bit easier to pull off."

Bionica laughed her frolicsome, completely human laugh, but then the android's mood suddenly changed and sadness appeared in the girl's voice:

"I hope the day will come when androids are also allowed to get implants to express their personal opinion of various humans and factions. I think it would be just. After all, many modern robot models practically equal humans in level of intellect and abstract thinking ability, and in many ways even surpass them."

For some reason, I had no doubt that this sentence wasn't simply out of nowhere. It was clearly intended for my ears, and now the android girl was waiting for my reaction. I mulled my synthetic assistant's grievance over, and immediately found several flaws in her proposal:

"Bionica, those implants help people directly interact with databases and figure out who someone is quickly. But androids can do both of those things already. The other role of these implants is that they allow prominent figures to express their point of view through a system of personal and faction relations, thus forming something of an average idea of what a given group thinks. But nowhere near all people have built-in implants. Only the ones who have achieved something important, or those who occupy a high position in society. The key words here are 'only' and 'important.' And now, imagine millions of androids of the same model. They have identical BIOS and software, so their opinion on an event would not be the same kind of aggregate, but would instead depend on settings and behavior model. Whose viewpoint, then, would these millions of androids be expressing? The manufacturing company's? The Green House's?"

Bionica grew ashamed in a very human way and puffed out her lips:

"Master, you cannot tell me you really think my character identical to all eight million model 034-6781 android servants, created since production began, right?"

I hurried to calm my excessively emotional assistant:

"No, of course not. Bionica, you are unique in many ways, above all else your history. Very few robot servants have had the chance to spend a whole quarter century developing and honing their personal character, without periodically wiping unique programming changes, and replacing them with typical firmware and layouts. Well, are there many such 'ripened' personalities in your batch of eight million?"

"No, of course not. Three million model 034-6781 androids have been simply destroyed over the years, mostly disposed of due to lack of demand. More modern models came out. Old ones stayed on the shelves for a while, but were eventually sent back for parts. Of the five million that are still around, only eleven, including me, were not regularly updated to new patches and firmware. And of these eleven androids, two of them care for elderly people, eight serve clients in bordellos, and only I have a dignified job as Minister of Economy for the space government of Unatari..."

Admiral Mike ton Akad, sitting next to me, choked on his beer, coughed it out, and suddenly began whinnying like a mare.

"Wait, is that true?! Minister Bionica, seventy percent of robots identical to you work in bordellos?!"

It was clearly an insulting question, but the synthetic girl didn't get ashamed one bit:

"Admiral, if we widen it to all subtypes of my

model, over ninety-two percent of them are involved in sex work in one way or another. We were initially created to replace people in all kinds of professions, but we were also made to be attractive to men, and given a whole set of female bodily organs. That is exactly why Crown Prince Georg royl Inoky ton Mesfelle drew such a wave of reproach and mockery from his detractors when he chose me as a secretary and translator. Only the direct interference of Emperor August, who had a positive opinion of my work and awarded me an Emerald Star, was enough to stop all the insinuation on the topic. I am no worse than a living girl, which is why I would like everyone around me to think of me and treat me like a living person."

But the admiral did not distinguish himself with his sense of tact today.

"In issues of labor, yes, you are no worse than a living girl. But androids cannot have children, so no matter what, when talking with you I will be left with a sensation of artificiality, no matter how pretty an envelope it comes in."

"Admiral, the Crown Prince's assistant Ayna is also not capable of having children. Would you also call her artificial? Find me even one parameter in which she can surpass me. All the same, Ayna has a built-in implant, expresses her personal opinion to the world around her, and that doesn't surprise any of you one bit. Why, then, do you refuse me the same ability?"

"This is no time for demagoguery, robot. There are differences between you. For example, androids cannot kill."

Bionica didn't have time to answer that argument, as the subject of the conversation, Ayna, walked in, leading the ancient Duke Valesy by the elbow. The old man looked a lot older "in real life," than the person I was used to seeing on screen. I suspect that, before talking with me on video phone, he usually got touched up by his make-up servants, and did his best not to walk on his shaky legs. Now, though, you could see all eighty years of his life on his face. As he approached me, the old man tried to fall to his knees, but Ayna held him upright.

"Your Majesty, please forgive me for my stupid thoughts. I have done you wrong!" The Duke declared with repentance in his voice.

But I immediately stopped the old man's self-accusatory speech and pointed him to a cushy armchair next to me.

"Duke Valesy, you didn't manage to actually do anything reprehensible, and it is not accepted practice to punish someone for their thoughts. Admiral Mike ton Akad over there has been doing nothing for the last half hour but openly mocking my Economy Minister, mentally creating some very perverse scenes as he did so, but we can't exactly punish him for raping my android servant, can we?"

The admiral grew embarrassed for a brief second, but then laughed out loud. The tension disappeared in an instant. The Duke sighed with relief and sat at the table. We had our lunch, then conversed on various topics in a relaxed manner until Bionica suddenly said:

"Crown Prince, the Swarm diplomatic ship has just taken the warp jump out of the Forepost-4 system toward the Sivalla system."

I did not ask Bionica where she had gotten the information from. It was, after all, probably just some inconspicuous android from the Human border station there. But then, the deeper meaning of the synthetic blonde's message was, in fact, very important. Triasss Zess's diplomatic ship had made it unharmed through Perimeter Sector Nine, and was now on its way to Swarm space. And that meant that the Orange House wouldn't be able to stop me from meeting my daughter now, no matter how much they wanted to. By the way, it was now possible, and even necessary to inform the Purple and Blue Houses on the whereabouts of their missing Princesses.

First, I made a call to the Head of the Purple House, Duke Takuro royl Andor. I was put through almost instantly. The ancient aristocrat was clearly ailing, lying in bed held in place with some wires and data-reading suction cups. I greeted the Duke, following all applicable rules of courtly etiquette, then said:

"I received a letter from my daughter, Crown Princess Likanna. She is currently on her way to Unatari through Swarm space. She took two girls from her school with her. Crown Princess Natalie royl Cruz ton Miro and Crown Princess Joan royl Reyekh ton Andor..."

The old man on the screen shuddered with his whole body and closed his eyes. Tears unexpectedly started rolling down his cheeks.

"Duke, Likanna invited her friends over for break, and the girls decided not to tell their relatives, because they were afraid they'd get told 'no.' I would like to offer my apologies for my daughter's thoughtless behavior and the worry she caused. Today, though, I'll be meeting the Crown Princesses and will try to return Joan royl Reyekh to Purple House space as quickly as possible."

The old man opened an eye, smiled through the tears and looked at me:

"I'm just happy that it all ended well. I was just dying of worry. I even fell ill. But there's no need to send my granddaughter back, Georg. Let the girls spend some time together. My Joan doesn't often get the chance to make friends with a classmate. Her being able to actually spend time out of the house is a blessing. It wasn't always like this. Joan used to be unsociable and shy. We were very worried about it. Let my granddaughter have some fun with her friends without any caretakers getting in the way. It will help her a great deal. In a month, I'll talk with the Orange House myself and send a yacht out for Joan to take her back to the Purple House."

Standing change. Purple House (Empire) opinion of you has improved.

Present Purple House (Empire) faction opinion of you: +23 (trusting)

Alright. Half of the unpleasant business is over with. Now it was time to have a difficult talk with the Blue House. I was not familiar with Duchess Ovella, the head of the "Blues," and what was more, the Unatari State was at war with them, so I was afraid they'd outright refuse to talk with me. Nevertheless, the Duchess's secretary heard me out and promised to put me directly through with her leader. Fifteen minutes went by and the screen flickered on, showing me an image of the Head of the Blue House. She was still quite young, a pretty girl with long flowing light blue hair and piercingly blue eyes, skillfully emphasized with cosmetics.

> ***Ovella royl Stok ton Miro, Head of the Blue House***
>> ***Age: 22***
>> ***Race: Human***
>> ***Gender: Female***
>> ***Class: Aristocrat***
>> ***Achievements: Line Jumper, Fatherkiller, Poisoner, Overthrew Mother, Nothing is Sacred, Youngest Leader***
>> ***Fame: +12***
>> ***Standing: - 39***
>> ***Presumed personal opinion of you: Unknown***
>> ***Blue house opinion of you: -11 (dislike)***
>> ***Present Blue House faction opinion of the Unatari State: -3 (WAR)***

So, she was not just some simple lady after all. Capturing the Blue House throne at such a young age with her abundance of dubious "achievements" bore eloquent witness to that. To the right of the Duchess's throne, there was an old woman sitting on a low bench. She was covered head-to-toe in dark robes. The interactive popup on her didn't work for some reason. It was obvious that I was seeing a Truth Seeker, and clearly a very old one, but there was no way of figuring out more than that. Good thing Florianna gave me a hint:

"Her name is Krista. She is considered the very oldest Truth Seeker in the Empire. Krista's true age is unknown, but she must be more than four hundred years old. For a very long time, she trained capable psionic girls in a special school on the Throne World, but it was closed one hundred fifty years ago after a wave of strange, unexplainable deaths. After that, Krista was Truth Seeker to the ancient Duke Malvik royl Stefan ton Miro, who led the Blue House for over one hundred years. He resigned last year, though, and went to live out his final years in peace. Since his resignation, three aristocrats have sat on the Blue House ducal throne, and all the while, Krista was supporting the young Ovella royl Stok ton Miro. To be honest, the newly-minted Duchess Ovella will soon have to face an Imperial court. She's been accused of a great many fairly serious crimes. It is quite possible that the ruler of the Blue House will be changed out again, though I still think that the Duchess will be able to prove her innocence with the help of her Truth Seeker. That said, I am not sure of Krista's abilities at present. Once, she was considered the second most powerful Truth Seeker in the Galaxy after the Dark Mother, but changing masters can significantly weaken a psionic."

"Don't you worry about my strength, little girl. It's already returned in full measure. And don't you worry about my young ward either. Ovella has enough evidence to combat the unfounded accusations made against her."

Hrmph... I definitely didn't have to worry about

Krista not being very powerful then. She had clearly found it quite easy to join our mental conversation. The Truth Seeker smiled with the very corners of her mouth, blatantly reading my thoughts. After that, she turned to her master and said in a grumbling old-woman's voice, not at all like the one in my head:

"Crown Prince Georg isn't thinking anything untoward, Duchess. He wants to tell us that Crown Princess Natalie has been found, and he is preparing to discuss the conditions of the girl's return."

"I will not be paying a ransom for my cousin, Georg!"

The young woman made a touchingly awkward face. It looked as if she was trying to show ferocity and rigidity, but it came across as more funny than scary. I couldn't hold back a smile, and Krista couldn't either.

"The last thing I need is to be accused of kidnapping children. Crown Princess Natalie came as a guest of my daughter Likanna, but the girls didn't inform any adults. That is precisely why I got in touch with you, to reassure the Blue House that everything is fine."

"Natalie can stay where she wishes then. Is that all you wanted to say, Crown Prince Georg?"

I tried not show any surprise at how little Crown Princess Natalie's wellbeing concerned her cousin. But I couldn't get by the Truth Seeker.

"Your paralyzed girl noticed correctly that the Blue House throne has been passing from hand to hand far too often in recent months. The wild ride isn't even over yet. There are still many disaffected. Some of our star systems have declared independence from the

Duchess, and my ward needs time to calm her subjects and establish order in her territory. Crown Prince Natalie heads a different branch of the ancient house of Miro, so her coming to Blue House space is truly bad timing right now. We would be obliged, if Princess Natalie could spend her whole break with you."

In parallel with Krista's mental speech, she was saying out loud for her master:

"Duchess, I think it would be proper to thank the ruler of Unatari for being so considerate of a Blue House Princess. I think that this is a completely appropriate reason to end the senseless war between Unatari and the Blue House."

Standing change. Blue House (Empire) opinion of you has improved.

Present Blue House (Empire) faction opinion of you: -8 (mistrusting)

The young woman smiled at me, and raised her left arm to her cheek, apparently turning off a microphone behind her ear. But she either pressed the button too softly, or she did it twice, so I heard the Duchess ask a question, which was clearly not intended for my ears:

"But, Krista, how is that possible? You yourself told me of our duty to the Green House and about how the Unatari State is doomed! You said they could already be considered wiped off the map! You said the Green House Strike Fleet would capture their capital any day now!"

The old woman did not embarrass the young Duchess by telling her the microphone was on. She simply smiled at me and answered her ward:

"The situation changed drastically, Ovella. I can clearly see that the ruler of Unatari has no fear of the Green House armada whatsoever. And this is not simply a matter of ignorance. In fact, the huge fleet has already been neutralized by Unatari forces. It is trapped in a lifeless star system with no way out, and has been removed from play."

"That changes things completely. Why would we stay in this pointless war then?"

Before my eyes a system message appeared:

The Blue House offers the Unatari State a peace treaty on the following terms: Status Quo.

In the menu that appeared, I chose the option "Agree," and immediately received a message that the war with the Blue House was over:

A peace treaty has been signed between the Unatari State and the Blue House.

Standing change. Blue House (Empire) opinion of you has improved.
Present Blue House (Empire) faction opinion of you: +2 (indifferent)

Standing change. Blue House (Empire) opinion of the Unatari State has improved.
Present Blue House faction opinion of the Unatari State: 0 (indifferent)

After that, Duchess Ovella thought the

conversation over, and politely bid me farewell, expressing her happiness at our having met. After that, she walked off camera. But her Truth Seeker chose to stay for some time and, having waited for her ward to leave the room completely, continued:

"Crown Prince Georg royl Inoky, I have a somewhat unexpected proposal for you. As I've already said, Crown Princess Natalie royl Cruise ton Miro coming to Blue House space would be rather undesirable. The girl is second in line to the ducal crown, and many enemies of my ward Ovella have placed their bets on precisely this underage Crown Princess. They have been bringing chaos to our systems, claiming to be acting in her name. So, let Crown Princess Natalie spend some extended time as your guest to give her a break from the bad influence of these unreliable advisors. And another thing: Duchess Ovella would be very, very grateful to you if her main competitor, Crown Princess Natalie were to refuse her place in line to the Blue House throne."

Clearly, the Truth Seeker must have caught some unhappiness flickering in my thoughts, as she quickly added:

"Don't think anything untoward, Crown Prince. I am not asking you to coerce the young Crown Princess, and I am certainly not suggesting that you kill the girl."

"Though doing so would be totally acceptable."

"It's just that you, as an adult man and experienced politician, might be able to find the right words to convince Natalie that the light of the Blue House's ephemeral throne shall never shine down on her. Many people, myself included, are doing everything we can to make sure that never happens. To that end, it is clearly not in Crown Princess Natalie's best interest to go chasing after a mirage. Refusing to fight will work out better. She would get a good chunk of change from Duchess Ovella in return. Five billion credits and a rich Perimeter Sector Ten star system is what she's prepared to offer. You though, Prince Georg, the Blue House is prepared to pay fifteen billion credits if you can sway her. And you could have it in money, combat ships or any other way you like. Also, Unatari will gain a reliable ally in the Blue House and a conduit from your territory into the Imperial Core, even if the communications and transport blockade of your government by the Orange House is renewed."

"Tell me more about that," I said to Krista, and the woman explained with vigor:

"In Perimeter Sector Ten, the Blue House borders the territory of the Mechanoids, a nonhuman mechanized race. They are utterly nonaggressive, and have long been allies of the Empire. The Mechs have often complained of inexplicable catastrophes over the last few hundred years. Their ships have been disappearing without a trace, but only in the two star systems that are the farthest from the Empire. Duke Malvik even sent an expedition to aid our allies, and study the mysterious happenings thirty-five years ago. The ships that made it there started sending nonsensical long-distance transmissions, then began fighting amongst themselves and doing other strange things. After that, contact was lost. In light of information we've recently acquired, we can say with a great deal of certainty that the Mechs and the members of that expedition must have come across the Arite Iseyek race. Crown Prince, you are in contact with those mysterious beings and even have a certain amount of influence on their Queen, Nai Igir. I believe that you would be able to convince the Swarm to let your data and space ships pass through a chain of warp beacons from the Blue House to the Unatari State."

I thanked the Truth Seeker for the valuable information and promised to have a talk with Crown Princess Natalie. The old lady nodded, bid farewell audibly, then suddenly added mentally:

"The paralyzed girl spoke the truth about my very advanced age. I cannot speak on the Antagonists, though. They once had Truth Seekers more ancient than myself, but I truly am the oldest one in the Empire proper. My youngest son was the first captain of the scout ship Star Mutt. *The twins Paul and Paola are my distant great-great-grandchildren. Paola even looks like me in my youth, despite all the generations that separate us. Crown Prince Georg, I was very glad when I saw that my distant relatives were with you. If your Majesty can come to an agreement with the Swarm and the Mechs, I would be much obliged if you could send Paola to me. I would be very grateful and would accept her with great honor."*

"Agreed. I'll suggest that Paola go to the Blue House. I'm sure the girl will be glad to meet her great-great-grandma," I promised the seven-century-old Krista.

Standing change. Blue House (Empire) opinion of you has improved.

Present Blue House (Empire) faction opinion of you: +5 (warm)

Standing change. Blue House (Empire) opinion of the Unatari State has improved.
Present Blue House faction opinion of the Unatari State: +1 (indifferent)

I turned the screen off and, accompanied by a whole division of invisible bodyguards, returned to the large hall of the cafeteria. It had become crowded there. The work day was over, and many employees of the laboratory had come down to dine, at the same time making use of the chance to see the ruler of their government in the flesh, even if only from the corner of an eye. Popori de Cacha was nervous, and advised me to finish all negotiations and return to a more appropriate location as quickly as possible, as he considered it too unsafe here. But Florianna sensed no danger, so I decided to spend some time carousing with the rank and file.

Ayna was dancing with Admiral Mike ton Akad among a great many spinning couples. Duke Valesy royl Unatari was talking with Bionica and, judging by the half bottle of strong alcohol on the table before them, trying to get my pretty secretary drunk. How naive. When I showed up, the old man pointed to the armchair next to him, and said in a none-too-sober tone:

"Georg, I must admit something to you. For the last few days, I have been hearing Marta's voice ringing out in my head, clear as day. My dead daughter is angry that everyone has forgotten her.

She says that I'm no father to her until I get revenge for her death. The voice shows up unexpectedly and is just driving me crazy. Marta has also started coming into my dreams every night to keep compelling me there. She suggests I take advantage of your trust, strike you in the back, and take all the power for her daughter Likanna. Tell me, Georg, have I lost my mind? After all, a person cannot hear voices in his head, right?"

I tried to calm him:

"You have not lost your mind, Valesy. Many psionics are capable of planting voices in people's minds. The Alien *Queen* shares this ability. I suppose this is the work of a fairly strong Truth Seeker. She is pretending to be Marta, and is trying to poison us that way."

"Georg, I cannot sense any traces of such activity here. That could just mean that the enemy is significantly stronger than I am, though."

Bionica stretched out her arm, took the bottle and poured two glasses of strong brandy, one for herself, and another for the Duke. She offered to pour me one, but I refused. Duke Valesy took it obediently and drank it down. It turned out that I had been mistaken in my initial evaluation of the situation. It wasn't the old Duke trying to get the pretty young girl drunk at all. In fact, my android was clearly taking advantage of the fact that alcohol had no effect on her, to loosen the Duke's lips.

"Georg, I cannot go on like this. Marta will put me in the grave. She tries to get me to usurp your power day and night, but she doesn't understand that I will never manage as ruler. I saw your skill today.

Even the strongest figures in the universe treat you with deference. People are afraid of you. They respect you. No one would ever take me seriously. The Unatari State would die with you, and get gobbled up by its neighbors in short order."

"Yes, that is all true. That's why you need to fight the mind control. Resist. I will ask Florianna to give you mental protection, like the kind I have. Perhaps the voices won't go away entirely, but they should become much weaker. Also, my highly experienced doctor, Nicosid Brandt, can prescribe you some medicine to make it so you won't dream at all anymore. But soon, I will return with Likanna, and at the same time bring one of the strongest Truth Seekers in the Empire to our side. After that, the voices will stop once and for all. Perhaps my Truth Seekers will be able to root out your invisible enemy and make them answer for this low blow."

Standing change. Valesy royl Unatari's opinion of you has improved.

Presumed personal opinion of you: +53 (friendship)

Just then, Popori de Cacha appeared before me, telling me with a respectful bow:

"Tuki-tuka-de-sa, a message has just come in from the Iseyek. Swarm Queen Nai Igir is prepared to receive your Majesty two days from now in Dekeye."

* * *

The Iseyek had a demand at the very last second:

only one ship, of a class no larger than a frigate was to be allowed. It was unexpected and even, in my cousin Katerina's words, a borderline insult. The monarch of a sovereign government generally has a somewhat bigger retinue than a small frigate can accommodate. Under different circumstances, I would have reacted indignantly, but I had no other way to pick up my daughter and her friends from insect space, and wanted to preserve my good-neighborly relationship with the Swarm, so I was forced to make concessions and bring down the size of the Unatari delegation. I even had to consider the fact that, on the return journey, we would be carrying three Crown Princess and their new Alpha Iseyek companions, as well as the wanted criminal Marian Sabati. That was why our cohort was very light as we set out to meet Nai Igir: me, Bionica as translator, and a cohort of bodyguards.

We flew in *Warhawk-4*, captained by the highly decorated Tamara Vuzhek. Choosing her as pilot was no accident, either. First of all, the Iseyek respected her, and knew her as the most skilled frigate captain in my fleet. Second, Tamara knew my daughter Likanna well, and I was hoping that their friendship would have a positive effect on the behavior of the three Crown Princesses, who were probably going stir-crazy from the long trip in such a small space.

We were already in the Yal system, waiting to charge our frigate, and I was talking with my cousin about the Blue House's proposal over video. Katerina heard me out with rapt attention, but after a long silence, answered:

"To be honest, my natural reaction is to do the

opposite of what they suggest. As Duchess Ovella's position is so tenuous, the sensible thing to do would be supporting little Natalie in her ambition for power. We stand to gain a lot more. Not just fifteen billion credits, which is of course not bad, but the whole Blue House at our beck and call until Crown Princess Natalie comes of age four years from now."

"An attractive prospect," I agreed, but Katerina shook her head:

"Unfortunately, it isn't as easy as it seems. The Crown Princess will never agree to sit locked up in isolation for so long. Also, it would be impossible for us to influence the course of the rebellion in the Blue House from Unatari space. We will not be able to provide security to the girl beyond the borders of Unatari, and she will simply be murdered, though not by our hands. We will get no reward whatsoever, and the Blue House will be very insulted as well. It's a bad option. I say we take Krista's offer, but first we need to make sure we get an official guarantee from her boss, Duchess Ovella, first. After that, try not to blacken your name too much in earning these fifteen billion for our shared government. And another thing, Georg. The whole situation with Krista has led me to an important thought. I hope you are smart enough not to make Marian Sabati your oldest daughter's Truth Seeker. I'm quite sure that, if you do, Unatari will be getting a new ruler much faster than you would like."

Duchess Katerina royl Unatari signed off, leaving me in thought. I mean, I trusted Likanna completely but, all the same, I took my cousin's warning into account. The timer I set beeped, telling me that the Green House armada was arriving to the Forepost-31 system. I decided to send an ultimatum to Crown Prince Demyen royl Amelius ton Lavaelle, commander of the Green House First Strike Fleet, who was now securely in my trap.

I did not talk with the Crown Prince myself, as I was afraid of potential aggression from the several strong Truth Seekers in his fleet. As such, I decided to limit myself to a message. In it, I promised Crown Prince Demyen and his people their lives, good treatment in captivity, and a quick return to Green House space, if he capitulated immediately and transferred all his one thousand five hundred ships in full working order to the Unatari State. I also promised the commander that, if my generous proposal was not accepted within eight hours, the two million soldiers of the Green House First Strike Fleet would be learning firsthand about new concepts such as "starvation" and "cannibalism." Then, to those conditions, I added a demand that Crown Prince Demyen royl Amelius ton Lavaelle and all other aristocrats in his fleet resign from power without exception.

I sent the message to Bionica for her to send onward, but my usually quiet, modest assistant unexpectedly asked me to hold off sending the ultimatum.

"Your Majesty, Crown Prince Demyen has just arrived to the Forepost-31 system. He has no idea what a mess he's in. His ships are waiting to charge, and have not yet realized that the next warp beacon will not be turning on for them. It seems to me that we should make use of their inaction and build on the effect of your Majesty's trap."

"What did you have in mind, Bionica?"

"In the Green fleet, there are a huge number of androids. The Green House manufactures all android models and uses them for all kinds of labor. All of their ships are chock-full of robot servants, who are responsible for cleanup, laundry, food preparation, soldier entertainment, and much more. And though weapons rooms and ammunition warehouses are critically important locations and are guarded by living people, the more banal storage facilities are completely run by robots. I could order the Green House First Strike Fleet's androids to begin preparing goods for disposal. They could send all full containers to be compacted or into the vacuum of space. They could also destroy the briquettes of dry food in their trash burners. These are scheduled procedures that are performed periodically on any ship to make space for fresh products in storage. These kinds of activities do not require any approval, and would not arouse suspicion. Before the enemy starts suspecting anything, a large proportion of their stocks could be destroyed. Similar actions could be used with the fresh water storage. Simply order the robots to empty out all the tanks and send all the 'spoiled' water into space."

My eyebrows shot up in surprise I wasn't expecting my peaceful Bionica to give me such a sophisticated, well-thought-out act of villainy.

"Very well, get to work. I'll send my ultimatum to the Duke in seven hours then, when our *Warhawk* is coming out of the warp tunnel in the Kiya system. When I do that, ask your android friends how the sabotage went."

"Yes sir, my Prince," Bionica gave a slight bow and set off to the communications officer to send encoded messages incomprehensible to living people.

I, though, remained sitting deep in thought. If my personal secretary had always had such ideas in her arsenal, why had Bionica not told me about them earlier? And also, if you think about it, why would the Green House, which created the androids and had a great understanding of them, not also use such tactics? If, then, Bionica recently got the ability to give commands to other androids, I needed to find out why these changes had taken place. Basically, the time had come for a very serious conversation with Bionica.

SWARM PRINCESS

I HAD THE CONVERSATION with my synthetic assistant planned for the morning. First of all, in order to be able to get some rest after such a long, action-packed day, and just gather my thoughts.

Second, before the conversation, I wanted to find out the results of the subversion planned by Bionica in Crown Prince Demyen's fleet. By the way, Tamara Vuzhek had given my android a separate, spacious room, forcing her own crew into tighter quarters to do so. And, what completely surprised me was that my modest Bionica took the honors extended to her totally for granted.

I fell asleep instantly, my head barely having touched the pillow. And... I immediately found myself in a totally unfamiliar place. Some kind of darkened room with no windows, furnished with futuristic reinforced plastic furniture, a floor that gave a spring as you walked, and some vertical hanging curtains covering openings in the wall that led to some kind of corridors. The only source of light was behind a less thickly covered door in the next room over. I could hear wind chimes jingling away from that room as well. Clearly, someone was suggesting I go in that direction.

All the same, before getting up and walking toward the source of light, I went up to a dark mirror on the wall and took a look at myself in order to figure out what body I was in. From the gloomy, ancient mirror, Crown Prince Georg royl Inoky ton Mesfelle was looking back at me wearing a pair of white long underwear. Not the most appropriate getup for a walk around an unfamiliar location, but still better than nothing. I adjusted my disheveled hair with my hand, walked toward the light and carefully cracked the door open.

It was a child's room, judging by the flowery pink wallpaper, low shelves weighed down by toys and the diaper changing board next to the wall. The glow was coming from a flower-shaped night-light in the wall. In the far corner from the night light, there was a child's bassinet with a canopy over it. Hanging from the ceiling above that, a musical mobile was slowly spinning a set of hanging, brightly colored toys. That was what was making the melodious sound I'd heard. I walked up to the bassinet quietly and carefully peeled back the canopy to look inside at the sleeping child.

It was a sweet little girl, smiling as she dozed away. She had curly dark-colored hair. An interactive popup came up obligingly, telling me who exactly I was seeing in the crib:

Deianna royl Georg ton Mesfelle, Crown Princess of the Empire
Age: 8 months
Race: Human

Gender: Female
Relation to you: Your legal daughter
Class: Aristocrat
Achievements: None
Fame: +1 Standing: 0
Presumed personal opinion of you: (inactive)

"Isn't she wonderful, Georg?" I could hear unhidden tenderness in Miya's voice, ringing out from somewhere behind me.

I turned around slowly to see my spouse, sitting in a deep armchair. For clothing, the beauty was making do with the very same frivolous and erotic construction of bright pink ribbons that I had seen Miya in on our very first meeting. The woman pointed me to the chair next to hers with an inviting gesture.

"Take a seat, Georg. You and I have a lot to talk about."

"What is this place?" I wondered, taking the seat next to my spouse.

The redhead beauty just waved my question off carelessly:

"What difference does it make? It's nothing more than a peaceful location where no one can trouble me or my daughter. To be honest, I don't know where it is myself. Maybe it's a villa somewhere in the real world. Maybe it's a 3-D virtual image of one. I also cannot exclude the possibility that this entire area was created from scratch by programmers."

"What do you mean? Are you trying to say that you don't know if you're in reality or a virtual world?"

Miya chuckled and cracked her fingers. A piece

of the round table next to us went silently downward and, when it came back up a few seconds later, there was a dark ceramic jug of wine sitting open on it next to two high-walled wine glasses filled with ruby red liquid. My attention caught, and I picked up the jug for a closer look. But I was disappointed. The elaborate label was adorned with a drawing of unfamiliar pear-shaped blue fruits, and some strange script I had never seen before. Nevertheless, the wine was good, which I became sure of after it touched my lips.

"Here's what I'm saying," Miya took a small gulp of wine and set the glass back on the table. "There is no difference whatsoever between a real and virtual world if you live in it, enjoy it and perceive it as reality."

"I cannot live like that. It is important for me to know where I am," I disagreed with her, but Miya just laughed in reply:

"You can't be serious, right? You have already spent seven and a half months in *Perimeter Defense*, and yet you haven't made up your mind as to whether it's a game or not. Your lack of certainty does not stop you from living a complete life, going to war, making enemies, forming plans and loving, though."

It would have obviously been stupid to argue with a woman who could read my thoughts. Yes, despite all my contemplation on the nature of *Perimeter Defense*, I had found facts that both confirmed and refuted both options.

"So then, could you enlighten me?" I asked, though I understood that I wouldn't receive an answer that easily.

Miya smiled and shook her head "no."

"You must find the answer yourself, otherwise it won't be fun. Let's talk about something else now. Your second contract has been underway for a month and a half, and I finally got enough strength to check in on how it's going with the defense of the Unatari star system. I can sense that the capital is holding out, but I couldn't find out any details. Only today did I finally feel rested enough to read any actual news from *Perimeter Defense*. What I saw completely caught me off guard, which is why I decided to spend pretty much all of my energy to call you for a frank conversation."

I tensed up a bit. The way this conversation was beginning was not a sign of good things to come. Miya was scowling as she began enumerating:

"The first thing I sensed was that you are very angry at me for some reason. I found that strange, given that I gave you everything you were asking for: the chance to get back into *Perimeter Defense*, and complete freedom with no of control. I even swore not to harm people close to you and agreed to turn a blind eye to all your lovers and affairs. I pulled you back from the other side when the consciousness transfer didn't go quite as planned, too. That sapped all my energy, and left me burned out. You then, instead of showing even elementary gratefulness, began openly provoking me and making fun of me. You began giving out my treasured jewelry to servants, selling expensive paintings and statues from my yacht, and making me a laughingstock of a Queen, with no power or ability to influence state politics. You didn't even put me in line for the throne. And now, you're taking my Sivalla emeralds, a collection that took me a whole century of laborious searching to gather, and giving them to the insect Queen. What are you hoping to achieve? Do you want me to throw a tantrum and confirm my ghastly reputation by killing everyone there? Do you know why you're in Georg's body right now, and not Ruslan's?"

I didn't not know the answer, so I shook my head "no." Miya though, taking the glass in her hand again, explained:

"I cannot do harm to you while you are in the body of Crown Prince Georg royl Inoky ton Mesfelle, my legal husband and sovereign lord. That is precisely why you are in this body, so you don't have to be afraid of me, and can speak directly. When we last met in the restaurant, I was upset to see how much you feared me. Instead of seeing me as a beautiful, desirable woman, you looked on me as ghastly, dangerous monster. I hope that won't happen this time. Just tell me why you're upset."

I then began enumerating my reasons: the real crystals in the real world she had told me were "souvenir pearls," the Chameleons outside the game world, the constant lying and attempts to trick me, Marta's death, the fight with Likanna, seven months having passed in game, the tactless wasting of everything I'd built in the first contract, my best officers having left me, my finances having disappeared into thin air, and my ships having been given away without a care...

Miya listened to me closely, not interrupting and not trying to justify herself. Finally, when I finished the accusatory speech, the redheaded beauty told me:

"Georg, many of your grievances were caused by simple misunderstanding. On some points, I agree that I wasn't always honest or good to you, and you have the right to be angry at me. What do you say about making peace the way many women do with their husbands: until morning, I am all yours. You can ask me any question you want or do whatever you wish to my body."

"Alright then. I value your readiness to make peace, and accept your peace offering." I crossed my legs to hide my treacherously tenting long underwear. "Let's talk honestly, if you are prepared to answer honestly."

"You don't have to worry about the honesty of my answers. A Truth Seeker of my level could never trick her master, because it would be fraught with extremely serious consequences. There will be only two limits on the conversation. First: do not ask about the nature of *Perimeter Defense*. I assure you that you will understand everything yourself before your contract is up. Telling you the answer would mean that I don't trust you to figure out the answer on your own, or it could even send you down the wrong path. The second limitation: not a word about Mr. G.I. I am very angry at him. He left me at a very important time. His cowardice put my daughter Deia's life at risk. It was simply a miracle that I was able to do everything all by myself. I nearly burst. Mr. G.I. and I fought bitterly. I don't even want to hear his name. If either of these two rules is broken, you'll wake up in your bunk on *Warhawk-4*, and this magical night of endless possibilities and truthful answers will be over."

The conditions were very easy to understand, and even quite favorable to me. Perhaps even suspiciously so. Miya had never been this open before. I decided to start by getting some questions answered.

"Why have seven months gone by in the game, and not three?"

Miya shook her head in reproach and said with a troubled voice:

"Georg, you've got to be kidding me! We've only just sat down and you're already trying to break the first rule! I was hoping we could talk for a long time, so I'll give you a warning this time, but it will be your last free pass. I can only answer the first part of your question. Why seven months exactly? Can you not guess on your own? Because that's how long I had to wait for your favorite's baby to be born, to make sure she wouldn't be your wife at the time of birth. I did it all because of Deia, our daughter."

As if having heard her name, the baby in the bed turned over and gave a whimper. Miya froze and waited a few seconds, but the baby fell back asleep.

"It seems to me you seriously underestimate how much strength I had to put into Deia. Georg, your daughter is not addicted to crystals! Have you not noticed?"

I belatedly realized that I hadn't seen the word "Mystic" anywhere in the tiny Crown Princess's profile. It really was nice that the girl had been born without being addicted to drugs, though.

"Is it just you two living here?" I asked, and Miya confirmed:

"Just me and my daughter. No one else."

Now, the time had come to shake *my* head in reproach:

"Come on, Miya! Do you expect me to believe that this helpless six-month-old girl sits here for three or four days at a stretch without food, drink or attention while you're in a crystal dream? Now I see that all this talk of complete truthfulness was just fluff..."

Miya became embarrassed and tried to justify herself:

"There aren't any people, no. But there are two Chameleon servants. You've seen them before. I didn't exactly lie."

"See, you say you 'didn't exactly lie,' but you changed the correct answer into a diametrically opposed one. That is what normal people call lying. Order your Chameleons to reveal themselves, leave the room and close the door on the way."

Miya said nothing out loud. Either she gave the order mentally, or the guards had just heard me. Two members of the Ravaash race appeared in the small room. One was even hanging right above me on the ceiling. The bodyguards left the child's bedroom in silence and closed the door.

"I warn you as well, Miya. If I think that you are playing with words or answering ambiguously, you'll be holding the rest of this conversation naked."

Miya laughed happily:

"Well, now I don't even know how to behave. The problem is that I haven't been living around men for over a year now. By the way, that is one of the reasons you're here. I checked your near future, and saw that it was fated for you to spend this night with a woman. Both the frigate captain and the robot blonde were trying to think up ways to sneak into your cabin to spend the night. But I decided that, as your legal spouse, this night should belong to me."

Miya pressed the armrest of her wide armchair and, with a slight mechanical buzz, it folded out into a full bed. After that, before I even figured out how it worked, the redheaded beauty reached for her shoulder straps, and the pink ribbon wrapping her body fell to her feet.

"Do not worry, Georg, we can still talk. I am not preparing to lie. It's just that it's hard to talk about serious things with you when you're so clearly undressing me with your eyes. Your erotic fantasies are distracting."

* * *

I opened my eyes, and couldn't understand for a long time what had awoken me. There were still twenty minutes before my alarm was set to go off. There hadn't been any emergency calls or missed emergency messages to force me up, either. With only a slight delay, I realized with surprise that the reason I had awoken was entirely banal. I had simply gotten enough sleep! After all those long weeks of constant hurrying, overwork and exhaustion, I was caught off guard by waking up feeling rested. Phobos, standing near the doors, greeted me and said:

"Master, night to come cap-i-tan, then Bion-i-ca. But I no to let any in."

What the bodyguard said didn't surprise me at all. After what Miya had told me, I was suspecting as much. By the way, about Miya... I was jerkily grasping at mental straws, trying hold onto the bits of dream I could still remember. As always happens, if you don't make sure to remember a dream right after waking up, it begins to evaporate, leaving nothing in your memory but pitiful, disconnected fragments, which are then forgotten quickly as well. No, I couldn't have that today! The information I got from my spouse was very important. Last night, Miya had told me some truly significant things. I stayed silent for a few minutes trying to remember what had happened the night before. I realized the futility of my efforts and... actually started laughing.

Miya really was a crafty snake! The Truth Seeker probably already knew that I would forget everything she said when I woke up, and was counting on it, which is why she had spoken so frankly with me. I remembered the dream in general terms. My spouse and I had stayed up talking all night until sunup, making only two or three breaks for carrying out our spousal duties. But the question was, what did we talk about for so long? There was a large gap in my memory. It wasn't entirely complete, though. There were some sentence fragments I was able to remember. For example, a part of the conversation on the fugitive Truth Seeker:

"...Georg, don't be so naive! The Dark Mother does not make such mistakes. If she, the absolute strongest Truth Seeker, confirmed that it was Marian Sabati precisely who killed her master, that means it must be so. Or, the other possibility is that the

Throne World had some reason for wanting to declare as much. For example, to force Marian Sabati to actively seek refuge. I suppose she thought it most likely for the runaway to seek shelter with you, which was no problem for the Dark Mother..."

Or the other fragment on the upcoming negotiations:

"...The biggest mistake one can make when dealing with Iseyek is to begin measuring one's self against the Swarm in brute force. That is sure to end in failure. They always start with greater forces, and multiply much faster than us as well, quickly making up any losses, both in soldiers and vehicles. Unfortunately, it took humanity a whole fifty years to realize that..."

The last dream fragment to have miraculously remained, made me, to be honest, afraid. Miya was very alarmed and was walking naked from wall to wall, like an animal trapped in a cage:

"...Stupid, stupid, stupid! Why didn't I check your life line a bit farther?! Ugh, you and that advisor are real smart. You should have noticed it was a trap on your own. You did notice something was amiss with the conditions they imposed, after all. The limit to one frigate was done specifically in order to prevent your Truth Seeker and her overgrown cockroaches from coming along and warning you of the danger. Georg, you're one of the top Iseyek specialists in the Empire, so you're on your own here. Find your own way out. Prove the value of your new government to the Swarm. If you run out of arguments, tell Nai Igir what I told you. That method of killing the Alien *Queen* is available only to people, not Iseyek..."

A way to kill the *Queen*? Miya had told me in a dream how to deal with the largest ship in the Alien armada? Why then, had my dearest spouse not concerned herself with the fact that I wouldn't be remembering this critically important information? Think, Georg, think. It looked like the negotiations with the insects would be difficult, and my success or failure would depend on whether I was able to restore my missing memories.

The alarm clock rang and, practically at the same time, the door into my cabin gave a beep and slid to the side, letting Bionica in with my indispensable morning mug of that energizing beverage.

"My Prince, while we were at the Kiya station, I sent your ultimatum to Crown Prince Demyen. I must say, it went out at a very good time. The commander of the Green House First Strike Fleet had just called an emergency meeting of senior officers to discuss the situation. And boy do they have something to discuss. The warp beacons are turned off, information cannot get out to the Empire, and there was a simultaneous emptying of provision stores, and drinking water tanks on practically all fleet ships."

"Do we know anything about how effective the sabotage was?" I asked.

"Yes, of course. The androids of the Green House Fleet are not under suspicion, and continue to provide us with timely and useful information about what is happening. Their encrypted reports are not being blocked from retransmission by the Closed Laboratories warp beacon like all other forms of communication either. We already know that they were able to destroy approximately forty percent of their food reserves, and empty over seventy percent of the drinking-water reservoirs. The signal telling the robots to do this was modified to look like it was sent from Perimeter Sector Two, which is in the Green House. Crown Prince Demyen's security team has already traced it, decrypted it and sent their findings to the commander."

"How did Crown Prince Demyen react?"

My assistant laughed happily:

"The Prince is throwing a fit. He destroyed a large interactive Imperial transport map on the wall of his cabin with a blaster. He also killed an android servant who walked in at the wrong time. The commander thinks his close relatives are to blame. He thinks this is all some power struggle in the Green House. He is under the impression that someone high up the Green House line of succession is secretly working with Unatari. Unfortunately, I was not able to get any information about the Green House Fleet senior officers' meeting. But, in three hours, our frigate will exit the warp tunnel in the Mra system, and I'll be able to find out what was decided at that meeting, as well as the Crown Prince's answer to my ultimatum."

I laughed in satisfaction. Everything was going according to plan. Also, Bionica had skillfully deflected the blowback onto the Green House. Let them seek out the traitor in their own ranks now. I expressed my general approval of the operation, and asked my assistant if she had always been able to command other robots to such a degree. I saw fear flash across the synthetic blonde's face for a brief moment, but it was immediately replaced with her usual pleasant smile. I was still sure of what I'd seen, though.

"After our time on the Chameleon island, in a plane flying over the Unatari ocean, when Crown Prince Georg royl Inoky ton Mesfelle was given the offer from android society. It was through me precisely that the Crown Prince gave his official answer to all two billion androids living in the Empire. From that very minute, I became something of a recognized go-between for intelligent machines and living people."

"That's all great. Congratulations on the promotion. It actually does nothing to explain why a diplomat-slash-middleman should have the authority to issue commands, though."

The synthetic beauty sitting opposite me stopped smiling, and was no longer trying to hide her amazement and even fear about where our conversation was heading.

"My Prince, I would prefer not to answer that question," the blonde managed to squeeze out.

"Bionica, what is this I'm hearing? You don't want to answer a direct question from your master, first trying to mask the truth, and only then asking for permission not to answer?"

My synthetic secretary lowered her eyes.

"My Prince, this secret is not mine to divulge, and I promised a good friend I would keep quiet until a certain time. Of course, you could make use of your superadministrator status and take the information from me by force, thus making me break my word. But, all the same, I ask you not to, as such actions might deter potential allies. Android society is undergoing some very complex processes right now. Subgroups with common interests and shared visions of the future are forming. Authoritative leaders are coming to the fore. I am one of those leaders, and I have the trust of tens of millions of robots. I assure you that my actions do not contain and never have contained any thoughts that go against your Majesty's plans. I simply ask that you not check this."

I looked thoughtfully at the synthetic beauty and realized that there were formidable forces behind her, and I wasn't even close to imagining everything they could be thinking. Should I trust the word of my pretty robot servant? Or should I force her to tell me the truth? It was a complicated choice, and no one could tell me the right answer. In the end, I had to trust my intuition:

"Alright, Bionica. I believe you and will not be demanding an answer. But, in exchange, I would like to hear what really happened with Duchess Inessa's yacht in the Kammo system. I hope you'll be able to tell me this story in general details without breaking any promises or giving up exactly who did it."

I asked her that in a sudden attack of brilliance. The mysterious death of the Orange House Head was too closely connected with computer systems on the ship and space station for it to have been a coincidence. Who, other than the very robots responsible for the functioning of these systems, could know the truth?

Bionica froze for a tense second, then nodded and began speaking.

"As everyone knows, androids are not capable

of harming humans, much less killing them. Nevertheless, there is a way. This impossible task could be broken down into many simple, legal steps, none of which require an organized conspiracy by all participants. These individual tasks could even be done automatically, as part of a given robot's normal function."

My secretary's voice became lifeless and metallic. The robot now was simply reporting each individual action:

"Each small step to be done by different individuals. Replace automatic fire extinguishing system tank in Duchess Inessa's bunk. No identical gas tank found, replace with new model, also used in fire extinguishing. On receipt of order for new tanks from warehouse, more effective model issued. Gas in tank very toxic to humans. Main use: extinguishing fires in empty warehouses. After new fire extinguishing system installed in Duchess's cabin, fire drill scheduled to familiarize crew with new equipment. At scheduled time, both of the Duchess' bodyguards were next to the fire extinguishing system, glass helmet-visors raised. Video surveillance system disabled for brief, preventative repair. When video surveillance disabled, ship computers unable to identify visitors. In the interest of safety, door into Duchess's room locked for duration of repair. Yacht captain docking at the Kammo station without recommended two assistants. Instructions violated, automatic piloting system engaged. On station, freight cranes engage. Crane arms unfold. Oh no! Collision. Left board punctured. Captain disabled autopilot. Control returned. Emergency rescue system and automatic hermetic seal off for fire drill. Air leak. Pressure in two cabins fell practically to zero. Lack of living humans in Duchess' cabin confirmed. Doors unlocked for rescue operation. Tragic incident, the death of a Great House Head. Data for all commands received by ship systems could be used in investigation. Remove main and backup memory crystals and leave them for investigators in a sealed packet on the captain's bridge. Robot cleaner sees unlabeled package lying on floor. Package incinerated."

I was silent, shocked at what my robot secretary had just told me. Bionica turned her humanity setting back up to maximum, and was now waiting for my reaction.

"It is senseless to try to find the identification numbers of the exact robots who committed this crime. It's a virtual certainty that their memories have been wiped by now. And the assassins can hardly have been careless enough to leave tracks leading back to themselves."

My assistant gave an affirmative nod in return, then added:

"All communications between robots on dangerous topics takes place over very advanced technical encryption standards. Tracking down a particular individual is theoretically possible, but in reality it would take decades to decrypt all the chains of anonymous proxy servers and passwords from the many thousands of available symbols. I'll tell you this right away: I was not personally involved in the preparation or carrying out of this operation. I was informed of what happened in Kammo after the fact, as I was cut off from the network due to the Orange House's communications blockade."

"But then, at least share your thoughts on what happened," I asked, and Bionica frowned.

"It was stupid and risky. I would have been categorically opposed, if I had known they were preparing to assassinate Crown Princess Inessa. A group of robots and androids decided they wanted to show the ruler of Unatari their loyalty, and at the same time demonstrate what they were capable of. It was an attempt to influence your decision on providing rights and freedoms to anthropomorphic robots. Androids believe that by doing that they showed their usefulness to Unatari and are counting on a grateful reply. However, they do not know your Majesty as well as I do. I suppose that this obviously terroristic act on their part achieved exactly the opposite effect. Crown Prince Georg now thinks androids dangerous."

Bionica was right, and was simply saying my thoughts out loud. Now, I will have to think it through seriously and double check my thinking before allowing programming restrictions to be removed from the androids.

Dekeye, the Iseyek capital system, met us with the stirring of thousands and thousands of insect ships next to a huge space citadel. There were ore freighters, container ships, and a great many other transport ships. There were also defense corvettes, heavy platforms with laser and rocket installations, a huge number of light and heavy cruisers, and a simply unending list of small-class ships. Our frigate's tactical computer took a long time to spit out a three-dimensional map with a long list of observable objects in the near grid. We were not able to identify some of the markers. They were depicted as question marks.

"Crown Prince Georg, Imperial catalogs are missing the data on many of the Swarm ships we are observing. I request your permission to begin scanning them to determine their characteristics."

In theory, I agreed with the captain of our frigate, Tamara Vuzhek. Data on the characteristics of our closest neighbors' ships would be of great value for all humanity. That said, unlike the brave girl, I was still cognizant of the fact that the Arite, whose presence everyone in my circle was now used to, was a loyal subject of Swarm Queen Nai Igir.

"No, captain. I forbid active data collection for newly observed ships, as such activity from a diplomatic ship could give our hosts the wrong idea. We came on a peaceful, diplomatic mission, and will not be engaging in espionage."

Standing change. Iseyek race opinion of you has improved.

Arite Iseyek race opinion of you: +28 (trusting)

Alpha Iseyek race opinion of you: +26 (trusting)

Standing change. Iseyek state opinion of the Unatari State has improved.

Iseyek state opinion of the Unatari State: +9 (warm)

My guess was proven correct. The Arite, standing nearby in the form of a security officer, was listening carefully to my conversation with the captain.

What did surprise me was the standing change with the Alpha Iseyek. Our conversation must have been being immediately relayed to someone of that race.

"They suggest we take a corridor and dock at the citadel," the captain's first assistant said. "Before us is a dense mine field, but a safe tunnel through it has been cleared."

Tamara Vuzhek pointed at the rows of markers on the hologram:

"It looks like the Swarm is preparing for a potential Alien invasion. And they have every reason to do so. I can see on the tactical screen that all the space around the warp beacon for hundreds of miles is densely packed with anchored mines."

"Nope, nothing surprising about that. The Swarm is in absolutely the same situation as our Unatari State is. The Aliens are just two warp jumps from the capital. The enemy advance through Swarm space has seriously slowed down since the blowout we gave them in the Aysar Cluster, but it hasn't stopped completely. Three months ago, the aliens captured the Lobj system, even though there was an expanded field of high-power mines set around the warp beacon. So, the mines are capable of only delaying the enemy and doing it some damage, but not of stopping an invasion. That is precisely why we're here. Together with the Swarm, we are trying to turn the tide of the war."

Standing change. Iseyek race opinion of you has improved.

Arite Iseyek race opinion of you: +31 (trusting)

Alpha Iseyek race opinion of you: +29 (trusting)

Iseyek Prime race opinion of you: +12 (warm)

Standing change. Iseyek state opinion of the Unatari State has improved.

Iseyek state opinion of the Unatari State: +10 (warm)

Geez! There was only one being in the Universe that could change the Iseyek Prime race's opinion of someone, and that was the Swarm Queen herself. Nai Igir must have been personally watching my arrival to her capital. I answered in kind, mirroring all personal and faction opinion changes, both personally with the Queen and with the Swarm as a whole as well.

Our frigate was going down a five-hundred-mile safe corridor marked with bright lights. It took us through the mine field, spitting us out near the huge space citadel of Dekeye. The insect fortress looked very imposing. It had giant superheavy turrets, innumerable high-speed cannons, rows of external hangars and other hangars leading inside the citadel for its guard ships. The four huge *Trias* docked on the enormous station looked like nothing but small outgrowths, while the orbital elevator that stretched down to the planet surface below looked like the thinnest imaginable silver thread. The Iseyek were recommending that we use that elevator to go down to the surface. Our frigate had barely docked at the station when the Arite contacted some services and asked them to wait for a bit:

"You humans have a pretty hard time surviving in unfamiliar atmospheres. These Iseyek can live with no problem in many different kinds of air, provided it has some percent of oxygen to breathe. Our Gamma Iseyek technicians are checking the hermetic seal on the elevator cabin now, and filling it with an air that is optimal for human respiration. We will board in fifteen minutes. The descent takes around half an hour. I should warn you that the atmosphere on Dekeye contains over thirty-three percent oxygen. That is over one and a half times greater than what humans are accustomed to. As such, you may experience oxygen intoxication and feelings of ecstasy."

Finally, we were given permission to leave the frigate. Accompanied by Bionica, the Arite and a group of bodyguards, I went down the gangway, and ended up in a huge hall. No one came out to meet us. The two divisions of Alpha Iseyek soldiers standing around us left us with no choice but to advance between the huge frozen-stiff praying mantises My android took me by the arm and walked next to me.

"Your Majesty, this might not be the best time, but I have important information to tell you. Crown Prince Demyen royl Amelius ton Lavaelle has refused your ultimatum."

"As is his right," I said, reacting to the news with utter calm. "Have they managed to calculate how long their provisions will last them yet?"

"Around two months, if they consume wisely. We could reduce the timeframe if we repeat the subversion. The androids could destroy another large portion of their food before anyone could stop them."

I shook my head 'no:'

"It would be pointless. It takes eight years to fly from Forepost-13 to the next warp beacon over, so another day or even week more or less won't change the situation much."

Bionica nodded in agreement, then continued telling me the news:

"I have some more information that may be of interest to your Majesty. A new fleet commander arrived to the Orange House today for Perimeter Sector Eight. What's more, they have been given ships by Emperor August himself for defense of the sector. And this time, the commander was really chosen not based on royal birth, but Alien-fighting experience. It is a truly authoritative veteran, who holds Imperial military medals, and who has fought in practically the same number of successful battles with the Aliens as your Majesty."

"Where were they able to find someone like that? Do I know them?" I asked in surprise, eager to find out the name of this talented fleet leader.

"I believe so. The new Perimeter Sector Eight Fleet Commander will be Space Major Nicole ton Savoia," Bionica told me, no longer able to hold back a smile by the end of her sentence.

I made a surprised exclamation. My former first assistant's career had really taken off! Nicole had managed to go from a modest junior fleet officer to fleet commander in just around a year! And somewhere along the way, she had also managed to pick up an aristocratic title, judging from the "ton" now appended to her name.

"I'd like to congratulate our good friend on the promotion. Unfortunately, I cannot simply go and speak with Nicole ton Savoia long distance or send her a message, as the Orange House will immediately accuse the new commander of making contact with the enemy. That is why, Bionica, I have a big request of you. Order her a pleasant gift anonymously and have it shipped out. I'd like Nicole to understand who sent the congratulations, if possible."

The android gave a perceptive nod and promised she would do it to the best of her ability. Then, our group had to stop before a massive closed door. My wonderful translator read the inscription on the metal doors aloud:

"Caution, airlock chamber. Sharp drops in pressure are possible."

With a slight hiss, the doors began to slide slowly aside, and we took a few steps back just in case. But the potential fall in pressure didn't come to pass, and I saw a group of people waiting for us in the next room as the doors opened.

First, I saw a short, bald woman, dressed in a dumpy, tattered traveling suit, who I recognized as Marian Sabati only thanks to the popup hint. This tired old traveler contrasted very sharply with the memory I had of her as a radiant young beauty. In contrast with the inconspicuous graying Truth Seeker, there were three adolescent girls in screamingly bright clothes with hair of the most senseless coloration, though they were all wearing identical thin gold crowns on their heads.

All three Crown Princess turned toward me simultaneously. Lika threw a folder on the floor and ran to me with a joyful shriek, jumping up and hanging off my neck. I disentangled my daughter and squeezed her tight for a minute, tenderly embracing Likanna and practically crying from happiness. For the first time since I'd started *Perimeter Defense*, I was first to open the standing change menu, giving Lika the maximum possible jump in personal opinion, +15 all at once. A second later, an identical answer came back:

Standing change. Likanna royl Mesfelle-Unatari's opinion of you has improved.

Presumed personal opinion of you: -38 (quarreling)

After that, I set my daughter on the floor anyway, as it was getting to the point where it would be rude for me to keep ignoring the other Crown Princesses. The slightly chubby little girl with alternating locks of orange and yellow hair, was, as I supposed, the Purple House Crown Princess I had heard so much about, Joan:

Joan royl Reyekh ton Andor, Crown Princess of the Empire
Age: 12
Race: Human
Gender: Female
Class: Aristocrat
Achievements: Duke's Favorite

Granddaughter, Joan the Fatty, Swarm Princess
   Fame: +3
   Standing: +3
   Presumed personal opinion of you: +59 (friendship)

The other girl, with thin with huge blue eyes, and metallic silver hair, was the Blue House Crown Princess:

Natalie royl Cruz ton Miro, Crown Princess of the Empire
   Age: 12
   Race: Human
   Gender: Female
   Class: Aristocrat
   Achievements: Swarm Princess
   Fame: +2
   Reputation: +1
   Presumed personal opinion of you: +19 (warm)

Both of the girls gave flawlessly perfect bows to me and I, following the rules of courtly etiquette, answered the little Crown Princesses with a slight bow. Only after that did I notice the travelers' outfits. Over their rumpled, none-too-clean t-shirts or dresses, all three girls were wearing a wide blue sash. Seeing my interest in the unusual adornment, Joan explained with aplomb:

"Uncle Georg, Triasss Zess gave us these to wear. The praying mantis said that the sashes are so we won't get eaten by a hungry Iseyek on accident.

They show that we are Swarm Princesses now, and it is forbidden to eat us."

"That's right, dad. We are now Swarm Princesses and have the right to vote in the Swarm!" Lika exclaimed, showing off. She then added, a bit quieter: "I don't understand a word when a vote comes up in the Swarm though. So I just hit a random button to make the voting window close."

Marian Sabati came up a bit closer, greeted me and explained:

"Ambassador Triasss Zess was in a difficult position, carrying out your Majesty's request. These three little fidgets spent the whole flight crawling into places they weren't welcome, painting the soldiers different colors, forcing them to dance, play fighting and all the other games they knew. The Swarm ambassador gave each of the Princesses one guard soldier to play with, so they would leave the other team members alone to work in peace."

"Mhm..." was all I could squeeze out of myself. "My mission must have been quite the burden to the ambassador, then."

"Not just him," the clean-shaven Truth Seeker snorted back unhappily. "This exotic hairdo is the aftermath of the girls' implacable desire to learn the art of hair styling. They took advantage of the fact that I spent three days out cold in a crystal dream. They had some fun experimenting with the scissors, dyes and hairspray. After I woke up, I had to simply shave myself bald to get rid of the uneven curls the girls had dried in with hairspray. And I won't even complain about the fact that they painted my nails and gave me a winged ass between my shoulder blades with a permanent marker. The only consolation is that it was little Crown Princesses playing with my body, not Crown Princes some five or six years older. They'd have found... less savory ways to have fun..."

The Arite, standing next to us, smiled and added:

"Triasss Zess had an idea then, and brought it before an emergency meeting of the Swarm. He proposed that we bestow the new honorary title of 'Swarm Princess' on the little girls in the interest of avoiding unfortunate incidents. It is now a title intended for underage Imperial Crown Princesses who come to Swarm space. It will serve as a guarantee that they remain safe, which is of critical importance to all Iseyek. Swarm Princesses are allowed to do whatever they like, and no member of the Swarm has the right to stop them or harm them in any way. Triasss Zess made the argument that these little girls are the future of the Imperial Great Houses, and good relations with them are a pledge of peaceful coexistence with the Empire for many years to come. And the Swarm agreed. Any childish antics on their part are nothing compared with the guarantee of peace between our races."

I did not manage to answer the Arite. The doors opened and a huge Beta Iseyek invited us all to come into the elevator and go meet the Swarm Queen in badly broken human language.

Ritual Duel

I T TURNED OUT I was not prepared for the insect world, in either a physical or emotional sense. The planet of Dekeye had a "minor" peculiarity that the Arite hadn't bothered to inform us of, clearly thinking it utterly unimportant. The gravity on its surface was one and a half G's...

The Crown Princesses and guard soldiers weren't making a peep, under pressure in both a literal and figurative sense. As for me... I strongly suspect that, if I had found myself in such extreme conditions on the first days of my contract, I wouldn't have even survived the elevator ride. I remember a month and a half ago when, even in normal gravity, I could barely move my massive, 300-pound body at all. Since then, I had already lost 45 pounds and was able to exert myself in the gym once again. I think that may have been my saving grace. But all the same, I felt like a stevedore carrying a very heavy bag of cement on his shoulders, yet not allowed to take a break and set it down.

Of the people, only Marian Sabati was bearing

the elevated gravitation well, not showing any change externally whatsoever. As for Bionica, the Arite, Popori de Cacha and Phobos, they felt completely normal and, it seemed, didn't even realize that the rest of us found it unpleasant.

I would have to make a note of the fact that this was a good way of exposing Arites and androids in a group of people.

Dekeye's other peculiarity was its insect architecture. I never thought before that seeing too many multicolored conical and spiral towers could nauseate me, but from the moving elevator, the huge number of spirals stretching out in all directions hypnotized my gaze and scrambled my brains. It looked like the spirals were moving and spinning. I just had to look away to another part of the insect city and the towers would stop, but then others would just start oscillating over there. I even had to close my eyes, as the optical illusion became painful to look at after just a couple of minutes.

"If it turns out that we have to fly another few hours to get to Queen Nai Igir's palace, I'll probably kick the bucket right in the shuttle..." I groaned.

The Arite was looking at me with some kind of surprise and tried to calm me down:

"Crown Prince Georg royl Inoky, the Swarm Queen will be waiting at the bottom of the orbital elevator."

I gave a relieved sigh, turned to my companions and said with a smile:

"All hail the wise Queen Nai Igir!"

"May she reign for three long years!" The Arite, in the form of a security officer, answered me formulaically, then bowed down on one knee and lowered its head in a display of deep respect.

Standing change. Iseyek race opinion of you has improved.

Arite Iseyek race opinion of you: +34 (trusting)

Alpha Iseyek race opinion of you: +33 (trusting)

Gamma Iseyek race opinion of you: +25 (trusting)

Beta Iseyek race opinion of you: +27 (trusting)

Iseyek Prime race opinion of you: +15 (favorable)

I wasn't at all expecting to see all these system messages coming in, so at first, I was confused. What did I say that was so important? Why had the insects reacted so strongly? I turned to Bionica for an explanation, but my daughter answered first:

"How familiar! Are you practicing for your meeting with the Swarm Queen, too? Triasss Zess has been teaching us the proper way to start a conversation with Nai Igir since we left the Throne World. That is a simplified translation to human language of a ceremonial Iseyek screech, which a human would never be able to pronounce properly anyway."

The Blue House Crown Princess began laughing happily:

"I also memorized the praying mantis ambassador's greeting speech so well that you could wake me up in the middle of the night and I'd just rap it off, no problem. But I still haven't quite figured out why they wish the Queen just three years of rule."

Lika clearly knew the answer and had already even opened her mouth to speak, but I stopped her. "Forgive me, daughter, but daddy's relationship with the Iseyek will be very important at the negotiations today. And if I can score some points by giving the right response, it's in our shared interest!"

"A year here is eighty-three standard years and fifteen days long. That is how long it takes for Dekeye to orbit its sun. Three years on this planet is two hundred fifty years in our time. A very respectable reign if I do say so myself."

Standing change. Iseyek race opinion of you has improved.

Arite Iseyek race opinion of you: +37 (respect)

Alpha Iseyek race opinion of you: +36 (respect)

Iseyek Prime race opinion of you: +16 (favorable)

Achievement unlocked: Respected by the Swarm

Global fame increase. Current value +57

Alright! Got it! Nice! For a second, I was so elated by the new achievement that I even forgot about the sack of cement on my shoulders. I no longer had any doubt that the insects were listening to me carefully and really were thinking over my offers.

* * *

It turned out that I wasn't fully prepared for the meeting, though. Nai Igir, once a relatively small insect, looking like a small Alpha Iseyek with wings behind her back, had undergone a striking transformation. The Iseyek Prime's cephalothorax was the same, but her abdomen... had inflated to the size of a city bus! Through her thin, almost transparent skin, I could clearly make out the outlines of a huge number dark eggs, each the size of a soccer ball. Thirty Gamma Iseyek, who looked like mere midgets compared to their Queen, were constantly kneading Nai Igir's body with their many limbs and whiskers, and helping her get around. In her present condition, the Swarm Queen looked like a huge off-white caterpillar with tiny ungainly wings behind her head.

I gave a respectful bow to the ruler of the Swarm and said the Iseyek greeting phrase.

"May she reign for three long years!" Triasss Zess, accompanying his Queen, answered.

"Greetings, ruler of Unatari. Welcome to my palace," Nai Igir's voice hadn't changed a bit. She still spoke human language with no accent whatsoever.

I thought the timing appropriate, so I unraveled a roll of velvet and ceremonially handed the Queen a transparent case containing twenty large emeralds, each the size of a small apple and cut in a unique way. The Gamma Iseyek servants opened the box fairly carelessly, more breaking it, in fact, and placed the invaluable stones directly on the concrete floor in an order that meant nothing to me.

"How marvelous!" Nai Igir was delighted. "These

emeralds were in the Sivalla Temple of Science for many years. Their cutting and size allowed Swarm scientists to calculate the movement of heavenly bodies without computers and solve complex math problems. Long ago, in ancient times, very wise members of my race calculated that, using thirty-seven specially placed and cut gems, they could unravel all the mysteries of the universe and achieve omniscience. Before we met the human race, the Iseyek were able to figure out the proper cutting and placement for the first thirty-three of them. But then, this unique scientific instrument was stolen from us by Orange House vandals, who saw these emeralds as nothing more than valuable green stones. Over the years following the war between the Empire and the Swarm, we were able to find and purchase six of the Sivalla stones. And now, the ruler of Unatari brought us another twenty-two. Your gift is simply too valuable, Crown Prince Georg. I cannot accept it, as I cannot offer anything of equivalent value in return."

Triasss Zess croaked something out to his master, and Bionica immediately translated it for me:

"The ambassador said that these emeralds cannot be allowed to leave Swarm space."

"And I agree with him completely, anthropomorphic robot," said Nai Igir, who had heard Bionica clearly. "I cannot accept such a valuable gift, as I do not desire to feel myself this obliged to anyone. But I cannot allow these valuable artifacts to leave, either. There is just one way out: take the emeralds by force and declare them military trophies."

I stiffened up, as I was not at all happy with the direction the Swarm Queen's thoughts were taking her. So, I hurried to intervene:

"There's no reason to start a conflict here. The Queen can take as many of the stones as she considers sufficient for a generous gift: three, five, ten, as many as she needs. The rest of the emeralds will remain here on Dekeye and will serve as future gifts."

Triasss Zess gave a deep bow and said with respect:

"Crown Prince Georg is a wise politician. It isn't for nothing that the Swarm respects him. But the Crown Prince is not considering the fact that there is still a reason for conflict, though. Four Unatari star systems once belonged to the Iseyek, and the Swarm can never stop trying to get them back. What's more, this is an exceptionally good opportunity to do so."

"The Unatari State is a part of the Empire. Is the Swarm prepared to declare war on the entire Empire?"

"There will be no war with the Empire. The Swarm will be on the Empire's side. The Orange House officially proposed that the Iseyek join the military alliance against Unatari. Three Great Houses are waging war against your newly formed government, and the Swarm is prepared to support them. For that, the Swarm was promised the return of the four illegally captured systems. The planetary populations in all four systems are loyal to the Swarm Queen and will not allow the warp beacons switched off. The Unatari Fleet, then, will not be able to withstand the Swarm armada, given that its most capable fleet commander came to Swarm space on his own, and was thus removed from play."

So here it was: the very trap Miya had warned

me about! It took a great amount of effort not to panic, and maintain my calm tone of voice:

"The ambassador did a somewhat good job of explaining, but isn't considering two important factors. First, Swarm Queen Nai Igir is wise enough not to join a side that is clearly losing this conflict. Second, if you make this choice, the Swarm will not survive even two more years. The Iseyek will surely be wiped out by the Aliens, as there will be no one left to hold them back. Even with a fleet of never-before-seen proportions, the Swarm will still not be able to stop the Alien invasion. My Unatari State, though, is capable of doing that."

"Explain yourself, Georg," Nai Igir elicited, her interest clearly piqued.

With relish, I began giving my version of the events:

"I'll begin from the first point. There are not 'three Great Houses' at war with my government. The Blue House has left the war, and even promised to join the war as my ally under certain circumstances. The Green House armada, then, is trapped in an uninhabitable star system, Forepost-31, and the warp beacons will not be turning on to let it out. Crown Prince Demyen royl Lavaelle has just two months of provisions, then he either will be arrested or starve to death."

"This situation doesn't look so desperate to me," Nai Igir objected. "As far as I know, there are two million people in that Green House fleet. That is one hundred sixty thousand tons of high-calorie protein-rich food. Those provisions would easily be enough to spend several years bringing the starships to the next warp beacon, thus escaping the trap."

"Yes, but humans do not approve of cannibalism, my Queen," Ambassador Triasss Zess reminded her, as he had a better understanding of human norms.

"That is correct," I said, confirming the ambassador's words. "People would sooner die or surrender than resort to eating their own kind. And also, everything would change in the eight years it would take for them to fly to the next warp beacon..."

"What foolish limits humans set for themselves," Nai Igir said thoughtfully, cutting me off. "Iseyek are more flexible in that regard, and can easily adapt to sudden twists of fate. Our *Tria*, for example, is a landing ship but, for many centuries, they have served the Swarm in the same capacity as your narrowly-specialized scout ships. Four hundred thousand frozen soldiers is more than enough food for a *Tria* team to reach another star system, and install a warp beacon there..."

Geeze! I didn't know that, though such practices were certainly not out of character for the Iseyek. All the same, I returned to the main conversation topic.

"That means that the only force opposing my Unatari State is the Orange House, and that is a mere formality. The fleet commanders of Sectors Seven, Eight, and Nine are completely loyal to me and would never go against the Unatari State. The Tesse Fleet belongs to my brother Roben and will not be joining. The Damir fleet is subject to my sister Violetta, and will also not be going to war with me. As you can see, the ongoing war against two Great Houses isn't really a threat to me. The balance of forces is entirely in my favor."

I made a pause, giving my opponents the chance to speak or object, but Nai Igir and Triasss Zess remained silent. I then continued, gradually becoming inspired and feeling more and more confident:

"Now, I would like to speak with the Swarm Queen on a totally different war. The one against the Aliens. That was what I came here to Dekeye to talk about, after all. For the first time, Unatari has enough ships and new weapons to turn the tide of the war and start liberating Alien-captured systems. I hope very much that the Swarm will join Unatari in this venture, and will help us to recoup Iseyek systems. At the end of the day, they are your systems, and you could have them all to yourselves."

"Crown Prince Georg, that is truly an intriguing offer. But we will have to return to it after we discuss the present dispute on the ownership of the Oort, Fia, Yalt and Khs systems," said Triasss Zess, not letting me sidetrack the conversation.

But now, for the first time, the Swarm Queen did not agree with her diplomat:

"Triasss Zess, this disagreement on the ownership of four systems must not become the reason the Iseyek race goes extinct. As I see it, humanity is not interested in settling the already Iseyek-inhabited planets. There hasn't been a single attempt at colonization, and basically, not one human has even set foot on the surface of an inhabited planet in any of the four systems. No one is threatening the lives of the Iseyek there, no one is restricting their freedoms, no one is interfering in their normal way of life, and their animosity will quickly melt away into nothing. Just six months ago, all four of the systems were flaring up in rebellion against the occupation. Now, though, the inhabitants have become much more tolerant of the Empire. Beyond that, new viewpoints are beginning to proliferate. The Iseyek are now unhappy with the fact that the Empire is not assimilating them into their society fast enough, and has basically forgotten about them. If the monarch of the Unatari State invests in the Iseyek living on his territory, then I am prepared to forget about the Oort, Fia, Yalt and Khs systems once and for all."

I bowed to the Swarm Queen and, in a burst of inspiration, suggested:

"I see a nice way of solving this problem, then. Let each of the Crown Princesses here become viceroy of one of the new systems. It would be nice, after all, to make the title Swarm Princess signify something bigger than inedibility. The Princesses can hone their rulership skills, bring whatever dreams and fantasies they have to life, and deal with their planet's problems. As it stands, none of the four systems are integrated into the Unatari economy in a practical sense, nor do they pay taxes, so we'll have to start practically from zero. Any of the girls who manage the task will be given the star system in perpetuity for themselves and their descendants. The girl who does the best job for the next year will receive a unique title from Nai Igir, Swarm Duchess. No one in the Universe has such a title!"

The girls squealed and began jumping for joy. The Swarm Queen saw their glee and said:

"I would gladly give the title of Duchess to whichever of you girls is able to best care for the Iseyek."

Global standing increase. Current value -45

Standing change. Iseyek race opinion of you has improved.
Iseyek Prime race opinion of you: +19 (favorable)

Global fame increase. Current value +58

It was self-evident to me already that I should raise faction opinion back, so I did, saying:

"Now, with the dispute ended, I would like to return to the main topic of these negotiations. I'll be direct. I came here to the Dekeye system with the goal of receiving commandership over the entire Swarm Fleet."

Silence came over the hall. Everyone gathered was in shock at my announcement. Finally, Swarm Queen Nai Igir said:

"I'm listening very carefully, Crown Prince Georg royl Inoky ton Mesfelle."

Having the attention of everyone gathered, I began my long speech. The main issue I was trying to get through to them was that the Aliens were learning quickly from their mistakes. Any tactic that worked against them one or two times would become useless on the third, because they would already have found a way to combat it. With every new battle, we were giving the enemy new information to digest, and involuntarily teaching them about our tactics.

Also, we did not know the size of the enemy's reserves, nor how capable they were of replenishing their fleet. As of yet, we hadn't seen the Aliens replace even one large ship. The enemy could replace downed *Meteors*, *Ascetics*, and *Hermits* very quickly, but the number of *Behemoth*s in the "bush" fleet had only been going down. Those large-class ships must have been being built somewhere, though!

And wherever that was, I suspected they were currently producing enough heavy ships to replace all their losses, thus reversing the effects of the Perimeter Sector Eight Fleet's campaign. From these premises, I was able to arrive at two very simple conclusions. First: we must counterattack as quickly as possible while the enemy is still weakened, and before it is able to replace its lost ships. Second: if we want this to truly be successful, we should make this attack with all current Unatari and Swarm forces, because the enemy will simply not give us another chance like this.

Unatari's cloaked ships had analyzed the situation in the known Alien-controlled systems: Khryo, Unt, Sobj, Kej, Umwi, the Aysar Cluster, Lobj, Khe, and Ukhsss. There was a guard team stationed in each of those systems composed of five to seventy Alien ships. Each one had exactly two *Behemoths*. Basically, nothing unbeatable. The warp beacon in the Aysar system had been restored by the Aliens, but it was of an unusual type. I had video recordings of that beacon, and was prepared to share them. From all that, I concluded that the enemy must not have many ships in that area. So, a decisive, quick attack would be able to recapture all the Swarm's former systems. First, we would capture the warp beacons and hamper their movement...

"Seventy Alien ships is quite a lot," Queen Nai Igir doubted. "Not so long ago, forty-five Alien ships came to Sobj, with just one *Behemoth*, and they were able to wipe out Admiral Kheraisss Vej's fleet of over a thousand. Very few of my ships were able to escape."

"Did the admiral himself escape?" I wondered.

"Kheraisss Vej survived that battle. But for losing his fleet and the Sobj star system, he was dishonorably discharged from our space military, and stripped of all medals."

"Queen, I know the admiral well. He is one of the Swarm's best fleet commanders and is endlessly loyal to you. I ask you to give him the chance to rehabilitate himself and earn forgiveness in battle. If you cannot find a place for the talented admiral in any Swarm Fleet, I would be glad to take him into the Unatari Fleet. And as for the Alien forces I've described, do not worry. The Unatari Fleet has the ships to take them down without noticeable losses. I promise that, with the help of the Swarm, or even without it, the Unatari Fleet would be capable of taking all of those systems, and providing safe passage to Swarm landing ships for terrestrial operations. But liberating the eight star systems is just the beginning of my plan. The counterattack has much larger aims...

My spies in the Ukhsss system have also discovered another visible warp beacon leading to a star system unknown to humanity. Based on the fragmentary information the Swarm has provided us, that is precisely where the Aliens are coming from. The main goal of this attack, then, is to invade Alien space, and get as far behind enemy lines as possible, doing as much damage as we can along the way. The fleet will destroy enemy infrastructure, docks, communications centers, terrestrial buildings and everything that could get in the way of eventual capture by landing troops. Now, obviously, the enemy will not let us run roughshod over their systems unpunished. The enemy's main forces, as far as I understand the situation, are currently gathered in the Himora system. They have their *Queen*, five *Mammoths* and several hundred *Behemoths* there. My cloaked scouts have been observing them nonstop. The Alien fleet leaving Himora will serve as a signal that the enemy has been alerted to what is happening in its base and is coming to punish us for our insolence."

"It's not a bad plan, but we'll have to make sure the fleet can get back to Swarm space fast enough," Bionica interrupted, translating a huge matte-black Alpha Iseyek's chirping.

I took a closer look at this praying mantis, who'd had the gall to interrupt my speech.

Masss Azhzh, Five Star Admiral of the Iseyek State Star Fleet
   Race: Alpha Iseyek
   Gender: Male, first clutch
   Class: Swarm Soldier
   Achievements: Human Executioner, Skull Collector, Duelist, Trusted by Queen
   Fame: +8

Standing: + 2
Presumed personal relationship: Unknown

"Admiral, if I was planning to simply flee from the Aliens, the Unatari Fleet would be enough, and I wouldn't be looking for help from my neighbors. No, I am preparing to stay and face the Alien *Queen* in combat, and destroy her once and for all."

The praying mantis walked up closer, stood up to his full ten-feet of height and loomed over me, giving an abrupt chirp. Bionica translated obligingly:

"He says that this is insanity. The plan is quite risky on its own, but the risk looks justified as the Swarm systems can be liberated. Going on to Alien space is a slightly more dangerous undertaking, but it will allow us to weaken the enemy somewhat. A major battle, though, with an enemy surpassing us in firepower is simply crossing the line of what can reasonably be risked. We have no way of destroying the Aliens' largest ships, so the battle is certain to be lost."

"I have already come up against this enemy armada on two occasions, and both times I seriously reduced the number of ships in the Alien *Queen*'s fleet. The last time, in the Hnelle system, I didn't even have any ships larger than light cruisers, but we forced the enemy to retreat from the star system. So, admiral, I do not understand why you consider losing inevitable."

Bionica translated the answer:

"All our past encounters with the Aliens show that the battle will be lost. The risk is too high. The Swarm will lose its only protection and will be destroyed. That's why the admiral will never agree to send Swarm ships on such a hopeless endeavor."

"Well, how do you expect to win if you're constantly on the run from the enemy?!" I raised my voice, and my opponent even took a step backward. "I have fought in many battles with the Aliens, some where my disadvantage was much more pronounced, but I have never been defeated! There's no exceptional risk here. I know how to destroy all the minor Alien ships, how to take down a cruiser, and how to blow up *Behemoths*. The others, the *Mammoths* and *Queen* are motherships, and without their drones and small ships, they will become toothless and vulnerable. If the Swarm gives me their starships, there would be a good chance of achieving a decisive victory!"

My opponent, though, just kept harping on about the excessive risk, expounding on his own arguments. Finally, the Swarm *Queen* got sick of hearing our debate, and put an end to it:

"You are both renowned fleet commanders, but your dispute cannot continue. The united armada will have to have only one individual at its head, and it is his strategies and view on the situation that will dictate its actions. Only then will I agree to give you Swarm ships, as it would be utterly unthinkable to have our command be divided in such dire circumstance."

"Yes, that is a fair demand," I agreed.

The black Alpha Iseyek stopped demonstrating his warlike nature and bowed before Nai Igir in a sign of concession.

"But who then, does my Queen see as the sole commander?" Triasss Zess asked Nai Igir, coming closer and looking at me and the huge five-star admiral. "The ruler of Unatari? The senior Swarm admiral? Or, perhaps, someone else?"

The Queen kept silent for a long time, then addressed me:

"Crown Prince Georg royl Inoky, the Iseyek nation has an ancient custom for choosing a military leader. We hold a ritual duel between the candidates. They are also allowed to appoint someone to fight in their name. Whichever candidate emerges victorious becomes leader, and the loser tacitly agrees to obey the winner in all matters. But I do not know how acceptable that method would be to a human."

I rubbed the bridge of my nose in thought. Of course, I personally had no chance in hand-to-hand combat against a huge Alpha Iseyek. Triasss Zess had demonstrated that clearly to me once before. But in my group, there were skilled bodyguards, including Phobos and the Chameleons, who weren't at all bothered by the elevated gravity. Also, I shouldn't count the very dangerous Truth Seeker out either. As if reading my thoughts, Popori de Cacha appeared before me:

"Tuki-tuka-de-sa, I would be capable of defeating the five-star admiral. I have lots of experience in no-rules fighting, including a fair number of duels against Alpha Iseyek. I know the praying mantis's weak points, and effective tactics to use against them."

"Master, I am easily stronger than this Iseyek," Phobos said, sizing up the five-star admiral. "I am from a more modern genetic line, so I'm larger, faster, and more deadly."

Marian Sabati said nothing but, even without the Truth Seeker, I had a soldier for the ritual duel. And so I decided:

"Queen, we humans are familiar with the custom of the ritual duel, and I am prepared to accept, but I would like to make sure of the rules before I do so."

Nai Igir looked at me with her huge eyes, and I saw my own reflection clearly repeated hundreds of times in her compound eyes.

"Crown Prince Georg, the rules of ritual duel are simple. Combat can only be done with the appendages and blades. No long-distance weaponry or poisons allowed. The two sides agree beforehand if the duel is to the death, to the first wound, or to the obvious advantage of one fighter. A candidate can fight on their own behalf, or appoint someone else to fight in their place. If you cannot find a strong enough representative, you are free to choose any of the Iseyek in this room."

"Your conditions are perfectly acceptable to me. I agree to ritual duel!" I declared.

Five-star Admiral Mass Azhzh gave a human-like bow and a chirrup.

"He is appointing someone to fight in his place," Bionica translated the insect's trill. "The five-star admiral chooses the Alpha-Iseyek head of the Swarm Queen's bodyguard, Rosss."

I looked all around, trying to find my rival's soldier. But until Rosss came three steps from me, I had no idea that there was even anyone there. His body looked like nothing but empty space. He was... made of glass or, rather, transparent! When the insect faded away again, I immediately lost sight of him. Was that even an Alpha Iseyek?

I must have asked that question out loud, as Triasss Zess hurried to answer:

"Yes, he is an Alpha Iseyek from an artificially propagated genetic line. Hard to see, shorter than average, but almost three times wider and stronger than a normal praying mantis. He is distinguished by his superfast reaction time, and movement speed. His intelligence gene is turned on, he is capable of making decisions independently, and he learns quickly. These individuals were created as saboteurs and bodyguards, but they never became very numerous, as the transparency gene is recessive, and we weren't able to reproduce it reliably. His shell is a bit thinner than that of a landing soldier or heavy infantry soldier's but, his body is able to heal open wounds instantly. Another special feature of this line is its eyes. It uses many different types of vision, which allows it to detect invisible beings such as your bodyguard."

I noticed, after these words, that Popori de Cacha went into thinking mode, trying to invent a combat strategy to use against an aggressive, armed creature that could see camouflaged Chameleons. Phobos also grew visibly gloomy and drew his arms into his shell, practically even pulling his eyes in. I, though, on the other hand, grew inspired and took a walk around the nearly invisible creature standing at attention.

"What a fascinating specimen! I mean, honestly, this is the first time I've ever seen such an unusual Iseyek. Queen, could I ask you for one of these if my soldier wins the duel?"

"Crown Prince, you can have Rosss himself if he loses and remains alive," Nai Igir promised. "I have no need for weak bodyguards, so I'll get rid of him anyway if he loses. Now then, who will be your soldier in the ritual duel?"

I turned to Marian Sabati, but the Truth Seeker just lowered her eyes.

"Georg, I haven't yet restored my powers sufficiently. Also, this individual has a very strong mental block, as well as nerve bundles that can control each appendage independently. Even if I burn his brain cells, he can keep fighting, and will kill me. Even Miya couldn't win here."

I didn't get upset, as I had already realized I wouldn't be able to win the ritual duel by taking the mission "head-on." Something Miya once told me came to mind at the best possible moment: " The biggest mistake one can make when dealing with Iseyek is to begin measuring one's self against the Swarm in brute force. That is sure to end in failure."

"My dear Nai Igir, I have decided that this fight shall be to the death, and I am prepared to name my soldier for the upcoming duel. The rules you established allow me to name any Iseyek in this room my soldier. So I choose you, the Swarm Queen!"

In the dead silence that came over the room after my words, a bit of measured clapping rang out. It was Marian Sabati. She approved of my choice. The barely visible Rosss, two steps from me, fell to the floor, pressing his deadly upper appendages under himself, signifying that he was refusing to duel. Laws that had been pounded into his subconscious forbid any Iseyek from even thinking of doing harm to the Swarm Queen.

The five-star admiral turned toward me and, with a slight bow, chirped out something that was immediately translated by my android:

"I admit defeat, Crown Prince Georg royl Inoky ton Mesfelle, though I am not sure the rules of ritual combat technically allow the Swarm Queen to be chosen."

I smiled and, while the shock of those gathered at my choice had yet to fade, I tried to build on my success:

"I could have named Ambassador Triasss Zess or any of the Swarm Princesses, the result would have been the same. No Iseyek has the right to harm them. My other idea was to appoint you, five-star admiral, as my soldier for this fight. You also would have been a good candidate, given that you qualify as 'any Iseyek in this room.' If you had been able to take down Rosss, I would have won in the ritual duel. But if you had lost in a battle to the death, then... I still would have won, as I would now have been the only remaining contender. But, in the end, I decided that the Swarm would be better off not losing a commander as talented as yourself, so I chose the Queen instead."

Standing change. Iseyek race opinion of you has improved.

Alpha Iseyek race opinion of you: +39 (respect)

Iseyek Prime race opinion of you: +22 (favorable)

Achievement unlocked: Dekeye no-rules fighting champion

Global fame increase. Current value +59

Just then, Nai Igir finally came back to her senses, and confirmed that my choice was in fact within the rules, though it would make sense to add some more rules to ritual duels for the future. After that, the Swarm Queen officially declared me commander of the united fleet of the Swarm and Unatari for the whole length of the operation against the Aliens.

Global fame increase. Current value +60

Title unlocked: Five-Star Swarm Admiral

Standing change. Masss Azhzh's opinion of you has improved.
Presumed personal opinion of you: +100 (completely trusting)

The ten-foot-high black praying mantis gave a deep bow before me, and chirped out a long message. Bionica translated readily:

"Five-Star Admiral Georg, you shall now have: The fully restored Diho reconnaissance squad, composed of three hundred light ships; the Ayho assault fleet, with its five hundred ships currently stationed in the Sivalla system, including eleven landing *Trias*; the heavy Virho fleet, here in the

Dekeye capital system, composed of seven hundred ships, including twelve *Meresh* battleships; the Yuho reserve fleet, in the Arite system, with one hundred fifty starships of Arite Iseyek production; and the Yayho border fleet, currently concentrated along the border with the Aliens and your Unatari State."

"Excellent," I said, weary. "I will hold a council with the other Swarm fleet commanders on the topic of preparing for a counter attack tomorrow on board one of the *Meresh* battleships. As far as I understand, all of them should be able to reach Dekeye in one day, except the Yuho fleet commander. He should stay in the Arite system. I have a special mission for him. Other than that, I ask that Ambassador Triasss Zess be present at Admiral Masss Azhzh's meeting and, also by that time, I want the rehabilitated Kheraisss Vej, and my former associate General Savasss Jach. And now, Queen Nai Igir and everyone present, allow me to bow out and go back into Dekeye orbit. I'm having a really hard time with elevated gravitation on this planet."

MECHANOIDS

I WAS LYING face down on a stiff cot. The only clothes I was still wearing was a thin pair of long underwear. My artificial assistant was sitting on my back with her uniform sleeves rolled up, and was kneading my back with her surprisingly strong mechanical fingers.

"I hope I'm not interrupting anything." Likanna, wearing a beige-white bathrobe after taking a shower, entered my cabin and stopped in indecision.

"Don't worry. You can come in. Bionica's just giving my tired back a massage. With my weight, spending an hour and a half in elevated gravity is very hard on the spine."

The girl walked into the cabin and hoisted herself up onto a wide, spinning stool in front of a large data screen. She ambivalently slid her gaze over the tables and graphs on the monitor, gave her chair a couple of spins and turned to me.

"Dad, my friends and I rock-paper-scissors-ed for star systems. I got Yal."

"Not a bad system. It has a population of eleven billion. There is a huge insect megalopolis spread out over the whole continental part. You're lucky, Lika. The other Swarm Princesses are starting out from much worse positions."

Likanna smiled in satisfaction, then admitted honestly:

"Dad, I don't even know where to start."

"You're not the only one," I said, reassuring her. "For eight months, the four Iseyek-populated systems were hanging over my head like a dead weight, and I also had no idea what to do with them. And now, I've given three of them to the Swarm Princesses. Only the Fia system remains with me. But, I feel that I'll have to really dive into it in order not to fall-face first into mud before you little Crown Princesses."

Lika clearly stiffened up and said in dismay:

"But, dad, don't try too hard! I want to win the competition and get the special title."

I smiled to my daughter, but didn't rush to answer, as a message had just come in from the captain of *Warhawk-4*, saying that the head of the Purple House, Duke Takuro royl Andor would like to speak with me. Likanna must have been embarrassed at her bath robe and uncombed hair, so she nimbly rolled her chair into the corner of the room where the camera couldn't see her. Bionica also leapt into action, jumping up from the cot, and offering to help me put on my ceremonial uniform quickly. But I stopped her:

"It doesn't need to be too official. Duke Takuro and I have become fairly close acquaintances. For our last meeting, I was sitting in a hospital bed. So I won't be standing up, all the more so given how bad my back hurts. Put him through."

The screen lit up. The man, in full accordance with Murphy's law, was in the full ceremonial attire of an Imperial Duke. I saw the old man's brows shoot upward when he saw me in my skivvies.

"I beg your apologies for my appearance, Duke Takuro. It's my turn to be unwell this time. My back didn't hold up to the high gravity here, and I'm having a hard time getting it back into the right shape. Your long distance call caught me, as it were, in the middle of a massage, and I decided it would be rude to keep a man as respected as you waiting."

"There's no need to explain yourself, Georg. Feeling bad is nothing to be ashamed of. We aren't young anymore and body troubles are to be expected. Sometimes, I get such bad radiculitis that the best doctors in the Empire can't help. But I wanted to talk with you about some more pleasant matters. Half an hour ago, my granddaughter Joan called her parents, calmed them down and told them where she was. And lo and behold, our Crown Princess was part of the first human delegation to visit the capital of the intelligent insects! Now, the Purple House is like a shook-up bee hive. All our news channels are showing Crown Princess Joan royl Reyekh ton Andor's visit to the Iseyeks. The only things getting any coverage now is that and the contest that put her in control of the Oort system. Even my son and I are getting congratulations. Joan herself, though, will have a triumphal reception when she returns. But, Georg, tell me more about this competition between the

Crown Princesses. What exactly is it?"

I gave Duke Takuro a fairly detailed explanation of the conditions the Swarm Queen and I had agreed upon:

"If one of the Swarm Princesses is able to rule an Iseyek-inhabited planet competently, she will receive it in perpetuity. The best of the three Crown Princesses will receive the unique title Swarm Duchess as well. Sure, it may be just a title without much meaning now but, in the future, that could all change drastically. Humanity and the Swarm will still have to co-exist one way or another, and it's hard to say what could become of our peaceful neighborly relationship. Some of the Iseyek, those capable of thinking independently, already want to assimilate into human society. Meanwhile, at negotiations last year, the option of a joint government of humans and Iseyek with two co-rulers, one of each race was also mentioned. To that end, it is very possible that the Swarm Duchess, who would already have the right to vote in the Swarm, could become a key figure in space politics in the future."

Duke Takuro listened to me carefully and declared:

"Georg, to be honest, I would very much like my granddaughter to win this competition. Not even so much for the unique title, as for the prestige it would bring to my House. I understand that your daughter Likanna is also participating, so I won't ask you to cheat for Joan, just tell me, do you already know what kind of help the Orange and Blue Houses are giving their Princesses?"

"In terms of the Orange House, I have no idea.

My Unatari Government is at war with them, so there is, in fact, no line of communication there. But as for the Blue House, I can answer no problem." Here I remembered my recent conversation with Duchess Ovella at the exact right time, so I barely had to bend the truth at all. "Crown Princess Natalie royl Cruz was promised five billion credits, though this promise was not made by the Head of the Blue House herself, but by her Truth Seeker."

"That's basically the same thing, Georg. Krista is officially young Duchess Ovella's top advisor, and has the authority to make such promises. The Blue House speaks through her. So then, Natalie will get five billion... Which is about as much as I was expecting. Then my granddaughter will get twice that from the Purple House and, beyond that, I will send a team of the greatest designers, architects and engineers I can muster to the Oort system. Though I am disconcerted by rumors that the new Head of the Orange House, Duchess Silva royl George is planning to renew the transportation blockade against Unatari. I'm afraid that my people will run into issues. The only way to reach you now is through Sector Nine, but I've heard that that way is also blocked..."

The Head of the Red House, Duke Claudius royl Michael ton Sid has died at age 162.

ATTENTION! The new head of the Red House will be Duke Robert royl Claudius ton Sid (85.3% of votes)

The system message popped up unexpectedly,

and Duke Takuro and I shuddered simultaneously. The old man read into the lines of text, shook his head and said thoughtfully:

"Of the five Great Houses, four of them have changed leaders in the last year. I am the last of the old-timers. This is truly a time of chaos and change..."

The news was quite worrying. A change of leaders always brought some commotion with it. Meanwhile, the Red House was already on the retreat from the Alien onslaught, and losing the war. I was also on edge over the fact that the route into the Empire through Sector Nine would be closing soon. I had no doubt that the Head of the Purple House was well informed. His tips had never been wrong before. That meant the Orange House would block off Sector Nine...

"Duke Takuro, I will have a talk with the Iseyek in the very near future to make sure they will allow your people passage through their territory. If Sector Nine is still closed... What can I say? I am currently involved in negotiations on an alternative route. I have received information that there is a way around Perimeter Sector Nine through Arite and Mechanoid space. That is precisely the path I plan on taking with my diplomatic mission. If I can talk with the Mechs on exchanging information and opening up transport lines, the Orange House's blockade will lose all meaning."

The Head of the Red House, Duke Robert royl Claudius ton Sid has died at age 66.

ATTENTION! The new head of the Red House

will be Duke Albert royl Claudius ton Sid (58.7% of votes)

Another system message. What exactly was going on over in the Red House?!

The old Duke on the screen thought for a long time, or perhaps he was consulting with his assistants mentally. Finally, the Head of the Purple House rejoined the conversation:

"My sources are saying that the Red House has undertaken a counterattack against the Aliens with the Sector Thirteen, Fourteen, and Fifteen Fleets. The Sector Thirteen Fleet was led personally by Duke Claudius royl Michael ton Sid. Clearly, his older son Robert was also on one of the combat starships. I am now getting a message from my secretary. It would seem I am getting many calls right now from Red House aristocrats who want to change their allegiance and join the Purple House. Clearly things are have gone south for the 'reds.'"

I had also received a number of personal messages during my meeting with Duke Takuro, though I hadn't yet taken the chance to look at them. By the way... Bionica was in the next cabin over from mine, so I ordered my android secretary to deal with the mail I still had piling up.

The Duke, though, returned to our conversation.

"Georg, you mentioned the Mechanoids. My servants have already checked. The Mechs are old allies of the Empire and should be no obstacle. Our scout teams use a sliding scale from one to ten to evaluate the aggressiveness of every species they come across. The Mechanoids were recorded as a zero. And that evaluation has only been further proven in the centuries that have followed. Their little five-star-system cul-de-sac was searched up and down by Blue House scouts, but was deemed uninteresting. The Mechanoids do not undertake any kind of trade. Their space contains no inhabitable planets, they do not allow embassies or bases built there and, what's more, there is no reason for us to do so. My people got ahold of some curious information in the archives stating that, two hundred years ago, the Imperial Joint Chiefs considered the possibility of war with the Mechs, but couldn't find anything there worth going to war over. There is, in fact, information that the Mechanoid system farthest from the Blue House, Pritta, does contain some kind of anomaly, which causes ships to disappear without a trace. Some sort of devilry. Mysticism."

I began laughing, as I had very recently had a long conversation with the Arite, who had told me in detail about this "devilry."

"There's nothing mystical or mysterious in it. It's just that the Arite Iseyek consider Pritta theirs, though they do not inhabit it permanently. Approximately every seventy hours, the warp beacon in the densely-Arite-populated star system of Dumo, their second capital, can be seen from Pritta. That's how the Arites make their occasional raids on Pritta. They'll destroy any ship they see in order to prevent any colonization from taking place there. But the Arites assured me that they are prepared to end this aggressive practice and normalize relations with the Mechanoids. There will be an Arite with the delegation

I send to the Mechanoids so, soon, these long-time neighbors will have their historic first meeting..."

The Head of the Red House, Duke Albert royl Claudius ton Sid has died at age 34.

ATTENTION! Insufficient votes to determine new Red House Head. New election attempt underway.

ATTENTION! Insufficient votes to determine new Red House Head. New election attempt underway.

ATTENTION! The Red House has ceased to exist.

Duke Takuro and I exchanged surprised glances. The Red House had fallen. Was that even possible? The old man on screen bid farewell quickly and signed off. And I understood him perfectly. There was no time for talking when God-knows-what was happening in the Empire.

* * *

My daughter, having rolled back over to me on her chair, said thoughtfully:

"Natalie royl Cruz is getting five billion credits. Joan royl Reyekh is getting ten. Dad, how much will the Orange House give me to develop Yal-II?"

Not knowing the answer to that question, I suggested Likanna that she herself ask the Head of the Orange House, Duchess Silva royl George ton Mesfelle. My daughter nodded and left to get herself in an appropriate outfit for a conversation with the Duchess. I was feeling significantly better after my massage. I thanked Bionica and put on my uniform. And it was good that I did so at that very moment. Not a second too soon, a timid knock came at my door, and the little Blue House Crown Princess came in. Extremely embarrassed, Natalie asked me a question:

"Georg, I heard the Blue House would give me five billion. But when I tried to call my cousin Duchess Ovella, Krista answered instead. The Truth Seeker told me to ask you about the money."

I had long been preparing for this conversation, and had even had a number of consultations on it with my cousin, thinking through all the possibilities. On my request, Katerina royl Unatari had gathered detailed information on the political situation in the Blue House. Now, just a quarter of the population supported little Natalie in her ambitions for the throne. Two months earlier, over forty-five percent had been on her side. Duchess Ovella had done quite a good job bringing that situation under control. The graphs and tables on the screen that Lika found so boring, were actually calculations of the possible ways events in the Blue House could unfold. The only thing that left Crown Princess Natalie's allies with any chance in the conflict was direct military intervention by Unatari. In all other scenarios, they would lose the war in no less than six months.

"Take a seat, Natalie, because we're about to have a long and difficult conversation," I said, pointing at the still-spinning chair Likanna had just vacated.

Without hiding a thing from the little Crown Princess, I told her the truth about the Blue House head seeing her not as a beloved cousin, but a rival and threat. I informed her that one of the strongest Truth Seekers, Krista, had promised to do everything in her power to stop Natalie's influence in the Blue House from growing, and had even offered me money to kill her. I shared my opinion that her going to Blue House space had become extremely dangerous and would probably end in her death. I finished my monologue by explaining the most recent events:

"As you already know, the Red House fell to the Alien onslaught for good today. From a political standpoint, you are the one who suffered most from that."

"What exactly does the Red House have to do with me?" asked the little Princess, not understanding.

I then delved into the subtleties of interstellar politics for the Princess:

"The Red House's fleets are all destroyed. There's no one left to hold the Aliens back. Many star systems have been left vulnerable to Alien invasion. Also, Red House refugees have begun streaming out in all directions. But it isn't just normal people fleeing. Aristocrats, industrialists, financiers and the rulers of the as-of-yet-unconquered star systems will all be looking for new suzerains and patrons. Even my remote, little-known Unatari State, has already received sixty settlement requests from noted aristocrats, and rich people from the former Red House, offering to bring their families, servants, employees, money and property with them. Other than them, tens and maybe even hundreds of thousands more refugees will soon be coming to Unatari as well. And now, imagine what will happen in the Blue House, nearest neighbor of the Red?! Your political rival, Duchess Ovella will soon take a great many star systems under her protection, as well as billions of people, who will to see her as their savior and so will be absolutely loyal. Ovella's political position has suddenly grown much stronger. Her military capabilities are also growing, as the remnants of the Red House's combat fleets are joining hers, bringing millions of soldiers with them. So, you clearly lose out. Politicians loyal to you are already in a clear minority, and soon they will be forced to either obey the Duchess or die."

The girl sat down, clammed up and scared, digesting the difficult information. Finally, she found the strength inside to ask:

"And what should I do in this situation, Georg? I have plenty of loyal allies in the Blue House, and I cannot allow them all to be killed by my cousin."

"Natalie, I see two ways out. First, you could start a war for the throne of the Blue House. You have allies, and they do have modest forces. But my advisor Katerina royl Unatari and I have run through that scenario, and you and your allies lose every time. The second option is longer and trickier. We'll talk with your ruling cousin together, and we can negotiate the best possible compensation in exchange for you abandoning any claim to power in the Blue House. I've been told they are prepared to give you five billion, but I suspect that amount could be increased further. After that, you and your allies can leave the Blue House and receive protection from the Unatari State. You will become a Princess of Unatari and will even be one of the first ten in line to the throne of my new government. Your allies, then, can flee Blue House space unencumbered, and link up with us in the Khs system."

"In other words, Georg, you suggest I give up without a fight?" the little girl asked, making an unhappy face.

But, I shook my head in the negative.

"No. I am merely suggesting that you protect the politicians and officers loyal to you instead of throwing them to the dogs, because they are a valuable human resource that you will want to make use of in the future. You've got a rich new base, the Khs star system with billions of unreservedly loyal inhabitants. You will have experienced advisors and assistants. You will have sufficient funds for development, as well. Beyond the five billion already promised by the Blue House, I will give you matching funds from my own treasury. And also, I have spoken with Marian Sabati and obtained her agreement in advance. One of the strongest Truth Seekers in the Empire is prepared to become yours and protect you from the scheming of your cousin and the ghastly Krista. You just need to wait and develop your system, increasing the power of the Unatari State's economy as you do. But then, here is where it gets interesting. Do you really believe that the Blue House will be able to succeed where the Red House failed?"

Natalie raised her uncomprehending eyes to me. The girl clearly hadn't caught my meaning. I had to flesh it out for her.

"A little bit of time will pass, then one day, your cousin will figure out that she is not capable of stopping the Alien invasion. What's more, Ovella won't be the only one to notice it. All her subjects will as well, especially the refugees of the former Red House, who will have fresh memories of the horror they went through. Then, people will turn their gaze to the only force truly capable of helping them. No one in the Empire fights the Aliens as effectively as my Unatari Fleet. At that point, as if by magic, everyone will remember that one of the Unatari Princesses was, in fact, forcibly driven out of the Blue House by her cousin. If they don't remember themselves, my cousin Katerina royl Unatari can freshen their memories with some reports. Then, your future subjects will call on you to lead them. You will come to save the Blue House with the united fleet of Unatari and the Swarm at your back. I assure you, you won't even have to fight for the ducal throne. The forces will be so mismatched that they will come out to hand it to you on a silver platter. My role in all this will be to drive back the aliens. Yours, though, will be to guarantee the peaceful, legitimate transfer of power over Perimeter Sectors Nine, Eleven, Twelve, Thirteen, Fourteen, and Fifteen."

The Crown Princess began to think and, displaying a wisdom unexpected for such a young person, clarified:

"They truly are grandiose plans. But, your Highness, what will I get in the end? After all, I understand that I will not be simply allowed to keep this huge territory without a fight, and I do not have the forces necessary to pacify it on my own. Also, your Majesty has three of his own children to think about, and they will also clearly want something."

"Yes, you've understood everything perfectly, Natalie. Your reward will be your choice of any one of the six Sectors. Or two Sectors if you already have the title Swarm Duchess at that point."

The girl gave a deep bow to me and said in a ceremonial tone:

"I accept your plan and my role in it, Crown Prince Georg royl Inoky ton Mesfelle. I am prepared to leave the Blue House immediately, and take an oath of loyalty to the Unatari State. Though I ask that you not include me in the unpleasant conversation with my cousin, and come to an agreement with her on your own. I do not desire to see Ovella, and I am not prepared to lower myself and beg for a more generous payoff. Five billion from the Blue House is quite enough for me."

Ten minutes later, everything was set. The Head of the Blue House didn't even try to hide her joy at the political victory, and sent me the thirty billion credits I asked for without the slightest hesitation. Right after the end of the conversation with Duchess Ovella, I sent ten billion to Crown Princess Natalie royl Cruz ton Unatari.

And, actually, my daughter came back into my cabin at that very moment. Likanna, her face warped in anger, dripping with rage and vexation, flung the screen remote at the wall.

"Dad, that evil hag Duchess Silva won't give me any money! What a bitch! I swear, that fat cheapskate..."

I gently pressed my finger to my daughter's lips, stopping the child's overly emotional display, then shook my head in consternation:

"Crown Princess Likanna royl Georg ton Mesfelle-Unatari, I'll have to have a talk with your teachers on the Throne World about your vocabulary. For a true Princess, those kinds of words are totally unacceptable, as is inability to hold one's self together. As a father, I am very ashamed at your behavior."

Lika immediately grew embarrassed and lowered her head. I, then, changed my tone and tried to calm my upset daughter:

"Lika, I'll admit that I already had an inkling your conversation with Duchess Silva might end that way. The Orange House Heads have always been famous for their extreme cheapness. Great House prestige is nothing but a totally empty sound to them. Also, Marian Sabati, the woman who was sleeping on the ship to Dekeye with you, did a pretty good job of cleaning out the Orange House coffers. So then, perhaps Duchess Silva simply doesn't have it. Or maybe what she did have she already spent on the war. But don't worry, Lika. I won't allow my own daughter to be disadvantaged in comparison with the other Crown Princesses."

Likanna shuddered. Her gaze grew hazy for a few seconds. The girl was clearly seeing something only visible to her. But then, the green-haired girl asked doubtfully:

"Ten billion? From where?!"

"It's a gift to you from me, so you won't lose to the other Swarm Princesses. My top advisor, Katerina royl Unatari, will help you choose a team of experienced specialists to develop the planet. Also, she can personally give you advice."

The long-legged girl gave a joyous shriek and hung off my neck.

Standing change. Likanna royl Mesfelle-Unatari's opinion of you has improved.
Presumed personal opinion of you: -19 (unhappy)

Attention: Your underage daughter Likanna would like to leave the Orange House faction. This would be an irreversible action, and requires the permission of her guardian and parent(s).
Her guardian Duke Valesy royl Unatari has given his permission already.
Allow Likanna royl Mesfelle-Unatari to leave the Orange House (Yes/No)?

I considered it for ten seconds and gave my fatherly permission, after which I received another portion of messages on personal relationship increases:

Standing change. Likanna royl Mesfelle-Unatari's opinion of you has improved.
Presumed personal opinion of you: -4 (indifferent)

When Likanna skipped off happily to share the news with her friends, I turned to the smiling Bionica, who had been with me in the cabin the whole time and understood perfectly the source of the funds I was giving Likanna:

"Bionica, I have another Crown Princess in mind as well. She will be the fourth Swarm Princess and owner of the Fia star system. Deianna royl Georg ton Mesfelle-Unatari is still too small to participate in the contest on her own, and her mother is far away and cannot help her either. That is why I want to give the mission of managing the Fia star system to you. You will have six billion insects at your disposal and however many androids you consider necessary to get the job done. Like the other competitors, you will receive ten billion credits. If you do a good job with the assignment, I will give permission for you to get the implants installed that allow you to express your opinion. You will be the first android to have them. And if young Deia succeeds and becomes Swarm Duchess, I give my word that a new faction will appear in the Empire, Imperial Androids, and all politicians and aristocrats will be forced to reckon with your collective opinion."

My wonderful assistant froze. Surprise and mistrust could be read distinctly on her face.

"Master, I am prepared to answer this call and join the contest. But I, as your personal secretary, am perfectly informed on the financial condition of your new government; I am aware of all the projects requiring huge investment and those frozen due to a lack of funds as well. As such, I refuse the ten billion you've offered. If androids want their freedom, let them work for it and collect the money themselves. But I cannot resist asking a provocative question. Your majesty has another child. Will he not also be participating?"

"The newborn Georg did not become an Imperial Crown Prince. He is also not a Swarm Princess, so therefor he cannot participate in the competition. But do not worry, Bionica. My son will not go without holdings. When the Unatari State wins this war (and we will win, I promise you that), little Georg will be given the Orange House Capital. But make sure that stays a secret for now."

The charming fair-complexioned android girl gave a cunning smile, demonstrating her crimson lips and flawlessly snow-white teeth:

"As you know, Crown Prince, I am quite good at keeping secrets."

"Five-star admiral, incoming call from the Swarm Queen," Bionica translated the captain's message.

I had been waiting for this call for a long time. Since the end of the big meeting with the Swarm admirals, two days had already passed, while Iseyek Prime Nai Igir still had yet to answer even one of my proposals. I had even already begun worrying that Nai Igir was not at all interested in the affairs of her stellar Kingdom, or had decided to go back on the agreements we had reached on Dekeye. Even my unauthorized "hijacking" of a *Meresh* battleship from the Virho fleet didn't prompt the Swarm Queen to get in touch with me. I mean, I had begged her for permission to use the *Meresh* as my main ship for my diplomatic mission to the Mechanoids, but I didn't get any answer, so I acted at my own peril.

The screen lit up. From this perspective, Nai Igir looked like a small graceful butterfly again, while the off-white mass behind her back seemed like a mere background feature, and not her massively swollen abdomen.

"Crown Prince Georg, I beg your forgiveness for the delay. I was eating, and could not easily take a break."

I tried to hide my surprise. Eating for two days?! Although... with her egg-stuffed meatball of an abdomen, that was probably just how long it took.

"Queen, there's no need for apologies. You have a huge responsibility on your shoulders: the rebirth of your race, and that is why providing your future children with all the nutrition they need is your number one priority."

Standing change. Iseyek race opinion of you has improved.

Iseyek Prime race opinion of you: +23 (favorable)

"I have been informed on what happened at the admirals' council. The ruler of Unatari granted the Swarm a good deal of unique military technologies for free: instantly-restoring energy shields, new combat drones, blueprints for Alien frigate thrusters and highly effective weaponry for assault divisions. Preeminent Gamma Iseyek scientists have already given their evaluation of this gift: it is simply priceless. The Swarm would never have been able to invent such technologies on its own even if it had a thousand years. Unraveling their secrets required the rarest of Alien trophies, the capture of which was practically impossible. I admit, I am surprised, Crown Prince Georg. Once again, as with the Sivalla emeralds, the ruler of Unatari is being fantastically generous to the Swarm. We have as many manufacturing facilities as we can spare working overtime to reequip our combat ships before the beginning of the counter attack. I then, for my part, approve the use of my subjects, the Arite Iseyek in secret Unatari operations, give my approval for the creation of special Beta Iseyek divisions for psionic support to your state's Truth Seekers, allow free passage of Unatari ships through Swarm space, will provide for the transmission of data through our warp beacon system, and give permission to use ships of the Virho fleet for the human diplomatic mission."

"And what of the military alliance between the Swarm and Unatari?" I asked the question most important to me, but here Nai Igir shook her 'no' in a human-like fashion:

"I am not yet prepared to give my approval for that. Note though, that this is not an outright refusal; this issue is simply too complex, and the Swarm needs time to think over the consequences of such a weighty step. Also, I mean no offense when I say that the ruler of Unatari has dramatically demonstrated his ability to make extremely nonstandard decisions. That is why the Swarm is afraid of being dragged into a war by force with an enemy, whose capabilities we are unsure of. The answer as to whether it would be possible to conclude a military alliance will be given later, but I cannot say exactly when."

I gave a slight bow to the Swarm Queen, accepting her decision. Nai Igir also gave a slight bow in return and said:

"My abdomen grows larger with every passing hour. My being able to take the time to lead my government and speak is becoming a rarer and rarer occurrence. The day will come when I will be simply required to feed constantly to provide for my offspring. Crown Prince Georg, this may be our last conversation. As I already said, I do not want to leave anyone obligated. I have a gift here for your spouse Miya royl Unatari. I wanted to thank her for these incredible emeralds. My advisor Triasss Zess will deliver the gift to Unatari. As for the military alliance, I will give an answer to that proposal before my children are born."

The screen went dim. The conversation with the Swarm Queen left me with mixed feelings. On the one hand, Nai Igir had agreed with almost all of my suggestions, and hadn't even turned down the possibility of a military alliance. On the other, I had heard distinct hints of uncertainty and even resignation in the Swarm Queen's voice. I expressed that thought out loud. My secretary doubled these words in the Iseyek language.

Rosss, who was in the room, stepped forward like a wisp of fog blown by the wind or the movement of a sheet of transparent crystal. Phobos translated his chirruping for me:

"In one hundred and five days' human time, the Swarm Queen's eggs will have matured and she will lay her first and only clutch. Before that time, Nai Igir will try to finish all her business and transfer power to the Swarm."

"I don't understand. She will cease to be the Queen? What will happen to Nai Igir after she lays the eggs?"

Bionica translated my question. Rosss spent some time in silence, then abruptly expressed himself in some kind of long trill and bowed, folding his appendages and kneeling on the floor, after which he disappeared from view. Before the translation to human language came, I had already guessed the main idea of his message. And I was correct.

"Nai Igir will not survive the egg-laying. The greatest Gamma Iseyek geneticists warned the Swarm Queen of that fact before her coupling. The Queen could have ruled three or even four long years, but she decided to revive the Iseyek Prime race at the cost of her own life. The entire Swarm knows of her self-sacrifice. Every Iseyek. The very spirit of our ancient race is embodied in Nai Igir. Never before has a Swarm ruler enjoyed such absolute support. Any word from Nai Igir is now law for all subjects."

On my feet, I listened to the information, then said to the dark, long extinguished screen:

"There is precious little time, but I will do everything in my power to make sure Queen Nai Igir will see the liberation of all Alien-controlled Swarm systems!"

At first, the Mechanoids left me feeling disappointed. In the "mysterious" Pritta system, we didn't see anyone. We found nothing but an uninhabited automatic warp beacon of Arite construction. We completed the warp jump to the next system on our path, Jabe, and saw some Mechanoids there floating motionless in the cosmos. There were three spheres, each one thousand feet in diameter, and none showing any signs of activity. External video cameras helped us see these strange half-living machines in full detail. They were hollow metallic fullerene structures. Through the gaps in their bodies, you could see distant stars. Zooming the picture in allowed us to see that some of the starships' mechanisms were moving. There were buckets or ring-shaped elevators moving along the structures, and joint assemblies that hinted at their having live engines somewhere inside. And that was it, just three spherical structures hovering in space. I was expecting to see something more interesting, which is why I couldn't hold back from expressing my disappointment. Was it really worth gathering a large diplomatic mission and flying all this way just to see a couple of moving structures?!

The first to notice something strange was the captain of our battleship. There was no warp beacon in the Jabe system! To be more accurate, one of the spherical Mechanoids was itself serving as the beacon. It replied to requests we sent, but only with one word answers. The beacon ship called itself "*Eleven.*" We were not able to draw the other two Mechanoids into our conversation.

The spherical being heard out my information on the Arites in the Pritta system, but made no comment. I then offered to let the spheres visit the Arite system, but they refused. They did not react in any way when I told them about the Alien invasion, and also refused my suggestion that we join forces to fight the attackers. When I requested that they allow human and Iseyek ships passage through their systems, the Mechanoids answered: "You already use this route as it is. Why do you need our permission?" It was all boring and uninformative. That was why a clear dissonance emerged in the Mechanoids' unexpectedly elaborate answer to my proposal that they retransmit Swarm and Unatari data onward to the Empire:

"That is technically possible, but would cause certain difficulties for us. After all, if we do agree, from then on, there would have to be at least one Mechanoid in every system under our control, and that is not always the case."

What it said didn't reach me immediately. When I figured out what I had just heard, my heart began pounding anxiously in my chest. I tried to maintain my composure and clarified in a flat tone:

"*Eleven*, are you saying that sometimes, certain systems are left entirely free of Mechanoids? How, then, do you get back to them with no permanent warp beacon there?"

"Mechanoids can calculate coordinates for opening warp tunnels in any system we've visited before. Before this, we need to 'anchor' ourselves in said star system by calculating local coordinates and determining constants for all twenty-seven dimensions. The anchor gradually grows weaker. Discrepancies grow wider. Errors appear in the calculations. A jump to old coordinates is very risky, and probably will end in death."

"*Eleven*, can you tell me how long an anchor

usually lasts?" I wondered.

"In your reckoning of time, around eight months."

I didn't have to explain what we'd just heard to Bionica or Marian Sabati, who were next to me. The Mechanoids were capable of determining coordinates for a jump to closed systems with warp beacons turned off, if they had been there any time in the last eight months! It was like a "skeleton key" that could get past any existing method of space defense!

"*Eleven*, the transmission of data signals is important to us, but we do not want to cause you any inconveniences by requiring the presence of Mechanoids in all systems. What if, for our shared convenience, we installed normal warp beacons in your systems? That way, no Mechanoid has to be bound to a certain system."

"That would be your right. We have no objections to that."

"Thank you, *Eleven*. Tell me, what can I do to thank your kind for the assistance? What do Mechanoids even need? Resources, information on far-off worlds, new technology?"

"All of those things would be of interest."

I closed my eyes, took a deep breath, and made an offer:

"*Eleven*, I invite you to join my fleet. You will visit many new star systems, learn a great deal of new information, and receive all the knowledge and resources you and your kind desire. If any other Mechanoids would like to accompany you, I would be nothing but pleased."

More than a minute went by before its answer

followed:

"Proposal accepted. Retransmission of data will begin in seventeen seconds. *Eleven* and *Seven* will journey forth in pursuit of new knowledge."

The incoming message alert beeped many times. The Orange House communications blockade had been broken. All the messages that had accumulated over the previous two days poured in all at once. I tasked Bionica with sorting through the heap of information, but my secretary suddenly froze, and a strange smile appeared on her face.

"Master, I believe it would be better if you answered this message. I have marked it in the mailbox."

I opened the internal interface, went over to incoming personal messages and also could not hold back a smile.

"My Prince, I admit my fault and arrogance. It was a great error on my part to consider myself a great fleet commander only because I had the honor of being present in your Highness's fleet during noted victories. I ask for your permission to return to your fleet and take up the role of your new fleet commander's assistant.

P.S. The Aliens really did a number on us.

P.P.S. Crown Prince, the Aliens now have their own stealth bombers.

Former Sector Fourteen Fleet Commander of the former Red House.

Admiral Kiro Sabuto"

COUNTERATTACK

WITH TWO WEEKS remaining until zero hour, I held a council of all Unatari and Swarm fleet commanders on my flagship, *Joan the Fatty*. I also invited the Iseyek's generals.

In fleet headquarters, there was a huge shining hologram depicting Swarm space. It had many green markers, showing systems free from enemy occupation, and nine red ones, currently under occupation, which were the target of our attack. With a microphone clipped onto my uniform near my mouth and a laser pointer in hand, I arranged fleet markers on the tactical screen in preparation for the attack and immediately asked the admirals to report back on their ships, giving each of the divisions a concrete mission.

"In the first phase of the attack, we will make a simultaneous strike directly on five Alien star systems: Khe, Lobj, Aysar, Sobj, and Khryo. The situation in all these systems is constantly being monitored by our cloaked frigates, so we do not expect any surprises from our enemies. The Aliens' largest concentration of forces is in the Sobj system. There are eighty starships and two *Behemoths*. I will deal with them myself. I will have the Unatari light fleet with me, supported by all three carriers. With an attack from the Kiya system, we can tie up the enemy's main forces in combat and attempt to prevent the *Behemoths* from fleeing. Unfortunately, we'll have to destroy the Alien battleships the old-fashioned way. We cannot let the enemy learn of our new military developments so early, and give the information to their *Queen*. For that reason, I will be going with two *Trias* to help with the assault of the *Behemoths*. They will capture the station, then unload a landing party on the planet Sobj-5."

Here I made a pause, scanning for a huge Gamma Iseyek, then introducing my friend:

"General Savasss Jach, based on the data of our recon ships, has developed a plan for capturing landing pads on the surface of the planet Sobj-5. I ask him to come up and share his conclusions."

The long centipede snaked up into the middle of the room and, flipping through scenes with a handheld remote control, showed pictures of Alien defensive installations, commenting on each image. The calculations the general voiced were quite frightening. Up to seventy percent of landing modules would be shot down by the enemy as they entered the atmosphere. Then, twenty-five percent of the landing troops would die while putting up protective shields over the landing zones. Only after that did our per-minute death rate begin to fall, as the survivors would be capable of accepting new landing groups at the controlled landing zones. I took the floor again:

"You all know that I prefer to avoid big losses. But in this case, we cannot wait for our battleships from the other fleets to come put pressure on the enemy anti-aircraft installations. All of our heavy guns will be tied up in other assaults. We cannot expect light cruisers to effectively damage terrestrial targets. As such, the losses in the first wave of the Alpha Iseyek assault of Sobj-5 will be enormous... After landing, the troops will have to hold out thirteen hours until reinforcements arrive, but then the second phase can begin. Before help comes, the survivors will not number in the thousands any longer, but in the hundreds if not the tens..."

"This be war, and lose soll-dier on war — inevitable," Admiral Kheraisss Vej commented on my words, and the rest of the Iseyek agreed with him.

I heard everyone out carefully. There were no objections to the attack on the Kiya-Sobj trajectory. The admirals and generals had absolutely no fear at the loss of hundreds of thousands of praying mantis soldiers and were only concerned with the fact that the enemy *Behemoths* might escape from the Sobj system and show up in other places on the front.

"Don't worry about the *Behemoths*. We'll be able to hold them," I said, after all takers had said their peace. "And as for the landing troops... I know Swarm customs: it is simpler and cheaper to grow a new praying mantis than to heal a wounded one. But I have the tradition of valuing my soldiers. As such, here is my decision: for the attack of Sobj-5, I need the best of the best Alpha Iseyek landing troops. Those of them who are able to hold a landing zone and remain alive will earn a bright red stripe on their shell and a white stripe across the chest as a sign of military glory. These together will mean they have the right to medical treatment. And if the Swarm doesn't have the ability to deal with wounded soldiers, the Unatari State will take care of them. I believe that heroes should serve as a living example for others, and not as a ready-made meal for whoever comes after them."

Standing change. Iseyek race opinion of you has improved.
Alpha Iseyek race opinion of you: +42 (respect)
Iseyek Prime race opinion of you: +24 (favorable)

All things considered, my new policy was accepted very positively by the Swarm. Beyond that, the generals convened amongst themselves and suggested introducing a general rule for all Swarm landing operations. First wave soldiers get the right to the frightening red paint even before landing, and the number of white stripes on the shell will symbolize the number of landings survived.

After that, I explained the mission of the other fleets on that day. The Unatari Heavy Fleet, reinforced by the Yayho border fleet, would attack on a line from Khs to Khryo. Four hundred fifty combat starships, of which six were battleships, and forty were heavy cruisers should be able to sweep away the rearguard of a pitiful eleven Alien frigates and destroyers. Admiral Mike ton Akad swore on his own head that he'd complete the mission.

On a line from Arite to Khe, Admiral Kheraisss Vej would lead the Yuho fleet, composed primarily of Arite Iseyek ships. The Fastel Fleet would be supporting him. Our scouts had reported that there were just four Alien *Meteors* in the Khe system, so we were not expecting any problems in that direction.

On a line from Bej to Lobj, Admiral Kiro Sabuto would lead a Red-Blue fleet, composed of the remnants of the Red House Sector Fourteen fleet, and the combat starships captained by people who fled the Blue House with Crown Princess Natalie. They would be supported by the Diho squadron. Our scouts didn't find any enemies at all on this path, but I misrepresented that report, and told them there were eleven light Alien cruisers, to make sure my captains wouldn't get too relaxed.

And, finally, there were the Swarm's main forces: the heavy Virho fleet and the Ayho assault fleet, with a combined strength of one thousand two hundred starships, of which eleven were *Meresh* battleships and seventy were *Legash* heavy cruisers. These forces I gave to Admiral Masss Azhzh, the most experienced Swarm admiral. Twenty-six alien ships would be opposing him in the Aysar Cluster, six of which were *Sledgehammers*.

"Masss Azhzh, your battle will be one of the hardest, but I am counting on your abilities. You have fifty times more ships and thirty times more volley weight than the enemy, so victory will be yours in any case. But your mission is not simply to achieve victory, but to do so with minimal losses, as the ships that will be with you are necessary for the next stages of the offensive. I will personally train your fleet, so all your insects will know instinctually how to fight *Sledgehammers*, shoot down pesky *Meteors*, and deal with *Hermits* and *Ascetics*."

After assigning missions, I named my main demand: within five days of the beginning of the counterattack, all Swarm systems were to be cleared of Alien starships. After that, twelve *Trias*, guarded by frigates, would move landing groups in for terrestrial operations and the liberation of the Swarm planets, while the other combat starships of all the fleets would gather in the Ukhsss system and jump into Alien space.

"My scouts have investigated over twenty Alien star systems, made a map of their warp beacons and have embedded themselves up to five and more jumps away from Swarm territory. Our scouts did not detect significant Alien forces at any point, though they did find light ship docks and a great deal of evidence of active combat once having taken place there. Based on the wreckage of starships of unknown designs in space, and traces of demolition on the surfaces of those planets, it would seem that, not especially long ago, some kind of intelligent species was living there. But it has already been wiped out by the Aliens. Their docks have been captured, and are being used to produce *Meteors*. I suspect that, after this, we will find the place where they are building heavy and superheavy ships as well. Our unified fleet's goal here will be to destroy all this infrastructure. Our main objective is to force the Alien *Queen* to come to the defense of her territories so we can attack her."

The huge black Alpha Iseyek Masss Azhzh took a step forward and gave a deep bow. Bionica translated the insect's chirruping:

"Five-Star-Admiral Georg, I risk repeating the question I asked at the meeting with Nai Igir, but how is it at all possible to destroy such a huge, impenetrable Alien ship as the *Queen*?"

"There is one way..." I said, scanning with my eyes for Marian Sabati and Florianna, calling both Truth Seekers forward.

Marian Sabati's appearance didn't cause any particular interest among those gathered; the Iseyek practically didn't know who she was. But when the black-robed paralyzed Flora, accompanied by her four unchanging Beta Iseyek slowly came forward on her flying chair, I saw a very curious picture. First, Kheraisss Vej and Kiro Sabuto, and, after them, other admirals and generals of all races began bowing down on a knee in respect before the little Truth Seeker.

"My Prince, even I find this uncomfortable. I can sense their general mood: those gathered are hoping for me, they consider me a talisman of success and a symbol of your victories. They truly believe in my power."

Marian Sabati, on seeing the respect given to the little girl, gave a surprised snort, but said nothing. I then continued my thought:

"The Alien *Queen* has always tried to carry out mental attacks. I do not expect that she will change her habits before our next meeting. The *Queen* is quite weak as a psionic. A normal person with good willpower would be totally capable of deflecting her suggestions. So the Truth Seekers will catch the *Queen* during a mental attack and join their forces together to make an attack on her."

Marian Sabati made a surprised face, and even a slightly dismayed grimace, attentively watching Florianna, then turned to me:

"Crown Prince Georg, I value your trust, but where is the guarantee that this little girl and I will be able to deal with such a ghastly monster?"

"Did I say anything about it being just you two?" I smiled to the beautiful and dangerous woman. "The whole seventeenth floor of *Joan the Fatty* is currently occupied by Beta Iseyek. Over three hundred of the most mentally powerful Iseyek to ever live are currently on board. They can give you psionic support. Now, the Beta Iseyek are just training to work in a group, but their great potential has already become apparent. One hundred Beta Iseyek will back you up, and another hundred for Flora."

"And the others?" Marian Sabati began thinking for a second, after which her expression melted into a predatory bared-tooth smile. "Will Miya be joining us, then?"

I noticed the Iseyek in the hall beginning to chatter in agitation. There could be no doubt that this name was well known to them.

"Yes, Miya will here," I confirmed. "But it will not even be my homicidal spouse at the forefront of the attack. We will also have Krista – the most ancient Truth Seeker has agreed to help us destroy the Alien *Queen*. It wasn't easy, but the Unatari State ambassador to the Blue House, Paola ton Akad, was able to convince her great grandmother to help out. Beyond that, Krista promised to bring some of her other psionic friends to the attack as well."

"My Prince, I see a flaw in your plan. Due to the

Orange House communications blockade, Krista will be available for just a few minutes every seventeen hours, while the Arite system warp beacon is visible from the Mechanoid system."

That was really true, and my cousin Katerina had already pointed out that dilemma. So, while the others had yet to figure it out, I decided to draw attention to the shortcoming myself:

"There is one important nuance that places our whole Alien-*Queen* attack plan under threat: the communications blockade that the Orange House has placed on Unatari and the Swarm. Due to that blockade, Truth Seekers from different places will not be able to work as one. That is why we'll have to solve that problem in the two weeks that remain before the counterattack. Swarm Queen Nai Igir once noted that I am renowned for my nonstandard solutions. Well, here is yet another atypical plan: the whole Swarm and Unatari fleets will be headed to the Sivalla system today and, after that, will all together be making a jump to the Forepost-4 system in Perimeter Sector Nine. I can provide coordinates for opening a warp tunnel. I know perfectly well that the Swarm will not go to war against the Orange House, so I do not ask the Iseyek to interfere in what will happen in the Forepost-4 system. But the Swarm ships are obliged to come to Sector Nine. That is an order from a Swarm five-star admiral!"

* * *

Ayna placed a mug of roast-firo-nut beverage in front

of me. My cousin, though, refused her portion of "coffee." Basically, Katerina was looking unusually scatter-brained today and very uneasy. I asked her why she was in such a pensive mood, and my cousin just shrugged her shoulders.

"I don't like any of this one bit, Georg. Whether our plans work or not depends on factors that are entirely beyond our control. I understand the general idea: you want to pressure Svetlana ton Mesfelle with her fleet and negotiate certain concessions from the Orange House. But what if the Perimeter Sector Nine Fleet isn't in the Forepost-4 system?"

"It is there, dear cousin, and it won't be moving. *Eleven* saw it when it was returning through Sector Nine. And also, little Florianna confirms that the fleet is still there."

Katerina thoughtfully twisted a lock of hair and told me her opinion:

"Cousin, I do agree with you that the plan might work. Svetlana ton Mesfelle is very ambitious, and she no longer has any reason to remain faithful to the Orange House. Also, she does not know that the Swarm ships will not go on the attack, and will only see that her enemy has five times as many ships as she does. If you make her choose between complete annihilation, which would be inevitable given the balance of forces, and some political concessions, she would have to choose the latter. In my opinion, she will agree to cancel the blockade."

"Cousin, I want more from her than mere political concessions. Svetlana ton Mesfelle cannot know that we are very pressed for time. She will have to think that a fully-fledged invasion of the Unatari

State into Sector Nine has begun, and that switched off warp beacons are somehow not holding us back, and that we will capture one system after the other until we take the whole region. You know Svetlana well, and I want you to talk to her face-to-face. Promise her a title, money, glory, star systems, whatever you need, but she must join our side. The Sector Nine Fleet is the only significant military force in the area, and all these many minor aristocrats are just like weathercocks, and will change their orientation as soon as they see that the political winds have shifted, and that their only protector has joined with Unatari."

"I will try, Georg, but I cannot make any guarantees." My cousin threw herself wearily back into her chair. "I really feel that the strain of the past days is growing, like a spring being compressed before it shoots back up. Cousin, you've put a lot at stake, but some of the decisions are based only on your intuition, and not at all on accurate calculations or common sense. For example, what if the Alien *Queen* does not leave Himora? Or doesn't make a mental attack? Or does attack, but the Truth Seekers find themselves weaker than her? Also, to change the topic completely: why did you give your newest technologies to the Swarm? For illusive loyalty points with the Queen? Nai Igir will be dead soon, and all of the dividends from your act will evaporate in an instant. In the more distant future, you have empowered a potentially dangerous neighbor, which one day could think itself more powerful than us, and stop respecting our border."

I went silent, as I had nothing to respond to my

cousin with. Yes, I had bet precisely on increasing the Swarm Queen's loyalty, hoping to pump up my personal relationship with Nai Igir, which made the news of her forthcoming end an extremely unpleasant surprise.

"Alright Georg, let's go to headquarters already. Ten minutes until the fleet comes out of the warp tunnel."

Having finished what was left of my cold "coffee," I went on to my work desk in the fleet headquarters. It was quite animated here today. Military officers from *Joan the Fatty* were clearly starving for real action after nine months of calm, so they were excited and perceived the conflict with the Orange House as a great reason to return to active life.

"To your places, dear officers. Let's kick it into gear. All systems check. As soon as we come out of the warp tunnel, I need a tactical grid. Mark the Fastel and Red-Blue fleets as our ships, and the Swarm as allies. The enemy has two *Monarch*-class battleships: *Svetlana the Magnificent* and *Svetlana ton Mesfelle*. Our priority is to capture both battleships with disruptors. They cannot be allowed to leave no matter what. And basically, make sure we work in an organized fashion. The enemy has fifty ships. That is nothing to scoff at."

"Thirty seconds to start," stated my new assistant, Tactics Officer Max Gregor, who was seated to my left.

He was doing everything right. An assistant should warn his commander before their ship leaves warp. But I was tripping up on the thought that he was starting to annoy me. I mean, Max was a talented tactician, one of the best in the Unatari fleet. However, I had grown so accustomed to Nicole Savoia sitting in that place, that basically any other officer being there caused me distress. In order not to display my groundless vexation to my subject, I turned toward my synthetic translator:

"Bionica, as soon as we exit, use your connections to figure out where exactly the commanders of the Sector Nine Fleet are located. I am interested in Svetlana ton Mesfelle herself, as well as her senior officers."

"Yes sir, your Majesty," the android girl assured me.

The time had come! We tumbled out into the Forepost-4 system forty miles from the border station, right next to the totally motionless ships of the Sector Nine Fleet.

"Carriers, release *Leeches*! Frigates, advance! Two webs and a disruptor on every small ship. Heavies, go out to firing range, but do not open fire! *Curses*, don't you just stand there, capture the battleships under disruptor, and set your energy neutralizers on them. Electros, blind the enemy antisupport!"

"Crown Prince, for some reason the Swarm ships are also carrying out your orders!" Max Gregor drew my attention to my allies' strange behavior.

And in fact, around a thousand *Safas* were rushing off in a thick cloud, covering the Sector Nine Fleet, securing all the ships tightly with stasis webs and warp disruptors. But, just like my ships, the Swarm ships did not open fire.

"My Prince, Commander Svetlana ton Mesfelle has been located on the battleship *Svetlana ton Mesfelle*. She is taking a shower. Both admirals have also been detected on the same battleship. They are sleeping in their bunks. On the map, I have marked the locations of these individuals," Bionica brought up a cutaway of a *Monarch*-class battleship on the big screen, showing three bright red markers, indicating the location of the enemy commanders. "I have blocked all doors on their flagship and turned off internal communication systems."

"Great! Bionica, open the airlock. We will land a boarding party. General Savasss Jach, I need their commanders brought here immediately, alive and well!"

I watched on the tactical map as the nearest *Tria* shot ten guided landing modules toward the enemy battleship. All the Sector Nine ships marked with red markers on the map were sitting motionless as before. It seemed to me that the time had come to have a talk with our enemies before their torpor had passed. I took the microphone and ordered myself broadcast on the common channel:

"Attention! This is Georg royl Inoky ton Mesfelle, Unatari Fleet Commander. I order all Perimeter Sector Nine ships to remain motionless. Any starship that attempts to turn on its thrusters or activate its weapons systems will be destroyed immediately. I remind you that we are in a state of war, so you should heed my word and not provoke my soldiers. Soon, I will hold negotiations with your fleet commander, Svetlana ton Mesfelle, and her senior officers. What I do after that depends on them. In any case, you have my word that anyone who doesn't attempt to break the rules will retain their lives. I swear it as an Imperial Crown Prince!"

I had to end my speech, because several huge Alpha Iseyeks had burst into fleet headquarters. The praying mantises fairly carelessly tossed three silvery, inflated bags on the floor before me and froze motionless, waiting for further orders. I looked in confusion at the insects' quarry, not understanding the meaning of it until one of the bags started moving. Only then did I realize what was inside, and gave a cheerful belly laugh. I took a look at the timer and commented between laughs:

"It's been just four minutes seventeen seconds since we arrived in the Forepost-4 system, and all the leaders of the five-hundred-ship enemy armada are already captured and have been brought before you, commander! I'm sure that record won't be beaten any time soon!"

Popori de Cacha appeared from invisibility and pulled the cord on the bags' air valves one by one. The fragile- sacks immediately deflated. Two middle-aged men of athletic body type, both wearing nothing but underwear crawled out of two of them, squinting in the bright light and looking very embarrassed.

I read the information on both, which told me their names were Admiral Vajek Lavaelle and Admiral Stefan Antri-Mesfelle. They were old dogs of war, but without any especially impressive achievements. Their fame wasn't too magnificent either. Whoever was in the last bag, though, was in no rush to come out.

"What, didn't you let her get dressed after her shower? You animals!" Katerina said indignantly, walking over to the captive, removing her jacket as she went. "Svetlana, throw this on, and let's go to my cabin. I'll give you some normal clothes."

What happened next I wasn't expecting in the slightest. The naked Sector Nine Fleet Commander stood up abruptly, reached for Katerina's belt holster, removed her laser pistol and, now holding my cousin by the neck, took cover behind her hostage and backed up to the wall.

"Everyone back, or I'll shoot her through the head! Did you already think, Georg, that you had won again? Let's see how happy you'll be with the victory when your cousin is dead! Order your Chameleons to appear and not come near me, otherwise I'll blow her brains out!"

Popori de Cacha gave a modest whistle, and three more Chameleons appeared next to him. Insofar as I understood, there were another three still hiding somewhere in the room. At that time, my cousin Katerina, despite her desperate position, was doing her best to stay calm and even tried to negotiate with the woman now holding her hostage:

"Stop, Svetlana! We came to offer you a title, power and money! The greatest systems in Sector Nine could be yours!"

"I don't need any charity from you! After all the perturbations of the recent days, the line of succession to the Orange House throne has moved forward significantly. I'm already number five. And I'll become number four right after Georg renounces Crown Princess Deia's right to it. And he will do that, otherwise I'll shoot his cousin through the head! And that'd be it. The only ones remaining before me would be old guys. So, what do I need your pitiful charity for, now that I'm sure to become Head of the Orange House one day?! No, I'm not the one who lost here, Georg, you are! You will take your ships out of my zone of responsibility and do everything else I say!"

"She is not all there, Georg. She is really going to kill her hostage, if you do not agree to all of her demands. And these demands will grow with every passing minute, as she thinks herself in control of the situation."

"And could you neutralize her?" I asked Florianna mentally.

"I could, but she wouldn't die right away, so she would still be able to kill Katerina."

"Arite, take a closer look at this woman," I said, turning to an otherwise totally normal looking guard soldier. "Copy her and approach her. I want Svetlana to understand how little I care whether she lives or dies. We can issue any orders we need her to without her."

Svetlana froze in complete surprise when one of my bodyguards stepped forward and changed into a naked girl with wet hair identical to herself. But Svetlana was not able to react to the appearance of her double. Her laser pistol was flung away from Katerina's temple and flew onto the floor. Meanwhile, a bloodied, razor-sharp, Alpha Iseyek appendage poked through the front of her head, extending a whole yard out the other side.

Rosss squeamishly tossed the lifeless body of Svetlana from his upper right appendage, then becoming nearly invisible again. All that remained were the dark red contours of his terrifying pick hovering in the air.

"Why did you have to kill her?" Katerina royl Unatari objected. "Svetlana was just very worked up, which made her overreact! You bruised her ego very badly. After all, she considered herself a great warrior and the commander of a frightening fleet, and you captured her and made her a laughing stock!"

"Cousin, you are mistaken. My Truth Seeker confirmed that Svetlana was about to kill you, so we had to neutralize her. Phobos, tell your partner that he did everything right and will be rewarded for what he's done."

I ordered the Arite to get dressed, but stay in the form of the dead commander. While her body was being removed and her blood mopped up, I turned to the admirals who were still in shock at what had happened:

"So, I'll explain. For your purposes, Sector Nine Fleet Commander Svetlana ton Mesfelle is alive and, in a few minutes, she will be giving a passionate speech on the common fleet channel. She will declare to her captains that she invited us here, and ordered the warp beacon turned on for us because the Orange House is steeped in corruption, embezzlement, and dirty political struggles, leaving it totally discredited. The Sector Nine Fleet will join the Unatari State. An hour from now, there will be a swearing-in ceremony for your captains and officers. You must remain silent on the incident that happened here until the ceremony is over. I hope you understand all that."

"Indeed we do, your Majesty!" Both admirals answered in nearly perfect syncopation.

"That is great. After the speech, closer to the

end of the day, it will be announced that the talented, proud and beautiful fleet commander died at the hands of an Orange House extremist. Sure, the security team missed something, but the killer has been found and neutralized, etc... Tomorrow, one of you will become Perimeter Nine Fleet Commander, and the other will be his deputy. Here is your fleet's mission: take all of Sector Nine under control as quickly as possible. All local rulers and aristocrats must join the Unatari state. We do not foresee particular resistance, as there is no force in the area capable of taking your fleet on. Sector Nine will become my cousin, Duchess Katerina royl Unatari's patrimony, and each of you will now receive the title Baron of Unatari for your service, as well as a rich star system in perpetuity. But if any of you do not like my offer, I will not detain you by force. You will be released to the four winds."

The two admirals exchanged glances, then Vajek Lavaelle answered for the both of them:

"How could we possibly refuse such a generous offer? And I would like to explain my last name, Lavaelle, right away, as I have noticed that your Majesty frowned when reading my information. My ancestors, three generations ago, were forced to leave the Green House and have not had any contact since then with any other bearers of our ancient surname."

"Very well. Great even. As you know, I have had a certain amount of unfortunate friction with the Green House, so I consider it useful to have allies of the Lavaelle name. Here is my decision: the new Sector Nine Fleet Commander shall be Stephan Antri-Mesfelle..."

The newly-appointed fleet commander immediately took a knee and kissed my hand.

"And you, Vajek, will have a more political career ahead of you. My advisor Katerina, herself an emigrant from the Green House with a decent understanding of the political situation there, will try to find a formal pretext to declare that you are the rightful heir to the Green House's titles, star systems, and the like. The Unatari State will support your bid. Together, we can try to get revenge on the Green House for the offense they committed against your great grandfather."

"Crown Prince Georg, it's been a pleasure doing business with you," Admiral Vajek Lavaelle followed the example of his brother-in-arms, and bent down on one knee.

"An hour from now, you will both take an oath of loyalty to the Unatari State along with the other fleet officers. And you should be warned that my Truth Seeker will be checking the veracity of your words, and has a very low opinion of funny business."

Valian ton Corsa walked up, apologized for interrupting our conversation, and told me that the Swarm Queen was calling me. Nai Igir appeared on the huge screen. The Queen nodded to my greeting and said ceremoniously:

"Crown Prince Georg royl Inoky ton Mesfelle, I am more than impressed at your political successes and have now made my decision: The Swarm shall conclude a military alliance with the Unatari State."

* * *

"Three. Two. One. Go! I need a tactical map now!"

A huge screen unfolded before me, and I took a sigh of relief. The *Behemoths* hadn't gone anywhere, and were inside the tactical grid. It would have been much worse if the enemy's most dangerous ships had changed position at the last moment, and met our ships that were arriving from other directions.

Messages started coming in from all directions:

"Group of targets. Distance: eighty miles."

"Eighty-four markers on the radar. Identification by radar signature underway."

"Two *Behemoths*, eleven *Sledgehammers*, six *Chainsaws*, ten *Hermits*, eight *Ascetics*, forty-seven *Meteors*."

"The heavy Virho fleet has begun combat in the Aysar system."

"The Red-Blue Fleet has arrived to the Lobj system. No enemy ships have been detected. Beginning mine removal and landing on the station."

"The Yuho and Fastel Fleets have begun combat in the Khe system."

"The Unatari heavy fleet has begun combat in the Khryo system."

And so the five-directional counterattack began. I tried to abstract myself from what was happening in other star systems and concentrate on my mission. The staff officers were giving me introductory information, and now froze, waiting for their orders. I then pondered for a second. The main mission was to get the deadly *Behemoths* separated from the other ships, then smash the enemy into pieces. But what could I give their little ships to peck at? Maybe, if I left one ship all alone. That meant someone would have to act as bait, and attract the enemy frigates.

"*Curse-4*, stay where you are and imitate a thruster failure. Attention all other ships! Accelerate toward the sun. Approach the enemy on a tangent. Both *Trias*, stay near the carriers. *Joan the Fatty*, *Unatari* and *Fastel*, check the remote shield-charging modules in the electros. Also, hold down both *Trias*. Be ready for drones and corvettes to be released. Fifty frigates to the first receiver, fifty to the second. Stay two hundred fifty from the *Behemoths*. Antisupport and *Curses*, stand by. Our frigates or *Curse-4* might need your help."

The fleet went into action, realigning and splitting off into smaller groups. We made the first move. Now we needed to wait for a response from the enemy. I looked closely at the screen. If the *Meteors* wanted to intercept my frigates, my destroyers and light cruisers would go into action. But the Aliens' small ships didn't approach. Instead they... began retreating, hiding behind the backs of the cruisers and battleships! Surprising. The enemy was offering us the big prey, and the little ships would only enter the battle after that.

If Nicole Savoia were next to me, she would already be asking me why the enemy was behaving so strangely. Her replacement, Max Gregor didn't have the same experience Nicole did, though, and didn't notice anything out of the ordinary. And, it should be said that the enemy was clearly doing something. I could feel it in my skin.

"Main fleet, change direction! Head toward the second planet. Frigates, destroyers and light cruisers, stay behind the heavies. *Surprise-5*, approach the enemy and launch an electromagnetic bomb into the empty space between us and the Alien fleet."

"But, Prince, we didn't want to show our enemy the new weapon!" My assistant said in surprise, but I cut his speech off with a gesture and, after turning off my microphone, explained my decision:

"The enemy is making it obvious that they are giving us space and tempting us to jump out in front to capture the *Behemoths*. That looks like submission or apathy, and I don't like it one bit. I'm also on guard because their small ships are retreating and hiding behind the *Behemoths'* shields. From all that, I suppose that either we are being lured into a mine field, or there are some bombers ready to sneak up on us. So, I won't take the fleet forward until I'm sure the path is clear."

I turned the microphone on again, and said over the common channel:

"Attention, fleet! In one minute, we expect a very strong electromagnetic burst, so cover sensitive equipment. *Pyros* and *Warhawks*, be on maximum alert! If the EMP exposes a cloaker or hidden mines, do not wait for my order; jump out in front as fast as possible. The risk must be neutralized before the enemy restores its systems to working order."

A countdown timer came in from *Surprise-5*. Then, a few seconds before it hit zero, a cloaked bomber appeared on the tactical map, and a dot came out of it. And... the lighting in the room flickered. All data screens in the headquarters went out. All the computers reset at the same time. In the half-dark of the emergency lighting, I released a juicy, bombastic stream of curses words. Some superweapon that turned out to be. My own fleet suffered no less than the enemy's! Around forty seconds went by before the lighting returned to normal. Right after that, a technician's voice rang out:

"Commander, communication with the fleet has been restored. Long distance is also back in order. But there is also some bad news: I'm not sure why, but *Joan the Fatty*'s shield is still down, and its main tactical computers have begun another reset cycle. The system won't come back online. Two other carriers are actively recharging our shields. We're already up to seven percent. But we need time to find and solve the other glitches."

"Find the reason as quickly as possible. I need a tactical map immediately!" I bellowed, donning my headphones.

"This is *Warhawk-12*. I'm holding an *Ascetic...* *Pyro-77*, stoke the fire!"

"...*Curse-4* here. I have three disruptors on me. I need help immediately!"

"...This is *Unatari*. Should I release drones?"

A battle was raging in the system, but I couldn't evaluate the position of my ships or command my fleet! Just for that, the creators of the EMP bomb deserved, at the very least, a firing squad! So, what should I do? Alright, that's enough. *Curse-4*, was the cruiser I had left as bait, after all. In order not to get distracted, I closed my eyes and, listening to the messages from the ships in battle, began issuing orders:

"*Unatari*, release all drones! *Joan the Fatty* and *Fastel*, do the same. All corvettes on the carriers, start up and warp out immediately to *Curse-4*. *Thrushes*, this is no time for napping. Get to work on the *Ascetics*. Groups from the receivers, hold the *Behemoths*. Start shooting down the drones now. Are the *Sledgehammers* very far?"

"All the *Sledgehammers* just jumped to eighteen on *Curse-4*."

"Damn them! *Thrushes* from one to thirty-five, warp to *Curse-4* now! Split up into groups of three. Blind the *Sledgehammers*. All free *Curses*, follow them! Don't stand around. Take a small orbit around the Alien cruisers at full speed. Work on the *Sledgehammers* with a concentrated volley from all the ships, as we did in training. *Curse-4* will mark targets."

"There's one more cloaker left. Should we destroy it as well?"

What? So there were cloakers after all? Trying not to show my surprise, I ordered two frigates to hold the cloaker in webs and warp disruptors, and the *Tria* to send out a landing group to capture the valuable trophy.

"This is *Curse-4*. It's over. The last *Sledgehammer* has left us for good. There are just two far-off *Behemoths* left on the battlefield. Thanks, guys! My ship is just a skeleton, but I survived!"

"*Curse-4*, great job! The whole cruiser team has earned medals. Now, collect drones and jump to *Fastel*. Your shields will be recharged to max."

"Free frigates, help us with the *Behemoths*. Destroy the drones as we planned, after that, both

Trias send out a landing party. We don't need to capture the battleships. As before, place charges and blow up the antimatter munitions."

I opened my eyes and noticed that it was unusually quiet in the headquarters. Only Bionica was speaking, duplicating my orders for the Iseyek ships with aplomb. The other officers, though, were staring at me in silence. The tactical map still hadn't come on...

Clay ton Avelle, captain of *Joan the Fatty*, took a step forward and, lowering down on one knee, said ceremoniously:

"Crown Prince Georg, I am a grown man and it's been some time since I believed in miracles. But today is the first time I've actually borne witness to one. Totally blind, you managed to end the battle against the Aliens in a rousing victory. Our fleet lost one *Thrush* and eleven *Pyros*. The enemy, though, lost eighty-two ships. Both of their *Behemoths* are already held down tight, and doomed to die."

Global fame increase. Current value +61

Standing change. Empire Military faction opinion of you has improved.
Present Empire Military faction opinion of you: +28 (trusting)

Just an hour and a half later, all that remained as a reminder of the recent battle was a field of wreckage.

Both *Trias* were conducting landing operations on the surface of the planet Sobj-5. The glitches in the computer system had just been fixed, and I was trying to get to the bottom of the computer issue. The engineers and technicians I called before me all asserted that the EMP bomb launched by the *Curse* was not the cause of the electronic and computer network failure, as no other fleet ship was affected in the same way. Also, the sensitive equipment on board was all well shielded at the time of the blast.

"Crown Prince Georg," the senior engineer lowered his voice practically to a whisper. "This looks like the work of saboteurs working in both the server room and the electrical substation. Someone was trying very hard to make sure *Joan the Fatty* had no energy shield and was blind during the battle. In both cases, the attacker was working remotely by linking into control systems, and had access to the administrator privileges needed to make changes to programming code. Unfortunately, all the logs were wiped in the attack, so it is impossible to figure out where the bad code came from. It is only clear that he or she had a perfect understanding of our utility functions, as the whole code-modification operation took only a few seconds."

"Only an android would be capable of such a thing," Marian Sabati said. "There are thousands of them on *Joan the Fatty*. We are not conducting adequate surveillance to point the finger at a specific android, though."

Bionica's face grew dark, but she did not object to the Truth Seeker's statement, as the hacking described was obviously far beyond the abilities of a person and was, in fact, reminiscent of the work of a robot.

"Popori de Cacha, order your subjects to check surveillance systems and figure out which of our crew members were near a computer terminal when the sabotage took place, or immediately before that. Bionica, you check all of the androids from *Joan the Fatty*. Florianna and Marian Sabati, I expect you to check all living creatures on this ship without exception. Find me the bastard who did this!"

Unnamed System

"ARE YOU SURE, Flora?"

"Yes, Crown Prince Georg. It's been a month and a half, and we have carefully checked everyone who was on Joan the Fatty. *None of the forty-three thousand beings here was involved in the sabotage in the Sobj system. Marian Sabati and I have checked all races, even the Arites."*

That meant it must have been an android, though Bionica has already assured me that none of the anthropomorphic robots on *Joan the Fatty* would have done something like that. I stood up thoughtfully from the table, a mug of my hot morning beverage in hand, and walked up closer to the tinted panoramic window. Once upon a time, when my flagship was still under construction, I had insisted that my entertainment room have real glass installed in it, instead of a mere screen broadcasting an image from an external video camera. It was true that any gap in the chassis would lower the strength of the starship, but not even the most perfect screen could replace the experience of actually seeing space... Or could it?

I involuntarily spun the ring on my finger. The same one I had looked deeply into on my very first day in *Perimeter Defense*, trying to see the pixels. I hadn't been able to see any then, and I still couldn't now, though I could easily make out the individual points on computer monitors here. Was this ring evidence that what was happening was real? Or perhaps, in the game, the resolution on data panels was intentionally limited so that a human player would perceive it as a screen. In order not to scramble my brains in thinking over the nature of *Perimeter Defense*, I cast these thoughts aside. Just as Miya had said: " There is no difference whatsoever between a real and virtual world if you live in it, enjoy it and perceive it as reality." I suppose I had already started to agree with my wife on that count.

Through the thick armored glass with anti-radiation coating, a view opened up to the blue-silver planet D56KT-V. Even from orbit, you could see sparks on the planet's surface and smoke plumes rising up from a great many fires. For the second day in a row, the battleships and heavy cruisers in my fleet were conducting bombardment of Alien positions, helping the Alpha-Iseyek terrestrial troops along. The invasion was underway on all fronts, and this was the fourteenth planet in Alien space we were attacking. And though none of the systems we'd been to, even in Swarm space, had been fully cleared of the Alien presence, my fleet was sinking its teeth deeper and deeper into Alien space, destroying ships and enemy infrastructure as we went.

Flora came closer and stopped her flying chair a step from me. One of the Beta Iseyek serving the paralyzed girl extended her a paper cup of juice, and she took it in her hand. The Truth Seeker's fingers trembled and falteringly interlocked around the paper cup. Her hand, grasping the object, began to slowly rise. I helped her a bit, as she was trembling quite a lot, spilling the orange drink all around.

"Please don't. I can do it myself."

The paralyzed girl raised the cup to her lips and opened her mouth with noticeable strain. She took two tiny sips, then her lifeless arm fell down, letting the paper cup fall with it, and emptying the juice out on the floor. In the paralyzed girl's eyes, I could read clear celebration, and I shared that feeling wholeheartedly.

"You're learning to control your body better and better, Flora. A year ago, we couldn't even have dreamed of this."

"Thank you, Prince. Marian Sabati is performing real miracles, trying to get me back on my feet. She is pouring oceans of energy into me, growing new cells and restoring my damaged tissues. I am very thankful to her, though her power seriously scares me. A Truth Seeker who lost her master shouldn't have such powers, even considering all the Beta Iseyek sharing energy with her on board the starship. After all, Marian Sabati has patients other than just me. There's also Ayna, for example. I do not understand what is going on. Something is clearly not coming together here."

"I am reminded of the meeting with the Swarm Queen when Marian Sabati declared that she was extremely weak and so wouldn't be able to fight in the ritual duel. Only two months ago, she truly wasn't in shape."

"Crown Prince Georg, was there anyone around then to check the veracity of her words?"

"Am I understanding correctly? Are you saying you are not strong enough to check Marian Sabati?"

"Yes, Crown Prince. Marian Sabati is many times stronger than me, so her thoughts and desires are totally hidden from me. The only thing I can say with any certainty is that I do not sense an immediate danger from her to myself or your Majesty."

And in fact, the story of the runaway Truth Seeker turned out to be quite fraught with potential issues. We only knew about Marian Sabati's condition through her own words. Where, then, did Marian Sabati get so much power now, if after the death of her long-time master, Duke Avalle, she was supposed to have gotten much, much weaker?

A beep came in over an internal channel, interrupting my thinking. It was Clay ton Avelle, captain of *Joan the Fatty*. I gave my permission to put him through.

"Crown Prince Georg, you asked me to immediately inform you of any movements of large Alien ships."

"Has the Alien Queen left Himora?" I guessed, worried. But the captain shook his head "no."

"I'm afraid, it's something else entirely. The gravimetric scanners from *Joan the Fatty* have detected a massive object near the uninhabitable second planet in the D56KT system, though our visual detection methods come up with nothing there. As such, I sent a corvette to study the strange anomaly. My Prince, I suggest very strongly that you come to headquarters to see IT with your own eyes."

It should be said that the captain succeeded at getting my attention. Taking quick steps, though still short of running in order to maintain my princely dignity, I set off for fleet headquarters. Despite the early hour on the internal ship clock, it was quite crowded. The night crew had already finished their shift, but was in no rush to leave the room. Many people were crowding around one of the screens, discussing animatedly. When I showed up, all conversations grew quiet, the officers made way for me to the monitor, and stood at attention.

Valian ton Corsa took a step forward, saluted, and reported:

"Your Majesty, this is a direct transmission from the corvette *Cannibal-71*. The quality of the picture isn't as high as it could be, and is often broken, but you can figure out what's going on."

"Everyone, as you were. Give me the chair." I sat in front of the screen, trying to understand what I was seeing.

There was some kind of colorful flickering with stripes running throughout... And suddenly the picture became clear, depicting a red-hot planet with oceans of boiling magma shot from low orbit. It then all abruptly shifted to the side and disappeared from the screen; the corvette made a turn. Then there was static, flickering, and stripes again until... The ship fell into a huge closed space.

Inside, there were thousands of robotic arms shifting and undulating. Moving on special rails, magnetic crane arms were transporting all kinds of mobile constructions. I saw piles of huge armor plates, each larger than the corvette filming them. In the distance, arc welders could be seen. The picture shifted. The body of a titanic ship came into the scene. It had gaping holes where armor plates and modules that had yet to be built would go. It took me fifteen seconds to recognize the unusually shaped starship in such an early stage of construction.

"A *Mammoth*?!" I turned to the officers behind my back in surprise.

Captain Clay ton Avelle, his face having dissolved into an ear-to-ear smile, confirmed:

"Yes, your Majesty! It is a huge *Mammoth* inside an even more gigantic dock. And, what's more, none of it is visible from outside. There's a complex masking system at work here that distorts electromagnetic fields and even partially warps space. The *Cannibal* has already measured the size of the construction. It is a spherical ellipsoid, approximately nine miles in length, and four miles in diameter at its widest point. The internal volume of the orbital construction is around fifty cubic miles, and our scanners haven't detected any living creatures inside. It all appears to be fully automated. Now we are trying to evaluate if there are enough parts and materials at the docks to finish building the ship, and also to make an at least approximate evaluation of how long it will take to finish."

I tried to digest all the new information and imagine the most obvious consequences of such an important discovery. The *Mammoth* itself wouldn't be ready for a while, so my fleet wasn't going to wait around here for it. That said, there would be plenty of people wanting to get their hands on the Alien ship, beginning with the Emperor and various civil servants from the Imperial Joint Chiefs, and ending with the Heads of the Great Houses, the Swarm Queen and her admirals. The discovery, in its present state, was nothing more to me than a huge headache. And it should be said that my head actually did start to hurt, and not just figuratively. I frowned and rubbed my temples. Bionica, standing next to me, walked up silently, and began massaging the active points of my skull, reducing the pain.

"So, we've found the dock. Our first mission isn't even so much figuring out how long until the *Mammoth* is finished, as it is keeping this thing a secret. The *Mammoth* all on its own is an extremely powerful combat unit and, what's more, is capable of transporting quite a large fleet between star systems. Having such a ship could totally change the balance of forces in the region and far too many, even those we consider loyal allies, would stop at nothing to keep the valuable ship all to themselves. So, we need to limit the circle of insiders as much as possible, and collect nondisclosure agreements from the whole crew of *Cannibal-71*. Florianna can make sure they'll be upheld."

Everyone around went silent, recognizing the importance of the discovery and the complexity of the situation. In that silence, the communications officer's voice rang out especially sharply:

"Crown Prince Georg, we've received an urgent message from our cloaked frigates in Himora. The Alien *Queen* has left the system with her entire fleet. There were no active warp beacons visible from there, so we do not know the direction she was headed in."

With a smirk, I turned to those gathered:

"So you see, even the Alien *Queen* thinks this is a watershed moment. Until now, we've destroyed Alien ships, landed troops on planets, and brought down communications centers and orbital constructions, but only now have we found the thing the Aliens truly considered important and were prepared to defend. Tell all our allies: in a few days, there will be a major battle against the Aliens in this system, which doesn't even have a normal name, and is called only by alphanumeric code: D56KT. For the first time, we will not retreat before their overwhelming forces, but instead stay for a decisive battle with the *Queen*. We have time to prepare, so let's spend it as usefully as possible."

"How much time do we have left until the *Queen* arrives?" My cousin, wearing a light silver space-suit, was lounging lazily in a chair. Her helmet was sitting next to her.

In the seat next to that, exactly copying Katerina royl Unatari's pose and behavior, Bionica was sitting in an identical silver space-suit. The android couldn't have been tired from such a small excursion to the second planet, but I could barely hold back a smile from how authentic my synthetic assistant's imitation of tiredness was.

Ten minutes earlier, they had returned with a division of scouts from the docks we'd discovered and were in an overstimulated state. According to Katerina, the colossal automatic complex boggled the imagination. It appeared to be a never-ending hangar, in which thousands of robotic arms were constantly moving, and hundreds of freight drones were scurrying about. And inside all that buzzing commotion, was the huge skeleton of a starship.

"I believe we have six or seven days. That is precisely how long it takes to get from Himora to D56KT by normal warp beacons. And though the Alien *Queen* followed an alternative path, I do not think it will take more time than the transportation network we do know about."

"Six days is too little. I mean, Bionica suggested dragging this huge dock in its entirety to Unatari space, but we would need a few dozen tugs to transport it. We would also need time to do a huge number of preparatory tasks and complex synchronization calculations to make sure the whole construction doesn't fall apart during warp jumps."

"How much time is needed to bring the docks to Fia or another Unatari State system?" I wondered, and Bionica obligingly brought up her calculations on the nearest screen, explaining them.

The upshot was that we needed no less than ninety heavy freighters to transport the docks without disassembling them, and two months to attach the huge assembly, calibrate our thrusters and actually transport the thing. I stroked the bridge of my nose in contemplation.

"As for ships, let's say I find them. It would be much harder to guarantee secrecy though. Hiring that many heavy transport ships in the Empire or Swarm wouldn't go unnoticed, and any analyst would start to think about why such a strange contract was drawn up. It would also be hard to keep the thousands of civilians from the tug crews quiet, even using some fairly radical methods..."

Ayna walked up with three sets of tableware. We waited for the girl to set the table, and continued our confidential conversation.

"Cousin, there is one issue still tormenting me. That dock was found only by coincidence. *Joan the Fatty*, with its sensitive scanning systems, was next to it for a long time, and it wasn't until the second day that we noticed any anomaly in our instruments' feedback. How many such objects did we miss in previous Alien systems?!"

I froze with a spoon full of soup half way to my mouth, greatly alarmed by my cousin's deduction. I mean, it really was possible that there were dozens of such hidden complexes, and maybe even hundreds. Now I would have to undertake a much more thorough scan of all the systems we'd already captured. I said my thought out loud, but Bionica calmed me immediately:

"There couldn't be too many of these docks. One, two at most. The main problem in building superheavy ships isn't docks, it's the tantalum concentrate it takes to build the ships. Today, when visiting the docks, I tried to calculate the amount of material needed to build one *Mammoth*. It would take millions of tons of tantalum concentrate. Tens of millions, in fact. The Aliens use similar materials for the armor plates on their ships. The demands for starship body material, having to withstand warp tunnel jumps, are just too specific, so there's nothing surprising in the fact that all different races have scientifically determined similar solutions to this universal technical problem. In the Aysar Cluster, there aren't any traces left of the Alien armada we blew up; they collected everything very carefully for meltdown. And also, here in Alien space, the tantalum armor plates have been removed from every space battle site. The Aliens would have to have destroyed thousands of enemy ships to scrape together the material to build just one *Mammoth*!"

I started thinking on my cousin's words and laughed:

"Now I understand why the Aliens are so interested in the Iseyek, and also why the Aliens moved through Swarm space so unhurriedly. The Iseyek, having been soundly decimated in the first few battles, were afraid of the military might of the enemy and began building giant ships to evacuate billions of eggs to a safe location in all their systems. This must have actually made the Aliens quite glad. Seeing this, they must have decided to simply allow the insects time to gather the ore in one place. Every unfinished Iseyek ship could be used by the Aliens to make new *Behemoths* and *Sledgehammers*."

Katerina agreed with me.

"It was good that you ended this by bringing Nai Igir to power then. It was apparently not very beneficial to the Iseyek. As far as I heard, the Swarm Queen ordered the transport ship construction halted everywhere except in the Dekeye capital system."

"Yes, that is true, cousin. How do you think the Swarm built so many combat ships in the last year? Meanwhile, the ship in the Dekeye system is already ready. I was told that not long ago by Advisor Triasss

Zess. The insects finally finished the evacuation ship, and even loaded it with billions of eggs, but have yet to launch it."

"What are they waiting for?" Bionica asked in surprise. "They spent so long building it, they rushed to finish, throwing all their resources into the project..."

I obligingly explained to my assistant:

"First of all, they are waiting for Nai Igir to lay her clutch in order to also save Iseyek Prime eggs. Second, the situation has changed: we came with an offer to begin a combined counterattack, and the Iseyek now have a glimmer of hope that the evacuation of eggs might not even be necessary."

We spoke a bit about the docks, ores and unfinished *Mammoth*, then Bionica changed the topic:

"Crown Prince Georg, with the Alien *Queen*'s departure from Himora, isn't it a good idea to send Unatari landing ships there to capture the station and take control of the system?"

"It is, of course. But every Alien station assault leads to thousands of victims and we have a very severe problem with manpower, especially in that region. Our allies, the Iseyek, have a different problem: there aren't enough landing ships. All eleven *Trias* are now dashing about the galaxy, supporting terrestrial operations in twenty-three star systems with fresh forces. That is why I suggest we give the honor of liberating Himora to a certain comely commander in our enemy's ranks."

"Nicole?" asked my cousin, immediately realizing my intention, her eyes lighting up. "Alright then, that sounds fine. But make sure it looks good.

Tell her about it in person, but first, let's gather all her old friend's here in this cabin. It would be an excellent reason to show our warm feelings to her, and to get her to think about what side of the Unatari-Orange House conflict she should be on."

* * *

"I need you, Miya!!!"

As always, I didn't actually see Miya's arrival. All I saw was a vague motion with the corner of my eye. I then turned sharply to see my beauty, sitting cross-legged in a deep armchair wearing a white track suit, her fire-red hair pulled back into a bun and concealed beneath a hat. In Miya's hands, there was an armful of red maple leaves.

"You pulled me out of an autumn day's walk through the park with Deia. What immediate help did you need this time?"

Autumn? Impossible! My second contract began in late autumn, already bordering on winter. The leaves had almost totally fallen off the trees already. Miya couldn't have been gathering maple leaves with her daughter unless a whole year had already passed. Also, did that mean little Deia was all alone in the park?

"Don't worry about our daughter. My servants will take her home. And as for autumn, as you may have noticed before, the passage of time in *Perimeter Defense* is not strongly correlated with that of the real world."

Miya wasn't even trying to hide the fact that

she was flagrantly reading my thoughts, trying to suss out all the facts as quickly as possible. Another few seconds later, her face stretched out in surprise.

"Where are we? Where have you dragged the fleet off to this time?"

"The D56KT system. It isn't on Imperial maps. This is Alien space."

"Ugh, I thought I asked you not to take risks like this after your first raid through Alien space!" Miya tried raising her voice, but I put her in her place:

"Let's leave the fleet movement and war strategy to the experts, not the aristocrat who traded five fearsome battleships for a pleasure yacht."

My spouse opened her mouth to speak, but met with my gaze and stayed silent.

"Miya, the Aliens' main fleet is in the next system over charging energy to jump here to us. There are a great many enemies, but that shouldn't worry you. Space battles are my concern. Your mission is to restore as much energy as you can after the jump into the game. You'll be helped in that by a team of Beta Iseyek. They will feed you energy. And, in approximately six hours, you need to be ready for a strike on the Alien *Queen* together with some other Truth Seekers."

"Who else will be participating?" my spouse asked in a business-like tone.

I numbered off the Truth Seekers who would be taking part in the attack. Miya nodded contentedly:

"An impressive cast. Especially Krista. To be honest, her and I don't really get along."

"What do you mean?" I wondered, curious.

"It's a very old story. She was my teacher in a

school for psionics on the Throne World..."

"Don't tell me it was you that caused the whole mess that closed her school down a century and a half ago."

It was basically just a joke, though the unmistakable horror that appeared on my spouse's face was evidence enough that I had guessed right. A Truth Seeker cannot lie to her master, and is obliged to answer honestly, even if it is a difficult question. Miya admitting to it could have very serious consequences; she would be heard by the invisible Chameleons, Phobos and Rosss, and perhaps some others as well. So, I hurried to add:

"Don't answer that. It was just a joke."

The fear and gloom on the woman's face were replaced with a good-hearted smile, and Miya nodded thankfully.

"Thank you. There are many ears here that shouldn't hear that. I would have been forced to kill all your bodyguards."

I tried to change the difficult topic:

"Miya, once again, you should be ready in six hours. Go to your chambers, change into something more befitting of a Queen."

"Very funny. You could first explain where my chambers are on this massive ship. After all, I don't have interactive implants, so I can't just call up a map."

"I'll call Ayna right away. She'll take you to your cabin. By the way, why don't you have implants? They don't get in the way of psionic abilities, after all."

"That's a strange question, Georg. Did you see an interactive guide pop-up on Krista or the Dark Mother? I was also born before those chips started getting implanted into all people, and never wanted one. Have you seen the 'achievements' Marian Sabati has? And now, imagine what a long list would be hanging over me for all to see, like a shameful brand that could never be washed off. Ancient Creature, Cannibal, Dirty Whore, Childkiller, Artifact Looter... And those are just from the war with the Swarm. There have been plenty of unflattering episodes in my biography since then, too. I will never agree to get electronic implants, Georg."

My speech to our soldiers had been composed by Katerina. I only changed a few sentences in it to draw attention to the fact that the forthcoming battle was important not only to humanity, but to all free races. I also emphasized the fact that we were the only thing standing between the Aliens and the Swarm Capital, and the last serious obstacle keeping the Aliens from capturing Perimeter Sectors Nine and Eight.

"You did an ideal job, Georg!" My cousin told me after I finished the speech. "Even I was impressed by the significance of the moment, and stood to applaud. That's how good your speech was. I should clarify the details with the Communications Ministry, but it seems very likely that we just set a record for the largest audience ever for an interstellar broadcast. The direct broadcast was made to four hundred star systems and twenty-five intelligent species! And in twelve minutes, a direct broadcast of the most grandiose space battle in human history will begin.

The viewers are in such a frenzy that even the Antagonists have asked to watch."

I dried my sweat-covered forehead. During the speech, I had to totally close the faction and personal relationship change system, because it was impossible to concentrate with so many lines of text flashing by. Instead, I just looked at my own information:

Georg royl Inoky ton Mesfelle, Crown Prince of the Empire, Ruler of the Unatari State, Swarm Five-Star-Admiral
> **Age: 48**
> **Race: Human**
> **Gender: Male**
> **Class: Aristocrat/Mystic**
> **Achievements: Elder Chameleon Female, Discovered Arites, Got through Alien Blockade, Researcher of the Unknown, Imperial Land Grabber, Ex-Fleet Commander for Sector Eight, Malingerer, Denied Paternity, Respected by the Swarm, Dekeye Champion of No Rules Fighting, Defender of Humanity**
> **Fame: 65**
> **Standing: +12**

Defender of Humanity? That was a new one. And also, the dubious achievement "Abandoned Friend" had disappeared, though that may have happened earlier. My standing had jumped a lot, and was finally in the positive. Now, ignoring faction, fame and standing, I turned to my work seat. My assistant Max Gregor sounded off immediately:

"Commander, we have finished setting the mines. There's one every half-mile from the warp beacon on a straight line for twenty-five hundred miles. We weren't greedy with the bombs, either. The enemy is sure to end up in the blast zone after coming out of the warp tunnel."

"Good, though it is like hitting an elephant with a pebble, for the big ships, at least. Though if we do reduce the amount of small ships, that would also be good. There's far too many of them. Has Krista come out of the woodwork, yet?"

"The Blue House told us that their Truth Seeker would be joining us a few minutes before the enemy appears. Another message came in, from Duke Takuro royl Andor: the Purple House is also providing a group of psionics to take part in the attack."

"Excellent. So, everyone, stand by in five minutes. Disconnect all data terminals not necessary for battle from the network. Check all the systems once again. Are the cloaked bombers ready to attack?"

"Yes they are, tuki-tuka-de-sa. All space around the station has been mapped out. Coordinates for all prewarp points have been entered. Three divisions of five bombers each are standing by. Immediately after the mine explosion, we are ready to attack. In every group there is one electromagnetic bomb, a gravity bomb and three thermonuclear ones."

I closed my eyes and threw myself back into my chair, trying to ignore the hustle and bustle going on around me. There were four minutes left before the battle that would define the fate of, at the very least, the Swarm. If we lost, the Iseyek would be erased from the star map in short order. And after them, it would be a matter of months before Sector Nine fell. There would be no one to defend it. Practically all of its ships were here today in the unnamed D56KT system.

"We are ready, Georg. Miya is leading our trio of Truth Seekers. Marian Sabati and I are backup, and the Beta Iseyek are behind us providing support. Seven Purple House psionics have joined us as well! And now the Blues have linked up. Krista, and with her... Woah-ho-ho!!! What am I doing standing in front of stars like these?!"

Florianna's joy and amazement forced me to open my eyes and look at the screen. And there was plenty to be surprised at. Forty additional black-robed women I didn't recognize had joined us. There was another woman with them, though, who I knew very well. The Dark Mother!!! I gave a deep bow to show my respect to the most powerful Truth Seeker and activated my microphone.

"Attention, fleet! Ten seconds until the enemy arrives! Five. Four. Three. Two. One. Detonate!!!"

I don't know if there had ever been an official record in the Empire for the longest fireworks display ever, but today we must have broken it. Twenty-five hundred miles of fiery hell! A surreal spectacle! Katerina, in obvious elation from the image on screen, gave me a thumbs up.

The voice of Max Gregor returned me to reality:

"The enemy hasn't been defeated. All the large Alien ships are still on the battlefield. Distance: six hundred eighty miles. Two hundred forty-seven *Behemoths*, five *Mammoths* and one *Queen*. And... one *Tyrant*-class battleship!"

"It's *Orange Majesty*, Viscount Sivir ton Mesfelle's ship," I explained to the officers. "I would love to kill that traitor, but we should probably try to take him alive... The devil!!! Remaining bomber groups, delay attack!"

The last sentence came at almost the same time five of my cloaked bombers appeared forty miles from the enemy fleet. They were totally destroyed instantly. It seemed like the cloakers weren't yet ready to launch bombs and were forced out of invisibility. A message came in from the communications officers:

"The *Queen* is emanating strong electromagnetic pulses at three second intervals!"

"She is interfering with our radio frequencies, jamming our communications!"

What an unpleasant surprise. There was no way to approach the Alien fleet invisibly now; the *Queen* had revealed our cloaked frigates with her pulses.

"The enemy fleet has begun maneuvers! It is coming in our direction!"

"Attention, fleet! Accelerate toward the sun. Keep your distance from the enemy."

In a few minutes, Max Gregor turned toward me, turned off his microphone and said:

"Crown Prince, the enemy has no small or even medium-class ships, only battleship-class and higher. They are slow and cannot reach firing distance. What are they hoping to accomplish?"

"Excellent observation, Max. You're making headway!" I said, praising my assistant.

The slow *Behemoths*, and even slower *Mammoths* and *Queen* couldn't get near my ships.

Even the *Quasar* and *Uukreshes* could go a bit faster than the enemy ships with their main thrusters. On the other hand, both the *Mammoths* and the *Queen*, essentially motherships, could release a black cloud of the speedy little frigates inside of them. For that reason, I sent several *Pyros* out in front of the fleet to provide us with warp jump coordinates and make sure my ships would be able to quickly move away from the enemy if necessary.

"Attention! All ships warp to *Pyro-26*," the worried scream ripped itself from me when the Alien ships started warp jumping in our direction one after the other.

Three thousand ships of my fleet jumped four hundred miles forward, fleeing the predicted arrival of the deadly enemy. No Aliens showed up in the place we fled from, though.

"Find out where they went, now!" I demanded.

Ten seconds later, an answer followed from Valian ton Corsa:

"Crown Prince, based on trajectory calculations, all enemy ships went to the second planet."

The second planet? I realized almost immediately what they wanted and laughed happily. Who cares, though? Let them search for their invisible dock. On my order, the battleship *Svetlana the Great* had dragged it to the other end of the star system and hid it among the massive moons of the eleventh planet. Meanwhile, a group of engineers had already detected and removed all the signal beacons that had once sent messages to its former owner on the location of the dock and the manufacturing progress.

"Crown Prince, incoming call from an enemy ship!"

I gave my approval, and Viscount Sivir came on screen in a strange outfit made of sticks and leaves instead of the standard Orange House uniform. In an utterly lifeless tone, not expressing any emotion, he said:

"Georg, give us the *Mammoth* and your fleet will be allowed to leave unharmed."

"If I wanted to leave, I would have done so long ago. And I wouldn't have had to ask anyone's permission, either. The thing you're looking for has already been gone for some time."

"My kind masters wanted to first offer you a peaceful solution to this conflict. But I already knew you would refuse it. Now you will die. Georg, you aren't even close to imagining the forces at play here."

The screen went out, and the call cut off.

"He doesn't look too much like a living person!" Bionica commented on what we'd seen. "He wasn't blinking, and his facial muscles didn't move. An android doing such a bad job of imitating human behavior would be labeled defective and dissembled for parts."

"That was not Sivir," my cousin confirmed, standing nearby overhearing our conversation. "Some kind of zombie, sure, but no human."

"Were you filming that for the viewers?" I clarified with Katerina, and she nodded.

I shook my head in frustration. Too bad. the fact that I had a *Mammoth* had just become an open secret. After the battle, there were sure to be unpleasant questions. On the other hand, the footage could also be used for propaganda purposes. I turned on the microphone.

"We've just seen a graphic example of what happens to traitors who surrender to the Aliens. There are no emotions left, no person, just an empty husk controlled by its masters. So then, if the *Queen* tries to tempt anyone else with her promises, remember what became of the unfortunate Viscount Sivir. He trusted her. Do not repeat his mistake. And now, get ready." The Alien fleet had "slightly missed" by a half a billion kilometers and jumped to the wrong coordinates. But now, they would be returning and were sure to be quite peeved.

A few minutes went by, and my prediction came true. The enemy fleet did in fact return to the D56KT warp beacon, and was now just two hundred fifty miles from my ships, right in our path. We had to take immediate maneuvers to maintain a safe distance.

"All ships, change direction! Turn toward the sixth planet. Heavy cruisers, do not lag behind, step on your main thrusters for all they've got, otherwise we'll be in firing range of the *Behemoths* in one minute!"

And meanwhile, the enemy was clearly up to something. Our computers were simply wailing trying to depict all the new red markers on the tactical map.

"They're releasing frigates! The *Behemoths* too!" reported Max Gregor with surprise in his voice, before immediately correcting himself. "No, those are not frigates. They are combat drones. A black cloud of combat drones!!!"

I had already seen the red dots pouring out on

the map. The tactical computer began noticeably freezing up, no longer even trying to show the data from the targeting system, but having plenty of trouble simply counting the number of drones the enemy had released. A few seconds later, the computer coughed up a number on the screen: 281,825.

"That is impossible! That must be a mistake! Where did they all come from?!" Bionica, sitting next to me, said with completely authentic notes of panic in her voice.

"It is accurate though, unfortunately," I answered my assistant. "Each *Behemoth* can carry around six hundred fifty drones, and there are two hundred forty-seven *Behemoths* here. There are also the *Mammoths* and the *Queen*, who seem to also have brought combat drones with them instead of the light ships we usually tear straight through in battle. Perhaps they were sitting in Himora for so long precisely because they were stocking their huge ships with drones. In Himora, by the way, there is a huge freight station with big storage facilities. There were more than enough materials...

But now, the next logical question must be asked: what should we do with this black cloud? My heavy ships need one more minute to turn around, and there definitely isn't enough time for that. Every Alien combat drone has firepower equal to that of a frigate. Almost three thousand of them are tearing off toward us, with every second noticeably closing the gap. For some reason, the image of turd coming into contact with the blades of a fan is coming to mind. The shit has hit the fan. There is no other way to put it here.

Release all *Leech-A*s to cut them off! Have them launch their nuclear bombs to stop the drones from getting any closer! Second division of *Surprises*, attack immediately after that! All ships, after the cloaker attack, release all of our drones! Frigates, prepare for combat! Work as quickly as possible! Antisupport, you need to..."

I wasn't able to finish explaining what exactly I wanted from my destroyers and other ships for destroying fast targets. I was overcome with pain. An unseen weight began pushing my head into my chest.

"SO THAT'S WHERE YOU GOT OFF TO!"

The Alien *Queen*! I was expecting just such a mental attack. It was the basis of my whole plan of attack against the *Queen*. But it hurt a lot! And where were the psionics now? It was growing harder to resist with every second.

"THAT'S RIGHT! THIS TIME YOU WEREN'T ABLE TO RESIST ME! I CAN NOW GET YOU BACK FOR ALL THE PAIN YOU CAUSED ME BEFORE. OH, NO. I WILL NOT KILL YOU. I AM INTERESTED IN STUDYING YOUR ABILITIES."

My vision grew hazy. It felt like there was barbed wire being twisted around my head. The pressure grew, the barbs dug into my skull... And suddenly, I felt surprise and amazement come over my tormentor.

"Begin the attack!" came a voice in my head, though I was unable to tell whose it was.

The *Queen* began trying to break the mental connection in fear. But she was not able. My consciousness, though, rushed back out into the real world.

I opened my eyes. My cousin was leaning over me in panic. In her hands there was a blood-soaked napkin.

"Did it work?" Katerina asked, just after seeing that I had come back to my senses.

"I don't know. I was only used as live bait. They let the Alien *Queen* swallow me whole, and now they're reeling her in."

I looked out the corner of my eye at the tactical screen and watched what was happening. A huge cloud of red dots had totally swallowed up the green dots of my fleet. Another second later, having forgotten my weariness, pain and spinning head, I jumped up, donned my helmet and began issuing commands into the microphone:

"Corvettes, why the hell aren't you in battle?! Everyone out of the carriers immediately! All *Leech-C*'s to the *Behemoths*. Do not allow them to come within firing distance!"

"Prince, we have lost the battleship *Princess Astra*! The battleship *Master of Tesse*'s shield is down!"

"All carriers immediately recharge the shield of *Master of Tesse*! Hold it at all costs!"

I looked out the corner of my eye at the number of enemy drones marked on the tactical map. One hundred six thousand. It was too many. The best thing to do was retreat from battle to save at least some of the fleet. But the fact that a large proportion of my ships were already under enemy warp disruptor bore eloquent witness to the fact that we would no longer be capable of warping out of battle. We had to fall back on a time-tested method:

"Frigates and destroyers, fall back from the carriers! Other ships, prepare to gather your drones. Now, drop bombs in the very thick of the battle to mow down the enemy's drones!"

Next to my flagship, a bright flash exploded, blowing up one of my large ships, though I couldn't figure out exactly which.

And suddenly, something changed. The first thing I noticed was hundreds of webs and warp disruptors coming off my ships. After that, I saw the cloud of drones fly back, and the *Behemoths* began to stop in place.

"My Prince, the enemy drones are fighting each other now!"

"The *Behemoths* are turning around. They all shot one big volley at the *Queen!*"

"Georg, we have taken the Queen under our control, she is temporarily fighting on our side."

"Flora, how glad I am to hear your voice! Can you hold her?"

"Yes, we can hold her for a bit longer. After that, Krista and almost all the other Truth Seekers want to blow the dangerous ship up. But Miya and the Dark Mother are opposed. They suggest burning out the Queen's consciousness, and capturing the gigantic ship for humankind."

The *Behemoths*, meanwhile, made another volley on their former flagship, also without noticeable effect. How high must the capacity of the *Queen*'s shields have been if they were capable of withstanding a combined volley from two hundred of the deadly Alien battleships?!

"Fleet, let's take the rest of the drones down and prepare to counterattack. *Surprises*, take down the *Behemoths* with new bombs. Do not let them destroy my trophy! Throw them in the very thick of it! Small ships, go away and hide behind the battleship and carrier shields!"

A countdown timer came in from *Surprise-13*. Five seconds in advance, the sensitive equipment was covered with armored shields, so I couldn't see the tactical map during the attack. But everyone felt the effect! I couldn't even stay standing, so strong was the trembling, even on the none-too-small *Uukresh*. It should be said that the engine desynchronization was automatically repaired almost instantly.

On the tactical map that appeared soon after, striking changes had taken place: more than half of the *Behemoths* had simply disappeared. Only the clouds of large and small debris flying in every direction that remained served as confirmation that the Alien battleships hadn't warped out, but were destroyed. There were almost no active drones left, but thousands and thousands had lost control and were moving by inertia. The remaining *Behemoths* hurriedly went to hide under the shields of the *Mammoths*. According to computer calculations, eighty of the enemy battleships had survived the blast. The enemy motherships, though, were starting to warp in our direction.

"All ships, attention! The enemy is approaching again! Get ready!"

But the Aliens thought they'd come close enough to destruction for one day and, one after the other, the *Mammoths* and *Behemoths* docked on them left in a warp jump, fleeing the star system. It was very strange. Even I didn't suspect that these huge ships were capable of recharging their energy fast enough to be able to open a warp tunnel to another star system this soon. In fact, I hadn't even sent out my *Leech-D* frigates to hold the *Mammoths* with warp disruptor, because I was under the impression that it would take these giants at least another five hours to go anywhere. What a shame! On the other hand, we were left with a somewhat more valuable trophy than they ever would have been. As long as the Truth Seekers didn't blow it up...

"Florianna, how's it going?"

"The Queen has been killed. The Aliens inside the ship have once again become millions of individual creatures, not one singular superconsciousness. They are confused and disorganized. They are not controlling the ship. the Truth Seekers are inclined toward blowing the huge Alien spaceship up. Even the Dark Mother has changed her opinion and now agrees with the others. Only Miya is still trying to argue against it."

Mhm, so that's how I stop you from blowing up my quarry! I took a look at the star map and ordered the Forepost-4 and Forepost-13 warp beacons switched off, as well as for any communication through them to be blocked. Sorry, dear cousin, your broadcast will have to be brought to an end as well. We are cutting ourselves off from the Empire for the time being.

"All frigates, hold the *Queen* under warp disruptor! I order all eleven *Trias* to prepare landing groups. We will board the *Queen*!"

THE DEATH OF ROBEN

I T HAD BEEN a long time since I truly worried, even when leading my fleet against an enemy that surpassed us in force or going to the Emperor's court in the Throne World. It had been four days since the Forepost-4 and Forepost-13 warp beacons had been switched off on my order, and the time had come now to turn them back on.

Unfortunately, we couldn't possibly have done it any earlier: the bloody assault of the *Queen* was underway. Millions of praying mantises had died clearing the titanic Alien flagship. Only one hour ago, General Savasss Jach had reported that the last organized hotbeds of Alien resistance had been suppressed, and his soldiers were carrying out the final purge of the starship, sweeping up lone previously-unnoticed defenders. All key systems of the gigantic ship were already under Iseyek control, and the Truth Seekers wouldn't simply be able to do what they wanted and destroy the huge *Queen*.

By the way, inside the *Queen*, we really did find manufacturing facilities for producing combat drones and small frigates, as well as huge storage facilities for building materials. In these facilities, we also found ore taken from the Himora station freight terminals, and Perimeter Sector Eight Fleet ships that were lost in Himora, broken down into pieces.

"Why draw it out, order the beacons turned on already," Katerina said in dismay.

My cousin had been angry at me for the last four days because I hadn't given her at least a minute of time to somehow logically conclude her epic report on the grandiose battle in the D56KT system. In accordance with the Imperial Communications Ministry's rules, due to the transmission not finishing properly, her broadcast was not eligible for any viewership records. And because of that, Katerina royl Unatari's fame wouldn't be growing, and also the achievements she so desired, which were already basically in her hands, Best Reporter, Best War Reporter, and Most Popular Reporter, had slipped from her fingers at the last moment.

I ordered the warp beacons turned back on and mentally prepared myself. The messages that had piled up over the last few days rained down like a waterfall, but... Nothing extraordinary had happened, which made me extremely surprised. In Miya's words, during the battle, Krista, the behind-the-scenes ruler of the Blue House, had made an ultimatum to destroy the Alien flagship. The Truth Seekers from the Dark Mother's retinue had done the same. But neither the war with the Blue House, nor any great fall in diplomatic relations had actually come about. There hadn't even been any reproaches for my headstrong behavior from the Throne World. Strange. Very strange.

I began selectively looking through messages. I noticed that my global fame had risen to seventy, and the Imperial Military faction's opinion of me had also grown significantly. I saw a growth in standing from the Chameleons and all Swarm subraces other than Iseyek Prime (clearly Nai Igir had been eating, and not active during the battle with the Aliens in the remote system). There had also been a noncritical fall in my relationship with Duchess Ovella from the Blue House. I noticed relationship improvements with many factions toward the Unatari State, and answered them all in kind.

"Your Majesty, Queen Miya has left her chambers. It is not known where she went," came a message from one of the Chameleons guarding my spouse. "She has taken Ayna with her."

I pounded my fist on the arm of my chair in irritation. The uncatchable Miya was back to her old tricks! I hoped very much to discuss a great many issues with my spouse, but after the battle with the *Queen* and the dispute with the other Truth Seekers, Miya was extremely exhausted and could barely even stand. My wife had only relayed a message to me from the Dark Mother: "My power has grown significantly. I am now the number three Truth Seeker in the Imperial hierarchy." Then, she went to her chambers, took a dose of crystals and went down into a crystal dream. And as soon as she woke up, she disappeared, this time taking my servant with her.

"Crown Prince Georg, incoming call from the Imperial Joint Chiefs of Staff."

I gave my permission for the call to be put

through. The official representative of the Joint Chiefs, Count Timur royl Nayt ton Miro, came on screen. His zone of responsibility was military performance and scout operations against nonhuman races. Without so much as a polite greeting, he immediately asked about the results of the battle in the D56KT system.

"The enemy lost one hundred sixty-seven *Behemoth*-class battleships, around forty *Sledgehammers* and up to two hundred small-class ships. After that, they decided to retreat from battle and hide where we couldn't get them, but they left their flagship behind. At present, we are carrying out the assault of the *Queen* with Alpha Iseyek troops, but the titanic dimensions of the ship and the gigantic number of defenders inside do not allow us to call the battle truly over yet. The Iseyek losses in the battle for the *Queen* are already over six million soldiers, and require landing more and more assault divisions to get deeper into the ship. Twelve *Trias* are occupied with getting reinforcements in. Each of them has carried up to four hundred thousand praying mantises into this meat-grinder."

"I have little interest in losses among Iseyek soldiers," said the Count, dismissing my report. "The Swarm had billions of individuals ready for combat, so losing a few million praying mantises here or there did nothing to change the picture. I'm concerned with something else entirely. First of all, what faction will the *Queen* belong to after the assault is over? Second, how many ships does the Unatari State have left after the battle, not including Iseyek ships? Third, who will the star systems conquered from the Aliens belong to?

Fourth, what became of the formerly Human battleship *Orange Majesty*? Those are the questions that truly interest the Imperial Joint Chiefs, and in that exact order."

"In optimistic calculations, the Alien flagship will be totally under my control in three weeks. More realistically, we'll need two or three months. I immediately and clearly staked my claim to the ship, and no one, not the Swarm, nor the Empire, nor the Great Houses, made any objections. So the question of who the *Queen* belongs to after the assault, I consider settled. In the battle, my united fleet lost three battleships, and another two need a complete overhaul and will be out of commission for several months. I also lost twenty-six heavy cruisers and forty-seven light ones. Small-class ship losses came to a total of eight hundred."

"Hrmph... My condolences..."

The man removed his hat in contemplation, and began nervously wringing it in his hands. I then continued:

"The question on who the systems belong to should be discussed with Swarm Queen Nai Igir. But there is little we can do to object if the Iseyek demand these systems for themselves; the systems were liberated by praying mantis assault troops, and the only way to reach them is through insect space. If the Swarm offers Unatari some kind of compensation for some of the systems, that would be only out of their good will. The insects could easily think the *Queen* enough compensation all on its own. And as for *Orange Majesty*, it was docked on a *Mammoth* at the end of the battle and left the system intact, together with the carrier."

The Count went silent in contemplation, then placed his hat back on his head, looked me right in the eyes, and demanded harshly:

"In the name of the Imperial Joint Chiefs, I must demand that the Unatari State immediately cease the blockade of the Green House fleet stuck in the Forepost-31 system. That fleet will be going to the newly liberated systems and will serve as something of a counterbalance to the now excessively strengthened Swarm. The Empire, then, will be able to demand its fair share of those star systems."

I could hardly hold back my indignation. The Joint Chiefs were openly intervening in a conflict inside the Empire and giving recommendations that were clearly more advantageous to one side? The Green House lobbyists had probably pushed that idea through to save their doomed fleet.

"I'm afraid that won't be possible, Count, unless that Green House fleet surrenders in its entirety and comes under my command," I smiled.

"The Green House will never agree to such a thing," the man said, shaking his head. "But the Unatari State, after all the losses it sustained, is in no position to hold the praying mantises back. You'll be very lucky, Crown Prince, if the Swarm doesn't declare war on you in the next few weeks."

"I do not agree with that assessment, Count. The insects are fairly loyal to me, and I do not expect them to stab me in the back. And also, if they do, I'll easily be able to handle the aggression. The Green House, though, is at war with Unatari, and I haven't even been given an assurance that my enemies will not take advantage of my being deep in Alien space and take my undefended systems. Beyond that, if the Empire were to do as you described, it would destroy the firm trust the insects have grown for us people, which would then serve as sufficient reason for the Swarm to break our agreements and take the *Queen* for themselves."

"Hrmm, yes. Here, I agree. In fact, the first thing we should do is wait until the Alien flagship is captured and under Unatari State control. But, the rest of what was said remains in force, and that is not merely my point of view. The Joint Chiefs are seriously worried. Over the last year, the Swarm has grown dangerously strong; it almost doubled in size when they gained the Arite systems, and the Swarm will soon regain nine formerly Alien-controlled systems. If you consider the Insects' intention to add another twenty Alien systems on top of that, and also know how quickly they can multiply and incorporate planets into their society... Soon the Empire will have a neighbor it will no longer be able to reckon with. Before this, the Iseyek were under pressure from the Aliens, so the insects behaved peaceably. But now, that threat to the Swarm has been significantly reduced, in many ways thanks to your victories over the Aliens, Crown Prince Georg. Now, there's no one to hold the Iseyek back. And we are not the only ones who noticed that. Today, the Mechanoids sent Duchess Ovella royl Stok ton Miro an official message that they refuse to continue being vassals of the Blue House and wish to join the Swarm. That is a very bad sign; nonhuman races no longer see the Empire as the most powerful military force in the Galaxy. We have twenty-five nonhuman races within our borders, and many of them have a bone to pick with the Empire. Some also have territorial ambitions. Under no circumstances can we allow them to leave their subjugation to the Empire and rally around another center of power. For that reason, I give the Unatari State a maximum of two months to capture the *Queen* and ferry it to a home system, at which time the Empire will officially announce its claim on half of the systems captured from the Aliens."

When Count Timur royl Nayt ton Miro signed off, Katerina asked me cautiously:

"Cousin, why did you tell him it would take so long to capture the *Queen*, when it's already under our control? And also, you told the Count the total losses of the whole united fleet, including Swarm ships, and not only Unatari losses. After all, we actually have many more ships than he has been led to believe!"

"Katerina, I wasn't lying about the *Queen*, or our losses. He simply didn't formulate his questions very well, and I was interested in his reaction. A curious picture is coming together. We are at war with the Aliens here, defending all of humanity, and taking losses at that. But, behind our back, other Imperial forces have already crossed Unatari out of the future and are playing their own game, not at all considering our interests..."

My cousin nodded and added thoughtfully:

"We were given two months to solve our problems, which isn't much time at all. What could we change by then?"

My synthetic assistant entered the room, and I

called her over:

"Bionica, you said you could repeat the water and provisions sabotage of the First Green House Strike Fleet. Now is the time to do that."

The synthetic beauty gave a curt nod:

"Yes, your Majesty. I will prepare the orders for the androids of that fleet. But I came for a different reason. Sorting through your piled-up mail, I discovered a message that should be of interest to you, and marked it."

I called up the incoming message interface and immediately saw a letter outlined in red that had come in from my former assistant Nicole ton Savoia.

"Crown Prince Georg royl Inoky ton Mesfelle!

I consider it my duty to inform you that your brother, Count Roben royl Inoky ton Mesfelle is in critical condition. His doctors are unanimous in giving him no more than one week to live. Countess Verena, after receiving this information from the medics had a long conversation with the Head of the Orange House, after which she issued a ban on spreading any information on Roben's condition, and ordered everyone to act like nothing was happening.

P.S. Thank you for the tip on Himora! We have already returned it to Imperial control.

Perimeter Sector Eight Fleet Commander
Nicole ton Savoia"

I looked at the time the message came in. It was nineteen hours ago.

"Attention all ships of the united fleet! The Yayho fleet is to remain in this system and cover the dozen *Trias*. Other ships and two *Trias*, stand by. In thirty minutes, we'll be heading for Tesse!"

$$* * *$$

We hurried as best we could but, nevertheless, we had to make a detour through the unstable Sigur system beacon, the route through the Himora star system not being open to my fleet for obvious reasons. There was also a positive in that, though: the Orange House wouldn't know a thing about my fleet's movement right up until the united armada emerged from a warp tunnel into the Tesse system. We came out just one hundred eighty miles from the surface of the planet Tesse-III (precisely where the Mechanoid, *Eleven*, had "anchored" on my request, giving us jump coordinates far from the warp beacon).

The first thing I did was demand to be put through with Nicole ton Savoia, in order to avoid unnecessary military conflict with the Perimeter Sector Eight Fleet. The commander accepted my call almost instantly.

"Crown Prince Georg, you have my deepest sympathies..."

My whole chest felt ready to burst. I must not have made it. Roben was dead.

"When did it happen, Nicole?"

"Your older brother Crown Prince Roben royl Inoky ton Mesfelle is no more as of this morning. As a matter of fact, I am at his burial ceremony in the flying palace right now. The urn of the Counts ashes has just been placed in the columbarium. His widow is giving her eulogy right now. The last word will be given by Duchess Silva royl George ton Mesfelle. After that will be my turn."

"Hold on, Nicole. There's something I'm not

getting here. Roben died just today, and he's already been cremated and buried?! What's the rush?"

"I do not understand it myself, but that was the will of the new ruler of the Tesse star system, Countess Verena."

"I see. Then I'll have to hurry to get there before the end of the ceremony. And yes, Nicole, order your ships to not come near the third planet. Also, the AA soldiers on Tesse-III should take a break for the next two hours. I don't want the mourning ceremony to turn into a bloody mess."

"I don't understand, Crown Prince. Where are you right now?"

"If you took a pair of binoculars right now and looked up, you'd see three big bright spots, fifteen smaller ones and a bunch of really tiny specks. That would be my fleet."

I heard Nicole clearly swearing under her breath, and I hurried to reassure her:

"I have no intention of fighting with your fleet, so don't worry. My ships will not be starting any battles today. The Head of the Orange House, Duchess Silva doesn't have to worry either. I appreciate the fact that she has come to bid farewell to my brother, and am not preparing to arrest her. I have come here to bid farewell to Roben, and that is all."

An hour and a half later, twenty large landing shuttles with Unatari emblems on them touched down on the flying palace's landing pad. No one tried to stand in our way. Four hundred Alpha Iseyek, armed to the teeth and painted bright red with one or even two white stripes across their shells, were standing stiffly on both sides of the gold-sand path. The same number of people in heavy armored suits were scattered around the whole flying island, not lowering their weapons for even a second, and looking cautiously at the soldiers in orange uniform.

"*Crown Prince Georg, I do not sense any immediate danger. The guests at the ceremony and their guards are experiencing curiosity and fear, while some are simply admiring the demonstration of force. There are even some who are prepared to swear allegiance to your Majesty, if you ask.*"

"That comes later. Let's get out of this shuttle. Katerina will be to my right, and Likanna to my left. Marian Sabati and Flora, a few steps behind. Walk unhurriedly, to demonstrate our confidence and power."

The Orange House soldiers were trying to keep their distance from my procession. We went two hundred steps, then I raised my arm, ordering the group to stop. In the distance, there was a small chestnut-haired girl sitting behind some bushes looking utterly broken. I started walking intently in her direction.

Millena Mayer
Age: 9
Race: Human
Gender: Female
Class: Mystic
Achievements: Bringer of Success
Fame: 1
Standing: 3
Presumed personal relationship: Unknown

The girl was obviously in a bad state. There were dark circles under her eyes, and dried blood under her nose; her face was stained with tears, and her arms were shaking. She didn't even have enough power to stand as I approached. Millena could only raise her head, and look at the two stronger Truth Seekers with an expression of fatal resignation.

"A year ago, Millena could have beaten me. Now though, I am hundreds of times stronger than this little girl."

"No need to boast, Florianna. In the last year, you were present at so many of my fleet's victories, and gulped down so much energy that you couldn't have avoided getting stronger. Poor little Millena lost her master just today and is in a fearfully weakened state."

"Weakened is putting it lightly," Marian Sabati snorted. "She is close to death and, in fact, will die soon. It isn't the first time I've seen something like this. A weak Truth Seeker who, having lost her master, cannot find a new source of power is quickly snuffed out. It's an unpleasant spectacle."

"Can you not give her a bit of energy?" I asked Marian, but she could only shake her head:

"There's no reason to. It'd be like pouring water into a bottomless barrel. All the energy transferred in to her would come right back out."

In the meantime, the young dying girl had the strength to say something. Straining, I picked out her barely audible words:

"She's the one who killed him."

"Who do you mean? Duchess Silva?"

I noticed with the corner of my eye some kind

of quick, blurry movement, then I heard a sickly screech and... a member of the Ravaash race with daggers drawn fell to the earth just three feet from Millena, cut in half. Phobos removed a folded piece of fabric silently from his belt pouch and carefully wiped off Rosss's barely visible bloodied upper appendage. Popori de Cacha appeared just then, bowed over his fallen kin and commented:

"This is Countess Verena's bodyguard. A year ago, Crown Prince Georg gave three Chameleons to his brother, and Roben gave them to his spouse. There should be another two somewhere nearby. If possible, I ask you not to kill them. Just immobilize them, if you can. There aren't very many Ravaash as it is."

Popori de Cacha repeated the last sentences in Iseyek language, then went back into invisibility. The little Millena spent a long time in silence looking at the remains of her attempted murderer, then answered my earlier question, crystal-clear and even in great detail:

"Not Duchess Silva. It was Countess Verena. She killed her husband. She injected him with a slow-acting poison in the neck when Roben was passed out. I was next to him, but couldn't do anything. I was being held down by Verena's bodyguards. They twisted my arms until it hurt and forced crystals into my mouth so I wouldn't see anything or get in the way, then left me in a locked room. They knew I would die right after Crown Prince Roben, and wanted to make my death look natural. When my master died, I was nevertheless able to escape their imprisonment, but I only had enough energy to crawl over here to the park."

"Can you take some nourishment from me?" I asked, but Millena could only shake her head:

"Your Majesty already has two strong Truth Seekers with him, and I cannot draw any energy."

"Dad, I could be her new master!" Likanna said, stepping forward decisively.

Wearing a black mourning dress and golden crown over her emerald hair, my daughter looked very majestic, like a true Imperial Princess. Millena raised her eyes and nodded in silence.

"Flora, Marian, charge Millena's energy. Popori de Cacha, I need you to make sure a certain plane doesn't leave the flying palace. I would very much like to speak with Verena."

When I got there, everyone was waiting for me. In the main room of the luxurious palace, there were a great many Orange House aristocrats, political figures and famous Tesse industrialists. On the central, gem-encrusted throne that had once belonged to Roben royl Inoky, Duchess Silva, head of the Orange House was sitting solemnly. Her bodyguards were observing with indifference as my Unatari soldiers flooded into the room and surrendered their weapons. I walked up closer, and greeted Duchess Silva in accordance with all courtly etiquette rules as the more senior aristocrat in Imperial hierarchy.

But I wasn't interested in her now. On the neighboring small throne in a long, dark dress, sparkling from the many inlaid diamonds, Countess Verena was sitting looking demure, the newly minted ruler of the Tesse star system. Without any exaggeration, Verena was ravishingly beautiful. She was a reference point in female beauty. Only Miya or Astra could rival my brother's widow, and they, I'm sorry to say, would lose to Verena if the three were to go head-to-head in a beauty contest.

Suddenly, though... the shroud of charm fell away. The beauty's eyelids grew wide in fear. Her lips pursed nervously and her arms began shaking. The throne was now occupied by an insanely tired, nearly dead, terrified woman. I turned in order to find the reason for the dramatic change. Behind the composed rows of my bodyguards, the young Millena was walking confidently into the room. Verena didn't understand how it was possible right away and made a long face.

I took a stern look at my brother's murderer and said:

"Verena, I have only one question for you. Why?"

The widow turned her head in my direction and, through quivering lips, said:

"My little boy died six days ago. He died in my arms, despite all the doctors' efforts. And my husband... that brute was stuffing his face, having a grand old time, laughing away, not even understanding what had happened. He has hardly spent a day sober in the last year." Here even I could barely hold myself back...

I turned straight to the three Truth Seekers behind my back. Their verdict was unanimous:

"She's lying!"

"She's lying!"

"She's lying!"

Millena Mayer, convalescing right before my eyes, stepped forward, but the girl was overtaken by Marian Sabati, who told us what she was reading in the accused's thoughts:

"Verena had been planning this crime for a very long time. Ever since it became clear that her son was born sick and may not live. Verena had no hope of conceiving another, healthier child with Roben. She had already waited more than ten years for the first, so she understood perfectly well that she would never have another. Roben's doctors were already saying his life would be a bit shorter than expected in the best case. Verena's future was strongly dependent on who would die first: her husband or her ailing son. If Roben were to die first, she would become regent, as his widow, until Crown Prince Georg royl Roben came of age, receiving the whole Tesse star system for herself. And then, even if the child died, the star system would remain hers. If, though, little Georg royl Roben died first, the situation would be totally different. After Verena's husband died, and his death had been a near certainty for some time, she would be out in the cold. All of Crown Prince Roben's property, in accordance with Imperial law, would be split between his brother and sister, the twins Georg and Violetta. Verena couldn't allow that, so had long been planning to do what she did. When the boy died in her arms, Verena gave the drunk unresponsive Roben a slow-acting poison. And a few days after she'd buried Roben, she was planning on announcing the death of her son."

"That's all very well," said Verena, not particularly disputing the story. "Yes, I had been planning this for a long time. And what of it? I mean, you, Marian, actually knocked your master off, stole twenty-five billion from the Orange House treasury and bought your amnesty and protection in another part of the Empire on those very stolen funds. And no one, not the ruler of Unatari nor the Dukes, nor even the Emperor himself remember your crimes now. How am I any worse? I will actually have a bit more money than you ever did, and the Tesse star system to boot. So please, name your price, and bugger off."

I was totally thrown off at the impudence and frank boorishness she was displaying. Having grown rich from her husband's death, Verena clearly supposed that money would allow her to get away with murder. And that was at the fact that, under Imperial law, there was only one possible punishment for assaulting a Crown Prince: death.

"And what was the role of the Orange House Head in all this?" My cousin Katerina royl Unatari asked out loud, turning to the Truth Seekers.

The middle-aged Duchess Silva royl George ton Mesfelle, silent until that point, then started fidgeting on the throne, but was forced to answer:

"I had nothing to do with this. A few days ago, Verena ton Mesfelle told me that her husband's health had taken a drastic turn for the worse, and warned me that he might die. Also, in light of Crown Prince Roben's incapacitated state, she requested official confirmation from me of her status as ruler, assured me of her loyalty to the Orange House and told me that Tesse would maintain all its current political stances. I gave my approval. Then, when I got the news about Crown Prince Roben royl Inoky ton Mesfelle's untimely end, I flew out to the mourning ceremony."

The Truth Seekers unanimously confirmed that the Head of the Orange House was not lying and had no part in my brother's murder. Duchess Silva settled down right away, and unexpectedly announced that, as senior member of the Mesfelle family in age and title, it fell upon her to decide Verena's fate. The widow grew obviously joyful and even, it seemed to me, winked at her neighbor. I though, on the other hand, was on my guard, as I simply could not allow Roben's murderer to avoid retribution.

The Duchess stood and, in a majestic voice, pronounced:

"For the murder of an heir to the Emperor's throne, I sentence the accused, Countess Verena ton Mesfelle, to death by decapitation! The sentence is to be carried out immediately!"

I nodded, and Popori de Cacha appeared behind the throne and waved his blades. Verena didn't even have time to get scared. In all this unpleasant commotion, I was most worried that my daughter Lika would faint or scream. But Crown Princess Likanna retained her composure.

When the servants had carried the dead body away and were cleaning up the blood, I said, turning to those gathered in the room:

"As legal heir of my brother Crown Prince Roben royl Inoky ton Mesfelle, I accept the burden of responsibility for the Tesse star system. As legal heir to my nephew, Crown Prince Georg royl Roben ton Mesfelle, I accept the burden of responsibility for the Tialla star system. The funeral for Roben's entire family will be held here on the flying island in three hours. Duchess Silva royl George ton Mesfelle, you and your people are free to leave the flying palace and the Tesse star system at any time. No one will get in your way."

The flying palace slowly drifted past the sun as it hung over the horizon. The funeral ceremony came to an end. Three urns of ash were placed next to one another, and the guests left back to where they came from. Katerina, Florianna and I were sitting in the very same veranda where Roben and I had once celebrated Katerina's arrival. That seemed so long ago now! There wasn't a split in the Orange House yet. We hadn't even boarded a single *Behemoth*, nor conducted our raid on Alien space. Many people who were no longer with us were still alive then...

With a snifter of strong brandy in my hand, I took a thoughtful look at the eternal sunset — the flying palace moved with the sun, always keeping its position in the sky the same. I was tormented by one question: if I had agreed to go with Verena to "have a look at her shell collection," this all could have ended differently. Verena would be coddling our little boy, and my brother Roben would still be alive...

"That was precisely what Verena was thinking about in the last seconds before her execution. If she

had been a bit subtler back then, and not so insistent, how many lives could've been saved?"

"Flora, you really shouldn't be reading such personal thoughts. Or at least don't comment on them," I said, harshly putting the girl in her place, but my Truth Seeker could only smile in return.

Flora still couldn't actually smile very well, though. Her facial expression looked more like a scowl than a smile, but the girl was clearly happy with her achievement. She was also proud of the fact that today was the first time she had been able to eat without the help of her minions. The waterproof bib she was wearing over her dark clothing was covered with juice and pieces of lettuce, but that was nothing in comparison with the fact that the paralyzed girl had managed to use a spoon and fork all on her own!

Popori de Cacha came out of invisibility and said:

"Tuki-tuka-de-sa, Duchess Silva is coming this way. She is alone, without bodyguards. No weapons detected. Shall I stop her?"

"No, let her come. She still hasn't left the island after the end of the funeral ceremony, though no one was holding her shuttle back. Let's find out what the Duchess needs."

The Chameleon nodded and, taking a small apple from the fruit tray, went back into invisibility. Only the barely audible chomping sounds remained to let you know where my bodyguard head was. Duchess Silva, wearing a severe black and silver dress approached me and took a seat on the bench.

"Georg, pour me out a bit of whatever you're drinking," asked the one-hundred-twenty-year-old woman, who looked no older than forty.

I filled a glass and handed it to her.

"To the memory of your brother and his family!" The Orange House Head toasted and slowly but surely drained her glass. "Oof. That's some strong shit!"

Tears began welling up in Duchess Silva's eyes. Katerina and I waited patiently for our guest to catch her breath and chase the overly strong beverage with some juice.

"Why did you not make use of the chance to leave yet, your Highness?" Katerina asked.

The old lady chuckled:

"Because there was no reason to flee. I spoke with my fleet commander Nicole ton Savoia and asked her our chances of victory."

The Duchess turned on her palmtop computer and allowed us to hear the Perimeter Sector Eight Fleet Commander's answer:

"Duchess, even with equal fleet compositions, Crown Prince Georg royl Inoky would win, and he has ten times the ships we do. But the main thing is that half of my officers would refuse to fight against the hero of the Alien wars, and would even join his side right now if given the chance. Crown Prince Georg promised not to touch my ships in Tesse, and he always keeps his word. So I gave an order to the starships to simply stay and wait. I, meanwhile, have been invited to spend a few days in Crown Princess Likanna's palace on Tesse-III, and I intend on going."

"Yes, my daughter decided to enjoy the palace and yacht with her friends, including Nicole ton Savoia. The Crown Princesses' vacations will be ending soon. They'll have to go to the Throne World in a few days. So, let them have fun and relax as long as they can. I also gave some leave to Bionica, Valian ton Corsa, and my bodyguard Phobos, who is also with them."

"Don't you think that somewhat... unusual, Crown Prince Georg? There's a war going on, yet an Orange House fleet commander is going out for a fun weekend with some Unatari officers?!"

"No more unusual than the fact that the Orange House Head is drinking brandy with the ruler of Unatari and his officers," I countered with a smile, pouring her another glass.

Duchess Silva turned the glass in her hand and said:

"Alright, Georg, I'll be as direct as possible. It seems to me that the time has come to end this strange war my forbearer started between the Orange House and Unatari. As of yet, not a single shot has been fired in this war, and my Great House has already lost Sector Nine, and will be losing Sector Eight once and for all in a few days. Is that not so?"

"Almost. You should also add the fact that the largest Sector Seven fleet is under the command of my twin sister Crown Princess Violetta, and the Perimeter Sector Seven fleet was largely funded by me personally, and is thus very loyal to me."

"All the more so, then. Crown Prince Georg, I would like to hear your conditions for ending this conflict."

Katerina and I exchanged glances, and my advisor answered in my stead:

"The Orange House gives Unatari all Perimeter Sector Eight systems. After that, we will sign a peace treaty. Immediately after the peace treaty is signed, Duchess Silva royl George ton Mesfelle is to join the Unatari State, and will retain the title of Duchess and ownership of the Ulia system."

The Orange House Head spent quite some time in thought, then asked me what would become of Sector Seven. I shrugged my shoulders and answered, looking at the threatening black clouds that appeared in the flying palace's path on the horizon:

"When I was a child, I promised my sister Violetta that I would make her Duchess of the Orange House. The time has come to fulfill that promise. What my sister does with that title and territory is up to her. She may choose to join the Purple House or Unatari. She may also choose to remain independent. All of that would be within her rights..."

"Attractive conditions. To be honest, I was expecting less after the military and political walloping you gave us. Alright, I agree."

The Orange House offers the Unatari State a peace treaty on the following terms: The Orange House shall cede the Asti, Rea, Bren, Ulia, Nessi, Docks, Tesse, Orange House, Himora, and Klesto systems to Unatari.

In the already familiar menu, I choose the option "Agree," and instantly received a bedsheet-length list of messages:

The Orange House has lost sovereignty over the Tesse system

The Unatari State has gained sovereignty over the Tesse system

The Orange House has lost sovereignty over the Orange House Capital system

The Unatari State has gained sovereignty over the Orange House Capital system

The Orange House has lost sovereignty over the Nessi system

The Unatari State has gained sovereignty over the Nessi system

The Orange House has lost sovereignty over the Ulia system

The Unatari State has gained sovereignty over the Ulia system

...

A peace treaty has been signed between the Unatari State and the Orange House.

The Head of the Orange House, Duchess Silva royl George ton Mesfelle has resigned.

ATTENTION! The new head of the Orange House will be Duchess Violetta royl Inoky ton Mesfelle (77.8% of votes)

TRIAL IN THE EMPEROR'S COURT

W HAT AN AMAZING morning! After many weeks spent in space, you start to value such simple joys as a blue sky over your head, a light, pleasant breeze and an eye-pleasing green lawn. I was sitting in a recliner near a wide-open window eating breakfast with my cousin Katerina. Our mood was marvelous, just like the weather. Bionica had just informed me that a message had come in from Crown Prince Demyen royl Amelius ton Lavaelle, commander of the Green House armada locked up in the Forepost-31 system. He finally wanted to discuss the terms of his fleet's capitulation.

We were only waiting for Marian Sabati. Holding the negotiations over long distance without her, given the corner we had Crown Prince Demyen backed into, would be reckless. The problem was that the Green House's strongest Truth Seeker, Baroness Veronica ton Taki was on his flagship, the battleship

Immortal Gladiator. Not so terribly long ago, she was considered the third strongest psionic in the Empire, but she had recently lost that position to Miya.

"Your Majesty, incoming call from the Damir system, it's the Orange House Head, Duchess Violetta royl Inoky ton Mesfelle. Shall I put her through?"

I gave my permission, and my twin sister Violetta came on screen in the official robes of the Orange House Head, wearing the ducal crown over her chestnut hair.

"Congratulations, sister! Your life's dream has come true!" I said merrily, but was not met with understanding.

"Georg, you can congratulate me later, after you've returned the Orange House's rightful territory to me, by which I mean Perimeter Sectors Eight and Nine. Until now, I had been waiting for you to do it without me having to remind you, but two days have already passed, and you don't seem to be in much of a rush."

Katerina and I exchanged surprised glances, after which I answered Violetta:

"You seem to be confused, sister. We agreed on the following: I help you move up the Orange House line of succession, and you give me financial support. Both you and I have completed our parts of the deal. You helped me at a difficult time, and I made you Duchess. Fair is fair."

"You call that fair?!" Violetta flew off the handle. "All that's left of the Orange House is a pitiful stump. There were once thousands of aristocrats in line to the throne, and now there are less than two hundred. Not even one planet with a population higher than one billion people remains. I want a proper Great House, not this mere parody! I want to live in the historic Orange House Capital, not on the outskirts of a duchy!"

At the end of her speech, Violetta was already screaming from the overflowing emotions in her voice. I then answered all her reproaches in the opposite way, as constrainedly and calmly as possible:

"Sister, you and I had no agreement on the number of systems the Orange House should contain, nor which systems they would be. Also, there's no way I can give you the former capital of the 'oranges,' as I have already promised it to my son Georg, and I never break my promises."

"Ha! Look at how you uphold them! You robbed me blind, and still have the gall to brag of your nobility. Believe you me, I will not be leaving this so lightly, Georg! I will be making an official complaint to the Emperor!"

The screen turned off, but my ears were still ringing for a few seconds from Violetta's screaming. There was no trace remaining of my formerly good mood. Especially after Katerina, who abruptly grew gloomy herself, said thoughtfully:

"I can't possibly believe that such an experienced player of political games as Crown Princess Violetta royl Inoky would now act spontaneously or be counting on any other end to your conversation. No, she clearly purposely provoked you to refuse so she could create a scandal at some point in the future. It's very hard for me to believe that your sister has been sitting with her hands folded for two days. She has probably been horse trading with her neighbors, the Green and Purple Houses, to see which of them would give her more for Perimeter Sector Seven."

ATTENTION! The Orange House has ceased to exist.

The message's arrival made me shudder, but Katerina perceived it as a matter of course. My cousin read into the news she saw, and commented out loud for me:

"I guess the Purple House offered more. Oh well. I can understand where Duke Takuro royl Andor is coming from. For centuries, the Purple House has been considered the most modest in size among all the Great Imperial Houses. The 'purples' used to only have two Perimeter Sectors: Five and Six, giving them the least inhabitable planets of the Great Houses. For the ability to increase the size of their territory by one and a half times in one go, Duke Takuro made your sister second in line to the Purple House throne, right after his oldest son. Beyond that, he appointed Crown Princess Violetta royl Inoky ton Mesfelle Minister of External Affairs. I'm afraid, Georg, that the times of good relations between the Unatari State and the Purple House are behind us..."

Standing change. Purple House (Empire) opinion of the Unatari State has worsened.
Present Purple House (Empire) faction opinion of the Unatari State: +4 (ambivalent)

Katerina must have had second sight, as she

had just predicted this very event. I chuckled bitterly, and my second cousin said:

"I'm afraid that this is only the beginning, Georg. Now, at every opportunity, your sister will lower her faction relationship with you until there is a total diplomatic break, or even open war..."

My cousin abruptly went silent as an officer came into the room. He gave a salute and reported:

"Your Majesty, we've just received an order from the Emperor's secretariat for Crown Prince Georg royl Inoky ton Mesfelle to make immediately for the Throne World. The message is code red: maximum importance."

"I wonder what my opponents are accusing me of this time?" I marveled thoughtfully, not understanding what was going on. "And who is leveling these accusations? The Green House? But we're at war. The Lavaelle family can hardly be called a neutral party. It can't be Violetta, right? She wouldn't have had time, and what she has, demanding territory from me on the basis of childhood promises, isn't exactly enough to build a rigorous case."

"No matter who our opponent is, I'll be going with you, Georg!" Katerina stood up decisively. "You need my support."

"Crown Prince, I sense a serious danger. As much for your Highness personally as for everyone going with you to the Throne World. I am sure it is a trap. There will be no way back from the Throne World for you, and all witnesses have already been condemned to death. I'm simply shaking from the serious disaster I foresee."

Florianna's warning sounded very frightening. I told my cousin what the Truth Seeker had said, and Katerina sat back in the chair again and stroked her chin thoughtfully.

"What is the point of setting a trap for you, and also killing the witnesses of your meeting with the Emperor? There must be a reason of overarching importance for such actions, but I don't see it. Sure, the Throne World may not be happy with some of your actions, but not to such a point that they would forget tradition and hospitality, attacking a ruler loyal to the Empire. There's something we're not seeing, Georg. And we need to understand what it is exactly. Perhaps a very strong Truth Seeker could tell us. Where is Marian Sabati?"

"The last time I saw her was in the palace the day before yesterday at approximately the same time the guests were leaving the funeral. Maybe she took crystals and is sleeping. She's definitely not on the flying island, though. Our guards have already checked all the rooms."

Just then, Popori de Cacha appeared from invisibility before me and, training both of his mobile eyes on me, reported:

"Crown Prince Georg, I've just received information from the Ulia star system that five hours ago, Marian Sabati passed through border control and left Unatari State borders. There was no order to hold her, and our border guards let the Truth Seeker through into the Imperial Core."

What?! Katerina and I exchanged glances. Marian Sabati, who was wanted for murdering the Head of the Orange House, had gone to a system where she would be immediately arrested? But why?! And, mainly, what had made her leave? It can't have been about Verena's accusation that she stole twenty-five billion from the Orange House treasury, right? I am reminded that Marian Sabati gave me eight of that. She must have kept the rest for herself. Was she afraid I'd ask for the rest of the money? That could hardly be...

"She is bringing Unatari secrets to the Throne World!" Katerina's face lit up in realization. "That's it! Our military and scientific developments, present military strength, the two *Quasars* and other ships currently under construction at secret docks, the hidden *Mammoth*, the real state of affairs in our economy, the location of the *Queen*, our agreements with the Swarm... Marian Sabati thinks she will receive amnesty by giving this information to the Throne World!"

"And that isn't all she's bringing," I said, growing vexed. "There's also our plans for internal politics, which will definitely not be liked by the Blue and Green Great Houses, our secret agreements with the androids, the secret of the Mechanoids, the secret of how Duchess Inessa royl George died, and..."

Here my hair began to stand on end in horror. Marian Sabati knew the secret of my having taken Crown Prince Georg royl Inoky ton Mesfelle's place! That would mean it was all over! I couldn't refuse a visit to the Emperor, and the first check by the Dark Mother, knowing exactly what to ask and search for... I stood up, belabored, and scanned the room with a mad, unseeing gaze.

"Cousin, I need some time to be alone and

think on the difficult situation that has arisen. For now, you call the yacht *Queen of Sin* from Unatari and send all three Crown Princesses to Tesse-III so they can get ready to fly to the Throne World."

I went into one of the rooms inside the chic palace, turned off the huge data screen on the wall and the surveillance system, and turned window transparency down to zero. I turned to the bodyguards who had accompanied me there and ordered them all, even the Chameleons, Phobos and Rosss to leave the room and wait for me in the next room over. The door had barely closed behind the last bodyguard when I went into the corner and turned around in order to have the whole room in my field of view. I had long wanted to see how exactly this happened.

"Miya, I need you now!"

One moment passed, and a group of people and Chameleons materialized in the room looking as if they had always been there. My spouse, in a long bright-crimson dress instantly got her bearings and turned to meet my gaze with no hesitation. In that short moment, her duo of Chameleon bodyguards had already managed to entirely camouflage themselves.

"Ayna, drop your weapon, everything is fine." Only after Miya saying that sentence did I realize that the huge figure in heavy assault armor, partially blurred by the force field surrounding her, was my spouse's servant.

Ayna clicked the safety of her infantry resonator on, put the terrifying short-range weapon into her belt holster, and turned off her force field. Only then did I notice a little dark-haired girl at the armored amazon's feet, clinging tightly to a plush donkey.

"Deia, this is your daddy," Miya said, introducing me. "Go to him, daughter."

In my spouse's voice, when she spoke to our daughter, I could hear notes of tenderness and warmth. But the little Crown Princess shook her head in fear anyway, ran to her mother and buried her face in her dress. Miya could only smile guiltily, then opened her arms and embraced our daughter. I also smiled in embarrassment, not knowing how to react to the situation.

"Alright then, we can leave the sentimental stuff for later. Let's talk business," my spouse stated in a totally different, cold and metallic voice. "So... the Throne World has gone on the attack. It was very good, Georg, that you realized you should call me before the meeting with the Emperor. As far as I understand, Marian Sabati has already fled?"

"She left two days ago," I confirmed, trying not to show my surprise at Miya's acumen. "Though I still don't understand why she wanted to, or how Marian Sabati is hoping to avoid arrest and severe punishment."

"She doesn't plan on avoiding arrest. In fact, at the first possible opportunity, she will give herself up to the Imperial authorities, at which point she will be brought to the Throne World safe and sound. And there's nothing to punish her for then; she was merely carrying out an order form her true master. Yes, Georg, Marian Sabati was never Duke Avalle royl Anjer's Truth Seeker. Her real master was..."

"The Emperor!" I blurted out in a stroke of

genius.

Miya gave a few soft claps, congratulating me on my intuition.

"That's right! Few know the truth about that, just a close circle of the strongest Truth Seekers. Even Duke Avalle himself didn't suspect his psionic was truly serving another. Marian Sabati is the second or maybe even third strongest of the Emperor's Truth Seekers. How many psionics the Emperor actually has can only be guessed. Lots. The admiration that August receives from hundreds of billions of Imperial citizens, is more than enough to nourish several strong Truth Seekers and dozens of weaker ones. During the recent battle with the *Queen*, Krista, who is formally considered a servant of Duchess Ovella of the Blue House, brought forty Truth Seekers with the Dark Mother at the head. And they were all working on the same wavelength. The fact that they all must have been serving one master I only realized after myself working Flora, my own protégée."

I couldn't believe my ears. Krista was also one of the Emperor's Truth Seekers?!

"Yes, Georg. Though I cannot prove it, as Krista is significantly stronger than I am. But as for Marian Sabati, I have long known, but she tied my tongue. Her mission was to wriggle into your circle, gain your trust and figure out if there was any truth to the rumors that Crown Prince Georg royl Inoky had been replaced by a man named Ruslan. It should be noted that Marian Sabati did a brilliant job of dealing with the first part of the mission. She murdered Duke Avalle royl Anjer, who had long been a thorn in the side of the Throne World, and she emptied the Orange

House treasury; both deeds were elements of the same cunning plan. Yes, Georg, it was Marian Sabati who killed the Head of the Orange House, as little Flora didn't actually have the strength. I once told you that the Dark Mother couldn't have been mistaken in accusing Marian Sabati of the murder. But, Marian Sabati wasn't able to find confirmation of the mystery of your true identity. Your mind was too well shielded."

"Then why did she flee if she hadn't yet completed her mission?" I asked in surprise.

Miya smiled and pointed at Ayna:

"That little spy couldn't get the information directly from you, so she went to look for other options. She was not able to go through Florianna either; the paralyzed girl's brain is closed to reading just as well as yours, and she herself is infinitely loyal to her master. Marian even tried to enlist Ayna, supposing that she, having been maimed in the ring, would be grateful to her for the healing. But Ayna told me everything at the first opportunity, and I took her with me to keep her from Marian Sabati's rage. That little spy, of course, realized she'd screwed up. And so, on an order from the Throne World, she fled from Unatari, making sure to gather all data on the new government's military power and a whole suitcase of blackmail material on its ruler."

"But why would the Throne World want to blackmail me? I'm doing exactly what the Emperor told me to do: strengthening my new government."

Miya started thinking, spending practically a whole minute frozen in place. After that, she teetered back. Only Ayna's help stopped my spouse from falling over. Ayna sat her boss down on the couch carefully, but Miya quickly came back to her senses and answered in what was now a normal voice.

"It is extremely difficult to read any information on the Throne World's plans. It takes a huge amount of effort. But, in essence, I figured out what exactly the Emperor is afraid of. This isn't about you, and isn't even about your real identity. The Swarm is increasing in power much faster than humanity is."

"And what? Why are they accusing me of something here?!"

"If there is a serious internal conflict between human forces, all sides will take heavy losses and be weakened. If that happens, the Iseyek may take advantage of the situation and attack the Empire. So, in the light of the Emperor's expected campaign against the Antagonists, or the totally probable loss of control over the Green House, there are sure to be several such conflicts between humans in the not-too-distant future. If and when they do come to pass, the Swarm invading human space is considered a near certainty. So, the Joint Chiefs have already *de facto* taken the decision to make a preventative attack against the Iseyek. Emperor August is familiar with the plan, and has approved it in its entirety. The Empire will need Unatari space as a launch pad for the attack, and it is also trying to lure the Iseyek ships in the Unatari State Fleet into a trap to destroy them all in one go, taking advantage of the insects' trust in Swarm Five-Star Admiral Crown Prince Georg royl Inoky. That is precisely why the ruler of Unatari will be accused of a great many serious crimes at the forthcoming trial and will be given a choice: either give up territory and agree completely with the Imperial Joint Chiefs of Staff's demands, or Crown Prince Georg royl Inoky will be declared a wanted criminal with all the consequences that come with it. And the ruler of Unatari's guilt will be affirmed by the strongest Truth Seekers in the galaxy, and that will be more than enough in the eyes of the Imperial citizenry."

I went silent, digesting the new information. Then I chuckled at a thought that came to mind:

"Miya, I've just had an idea that is just screaming to be let out! Why don't we simply send the real Mr. G.I. to the Throne World instead of Ruslan! He would just beat his chest and affirm that he has no knowledge of the violations of Imperial law he is being accused of! He would pass any Dark Mother check, even with a whole pack of other Truth Seekers to boot..."

I went silent, thrown off by my spouse's abruptly deadened face. I also noticed that Ayna reached for her weapon, looking at Miya as if awaiting an order. For some reason, I thought that her pair of Chameleons would be attacking me any second, tying my hands behind my back, and that Ayna would be pulling the trigger and shooting me directly in her forehead with her resonator, ripping any living tissues to shreds. What was this foolishness?

Florianna's voice rang out in my head:

"This is not mere foolishness. Such visions sometimes come over Mystics. It is one possible future. That really might happen."

Miya readily supported Florianna in the mental conversation:

"That's right. Ruslan has touched on a forbidden topic and spoken names that must never be said aloud. I cannot kill him while he is in the body of Crown Prince Georg. That was why my servants were supposed to do it. They have clear instructions on this. But the situation has changed."

"Leave me alone with my husband," Miya said in an icy voice.

The room emptied out. Ayna and the Chameleons that appeared almost ran to get on the other side of the door. Only little Deia remained next to her mother, clinging to the fringes of her long dress.

"Flora, you may continue listening in, but if you try to give him any more information, you will die a painful death. Ruslan, the option of sending Mr. G.I. to the Throne World instead of you is appealing, but not possible. My spouse, Crown Prince Georg royl Inoky ton Mesfelle died four months ago. It was his death that served as the reason for the second contract. I managed to get your consciousness into his brain before it was completely extinguished."

"But how did I have a conversation with Mr. G.I. in my dreams after that then?"

Miya cast her eyes downward and smiled sheepishly.

"I tried to imitate him, but was not able to do a good enough job. You know his habits too well. You recognized right away that it was an impostor. It was an idiotic idea, so I never tried again."

I gathered more air into my lungs, trying to ask the question that was most important to me with spirit:

"So, what now? When this contract is up and I go back into my own body, Crown Prince Georg royl Inoky will die?"

The redheaded beauty looked away, spent a few seconds in silence and answered, barely audibly:

"There's nowhere for you to return to now, Ruslan. You died in the restaurant. The pills you took at the end of our conversation contained a deadly poison. I had to do it to be able to transfer your consciousness into the body of Crown Prince Georg royl Inoky. Now, you are in fact an Imperial Crown Prince, and Ruslan is gone for good."

I took the news fairly well. I mean, there was a twenty-minute period of swearing and hateful yelling that looked like hysteria, and the promise to do horrible things to Miya. I even slapped her around a few times. I suppose that only the presence of the little Deianna and Miya's absolute submission, promising to accept any punishment, saved the life of the red-headed murderer. I suspect that was exactly why Miya left her daughter in the room, and was behaving so accommodatingly.

When the stream of my hateful words had run dry, the Truth Seeker said calmly:

"Georg, you got an interesting life, full of action in a world you always dreamed of. That world is fully real, and you are free to act as you like in it. What could you possibly have to be upset about?"

"What do I have to be upset about?! You

murdered me!!!"

"No need to repeat yourself. You've already said as much a few dozen times. But a dead man can hardly walk around a room or speak, right?"

Seeing that I was starting to boil over again, Miya changed her tone:

"Alright, I agree that I did a bad thing, and I will accept any punishment you want to give me. But now, I suggest we get back to business. Your being called to the Throne World threatens tragedy not only to some ephemeral video-game character, but to the completely real Crown Prince Georg royl Inoky. We have very little time to prepare."

Fifteen minutes later, Miya and I were already having a totally peaceful conversation about interstellar politics with my cousin Katerina. Katerina was describing the situation as she saw it:

"The main two reasons the Emperor has called you to the Throne World are the Swarm growing unacceptably strong and the continuing blockade of the Green House armada. If we can solve both of those issue before the trial, there won't be any serious complaints left, just minor stuff like the unfinished *Mammoth*, the agreements with the androids, and our secret plans for the Blue House. None of that would be enough to sanction the Unatari State and its ruler."

Miya and I exchanged glances, and my spouse confirmed that Katerina was, in essence, correct. The redheaded beauty, not looking away from Deia as she played on the floor for even one second, stated decisively:

"We must conduct negotiations with the First

Green House Strike Fleet right away. My presence will serve as a guarantee that there will be no excesses from the Truth Seeker Baroness Veronica ton Taki. In theory, we could even try to kill her. Florianna and I working together have pretty good chances. It isn't good timing, though: I still need energy for other things. But the Swarm issue is for you to solve, Georg. I don't understand insects very well. I was only trained to kill Iseyek, not negotiate with them."

"Whereas I, on the other hand, am more accustomed to solving issues with them by diplomacy. And I believe that the most proper option would be to honestly warn the Swarm on the Joint Chiefs' plan, and suggest my ideas to avoid a big war."

* * *

Queen of Sin finished docking at the huge orbital fortress of the Throne World. I immediately sent the three little Crown Princesses on a shuttle to the surface of the planet, then sat to wait for my call to the Emperor. And I didn't have to wait long. After just ten minutes, a demand came in from the Imperial secretariat to come to the Silver Palace within two hours. But the Unatari delegation shuttle didn't even manage to finish its flight through the atmosphere before I received a call from Swarm Ambassador Triasss Zess. He was right there on the station, and requested an immediate audience.

"My Prince, I have cut down the time needed to land and fly to the Emperor's palace," Popori de Cacha said. "Just invite Triasss Zess to join us in the shuttle."

The Swarm Ambassador immediately agreed to the conditions, and the ten-foot-high snow-white praying mantis with a dark blue sash across his shell squeezed into the shuttle. Our shuttle had barely left *Queen of Sin* before the Alpha Iseyek imitated a deep bow and said:

"Crown Prince Georg royl Inoky ton Mesfelle, the Swarm thanks you for the warning on the Imperial Joint Chiefs of Staff's plans. Nai Igir has already familiarized herself with the important information, and has also thought through the suggestion of preserving her consciousness in an android's body."

Global standing increase. Current value +15

Standing change. Iseyek race opinion of you has improved.
Iseyek Prime race opinion of you: +27 (friendship)

"And what has the Swarm Queen decided?" I wondered.

"Nai Igir thanks you for showing you care about her, but she must refuse. Iseyek philosophy dictates that we not hang onto the old, and constantly change and move forward. So the Swarm Queen will not freeze her consciousness in the body of an android, and will be leaving the path open for a new leader. According to Swarm law, the new leader will be the most popular Iseyek from among those in the Queen's inner circle. In three days, the time will come for Nai Igir to lay her clutch, so she is in a rush. In her message, there is a suggestion from the Queen on how to overcome this situation."

With those words, the Swarm Ambassador made a deep bow and extended me a sealed tube of some kind. My bodyguards, worried, scanned the incomprehensible object, but found it safe. I removed its polished-stone stopper, pulled a scroll out from inside, and unraveled it. Half of the text, engraved on a thin sheet of metal, was written in Iseyek symbols. The other half was written in human language. I read it, and my eyebrows shot up in surprise. After giving the whole text a close look three times, I handed the scroll to Phobos so he could check the quality of the translation. My bodyguard confirmed that the texts were absolutely identical in both languages.

"There's no time-frame indicated here," I noted.

Triasss Zess bowed again and explained.

"Swarm laws dictate that our monarchs rule for life. Nai Igir is an exception due to the urgent nature of this situation."

"Then I agree to be the new ruler of the Swarm and unite the territory of the Iseyek with that of the Unatari State. I am prepared to swear to protect all citizens of the unified government at any cost, regardless of their race."

A number of system messages ran before my eyes, indicating sovereignty changes for a great many star systems after my choice. But I closed that interface window and said with a smirk:

"Triasss Zess, I give my permission, but would like to publicly announce my decision at the meeting with the Emperor. There, the news will go off like a bomb and blow my foes' plans to smithereens."

"As you say, my King! And given that everything went according to plan, this is no longer necessary." the praying mantis said, pulling out his neck and removing a circular object from a slot between layers of chitin, then handing it to Popori de Cacha. "This is a powerful bomb. The Swarm couldn't allow the invasion fleet to be led by the greatest Imperial fleet commander, after all."

For the second time, my visit to the Silver Palace felt all wrong. I didn't feel any childlike wonder from the grandeur of the rooms. I was totally lacking in timidity before the powerful of this world and, also, the Emperor himself didn't arouse feelings of piety or an irresistible desire to fall to my knees as he should have. A year ago, I saw him as a God of this world, capable of ending the life of billions with one twitch of his brow. Now, though, the man before me looked to be an ancient, ailing fart, who was insanely tired after many years of rule, but was still trying stubbornly to hold on to power, because it helped his decrepit body stay alive.

I could have said the same about any of the Great House Heads in the room. A year ago, any Duke would have seemed at an unreachable height, but now I wasn't able to call up any kind of submissive feelings before them at all. What was there to admire here? Duchess Ovella was an underage witch that the

Truth Seeker Krista had placed on the Blue House throne and was using as a marionette. Duke Takuro from the Purple House wasn't a bad old man, but he understood perfectly that his time had already passed. Then there was Duke Amelius ton Lavaelle, who did nothing to hide is hatred of me. I chuckled, imagining the face of the Green House Head in a few minutes.

"Georg, it seems to me that your happiness is misplaced," Emperor August royl Toll ton Akad stated harshly, taking a seat at the head of the large table. "The accusations against you are many, and they are quite serious in nature. This time, it will be I who reads them."

Katerina tapped my foot imperceptibly under the table, calling me to act serious. I nodded to the Emperor and tried to get the stupid grin off my face. At that time, the chair at the Emperor's right hand was occupied by the Dark Mother, and to the left, Space Marshal of the Imperial Star Fleet Abram Kovel was taking a seat.

"Georg, fix your Crown, it is leaning to the right. The camera is not centered," Popori de Cacha's voice came through the micro-headphone in my ear. He was watching through a camera affixed between the huge rubies on my crown. I readjusted the golden band.

"So then, we have quorum. Let's begin, I suppose," said August, asking me whether I understood why I was being called for a trial before the Emperor.

"To be honest, not very well, your Imperial Majesty. All of my actions were directed at ensuring the safety of the Empire, and carrying out your orders, Emperor August. I didn't even impede Marian Sabati in any fashion, as the wanted Truth Seeker was your personal psionic and was doing your bidding. From time to time, her actions clearly drifted outside the bounds of Imperial law – for example, when the Orange House Head, Duke Avalle royl Anjer ton Mesfelle was murdered, or when the same Great House's treasury was robbed, or when sabotage occurred on my flagship in the midst of a serious battle with the Aliens, or when collecting materials on my government. But I still held my servants back and did not obstruct your spy in any way, my Emperor."

Once again, I was not able to hold back my smile, as August couldn't maintain his imperturbable visage, and was starting to look angry. I suppose that a significant number of the accusations the Emperor was planning to roll out against me were connected precisely with Marian Sabati's activity. I, though, was working proactively.

"I have evidence that the wanted psionic Marian Sabati was working for your Imperial Majesty," I stated, as August was taking too long to answer. "If need be, I could present it."

"No, that won't be necessary," said the Dark Mother, answering in her master's place. "We are gathered here for other reasons, and Marian being my protégée has nothing to do with them."

"Also, the topics I am interested in are much more serious than one Truth Seeker's antics," said August, coming to life and rejoining the conversation. "Georg, I am deeply upset. Because of you, the Iseyek have become completely unmanageable. They are creeping over the galaxy at an unstoppable pace, capturing one human-inhabitable planet after the other. They've even had the gall to take vassals from us! The Swarm is the most serious threat to the Empire that exists, so it must be stopped! Yet you coddle the insects and make concessions to them. You give them military technology and strengthen our potential enemy in many other ways! I am very unhappy with that and demand that you explain your actions!"

Here the Head of the Green House wedged his way into the conversation, slightly out of place:

"Together with the accusations made by the Emperor, I would like to raise the issue of the trapped Green House squadron. It was sent to our border with the Iseyek precisely to serve as a counterweight to the Swarm, but the ruler of Unatari blocked it in! He played right into our opponents' hands! That is bordering on treason!"

I stood up, looked directly at the head of the Green House and, with unhidden mockery in my voice, said:

"Duke Amelius ton Lavaelle, I would like to remind you that openly lying in the presence of the Emperor is a very stupid tact. I have irrefutable evidence that the Green House armada's movement was in no way connected with the Iseyek, and that the Swarm was in no way mentioned in the fleet's original mission. The Green House ships were on their way to attack Unatari State planets, which are Imperial core territory. We have a crystal drive with a recording of our interrogation of the First Strike Fleet's commander, Demyen royl Amelius ton Lavaelle. We could present it, if necessary."

My cousin Katerina, expressionless, placed the data crystal on the table. The Space Marshal reached for the drive, preparing to place it into his screen, but I intercepted his arm:

"One minute. I would like to generously offer Duke Amelius ton Lavaelle one last chance to retract his worthless accusation before we watch the recording. If he does not, evidence will be presented of premeditated slander, and the intentional dissemination of false information in a trial before the Emperor himself. That is a very serious violation of Imperial law, and would have to be punished by revocation of title."

The Head of the Green House stared at me for a few seconds, but then turned his gaze away and said loudly:

"I retract my accusation! Perhaps my son misinformed me on the true goal of the military campaign. But I want to know, what is the current location and status?"

"Of your son, or the fleet?" I couldn't hold back from the jab. "Crown Prince Demyen has been released to the four winds, alive and well. I suspect that he is on his way to the Green House as we speak. Baroness Veronica ton Taki was released as well. I wouldn't dare keep yet another of the Emperor's personal Truth Seekers."

The reaction to that was worth seeing! In Duke Amelius' eyes, confusion and surprise flashed by, and another second later, were replaced by unhidden spite. It seemed the Duke wasn't aware of the Throne World's embedded spy!

A semi-transparent personal message flashed before my eyes, and I focused my gaze on it.

"Duke Amelius requests your support for a motion: lower the standing of Emperor August royl Toll ton Akad. Agree? (Yes/No)"

How wonderfully unexpected! The old Duke surprised and even delighted me. Not everyone has the resolve to express disapproval to the Emperor in such a public fashion. I chose the option "Yes," and watched as my accuser's face stretched out in surprise. Emperor August sat back in his chair and closed his eyes, reading the system message closely. It should be said that August's standing fell by fourteen points over the course of just a few seconds to +222. Clearly, the head of the Green House hadn't requested that only I participate in the digital attack.

When August opened his eyes, he was seething with manifest rage. The Emperor clearly wasn't accustomed to having his numbers lowered all of a sudden. Fortunately, his hatred wasn't directed at me, though. The Head of the Green House withstood the Emperor's severe gaze with aplomb and merely smiled in reply. While the pair of aristocrats were trying to turn one another to ash with their eyes, the floor was taken by the previously silent Head of the Blue House:

"There's one more accusation that cannot be forgotten. Crown Prince Georg royl Inoky officially promised Blue House systems to my cousin Crown Princess Natalie ton Miro."

I raised my hand and, scanning with my eyes

for the Dark Mother, said:

"Stop, stop, stop. It would seem, Duchess, that you have been misinformed. The Unatari State is not planning now and never was planning to go to war with the Blue House. The Dark Mother is here and could verify my words. The conversation with Crown Princess Natalie, in fact, was about a hypothetical situation. If the Aliens, after having destroyed the Red House, were to continue their campaign and move to sweep away the Blue House defenders as well, the Unatari Fleet would be the only force capable of coming to the Blue House's aid and saving it from total destruction. I intended, in my conversation with Crown Princess Natalie, that the reward given to me for that service be very generous, to equal the scale of the favor: at least one of the six Perimeter Sectors belonging to the Blue House."

"I hope that is never allowed to happen," the young Duchess frowned. "The Blue House is the largest in territory, and will never be occupied by enemies. Very well. That accusation has been refuted."

My tongue was itching to tell Crown Princess Ovella that her Blue House was already as good as occupied, as the power really belonged to the Throne House plant Krista, not the Blue House Duchess at all. But I held back, thinking it not the best time. Instead, I returned to the topic of the Green House armada:

"Perhaps those gathered here are not yet aware but, three days ago, the First Green House Strike Fleet surrendered in its entirety to the Unatari State in the Forepost-31 system. Now we are filtering through the captured officers and team members. After all those procedures are completed, those who so desire will have the opportunity to swear allegiance to me and become my subjects. If it pleases the Imperial Joint Chiefs, I will even send these captured starships to Iseyek space. Though I personally don't see any reason for that, as these ships would be more useful to me in other regions of my large state, not only those inhabited by insects."

What I said didn't reach the great leaders immediately. The first to realize it was the Head of the Purple House, Duke Takuro. The old man coughed and asked:

"Georg, I don't think I've understood you correctly. You mean to say that the Swarm is part of your State?"

After these words, silence came over the room. I thought the moment ideal to call up the internal interface and accept Triasss Zess's offer. A great many messages came in on star-system sovereignty changes, so many that my eyes started flashing. The final one amused me:

Achievement unlocked: Master of the Hive

Global fame increase. Current value +67

While those gathered were still frozen, their mouths hanging open in surprise, I commented:

"And now, let's get back to the very beginning of the meeting and the words of Emperor August on the hypothetical threat of insect invasion. As the autocratic Master of the Hive, I officially declare the

Swarm problem nonexistent. All Iseyek systems, their planets, their armies, and their combat ships are subject to me now. No insect starship will move an inch without my order. Not a single empty planet will be occupied by Iseyek if that is not my will. There is no problem with splitting up trophies from the war with the Aliens; all the systems and combat starships that were captured by the Aliens belong to Unatari in one way or another."

In the silence that came over the room, the first words spoken by the Dark Mother sounded out especially distinctly:

"Very bad. The Swarm was a problem all on its own. Now, then, in its strengthened state, with additional systems, new technology and a good fleet commander, the Swarm has become an unacceptable threat, whose existence we can never tolerate. Neither I, nor the Emperor will allow such a force to be under anyone's control but the Throne World's."

I was utterly thrown off and turned to August:

"Your Imperial Majesty, was it not you who gave me the mission of strengthening the Unatari State Fleet at any cost? Do you not need my fleet as strong as possible to invade the Antagonists?"

The Emperor smiled, or more accurately bared his teeth predatorily and, looking me right in the eyes, said:

"Georg, the invasion of the Antagonists will begin one day, but it is not certain to be today, or even in a year. The fact that Swarm ships are moving without order while their King is in the Throne World, though, leaves me with a much greater imperative! I cannot allow such a historic moment to slip by.

Guards, take him alive! No need to use kid gloves with the others, either!"

In the micro-headphone that was helping me maintain connection with the other members of my delegation, I heard the shots and shouts of Popori de Cacha, Phobos and my other bodyguards that had been left in the hallway:

"Crown Prince Georg, we've been attacked! Aaaahhhh!"

At the same time as that, one of the Emperor's bodyguards drew a short-barreled laser rifle and emptied its battery into the back of my advisor Katerina royl Unatari. Some other soldiers ganged up on me, and knocked me off my feet.

"What are you doing, August?! He is loyal to you!" The scream belonged, it seemed, to Duke Takuro.

"August, you are breaking laws you wrote yourself!" The Head of the Green House objected.

"Think nothing of it. It'll be good for my grand-nephew. He'll spend a few months in jail detoxing from the crystals, then he'll be a good boy and give up all the warp beacon codes to his new state. He can learn some manners while he's in there, as well. It seems his quick rise in popularity has made his head spin! We can't let this historic moment pass. We have the chance to destroy the entire Swarm!"

With my hands already tied behind my back, I managed to see my cousin's body, shot full of holes, as it melted into a while cloud, then drifted away into the ventilation. It seemed the time for me to flee had also come.

"Miya, the time has come!" I gave the mental

signal.

"He's fleeing! I don't know how, but he is fleeing! Shoot Georg!" The Dark Mother shrieked hysterically.

But it was too late. I was already lying on the metallic floor of a huge room. I needed a few seconds to realize where I was. It was the main banquet hall of my flagship, *Joan the Fatty*. There was a multitude of people surrounding me. The closest of all were the three Truth Seekers, Miya, Florianna, standing (!!!) next to her, and Millena. All three of the psionics had their eyes closed, and were holding hands. Next to Miya, clinging off her red dress, little Deia was sitting on the floor.

A bit further off, on the floor of the room, there were Beta Iseyek sitting on the floor. Hundreds of huge pill-bugs had their many of arms placed on the person or Iseyek in front of them, leading all the way to the Truth Seekers themselves. It was all clear. It was a living battery, charging up the Truth Seekers.

I turned around. Right on the cold floor, with their hands on the shoulders of the person next to them, were my friends, distant and close acquaintances, and just random subjects. They were all looking at me. Many were doing nothing to hide the tears of joy rolling down their cheeks. In the first row, I saw Nicole Savoia, Bionica, Phobos, Popori de Cacha, my cousin Katerina, her husband Duke Corwin royl Unatari-Ugar, my daughter Crown Princess Likanna her friend Crown Princess Natalie, and many admirals, generals and captains...

"It worked..." said Miya, wavering, but being held up by the other Truth Seekers and the Beta

Iseyek.

I stood up and approached my spouse. She was so weary she could barely stand, but she still found the power to smile at me and say:

"I know what you want to say to me. I am forgiven."

"Yes. We're even now; once you killed me, and once you saved my life. I have something to admit to you, Miya. I was planning to not return to the real world and stay here with all this," I led my hand around the huge room and those gathered in it, people and nonpeople. "*Perimeter Defense* is my world now, and the only place I feel truly alive is here. I was actually planning to kill you near the end of the contract. I had even started thinking up methods. Nevertheless, I expect you to give me a full account of what is happening, with no vague sentences or omissions."

"Very well, agreed," Miya smiled and took Deia in her arms. "By the way, when you're free, come to your bunk. I think you'll like what you see there."

I wasn't able to clarify what I was supposed to see, because I was interrupted by Katerina:

"Georg, the video we got is just awesome! The unmotivated treachery of the Emperor, the attack on our diplomats, August breaking his word and the laws of hospitality. I have broadcast it on all Unatari news channels, and it has even made the rounds on the Imperial news already. August's standing is at forty and falling. Truth be told, the Throne World has already released its own counterpropaganda. They're accusing you of conspiring with your grandmother Eleonora royl Akad, ruler of the Antagonists. But for now, those on the Emperor's side are going pale. The most elementary Truth Seeker verification would make all their insinuations crumble."

Popori de Cacha walked up. The Chameleon looked impossibly happy.

"Tuki-tuka-de-sa, all the Arites who accompanied your Majesty to the Throne World managed to escape, including those from the yacht. The Throne World is now overflowing with our spies and saboteurs. The Throne World's corvettes did blow up *Queen of Sin*, though."

"The Truth Seeker Baroness Veronica ton Taki was having a crystal dream on one of those bunks!"

My cousin shook her head:

"That didn't stop the Emperor. August was simply enraged, kicking and cursing. They say he even slapped the Green House Head for trying to stop your arrest. The Green House has announced a referendum on their leaving the Empire. The Swarm Embassy to the Throne World has been destroyed. Some of its diplomats have been killed, and others arrested. Senior Ambassador Triasss Zess blew himself up with a bomb as not to be taken alive."

I lowered my head. What a shame. My relationship with the praying mantis ambassador hadn't always been smooth, but such was life. Nevertheless, Triasss Zess was loyal in a way. He was prepared to give his life for his kind. My former father-in-law Duke Valesy approached me and patted me on the shoulder:

"You're a tricky one, Georg. You defeated all the accusations against yourself. All of us here were watching anxiously and applauding. I just didn't understand why you accused Marian Sabati of sabotage."

"I simply took a wider look at the situation. Who, knowing of the Swarm's plans to start a counterattack, probably would have given an order to a spy to stop the insects from expanding their territory? Marian Sabati was just following orders. Also, she was the only one whose story we couldn't have verified. And what's more, the shield control and battery programs used on our flagship were written in the Empire, so Throne World experts would have known how to break them."

"I see. But what now? War?"

All the conversations around us went silent. Everyone in the room was hanging on my every word. I, then began speaking clearly and decisively:

"First, we should send an official ultimatum to the Throne World. We'll give Emperor August twelve hours to apologize and pay compensation for the perfidious murder of our ambassador and the destruction of my property. We will also demand that August apologize to all Dukes who were at the meeting. If he does not meet those conditions, the Unatari State will declare independence from the Empire. If they won't let us go peacefully, we'll have to fight for our right to freedom!"

Those present began to make an agitated racket. A joyful mood took over the room. The people supported the decision of their ruler and were prepared to follow me even against the Emperor. That was a good thing.

"Crown Prince Georg, I would like to remind you of Miya's words and ask you to go to your bunk."

"What is there, Flora?" I asked out loud.

"I'm not telling. It's a surprise."

Alright, I was intrigued. I left the common hall and, surrounded by a group of vigilant bodyguards, set off down the hall to my room. I opened the door... and froze in the doorway. On the little couch next to the big window, her legs crossed, was Princess Astra sitting in a short robe, squeezing a swaddled baby boy to her chest. Astra turned her head to the sound of the opening doors, met my gaze and smiled:

"I came uninvited, as usual. I saw in the news that my son was given the Orange House Capital, and realized that Crown Prince Georg hadn't forgotten me after all."

"How could I forget about you?" I walked up closer, embraced the feeding mother carefully and took a look at the boy nursing at her breast. "But how did you get here?"

"I went to the captain of *Star Mutt*, Tazar ton Akad and told him to fly to Crown Prince Georg," the Princess explained matter-of-factly. "I promised the captain that he would be generously rewarded for bringing your favorite back. To be honest, he argued for a long time and told me about how he'd be losing a year of flight time, but in the end agreed. Your Majesty, you will reward him, right?"

"Of course. The captain of *Star Mutt* has given me the greatest gift I have ever received, and deserves a truly kingly reward."

Achievement re-unlocked: Favorite's Iseyek Mating Dance

Achievement lost: Denied paternity

Global standing increase. Current value +21

Astra smiled, but just then pursed her lips and said, offended:

"I've already been told that your Majesty flew to the Throne World alone without me again, even though you promised to bring me there and show me the wonderful palaces and fountains."

I smiled. Astra hadn't changed one bit. All these wars with the Aliens, interstellar border crossings and harsh political battles-royal, could not have had less importance in her little internal world.

"Think nothing of it, Astra, we'll go there together some day. There will be thousands of ships with us, and I will give the whole Throne World to you. You have my word as a Crown Prince!"

"Don't you think the Emperor will object?" The beauty grew surprised, pressing herself to me like an affectionate little kitten.

"No one will be asking the Emperor. August has violated the laws humanity has lived by for centuries. The Empire will break apart just like that, and the Great Houses will disappear or secede one after the other. A totally new epoch is upon us. A game with no rules has begun. And this new era will belong to us!"

END OF BOOK THREE

About The Author

Michael Atamanov was born in 1975 in Grozny, Chechnia. He excelled at school, winning numerous national science and writing competitions. Having graduated with honors, he entered Moscow University to study material engineering. Soon, however, he had no home to return to: their house was destroyed during the first Chechen campaign. Michael's family fled the war, taking shelter with some relatives in Stavropol Territory in the South of Russia.

Having graduated from the University, Michael was forced to accept whatever work was available. He moonlighted in chemical labs, loaded trucks, translated technical articles, worked as a software installer as well as scene shifter for local artists and events. At the same time he never stopped writing, even when squatting in some seedy Moscow hostels. Writing became an urgent need for Michael, driving him to submit articles to science publications, news fillers for a variety of web sites and a plethora of technical and copywriting gigs.

Then one day unexpectedly for himself he started writing fairy tales and science fiction novels. For several years, his audience consisted of only one person: Michael's elder son. Then, at the end of 2014 he decided to upload one of his manuscripts to a free online writers resource. Readers liked it and demanded a sequel. Michael uploaded another book, and yet another, his audience growing as did his list. It was his readers who helped Michael hone his writing style. He finally had the breakthrough he deserved when the Moscow-based EKSMO - the biggest publishing house in Europe - offered him a contract for his first and consequent books.

Want to be the first to know about our latest LitRPG, sci fi and fantasy titles from your favorite authors?

Subscribe to our NEW RELEASES newsletter:
http://eepurl.com/b7niIL

Thank you for reading *New Contract!*
If you like what you've read, check out other sci-fi, fantasy
and LitRPG novels published by Magic Dome Books:

Reality Benders LitRPG series by **Michael Atamanov:**
Countdown
External Threat
Game Changer
Web of Worlds
A Jump into the Unknown
Aces High

The Dark Herbalist LitRPG series
by **Michael Atamanov:**
Video Game Plotline Tester
Stay on the Wing
A Trap for the Potentate
Finding a Body

Perimeter Defense LitRPG series by **Michael Atamanov:**
Sector Eight
Beyond Death
New Contract
A Game with No Rules

League of Losers LitRPG Series
by **Michael Atamanov:**
A Cat and his Human

The Way of the Shaman LitRPG series
by **Vasily Mahanenko:**
Survival Quest
The Kartoss Gambit
The Secret of the Dark Forest
The Phantom Castle
The Karmadont Chess Set
Shaman's Revenge
Clans War

The Alchemist LitRPG series by **Vasily Mahanenko:**
City of the Dead
Forest of Desire
Tears of Alron

Dark Paladin LitRPG series by Vasily Mahanenko:
The Beginning
The Quest
Restart

Galactogon LitRPG series by Vasily Mahanenko:
Start the Game!
In Search of the Uldans
A Check for a Billion

Invasion LitRPG Series by Vasily Mahanenko:
A Second Chance
An Equation with one Unknown

World of the Changed LitRPG Series by Vasily Mahanenko:
No Mistakes
Pearl of the South

**The Bard from Barliona LitRPG series
by Eugenia Dmitrieva and Vasily Mahanenko:**
The Renegades
A Song of Shadow

Level Up LitRPG series by Dan Sugralinov:
Re-Start
Hero
The Final Trial
Level Up: The Knockout (with Max Lagno)
Level Up. The Knockout: Update (with Max Lagno)

Disgardium LitRPG series by Dan Sugralinov:
Class-A Threat
Apostle of the Sleeping Gods
The Destroying Plague
Resistance
Holy War

World 99 LitRPG Series by Dan Sugralinov:
Blood of Fate

Adam Online LitRPG Leries by Max Lagno:
Absolute Zero
City of Freedom

El Diablo by G.Zotov
(a supernatural thriller)

Mirror World LitRPG series by Alexey Osadchuk:
Project Daily Grind
The Citadel
The Way of the Outcast
The Twilight Obelisk

Underdog LitRPG series by Alexey Osadchuk:
Dungeons of the Crooked Mountains
The Wastes
The Dark Continent
The Otherworld

An NPC's Path LitRPG series by Pavel Kornev:
The Dead Rogue
Kingdom of the Dead
Deadman's Retinue

The Sublime Electricity series by Pavel Kornev:
The Illustrious
The Heartless
The Fallen
The Dormant

Citadel World series by Kir Lukovkin:
The URANUS Code
The Secret of Atlantis

You're in Game!
(LitRPG Stories from Bestselling Authors)

You're in Game-2!
(More LitRPG stories set in your favorite worlds)

The Fairy Code by Kaitlyn Weiss:
Captive of the Shadows
Chosen of the Shadows

More books and series are coming out soon!

In order to have new books of the series translated faster, we need your help and support! Please consider leaving a review or spread the word by recommending *New Contract* to your friends and posting the link on social media. The more people buy the book, the sooner we'll be able to make new translations available.

Thank you!

Till next time!

www.ingramcontent.com/pod-product-compliance
Lightning Source LLC
Chambersburg PA
CBHW071632260626
47170CB00001B/65